D0981288

FREEWARE

Other Books by
Rudy Rucker

THE HACKER AND THE ANTS
THE HOLLOW EARTH
SOFTWARE
WETWARE

Avon Books are available at special quantity discounts for bulk purchases for sales promotions, premiums, fund raising or educational use. Special books, or book excerpts, can also be created to fit specific needs.

For details write or telephone the office of the Director of Special Markets, Avon Books, Dept. FP, 1350 Avenue of the Americas, New York, New York 10019, 1-800-238-0658.

FREEWARE

RUDY RUCKER

AVON BOOKS ◆ NEW YORK

FREEWARE is an original publication of Avon Books. This work has never before appeared in book form. This work is a novel. Any similarity to actual persons or events is purely coincidental.

AVON BOOKS
A division of
The Hearst Corporation
1350 Avenue of the Americas
New York, New York 10019

Copyright © 1997 by Rudy Rucker
Front cover art by Raquel Jaramillo
Published by arrangement with the author
Visit our website at **http://AvonBooks.com**
Library of Congress Catalog Card Number: 96-47375
ISBN: 0-380-79278-8

All rights reserved, which includes the right to reproduce this book or portions thereof in any form whatsoever except as provided by the U.S. Copyright Law. For information address Avon Books.

First Avon Books Trade Printing: May 1997
First Avon Books Hardcover Printing: May 1997

AVON TRADEMARK REG. U.S. PAT. OFF. AND IN OTHER COUNTRIES, MARCA REGISTRADA, HECHO EN U.S.A.

Printed in the U.S.A.

QPM   10   9   8   7   6   5   4   3   2   1

If you purchased this book without a cover, you should be aware that this book is stolen property. It was reported as "unsold and destroyed" to the publisher, and neither the author nor the publisher has received any payment for this "stripped book."

For Embry Cobb Rucker
October 1, 1914–August 1, 1994
"We live in hope."

Contents

Geneaology of Characters
in <u>Software</u>, <u>Wetware</u>, and <u>Freeware</u>

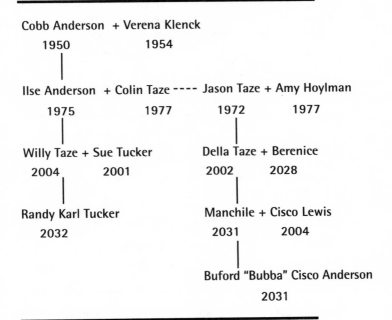

Cobb Anderson + Verena Klenck
1950   1954

Ilse Anderson + Colin Taze ---- Jason Taze + Amy Hoylman
1975   1977   1972   1977

Willy Taze + Sue Tucker   Della Taze + Berenice
2004   2001   2002   2028

Randy Karl Tucker   Manchile + Cisco Lewis
2032   2031   2004

                                 Buford "Bubba" Cisco Anderson
                                 2031

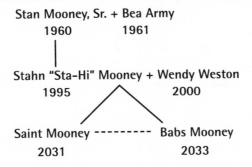

Stan Mooney, Sr. + Bea Army
1960   1961

Stahn "Sta-Hi" Mooney + Wendy Weston
1995   2000

Saint Mooney -------- Babs Mooney
2031   2033

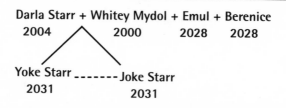

Darla Starr + Whitey Mydol + Emul + Berenice
2004   2000   2028   2028

Yoke Starr ------- Joke Starr
2031   2031

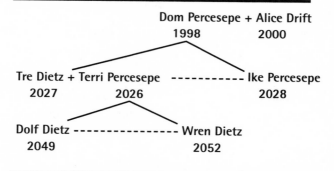

Dom Percesepe + Alice Drift
1998   2000

Tre Dietz + Terri Percesepe ----------- Ike Percesepe
2027   2026   2028

Dolf Dietz --------------- Wren Dietz
2049   2052

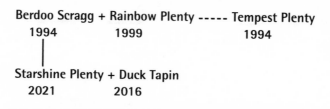

Berdoo Scragg + Rainbow Plenty ----- Tempest Plenty
1994   1999   1994

Starshine Plenty + Duck Tapin
2021   2016

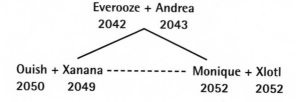

Everooze + Andrea
2042   2043

Ouish + Xanana ----------- Monique + Xlotl
2050   2049   2052   2052

CHAPTER ONE

MONIQUE

=== ■ ===

October 30, 2053

Monique was a moldie: an artificial life form made of a soft plastic that was mottled and veined with gene-tweaked molds and algae. Although Monique was a being with superhuman powers, she was working as maid, handyman, and bookkeeper for the Clearlight Terrace Court Motel in Santa Cruz, California. The motel manager, young Terri Percesepe, occasionally worried about Monique's motives. But the moldie's work was affordable and excellent.

The Clearlight was situated near the top of a small hill, fifty yards back from the Santa Cruz beach with its Boardwalk amusement park. It was a fine fall day, October 30, 2053, and the morning sun filled the town with a dancing preternatural light that made the air itself seem jellied and alive. On the ocean, long smooth waves were rolling in, each wave breaking with a luscious drawn-out crunch.

The motel consisted of a wooden office and three terraced rows of connected stucco rooms, each room with a double sliding glass door looking out over the sea. Pasted onto part of each

1

room's door was a translucent psychedelic sticker mimicking an arabesque tiling. The weathered motel office sat on a flat spot behind the highest terrace. The back part of the office held a four-room apartment in which Terri lived with her husband Tre Dietz and their two children: four-year-old Dolf and one-year-old Baby Wren.

Monique was making her way from room to room, changing the sheets and towels, enjoying the feel of the bright sun slanting down on her and on the faded blue walls of the motel buildings. She'd already finished the rooms in the two upper rows and was now busy with the rooms of the lowest terrace, which sat directly above the well-worn shops of Beach Street. It was almost time for Monique's midday break; as soon as her husband Xlotl called up, she'd go down for an hour on the beach with him.

Monique looked like a woman, sort of, most of the time, which is why it was customary to refer to her as a *she*. Moldies picked a gender at birth and stuck to it throughout the few years that they lived. Though arbitrarily determined, a moldie's sex was a very real concept to other moldies.

Each moldie was passionately interested in mating and reproducing at least once before his or her short life should expire. The moldies reproduced in pairs and lived in nests that were like extended families. Monique was in a nest of six: herself, her parents Andrea and Everooze, her husband Xlotl, her brother Xanana, and Xanana's wife Ouish.

Monique's mother Andrea was very strange. Sometimes, under the influence of certain chelated rare-earth polymers, she would form her body into a giant replica of the Koran or of the Book of Mormon and lie out in front of the beachfront Boardwalk amusement park, babbling about transfinite levels of heaven, chaotic feedback, and the angels Izra'il and Moroni. Her body was more mold than plastic, and it looked like she might fall apart anytime now, but Andrea had gotten rejuvenation treatments for herself before, and she planned to do it again—if she could get the money.

Monique's father Everooze worked as a liveboard for Terri

Percesepe's kid brother Ike, who ran a surf shop called Dada Kine out at Pleasure Point in south Santa Cruz. Like Andrea, Everooze was quite old for a moldie and had been rejuvenated several times. Ike had been going out surfing with Everooze every day for the last few years, and occasionally Ike might lend or rent Everooze to friends or to stuzzy big-time surfers. For his own part, Everooze got a kick out of giving free lessons to beginners and spreading the gospel of surf. Like Andrea, Everooze was starting to flake pretty badly. Without a retrofit he'd die this winter. But Ike worshipped Everooze and was prepared to pay for his rejuvenation.

When Terri had heard about Monique's birth to Everooze and Andrea—last August—she'd thought of hiring the newborn moldie right away, and she'd been able to convince Andrea and Everooze that it was a floatin' idea.

Monique quickly learned the ins and outs of running the Clearlight, and her diligent efforts left Terri and Tre plenty of free time. Not only did Monique make up the rooms quickly and beautifully, she managed all of the motel's books. Terri went out surfing most every day, and Tre liked to sit in an easy chair behind the motel office desk, whiling away the hours smoking pot while wearing an uvvy on his neck and doing complicated things with his brain. Although most people thought of an uvvy as a communication device, you could also use it as a computer terminal, which was something Tre did a lot. "Uvvy" was pronounced soft and cozy, like "lovey-dovey."

Tre earned a middling amount of money designing intricate uvvy graphics effects for Apex Images, a commercial graphics shop that did contract work for ad agencies and music producers. The number-crunching and brute programming of Tre's visions could be carried out by well-paid moldies, but it took Tre's unique sensibility to come up with juicy, tasty, gnarly images that people felt a visceral need to see over and over. Tre got royalties on the effects that Apex was able to use.

With Monique in their employ, Tre and Terri's motel responsibilities amounted to little more than providing a human interface for the guests to interact with. They needed to be there to buffer new arrivals from the unsettling sight and smell of Monique.

The guests, always tourists, usually middle-class and Midwestern, came to Santa Cruz because of its low prices and were often shocked at the number of moldies. There weren't very many moldies in the heartlands, for the people there hated them—many Midwesterners were Heritagists. The common Heritagist term for burning a moldie in a puddle of grain alcohol was "fryin' up an Iowa chop." "With truffle sauce," people would add sometimes, referring to the deep-buried nuggets of camote fungus that would crisp up as a moldie's twitching plastic disintegrated into the flames, sending off psychedelic clouds of blackened spores.

It was up to Terri and Tre to put the guests at ease in the free zone of Santa Cruz and to make them feel that Santa Cruz wasn't threatening, even though the town was filled with students, moldies, farmworkers, surfers, and homeless stoners. But, yes, prices were low, and there were a lot of entertaining things to do.

Monique's husband Xlotl worked at Los Trancos Taco Bar, just down the hill from the Clearlight. As well as chopping the vegetables and cleaning the kitchen, Xlotl maintained the tank in which the meats used for the tacos were grown. The tank contained four perpetually self-renewing loaves of meat: chicken, beef, pork, and wendy—*wendy* being the human-cloned flesh which had taken such a hold on people's palates in recent months.

Pulling clean sheets off her cart for Room 3B on this sunny October morn, Monique resembled a short Indian-blooded Mexican woman. Her skin was a coppery orange, with irregular veins of green and blue lichen just below the surface. Rather than forking into legs, her lower body was a solid tapering mass that fluted out into a broad bottom disk—Monique was shaped more or less like a chessman with arms, like a pawn or a queen or a knight. The exact appearance of her humanoid head and arms was something she could tweak according to the realtime situation. But when Monique relaxed, like now, she looked Aztec.

Monique's disk-shaped plastic foot had ridges on the bottom, piezoplastic imipolex ridges that could ripplingly glide Monique across level surfaces. For more rapid progress or on an irregular terrain, Monique could hop. If the utmost speed was called for, she could flip her body out of the "chess man" mode and go over into another of her body's stable attractor modes, a mode in which she could fly. In this alternate "pelican" mode, Monique became a set of great flapping wings attached to a tapered big-eyed body resembling the brown pelicans who dive for fish along the Santa Cruz coast.

Monique's tissues had at least three other basic attractor modes as well: the spread-out "puddle" shape she used for soaking up sun, the seagoing "shark" shape, and the rarely used "rocket" shape that moldies could use to fly back and forth between the Earth and the Moon, not that a moldie like Monique had any desire to go to the Moon with its fanatic loonie moldies.

The changes between body modes could happen quite abruptly, like a structure of springs and dowels that snaps into a new position if you pull one of its armatures just so—like the Zeeman Catastrophe Machine of the 1970s, which was an educational toy made out of cardboard, paper clips, and rubber bands that would unexpectedly and *catastrophically* (in the technical chaos-theoretical sense of the word) snap into one of two different positions, depending on how you manipulated it. Imagine being able to change your body into a rug or a bird or a fish or a spaceship simply by pretzeling yourself into a peculiar yoga position. Moldies could!

The pelican shape was Monique's favorite. There was nothing Monique enjoyed more than gliding high in the sky above the cliffs and the crashing sea of Monterey Bay, with the algae in her wings feasting on the impartially free energy of the sun. She'd been out flying with Andrea and Xlotl yesterday, in fact. But now today here Monique was, cleaning rooms and keeping the books for a flesher motel. It was fully a xoxxox bummer, and all just to have a baby?

There was a rapping noise from Room 3D, two doors down. A gangly young man was standing behind the sliding door and knocking on the glass with his ring, one of those heavy high school rings with a *hollow*, or hologram, of a rose or a skull or a school mascot inside the cheaply doped stone. The man gestured for Monique to come into his room. He wore a white plastic shirt and gray slacks. Monique made a quick mental check of the registration records and found that the man was named Randy Karl Tucker and that he was occupying the room alone.

Monique jumped to the conclusion that Tucker was a *cheeseball*, a person given to having sex with moldies. A cheeseball was not a high-class kind of person by any means. The name had to do with the fact that moldies didn't smell very good. Depending on the exact strains of fungi and algae that a given moldie incorporated, the smell might resemble mildewed socks or brussels sprouts or an aggressively ripe cheese. The most noticeable component of Monique's sachet was a tangy iodine smell suggestive of fecal black muck from the Santa Cruz harbor floor.

It went without saying that a moldie's intelligent, malleable flesh could provide a very unique multipronged personal massage for those humans who sought sex in strange forms. The unnaturalness of the act was of appeal to certain individuals; indeed the very reek of a moldie was something that most cheeseballs found powerfully arousing. Sad to say for the men of this world, cheeseballs were almost always male.

Behind the glass door of Room 3D, Tucker formed a cozening, humorless smile and winked at Monique. He had prominent cheekbones and thin lips; he looked like a country hick. The sly, insistent way that he kept crooking his finger made it seem almost certain that he was a cheeseball.

As it happened, when Monique, Xlotl, and Andrea had been out flying yesterday, Andrea had talked to the younger moldies about cheeseballs. Andrea had some very definite ideas about how to handle them.

"Persuade the cheeseball to accompany you to an isolated setting," intoned Andrea, who'd recently started talking like an engineer or, of all things, a robot. In the past she'd used the gaseous verbiage of the King James Bible, the Book of Mormon, and the Koran, but these days she modeled her speech patterns on the style of science journals. "Encourage the cheeseball to initiate mating behavior and then supply genital stimulation until the cheeseball is thoroughly distracted. At this point extrude a long tendril from your body mass and use rapid, decisive motions to encircle the cheeseball's neck with the tendril. Immediately tighten the tendril in the fashion of a noose, so as to produce a cessation in the cheeseball's respiration."

"You choke him to death? You just snuff him pronto?" asked Xlotl. Each moldie based its speech patterns on some different database. While Andrea had filled herself with science writing, Xlotl had steeped himself in hard-boiled detective novels and gangster *film noirs*.

"By no means," said Andrea. "The goal is to render him unconscious so that you can operate on his brain. During the interval that you are constricting his throat, you must monitor his pulse, taking care that it does not become too slow or too irregular. Allow him to respire small amounts of air as needed. Meanwhile you elongate your tendril and insert its tip into his left nostril."

"Eeew," said Monique. "Guh-ross. I mean like what's in his *nose*?" She had modeled her speech on the bubbly, questioning Valley Girl slang of the late-twentieth century. They were hovering on the thermals off the cliffs north of Santa Cruz, all three of them snapped into pelican mode, talking in the shrill, compressed chirps of encrypted sound that moldies could use to speak with each other. The moldies were like great birds, squawking high above the crawling, wrinkled sea—yet to each other, they sounded like people talking.

"One of the weakest spots in a flesher's skull is the upper nasal sinus," old Andrea explained. "Adjacent to the ocular orbit. This is where you must punch through with your tendril. At this point you will have free access to his brain. And you give him a *thinking cap*."

"Cripes! A brain control!" exclaimed Xlotl.

"Your thinking cap will live in his skull like the pith on a nut in its hull," said Andrea, cackling and flapping her wings. "The cap functions as an I/O port or like an internal uvvy. Once he has your thinking cap, the cheeseball is your peripheral device."

"This sounds totally hard, Andrea," said anxious Monique. "I'd be freakin'. What if I don't choke him enough? And then I'm all 'Where's the weak spot?' I am so sure. And how am I supposed to know how to like hook a *thinking* cap into some pervo flesher's *brain*?"

"Come close, children," said Andrea. "I can give you copies of the full specs for a human brain interface. Make a physical contact with me for direct transmission."

The three soaring pelicans brushed wings, and Andrea downloaded a petabyte of information to each of the younger moldies. Thanks to the conductive polymers which filled their plastic tissues, moldies could communicate electromagnetically as well as by sound.

"Andrea, have you ever *really* done it? Tell me true," sang Monique after storing the info.

"Yes, I have given thinking caps to two cheeseballs in the past," said Andrea. "I refer of course to Spike Kimball and Abdul Quayoom—of whom I have often spoken. As my servants, these men left their families and their old lives. All of their assets and possessions were liquidated, with the full proceeds being given to me. By use of these resources, I have been able to purchase rejuvenation treatments as well as to buy the imipolex necessary to bring you and Xanana into the world, Monique."

Spike Kimball had been a muscular Mormon missionary who'd asked Andrea for sex three years ago, and Abdul Quayoom had been an Islamic rug programmer who'd approached Andrea three years before that. If they'd been smarter, instead of trying to have sex with Andrea, they would have burned her in a puddle of alcohol.

"So what do you do with a mark after you bleed him dry?" asked Xlotl. "Make him shoot himself? Have him swan-dive off a building to cave in his skull?"

"The direct control of a cheeseball must be of limited temporal duration," said Andrea. "Otherwise the danger of discovery becomes too great. And it is indeed essential that the cheeseball be terminated in such a way that no trace of the user's thinking cap can be found in his remains. Do you want to hear what I did to Quayoom and Kimball? About how I helped them follow their death angels Moroni and Izra'il into the beyond?"

"Oh yes," cried Monique and Xlotl.

"I directed them each to swim a mile out into the ocean at night and tread water there until hypothermia enabled them to drown. Once the subject had experienced brain death, I had my thinking cap crawl out of his nose and swim like a fish to meet me, waiting upon the shore."

"Whoah, that's cold," said Monique.

"Many fleshers would treat us with equal severity," said Andrea primly. "And remember, dear Monique, it is only by these means that I was able to acquire sufficient resources to continue my life after having given birth to you and Xanana. Would you deny your own mother the chance to rejuvenate herself? Moldie flesh is exorbitantly precious. Certainly you wouldn't want to stoop to victimizing other moldies instead of fleshers. I've heard that's what the loonie moldies do. You wouldn't want to be like them."

So when the hillbilly cheeseball solicited Monique from the door of Room 3D, she started thinking about giving him a thinking cap—thinking a mile a minute. Should she? Could she? Dare she try?

Just then Xlotl's voice spoke up in Monique's head. "Time for lunch break, baby. Meet me down at the beach?" The Los Trancos Taco Bar liked Xlotl to take an hour or more off around noon, so that his presence wouldn't repel people wanting to have lunch. In principle, Xlotl could have sealed his pores and become nearly odorless, but human prejudice ran deep. It was better not to have him in the place when a lot of folks were eating.

"Totally," thought back Monique. "There's something I want to discuss with you in person." Due to the irredeemable promiscuity of electromagnetic radiation, *no* uvvy link could be secure enough for planning murder.

Monique waved enticingly to the cheeseball behind his green-and-red-stickered window glass, then flounced down the stairs to Beach Street.

A moldie bus full of tourists went quietly pattering past, followed by five moldies acting as rickshaws and carrying individual people. Monique boinged around them, chirping hellos to the ones that she recognized, and then she was on the beach. Looking up the hill toward the Los Trancos Taco Bar, Monique could see her darling husband hopping toward her. Xlotl resembled his wife Monique—he was shaped like a coppery Aztec chessman with a mouth like a purple slash in his face.

He bounced right into Monique, whooping wildly, and they wrapped their arms around each other and went rolling down toward the water. They came to rest at surf's edge and lay there writhing in a sexual embrace, each of them pushing branching tendrils deep and deeper into the other's body.

Monique loved the intimate sensation of having herself in Xlotl and Xlotl in her. They were linked up like fractal puzzle pieces, with as much of their surfaces in contact as possible. In the deepest cracks of their linkage, their skins opened up so that their bodies could exchange small wet seeps of imipolex, carrying along cells of their symbiotic fungi and algae. The more often two moldies embraced in this sexual manner, the more their bodies came to resemble each other.

The pleasure of contact reached an intense crescendo—an orgasm, really—and then the moldies slipped into puddle shapes so that their algae could soak up as much sun as possible.

"Oh, that was yummy," sighed Monique. "We're getting so tight with each other, Xlotl. If we can buy the imipolex, we'll be ready to have a baby soon."

After having sex enough times, two moldies would buy the

necessary imipolex plastic for a new body and fuck it into new life, creating a child infused with some combination of the parents' lichens and software. The plastic was expensive and could only be purchased from one of two or three large human-run companies with money earned (or stolen) from the fleshers. Like it or not, the moldies and the fleshers were uneasily allied, even though some moldies were capable of invading human brains and some humans were willing to burn moldies in pools of alcohol.

"It's gonna take a while to earn the dough, what with the crummy wages we're getting," chirped Xlotl cozily. "But we're having fun anyway, ain't we?" The foam lapped about them and Xlotl snuggled himself against Monique, making sure that they touched all along the edge that separated their two puddles. For a moment Monique slipped into sleep and started to dream. About whales. But then a bold wave splashed her and she was back awake. Something was wrong . . . oh yes.

"Xlotl, omigod, I forgot to tell you! This cheeseball in Room 3D is like coming on to me?"

"No kidding? A cheeseball?"

"For sure. I'm about to like clean the room and he's standing there behind the glass waving to me. *Beckoning* me? Just then you called and I jammed down here. I don't want to go back."

"Aw, go on in there and take him for every cent he's worth, Momo. Andrea taught us how to do it yesterday."

"I'm scared. And, Xlotl, don't you think it's a negative thing to trash a dook's brain and then make him like die? I mean of course it's only a flesher . . . but don't you ever flash that information is sacred? Even a flesher cheeseball's brain?"

"Honey, it balances out. A dog is sacred, a DIM is sacred. Everything's sacred. But with this mark's money we can have a child right away and use our own money to get ourselves retrofits. Like Andrea does. Hell, we can have two, three children *and* rejuvenate ourselves if your dook is well fixed. All this fine moldie consciousness for the cost of one less flesher? I'd call that a net gain of information. Move in on him, baby!"

"I'm like undecided? Let's fab about something else. How's Los Trancos today?"

"Same sleazy dive. This morning I had to goose the loaf of wendy meat with hormones to make it grow faster. All the tourists are gobbling it. I think they ain't got that brand outside of California yet."

"And wendy meat is human flesh!" exclaimed Monique. "It's all cloned from the same cells as that Wendy Mooney who's in the ads. I thought there was some heavy human taboo about *cannibalism?*"

"Fleshers will eat anything, Monique. They're like lobsters. How do you know the woman in the ad is the actual Wendy Mooney anyhow?"

"Tre told me. He just helped Apex Images design a wendy meat ad—the big one down at the Boardwalk?"

Monique and Xlotl laid back down in the shallow, lapping surf, enjoying the warmth of the sun and the coolness of the water. Xlotl formed a cavity in his flesh, filled it with water, and sprayed it up overhead like a fountain. Monique engulfed an even bigger amount of water and sprayed higher than him. Then break time was over and the two moldies shared a last intimate embrace.

Just then a little boy stopped to stare at Monique and Xlotl.

"Lookie, Paw, it's two moldies fucking!" he bawled. "I'll try and kill 'em!" The child picked up a stick and poked it into Xlotl. Hard. Xlotl pinched off his skin around the puncture before he lost much cell tissue, and then he twisted around so that he flipped into the shape of an angry chessman, with the stick still protruding from his chest.

"You want me to bust your sack for good, you twerp?" snarled Xlotl, rearing up like a six-foot nightmare centaur. He pushed the stick out of his flesh so hard that it flew past the boy's head like a viciously hurled boomerang.

The kid took off crying, only to return a moment later with his father in tow.

"What are you scummy moldies doing out here?" asked the man. Monique jumped up into her chessman mode as well.

"This is a public beach, dook," said Xlotl. "And we're citizens."

"Hell you are," said the man, not drawing any closer. He was balding and paunchy, with sunburned pale skin. "You leave my kid alone or else." He turned and moved back off down the beach. The little boy followed his dad, turning once to give Xlotl the finger.

"Fleshers," said Xlotl. "Why can't we ever get away from them? Why can't we kill them all?"

"It wouldn't work," said Monique. "You know that. You can't ever kill all of anything."

"The fleshers killed all of the boppers in 2031, didn't they?" said Xlotl. "With chipmold. All we need is a really good plague germ to kill off all the humans."

"They didn't really kill the boppers. Lots of the bopper software still lives on in us. The chipmold just helped the boppers move to a new platform. All at once. And really, Xlotl, you know that if the moldies start a biological war against the fleshers, the fleshers will come back at *us* with some really sick disease. Everyone knows that. It's live and let live."

"Also known as a mutual-assured destruction," said Xlotl. "Thank God for the Moldie Citizenship Act. Now what about this cheeseball situation. You ain't gonna punk out, are you? Get mad! Think about the kid who poked me."

"Maybe—why don't I go get a pep talk from Mom. I think she said she was gonna get high and lie out in front of the Boardwalk today."

"Shaped like the Koran or the Book of Mormon? Or maybe like the fuckin' works of Shakespeare!"

"Like the Bible. Remember? Andrea's into Christianity these days. She's all—" Monique broke into laughter, threw back her head, and delivered a pitch-perfect imitation of her mother's tones: " 'I am interested in a relationship with a God-fearing Christian man.' "

Xlotl nodded thoughtfully. "Andrea will get you to go through with it. If she don't take the job herself. I'll cool my heels at Los Trancos—with my uvvy tuned for you. Squawk if you need muscle."

"Wavy, darling. Wish me luck." Monique bounded down the beach toward the Boardwalk.

She stayed at the edge of the surf, where the glistening wet sand was the firmest. Some of the people she passed smiled and nodded, while others frowned and looked away. One guy—the father of the boy Xlotl had frightened—stood up and shouted, "Go back to the Moon!" He was holding a beer.

Instead of bouncing on farther, Monique stopped short and faced him. He was sitting on a blanket with his wife and another couple under an oversized beach umbrella. Their pale, weedy kids grubbed in the sand around them.

"I've never *been* to the Moon," shouted back Monique. "Why don't *you* get out of my town?"

"Fuck you!" hollered the man.

"Where do you want it?" screeched Monique, phallically thrusting her arm. "In your nose or up your ass?" She bounced menacingly toward the man. He sat down and gestured weakly for Monique to go away.

In a few minutes Monique drew even with the Santa Cruz Boardwalk, a classic seaside amusement park. All day long, the students, moldies, farmworkers, surfers, and homeless stoners of Santa Cruz streamed through the Boardwalk, diluting the valleys and Heritagists enough so that the place was never whitebread dull. The Boardwalk was six blocks long and half a block thin. Despite the name, the grounds were paved with concrete.

Monique went up from the beach onto the Boardwalk near the main snack bar, which had Tre's huge new ad for wendy meat on display overhead. The ad was a vast translucent hollow made up of seven kinds of funny-shaped creatures pecking each other's butts and heads and adding up to an image of an impossibly beautified man and woman whose expressions kept cycling through an ever-escalating but never repeating spiral of joy.

The man was modeled on ex-Senator Stahn Mooney and the woman on his wife Wendy Mooney, sexily wearing nothing but her Happy Cloak. It was a fascinating thing to look at, like an immense three-dimensional mosaic of pastel chunks. The shapes of the chunks were based on a four-dimensional Perplexing Poultry philtre which Tre had discovered in July. Monique had helped Tre a bit with the final computations for the ad, and it made her proud to see it.

As Monique crossed the Boardwalk, somebody mistook her for a worker and asked her where to get ride tickets. Monique pointed to the ticket kiosk and motorvated on past it, smoothly rolling the ripples of her base.

On the sidewalk outside the Boardwalk was Monique's mother Andrea, spread softly out on the pavement like a Colorado River toad, but a toad in the shape of a giant book lying open on the ground. The Good Book. Big gothic letters scrolled across the two exposed pages. Just now the letters read THOU SHALT NOT HATE MOLDIES.

"Moldies are sentient beings with genuine religious impulses," intoned Andrea. "I'm interested in pursuing a dialogue on this issue. Especially with single men!"

"Mom," said Monique in an encrypted chirp. "One of these days a Heritagist tourist is going to pour alcohol on you and light you. A lot of Heritagists are Christians. Do you really think they dig seeing you like imitate their sacred book?"

"Greetings, Monique," squawked Andrea cheerfully. "I am in an ecstatic state of consciousness today. A potent yttrium-ytterbium-twist compound was provided to me this morning by Cousin Emuline. It's made right here in California, they call it *betty,* I don't know why, maybe because *betty* is almost *ytter-bium* spelled backward, well that would be *muibretty*. Monique, your mother is lifted on fine, fine muibretty betty. But what is your request, my dear daughter?"

"I wanted to fab about this cheeseball who's after me? I'm trying to get like stoked to give him a thinking cap?"

"You can do it, Monique, you can!"

"I'm scared. And it seems wrong."

"Accept your sensations of fear, Monique, but don't let them dominate your behavior. Remember that your attack must be abrupt and decisive, otherwise—"

"Otherwise what?" asked Monique nervously.

"Cousin Emuline told me a rumor that someone is abducting moldies and shipping them to the Moon. My hypothesis is that it's the Heritagists working with the loonie moldies. Yes yes, those greedy loonie moldies are capable of anything. Emuline and I think they're getting their hired goon Heritagist friends to enslave moldies with a new kind of leech-DIM called super-leeches."

"What're they?"

"I've told you about the old leech-DIMs. They jam a moldie's normal thinking process. It's a bit like being asleep and on the whole a rather pleasantly stony ride, I'm told—unless some flesher slits you open and sells your camote to the sporeheads and your imipolex to the Moon. Your boss Terri's father used to be into that, by the way, which is why we executed him—not that you should ever ever mention this to Terri. The new su-perleeches are much worse than the old leech-DIMs. Emuline says a superleech is like a reverse thinking cap, like a psychic cage that—"

Three well-dressed California tourists had stopped to stare at Andrea. They were a yuppie mother, father, and daughter.

"What's that thing supposed to be?" asked the mother.

"I am the Bible," said Andrea in a sweet, reasonable voice. "The Good Book of your Savior. I'm interested in pursuing a dialogue on religious issues."

"Look, it has writing on it," said the little girl. "It says, 'Love thy moldie as thyself.' "

"Don't get close to it," cautioned the father. "It might try and get something from you. Everything that has anything to do with religion sucks, Susie. You might as well know that right now. Let's go look at the rides." They wandered off.

"Why do you do this anyway, Andrea?" asked Monique.

"To foster an enhanced peace and understanding between the species, my child. And to meet a cheeseball Christian man I can rob and kill."

"Well, I think you're crazy."

"The Bible says, 'Honor thy father and mother,' " said Andrea.

"Quite reasonable. Now you go and do what you're supposed to do. And use extreme caution. Did I tell you I'm way lifted on betty? Yes. I can almost see creatures in the sky, even now as I speak. Creatures from other worlds."

Andrea flipped a few pages of her Bible body and called out a greeting to another group of tourists. They ignored her and walked on.

"Has it ever occurred to you that everything is alive, my child?" mused Andrea. "Information is everywhere. Information rains down upon us from the heavens in the form of cosmic rays. In my exalted mental state, I can feel them. Oooh. Ummm. Ooooh. Aaaaaaah."

"Mom, are you sure that rare-earth stuff isn't bad for you?"

"All known life processes end in death, Monique. In an information-theoretical sense, becoming repetitious is like dying even before your body goes. You have to trade off some risk to your body in order to enhance the action of the mind. And in your case, you have a very dangerous and very specific mission for today. Don't avoid it."

"Wavy, floatin', I'll go for it. Bye."

Back up on the lower walkway of the Clearlight Terrace Court Motel, there was no visible action in Room 3D. But Monique had a feeling that her cheeseball was still in there.

She stretched her neck out backward over the balcony like a comic book Plastic Man, looking to make sure that Tre or Terri weren't in sight. Thanks to the contractible polymers in her piezoplastic imipolex body, Monique could stretch and bend her body at will—although it took a lot of energy to stay in any position other than one of her stable attractor modes, such as the chessman or the pelican.

There was no sign of Tre or Terri. Terri had probably gone

out surfing, leaving Tre in the office playing with his uvvy. Just
to make sure about Tre, Monique made an uvvy call to him. She
found Tre's icon in the midst of a weird four-dimensional collage
of warped animal shapes: his new uvvy philtre.

"Yaar, Monique," said the Tre icon, noticing her. "Is everything wavy?"

"Just fine," said Monique. "I'm back from break and I'll be
done cleaning the rooms in a half hour or so. I wanted to tell
you that we need to order more soap today. You'll have to authorize a payment."

"Floatin'," said Tre. "And come on up to the office later if
you could. Terri wants us to start fabulating about painting the
buildings. And there's some other stuff we gotta fab about. Some
of it's gogo, some of it's kilpy."

"I surf all, Tre," said Monique pleasantly. "Delish!"

After signing off with Tre, Monique used part of her computational space to follow the data threads that led out of the
registration information she had on Randy Karl Tucker in Room
3D. He was a native of Shively, Kentucky, twenty-one years old,
unmarried, and with a good bank balance. Apparently he'd been
overseas recently, but Monique wasn't able to access any information about the trip; this part of Tucker's data trail had been
covered with a security lock. The most salient point was that
Tucker had more than enough money to pay for the plastic for
a child. Randy the redneck seemed like just the kind of victim
Andrea had told her to look for.

Monique glided over to Randy Karl Tucker's door and
knocked. He opened it, and Monique mamboed on in. The room
smelled like Tucker's breath. Tucker's uvvy was sitting on his
desk, projecting a hollow of a pornographic soap opera.

"Yaar there," said Monique, synthesizing the sounds on a fluttering membrane near the back of her mouth cavity. "I saw you,
um, gesturing to me before? Is there something I can like do
for you?"

Tucker's thin mouth lengthened in a sly, lustful smile. "I
knowed you'd come back. That's why I been settin' here a-

waitin'. Just close the door to begin with, you little stinker. And pull the drapes. Before we start a-carryin' on." He was clean-shaven, and his eyes were flat and pale. Two women on the porno soap were arguing over a boyfriend.

"I'm not sure I can help you, sir," said knowing Monique, sliding the door closed and pulling the curtain across it. "Terri Percesepe, she's the manager here, she was just telling me this morning that it's not proper for me to have any kind of intimacy with the guests. 'The Clearlight Terrace Court Motel is a place for wholesome family fun.' Those were Terri's exact words." Monique set her arms akimbo, flexed the erectile tissues of her breast mounds, and waggled the hiplike swelling below her waist. "So, um, like what *is* it that you want from me, country boy?" She pouted out her lips and giggled.

"I . . ." Moving as stagily as one of the actors on the soap, Tucker paused to take a slurp from a cardboard cup of coffee printed with the logo of the Daffo Deli down on Beach Street. He looked solemnly up from his cup, only to lose his composure and break into a cackle at Monique's beckoning gyrations, for now Monique was milling her arms and flinging them out like a pom-pom cheerleader.

"*You're* a peppy hunk o' cheese, ain't you," said Tucker. "To hell with what your boss says, Monique. You show me a good time, and I'll pay you plenty."

Monique undulated forward across the motel room's carpeted floor, standing right up against the man, opening her skin fissures to release an even headier mixture of her bouquet. "Can you authorize a charge to your account now, Randy?"

"How?"

"I'm the bookkeeper as well as the maid, Mr. Tucker. Will you authorize the charge?" Monique reached out and undid one of the buttons of his long-sleeved white plastic shirt. His gray pants and black plastic belt were as cheap-looking as the shirt. His hair was short and unclean. His thin skin was spotty from acne and a faded tan, and Monique could see his faintly pulsing blue veins beneath the skin's surface. His nose was a bit crooked, and he had a large Adam's apple.

"Um, all right," the man mumbled reluctantly. "But put it down as, as . . ."

"I'll just average it into your like room rate?" said Monique. "It won't show. But you have to come out and say just what it is that you want me to do." Monique smiled hugely and released a cloud of spores. "So that you can't frame me for prostitution. In case you're a like Heritagist? So now please tell me what you want, Randy."

"I want you to blow me, damn it. And what's wrong with Heritagists anyway?"

"That's what you are?"

"I ain't sayin' that I hold their beliefs. But I knowed a few of 'em back in Shively. The Heritagists have done me some good from time to time."

"What would they think about your wanting to have sex with a moldie?"

Tucker sighed. "They'd understand it perfectly—why the hell you think they talk about it so much? I'm way past that loser guilt shit, Monique. All the things I've done—it's hard to believe I'm only twenty-one." Tucker stared intensely at Monique, as if trying to read her mind. Finally he reached some internal decision and looked away. "Let's just say I'm a peculiar man, and I got my needs. Can we git started now?"

"Love to," said Monique dryly. She finished unbuttoning Randy's shirt, and now she undid his pants. She paused, looking at him. He was weedy and thin, but with a certain amount of muscle. She was going to have to be sure to get a tight choke hold on him when she went up his nose and punched into his cranium.

Now he lay back on his bed and Monique pressed against him, letting her tissues flow and reshape to mold themselves so as to fully envelop Randy's private parts. Sexually, it meant no more to her than pushing a wheelbarrow would mean to a human. Monique set up some caressing rhythms, trying to rock the weight up to speed.

While Tucker wheezed and twitched in mounting excitement, Monique set her right forefinger to growing like a vine. She twined it up along Tucker's torso and wrapped it once around his neck.

Feeling leery of starting to choke Tucker right away, Monique went ahead and slid the tip of her four-foot-long finger into Tucker's nose, at the same time setting some chaotic ripples onto his genitals. But now, instead of lying back in blind ecstasy, Tucker suddenly sat up and started clawing at his face and neck.

"What the hell you think you're doin' in my nose, bitch? Thought you'd give me a thinking cap, didn't you!" Weirdly enough, he sounded not so much angry as excited, and he made a rattling noise that sounded almost like a cackle.

Monique tightened herself around his neck as much as possible and punched her tendril with all her might against the spot high up at the back of Tucker's nose. But it wouldn't give! She punched and punched again, but it was like Tucker's skull was patched with titaniplast or something—Monique couldn't get in!

And now Tucker had wormed his right hand between Monique's noose and his throat, and she couldn't choke him anymore. With his left hand, he yanked Monique's tendril out of his nose. He got to his feet and started kicking at Monique's body. Monique squeezed his testicles so hard that he screamed and fell sideways, crashing into the desk and plopping the uvvy and its holograms to the floor. This was turning into a full-scale disaster. If Monique ran off now, Tucker would tell people about Monique's attack on him and she'd be hunted down and exterminated. She had to finish him off!

Tucker was on his back now, and Monique was on his nude body like a savage vampire slug. There was a fight scene playing on the hollow too, which seemed to be drowning out Tucker's cries so far. Or maybe all the people in the nearby rooms were out on the beach where they belonged, instead of lurking inside waiting to have sex with a moldie like this skungy Heritagist bastard—

Tucker had hold of his travel bag now and was fumbling to unlatch it. A gun? A gun couldn't hurt a moldie. With his left arm out of the way, Monique was free to shove a fat tendril down his throat. She'd been on the point of calling Xlotl for help, but now she was sure she was going to win. There was a good weak spot in the skull right behind the roof of the flesher's mouth, and it wasn't armored like the spot in his nose. Bye, flesher. But just as Monique began to push, something leaped out of Tucker's suitcase and slapped up against her—and everything changed.

Instead of being on top of the struggling Randy Karl Tucker, Monique was curled up on the floor beside him. His voice was inside her, whispering to her. She could make no move without his permission. Even her thoughts were not fully her own.

"Yeah, you just lay still for now, Monique," Randy said, getting to his feet. "Nice li'l tussle you put up there."

A lively little two-legged imipolex creature was strutting back and forth on the floor like a chicken. It was the thing that had jumped at Monique. "Back in the bag, Willa Jean," Randy told it. "You done good. You pasted that superleech on her just in time." He coughed and went into the bathroom to drink some water. The chicken stood there staring at Monique. It had a fuzzy purple patch on its back. It moved tentatively closer and gave Monique's face a gentle peck, then a harder one, gouging out and absorbing a little strip of Monique's imipolex.

"Back in the bag, Willa Jean," repeated Randy, coming out of the bathroom. "Now." The creature hopped into Randy's bag and he closed it back up.

Randy dug in his pocket and examined a couple of small purple patches of imipolex he found there. Then he picked up the room's uvvy and called someone, using a voice connection alone.

"Aarbie? Randy here, ole son. Got me one. How soon can y'all get the boat out there? Copacetic. I'm startin' now." He turned off the uvvy.

"We goin' for a swim," Randy told Monique, this time without speaking out loud. "We'll walk outside and you'll rickshaw me down to the cliff at Steamer Lane. We gonna step lively so your boss don't stop us."

Monique had a sudden hallucination of the seabed lying all uncovered, with gasping fish lying on their sides and octopuses slithering about and great windrows of kelp filled with starfish of every color. She felt floppy and without force; she felt like a jellyfish.

"Up and at 'em, Monique." The voice goaded her upright, and she made her way out of Room 3D with Randy Karl Tucker close behind.

Tre was sitting in front of the motel office, but Monique walked right past him. Randy had some brief discussion with Tre behind Monique's back, and then Randy jumped onto her, riding her like a beast of burden. They raced down the hill to the water's edge, then hurried the half mile north to Steamer Lane.

"Now you be a wetsuit for me," Randy told her and forced Monique to flow out around him, forced his nasty body all the way inside her. They dove off the cliff.

The water broke around Monique in a dizzying explosion of color and light. She was hallucinating again. A whirlwind of pure energy boiled around her and through her. In the boiling she forgot herself entirely for a time and then, as the roar damped down, Monique realized she'd been swimming for ages; she could feel it from the fatigue in her body. The seabed looked odd; it was patterned with a grid like a map, and the fish around her seemed to have human faces. In the same dreamy way, the kelp plants seemed to be made of gears and metal.

And then she stopped, and near her was a white boat. Sun-dappled wave crests marched out to the horizon and suddenly she noticed something amazing, a great poisonous green bulk hanging over the water near the boat, a spot she'd seen but not registered before. It was a great translucent green whale hanging there in midair, and now that Monique saw it, the whale began to fall, its flukes threshing the air. "You gonna follow that," said the enemy who was nestled inside her, and the whale jumped backward in time, its great tapered tail rising up out of the water in an arc with the huge striped belly and giant mouth coming after, the whale hanging there in the air, smiling so strange and friendly that Monique began to laugh and laugh. She laughed so hard that her back split open, and the evil white worm man popped out of her and swam to the boat.

"Follow the whale," the man called, and now the dreamy ghost of a whale moved forward again in time, diving into the water, sounding for the ocean's very floor, with Monique swimming after, swimming down and down toward the whale's glowing green light.

CHAPTER TWO

RANDY

=== ■ ===

September 2048–April 2051

Randy Karl Tucker grew up near the Dixie Highway in tacky Shively, down in the southwest corner of Louisville. About a century earlier, the Dixie Highway had been the main road into town from the army base at Fort Knox, thirty miles south of Louisville, and Shively had been a place where soldiers would come to taste the calm pleasures of civilian life—or to gamble at Churchill Downs and get drunk and sleep with floozies. Many of the soldiers ended up marrying Shively women; over the years it became a solid little community, with its full share of godless lowlifes, professional Christians, and dazed white trash.

Randy's mother Sue Tucker was bi, on the butch side, though cutely tomboyish to some male eyes. She was a master plumber with her own business that she ran out of her truck and her little house's garage. Mostly she did repairs, though now and then she'd do contract work for remodeling.

Sue didn't like to talk about Randy's father, but children hear everything, and over the years Randy had learned that his father had been a random guy who'd happened to make it with Sue in

25

the course of a big sex party at the La Mirage Health Club in downtown Louisville on Halloween, 2031. According to Sue, the guy had been masked behind a flickercladding Happy Cloak, disguised as a woman, in fact, and she'd never found out who he was.

There were men around when Randy was quite young, but at the time he entered adolescence, Sue Tucker was in lesbian mode. One of Sue's favorite girlfriends was a femme named Honey Weaver—a stocky bleached-blonde waitress with large breasts and a weak chin. Soon after Randy's sixteenth birthday, Sue Tucker selected Honey to be the one to instruct Randy Karl about sex, the idea being that, as a lesbian, Honey would teach Randy a proper respect for women.

"Randy Karl," Sue said one September afternoon in 2048 after coming home to find Randy squirmingly watching porno on the uvvy once again. "Turn off that kilp. It's antiwoman."

"Oh, come on, Sue." He always called his mother by her first name. "It don't hurt none. At least let me do it till I need glasses." He was a mournful-looking lad with a long, thin face. He hadn't gotten his growth yet and was only a little over five feet tall. He wore his hair in a flattop. He was dressed in a white T-shirt and khakis; the khakis had a nasty bulge in them from Randy's watching the filth on the uvvy.

"Randy Karl, it's high time you learned what's what. I want you to go on over to Honey Weaver's right now."

"Huh? What for?"

"She's having a problem with her drain. You can fix that for her, can't you?"

Randy had often helped his mother on jobs, but this was the first time she'd offered to let him go out on his own.

"Will I git paid union wage?"

"And then some."

Randy put together a toolbox and walked down the street to Honey's—she lived two and a half blocks away in a house exactly like the Tuckers': a three-room bungalow with cheap ceramic siding and a concrete front stoop.

Honey came to the door in a loosely fastened pink wrapper. "Oh, hi there, Randy. Sue told me you were on your way. I just changed out of my waitress clothes. Come on in." As she opened the door, her wrapper slid a bit farther open, and Randy could see her bare breasts and a flash of her pubic hair. "What you starin' at, boy?" said Honey with a gentle laugh. "Ain't you never seen a live woman before?"

"I—" choked Randy, setting down his box of tools with a clatter. "Honey, I—"

"You're all excited," purred Honey. "You cute little thing." She stretched out her arms so that her wrapper fell wide open. "Come here, Randy. Hug me and kiss my tits."

Randy exulted in the smell and feel of Honey's pillowy breasts, breasts that smelled of sweat and perfume, breasts that rubbed Randy's face with stiff nipples. Honey snaked her hand down and undid Randy's pants. Before he knew what was happening, she'd gotten out his stiff little dick and he'd come off into her insistent, intimate fingers. He was so surprised and embarrassed that he burst into tears.

"There, there," said Honey, smiling down at him and rubbing his sperm onto her breasts. "That makes nice smooth skin. I like milking a little boy like you, Randy Karl. Would you like to see my vagina?"

"Yes, Honey, I surely would."

"Kneel down on the floor in front of me."

Randy knelt on the smooth plastic floor, and Honey stepped up close to Randy with her fragrant, bushy crotch right at the level of his face. She adjusted her legs a bit, straddling them wider, and now Randy could see the details of her genitalia.

"Kiss my pussy, Randy Karl. Lick on it all over."

Randy started in gingerly, but then Honey seized his head with both hands and pressed his face tight between her legs. Honey's slippery, soft tissues felt luxurious, extravagant, intoxicating. Randy kissed and licked and sucked and moaned. Honey began a rapid rhythmic bucking of her pelvis against Randy's mouth, a bucking that cascaded into chaotic shudders. And then she sank down to the floor beside Randy.

Randy crawled up onto Honey, hoping to sink his painfully stiff erection into her—but she balked.

"I don't want no man's dick in me never again, Randy Karl, not even yours." She sat up, looking a little dazed. Outside it was dusk; the door was slightly open, and through the screen door Randy could see people down on the sidewalk passing by. But the kitchen lights were off and the people couldn't see in. "If you do one more favor for me, Randy, I'll milk you off again."

"Sure, Honey. I'll do anything you say. This is the most fun I ever had." At this moment Honey looked sublimely beautiful to Randy, even with the roll of fat at her waist and with her stark lack of a chin.

"Wait right here."

Honey went into her bedroom and got something. A long, soft, plastic thing in the shape of a dick. It was dark blue with shifting highlights of gold.

"This here's my limpware dildo," said Honey. "Since I'm a dyke, I call it a *she*. Her name is Angelika. Angelika, this is Randy Karl Tucker. Randy, meet Angelika."

The dildo twitched and simpered in Honey's hand. It—*she*—actually had a little voice. Randy recognized that Angelika was made of imipolex with a DIM; she was like a moldie, only not so smart. Randy had hardly ever seen any moldies or even limpware in Shively before. There were enough militant Christian Heritagists around to keep that kind of thing out of sight.

"Stick Angelika in me, Randy Karl," said Honey, laying back on the floor. "It's what your mommy always does for me. And get over on one side of me so's I can reach your dick."

Angelika was lively and vibrant in Randy's hand. She hummed as if in pleasurable anticipation. Noticing an odd smell, Randy held the dildo up to his nose and sniffed it. The limpware gave off a gamy fetid odor quite unlike Honey's funky musk.

"That's the way moldies smell," Honey explained. "It seems

right nasty at first, but later you get used to it. It's sexy! Spray out more smell, Angelika!"

The dildo chirped and hissed, and the sharp moldie stink got ten times stronger. Randy could feel his blood pounding in his temples. He'd never been so aroused in his entire life.

"Come on, Randy!" urged Honey. "We're still just gittin' started!"

Over and over for the next two years—the rest of his time in high school—Randy kept coming back for sex with Honey, and Honey kept thinking of new things for them to do. When she noticed how interested Randy was in seeing her go to the bathroom, she bought a big moldie imipolex sheet that Randy would lie down on naked while Honey urinated all over him, especially on his face. The sheet's name was Sammie-Jo.

Randy's grades dropped as he wandered around in a haze, continually thinking of things like the scent of Honey's hot urine mingled with the rank odor of Sammie-Jo. He made some half-hearted attempts to date the girls he went to high school with, but nothing could come close to Honey Weaver, Angelika, and Sammie-Jo. Randy was becoming sexually addicted to imipolex.

One of Honey's motives for the whole affair was to focus Sue Tucker's attention on Honey's sexuality. Honey loved to tell Sue all the intimate details of what she did with Randy. At first Sue was compulsively, unwholesomely fascinated; during those unpleasant months Randy would sometimes catch his mother watching him with a bright, quizzical expression. But finally Sue's motherly instincts won out and she banished all interest in her son's sex life.

This turned out to be a net loss for Honey, because Sue's interest in Honey's sexuality got repressed right alongside the visions of Randy servicing Honey. Sue had several screaming arguments with Honey on the uvvy before she could get Honey to stop calling her up with the latest details. After a year or so, the irregular love triangle became so galling to Sue that she stopped talking to Honey entirely.

In the spring of Randy Karl's senior year in high school, Sue flipped back to being het. She started a steady relationship with an unpleasant, foppish man named Lewis. Lewis had a mustache grown out so long that it was possible to twirl the ends, which was something Lewis frequently did. Lewis was a site manager for the company building London Earl Estates, a cut-rate housing development in Okalona, Kentucky, twenty miles south of Shively. Sue was doing a lot of the plumbing contracting at London Earl, which is how she met Lewis, who spent his days there in a trailer office. Lewis was a martinet and a weakling, but Sue seemed to enjoy him. She was quite a bit smarter than him, and she was generally able to get him to do whatever she wanted him to.

As soon as Lewis moved in with Sue, he started pressuring Randy to leave, but Sue stuck up for her son. She moved Randy's room out into the garage so Randy and Lewis wouldn't get in each other's way so much, and she began passing Randy all of her plumbing work other than the contracts out at London Earl Estates. Randy already had his journeyman plumber certification, and she wanted him to make master plumber before leaving home.

"Technology can come and go, Randy Karl," Sue liked to tell Randy. "But people are always going to use pipes. These days we got soft pipes and smart pipes, but they're still pipes. There's no other way to move water around, and nobody knows how to handle pipes except plumbers. Once you're a master plumber, you're fixed for life."

Randy was happier than he'd ever been that spring. His sex thing with Honey was going hot and heavy. And he made great money after school and on the weekends. He was getting really good at the new plumbing technologies. His favorite was the pipe-gun that would grow a plastic pipe right under a house's crawl space, a snaky crawling pipe that would zig and zag where you told it to. He liked living in the garage, and Sue was proud of how fast he was learning.

The end to this golden age came on June 20, 2050, the day after Randy graduated from high school.

Randy woke up late; it was nearly noon. Some of his classmates had thrown a big party after the graduation and for once they'd let Randy come. He still felt giddy from the beer, pot, bourbon, and snap he'd had the night before. Randy wasn't used to drinking and doping. How had he gotten home? Oh yeah, he'd walked, stopping every few blocks to puke into people's yards. What a toot!

He rolled over on his side, taking a mental inventory of himself. He felt pretty good. He was all through with school. He sat up on the edge of his bed and looked around the garage—at his dresser and desk sitting among the drums of raw pipe plastic and the cabinets of plumbing machine parts. His clothes hangers dangled from a wire slung up under the ceiling. Sue's truck and Lewis's hydrogen cycle were gone. Randy was all through with school. He had a stubborn erection; the sensory amplification of his hangover/stoneover made him riggish. He decided to go on over to Honey's; today was her day off.

Randy put on a sleeveless T-shirt, baggy shorts, and plastic sandals. He ate some milk and bread out of his mother's fridge and ambled down the street toward Honey's.

It was a hot Kentucky day, the air so thick with humidity that your skin got slick with sweat if you moved fast. The cracks in the old concrete streets and sidewalks were lush with weeds. Gnats whined everywhere. The weeds and the bushes and grasses exuded a steamy warmth. Each of the Shively houses was just like the one next to it, each the same ceramic-coated box, each with a slightly different trim pattern around the front door.

Honey was home all right, but when Randy walked in, she turned red-faced and tearful. "Don't come near me!" cried Honey. "No more! All them things you and me did was wrong, Randy Karl!"

"Now what are you talkin' about, Honey? Are you mad Sue wouldn't let me ask you to the graduation?"

"Everything we done was wrong!" repeated Honey. "Especially the things with Angelika and . . . and with Sammie-Jo. Dr. Dicky Pride at the Shively Heritage House told me so. Yes, when you and your mamma didn't ask me to your graduation last night, I went to the service at the Heritage House. And now I've done been born again. I was up past midnight with Dr. Pride a-prayin' over me."

At first Randy thought Honey was playing with him, and he began to beseech her and to abase himself like she'd taught him to do. "Forgive me, Mistress Honey. Your will is my will. Do anything you like to me," said Randy, groveling at her feet and unzipping his fly. "But, um, please do *something*. I'm horny as hell from all that beer and snap I had last night."

"Only thing you and me might *ever* do together again, Randy Karl Tucker, is goin' to meetings over to the Shively Heritage House," said Honey, flouncing to the other side of the room and sitting down in a straight-backed chair with her arms crossed. "I'm through bein' the goddamn Whore of Babylon. I've cleansed my body's temple."

"Um—what about Angelika and Sammie-Jo? Can I have 'em?"

"Dr. Pride said I should bring them to the Heritage House, but—yeah, you take 'em. I'd be ashamed to bring them in. What if Dr. Pride asked me to hold them up and like go, 'This is my dildo that my boy toy and his mommy and me fucked each other with so many taahms, and this is the sheet I used to piss on him with, and—' " Honey's voice broke into shrill brittle laughter— or was it tears? She was still sitting in the chair across the room. She stretched out her trembling arm to point at the closet where she kept her imipolex sex toys. "Take 'em the hell out of here right now, Randy Karl! Take 'em and git!" She began crying hard, and Randy tried to pet her, but there was no way.

He took Sammie-Jo and Angelika home and masturbated with them. It was okay, though nowhere near as hot as it had always been with Honey at the controls. Angelika and Sammie-Jo weren't smart enough to be really fun. For the first time Randy started wondering what it would be like to have sex with fully intelligent and autonomous moldies instead of with these imipolex DIM-equipped toys. After he'd come, he washed Angelika and Sammie-Jo, let them lay out in the sun for a while, and then put them in the back of one of the cabinet drawers near his bed in the garage.

Randy kept on mooning around Honey's the rest of that summer—mowing her lawn, doing her dishes, anything at all—but to no avail. The only thing Honey liked to do anymore was to go to meetings at the Shively Heritage House. So in August Randy started going with her.

Randy was certainly no Mr. Sophisticated, but he'd never seen such a bunch of losers, geeks, and feebs as he found at the Heritage House meetings—all the people raving about Jesus and the Heritage of Man and about how much they hated the moldies. The Heritagists were highly exercised over the Moldie Citizenship Act that Senator Stahn Mooney of California had managed to railroad through Congress back in 2038. Even though Mooney had been out of office for years now, Congress still hadn't mustered the will to repeal that hellacious moldie-lovin' Act. What an outrage! Another big area of interest was, of course, all the perverse permutations of sex made possible by moldies, uvvies, and imipolex.

Randy would try and catch Honey's eye sometimes when Dicky Pride would go off about moldies and imipolex—Randy fondly remembering the steamy sessions with Honey and her toys—but Honey would just look away. Her small mind had shifted gears and there was nothing to do about it.

Meanwhile Randy was doing more and more plumbing. The customers Sue had given him were passing his name on to their friends; he was known for doing fast, solid work for the best price around. He was a whiz with the pipe-gun. But it was getting really hard to live at home. Lewis was in his face all the time, acting like he was Randy's father or something—what a joke. Lewis had picked up some kind of drug habit, a cocaine analog called pepp. Like coke, pepp had the effect of making stupid people think they were smart. And the smarter Lewis felt, the more insufferable he became. It was time for Randy to move out, but now it turned out that Sue didn't want him to, and she was stalling on the master plumber's certificate to keep Randy at home.

At Christmas, Honey's mother in Indianapolis died of cancer, and Honey, the sole child, moved there with her new Heritagist girlfriend Nita to take over her mother's comfortable estate: a paid-up retrofitted tract home near the Speedway and a well-deployed range of cash credits on the $Web. Dr. Dicky Pride alerted the Indianapolis branch of the Human Heritage Council, and they were prepared to welcome the grieving Honey and Honey's companion with open arms.

When Randy heard Honey was moving, he went over to her house and asked her if he could leave town with her and Nita. But Honey chose to be a real bitch about it.

"Face it, Randy, you was nothing more than my boy toy. A kid I liked to piss on. Get over it. It was only because of Sue that you was important to me. And by the way, you can tell Sue she's a cold-hearted xoxxin' bitch."

This was way too frank. Randy felt small and used, used and abused. His poor young heart broke clean through that day, and it would never really heal again.

What with his nonexistent social life and the bad situation at home, Randy kept going to the Shively Heritage House meetings that winter. No matter what he thought about the Heritagists' beliefs, he had the ability to blend in with them real well. He'd seen an uvvy show once about some beetles that live in anthills because they can trick the ants into feeding them. The Heritage House was an anthill Randy could live in.

Dr. Dicky Pride liked asking Randy to repair little things, and soon—it wasn't clear which of them originally proposed it—Dr. Pride arranged for Randy to move into the Heritage House as a "seminarian." The Heritage House—really just an oversized Shively home—had a big garage with a second floor, and Dr. Pride turned the garage over to Randy rent-free.

Sue gave Randy some of her older plumbing equipment, and Randy used his savings to buy his own pipe-gun and his own whipped-to-shit panel truck. The day Randy moved out, Sue finally pulled the right strings to get Randy his master plumber's certificate.

Randy lived alone up in the room over the Heritage House garage, and for sex he still had Angelika and Sammie-Jo. Whenever Randy asked them to, which was just about every night, Angelika would turn into a vaginal sheath with an extra flap that would ruck up tight and caressing around Randy's balls, while at the same time Sammie-Jo would smother Randy's face with a divinely smelly moldie hood pursed into the folded shapes of clitoris and labia. When he was finished, Randy always made sure to open the window wide to air out the toy moldies' cheesy reek. And in the mornings he let the algae-veined limpware goodies "feed" by sitting out in the daylight while he dressed and had breakfast.

One rainy night in March, there were footsteps up the stairs to Randy's room just as Randy was in the midst of an onanistic sex party. A passkey slid into his lock and the door swung open. A trapezoid of light came in from the stairwell to lie across Randy Karl's engorged nudity.

"Hi, Randy." Dr. Dicky Pride stepped into the room, closed the door behind him, and turned on the light. "Don't be embarrassed, son. I expected to find you this way. I've been able to smell what you do up here nights. And of course Honey told me all about you." Dr. Pride was carrying a pink imipolex dildo, slender and not so long as Angelika. He waggled it rakishly, then ran his nose along the length of the moldie imipolex penis— sniffing it full savourily. Though it was a cold night, Dr. Pride's face was damp with perspiration.

"Isn't he a beauty, Randy Karl? I call him Dr. Jerry Falwell."

"What do you want?" said Randy, pulling his bedsheet up to his chin to cover him and Angelika and Sammie-Jo. "You shouldn't of barged in here, Dr. Pride."

"Struggle though we might, we're both miserable cheeseballs, son. We've got to stick together. Do me like you did Honey. Or I can do you. You're a very attractive and virile young man."

"I ain't gonna do nothing with you, Dr. Pride. You've been

good to me, I know. But I just ain't interested in sex with people no more, and if I *was* a-goin' to do anything, it would be with a woman. I'll move out of here as soon as you like. But no way am I a-stickin' Dr. Jerry Falwell up your butt for you. Now, please git on out of here and leave me alone."

Randy and Dr. Pride didn't explicitly mention the incident to each other during the following days, but they both agreed that it was time for Randy to graduate from being a seminarian and to leave the Shively Heritage House.

"You ought to go on a mission, Randy Karl," suggested Dr. Pride. "The Human Heritage Council is very well connected— and I'm talking worldwide. We've got Heritage Houses and missionaries everywhere. The Council can act as a very effective placement service. I've already sent in my very top recommendation for you, by the way. Uvvy in to the Council's central server and see what they can find for you. A spirited young man like you needs to get out and see the world!"

Dr. Pride left Randy alone with the Heritage House uvvy, and Randy logged into the Council's central machine, a huge asimov slave computer located under a mountain in Salt Lake City, Utah, just like the Mormons' genealogy computer. The uvvy fed Randy an image showing an a-life clerk in a sterile virtual reality office. The clerk was meant to look like a wholesome young daughter of the Great Plains, but the illusion was unconvincing. The silicon computation was crude enough that Randy could see the facets of her body's polygonal meshes, and several of the facets were incorrectly colored in. For a few moments the figure sat stiff and blank, but then some signal from Randy's uvvy animated her.

"Hello there," she said. Her voice was shrill and perky. "You're Randy Karl Tucker from the Shively, Kentucky, Heritage House, I believe? Yes? Terrif. You can call me Jenny. How can I help you?"

"Um, I'm a-thinkin' about gettin' out of town," said Randy. "Like a mission or a job somewheres else? I've got me a master plumber's certificate."

"Yes, we already have that information, Randy." Jenny woodenly pretended to look through some papers on her desk. "Master plumber is very good. And your minister Dr. Pride speaks very highly of you. I wonder—could you tell me frankly what you think of *him*?"

"Well, he's a good preacher. He packs 'em in."

"We've heard some rumors that he's a . . . cheeseball?"

"I ain't never had sex with him, and I don't plan to. So don't ask me. Just help me get to heck outta here."

"What kind of sex *do* you like, Randy?" Jenny morphed her faces' polygons into a conspiratorial smile. A few of her cheeks' smaller triangles flickered to black, making it look as if Jenny had blackheads. Or stubble. "You can tell Jenny. Jenny knows lots of secrets. Do you like toy moldies?"

"Looky here, I thought this was supposed to be a job-search session. And what if I *am* interested in moldies? That's a good enough reason to be a Heritagist, ain't it? Just like it's all drunks that goes to AA."

Jenny emitted a laugh. "I won't pry any further, Randy. I just wanted to make sure you don't mind being around moldies and imipolex. Because the job I've found for you—have you ever heard of Bangalore, India? Look."

A world globe appeared in front of Jenny and rotated to bring India into view, hanging like a fat udder from the Asian landmass. A little red dot pulsed down in the center of the teat's tip.

"It's on a plateau and has a pleasant climate," said Jenny. "It's quite modern and Western, very high-tech. It's one of the only cities in India that sells beer on tap. Hindustan Aeronautics is there, also Indian Telephone Industries, Bharat Electronics, *and* Emperor Staghorn Beetle Larvae, Ltd. The world's largest manufacturer of imipolex. Emperor Staghorn needs a pipe fitter; a master plumber."

"The folks who make moldie plastic are gonna take the Heritagists' advice on who to hire?" said Randy. "That don't make sense."

"Oh, they'll take our advice," said Jenny. "Indirectly. Like I said, we've got a lot of contacts, and a lot of people owe us favors. We can get you hired, Randy, I guarantee it. And you'll be surprised how big the salary is. All we want is that you uvvy me every month or two and tell me about anything interesting you see. And remember, you'll be working around moldies and imipolex *every day*." Jenny smiled again and put on a Kentucky accent. "Hell, Randy Karl, you'll be happy as a pig in a potato patch."

"Shitfire!" Randy finally allowed himself to get excited. "India? Do they speak English there?"

"You bet! Just say the word, Randy, and you've got the job. We'll even find you a place to live and buy your plane tickets."

"I'll do it!"

"Be at the Louisville airport tomorrow at 9 A.M. They'll be holding your passport and your tickets for you at the Humana Airlines counter."

Randy packed his few possessions into his panel truck, told Dr. Pride good-bye, and drove over to Sue's house to tell her. It was six o'clock on a dark Friday evening.

Lewis answered the door. "Sue's not here," he said shortly.

"I'll come in and wait," said Randy.

"She's not coming back till Sunday night," said Lewis, fingering his mustache. He was twitchy from pepp. "She's gone up to Indianapolis to visit that goddamn dyke whore Honey Weaver. Your old girlfriend. And as long as Sue's not home, *you're* not welcome." Lewis made as if to close the door, but Randy stuck his foot in it.

"Don't slam my own door on me, you poncey son of a bitch."

"You mess with me, son, and you're in for a world of hurt," snapped Lewis. "I've got a gun. What the hell are you doing here anyway?" He peered out at Randy's laden truck. "Don't tell me you want to move back in! Xoxx-ass loser."

"I'll be spending tonight in the garage like I used to," said Randy shortly. "And you'd best not disturb me."

He cruised out for some burgers and brought a six-pack of grape soda back to the garage. The back of the garage was still set up more or less like Randy's room; he'd only taken a few of his things with him when he moved over to the Heritage House. Randy took out the suitcase he'd gotten for his high school graduation and carefully began going through his life's accumulation of stuff, trying to figure out which things he'd need in India. What the hell would it be like there?

Finally Randy's bag was ready, and he spent another hour unpacking the plumbing supplies from his truck and storing them back in with Sue's stuff. He was fooling around with his beloved pipe-gun when Lewis appeared in the garage, pepped to the pits. He had an old-fashioned Wild West gunpowder pistol in his right hand. What an asshole.

"I said you're not welcome here, Randy," said Lewis, pointing out the garage door like some kind of plantation overseer. "Out."

Randy felt himself looking down submissively. He always got scared when people yelled at him; he always gave in and looked away. But tonight he caught himself doing it, and he realized he didn't want to give in anymore. He touched the pipe-gun's controls, which set a growing white snake of two-inch plastic pipe creeping across the garage floor, hidden from Lewis's view by the truck.

"I mean it," said Lewis, stepping closer and waving his gun. "Get your trashy ass out of here, Randy Karl Tucker." He actually twirled his mustache after he said this.

Randy had the pipe form a right angle and flow out from under the truck just in time to tangle with Lewis's feet. Lewis stumbled, looked down, and suddenly the pipe grew a tee at its end and accelerated straight up, punching Lewis in the crotch. The man doubled in pain, dropping his pistol.

Randy's fingers danced across the pipe-gun controls, and in seconds Lewis was imprisoned in a tight cage of pipes. When Lewis opened his mouth to yell, Randy grew a skillful circle of pipe tight around his head, gagging him so that he could do no more than grunt and moan.

"How would you like it I send a pipe right up your butt and out the top of your head?" asked Randy rhetorically. "But I don't

need the hassle of the cleanup. After tomorrow I'm gone. Goin'
to India, Lewis. Not *Indiana*, my man, but *India*. It'll be real
different there, for true." Randy opened up the back of his emp-
tied panel truck and threw in a couple of canvas tarps. "Stay nice
and quiet, Lewis, if you don't want that there plastic pipe en-
ema." Randy found a dolly and used it to lever the caged Lewis
into the back of the truck, loosely wrapping the cage in the tarps
in case Lewis did try to make noise. "You can breathe, can't
you? Maybe I should trim off that mustache for you? To hell
with it. You'll be okay. Tell Sue good-bye for me when you see
her Sunday." Randy shut the truck door, took his suitcase, closed
up the garage, and spent the night on the couch watching porno
on the uvvy, just like old times, with tattered Angelika and Sammie-Jo for company.

It turned out that Randy liked India a lot. He liked the chaos
and disorganization of the city streets—the sweepers, the priests,
the bright-clothed women with alert eyes, the thin barefoot men
in plastic shirts or no shirt at all, the older men in white jackets,
the wildly bearded holy men, the nose rings and pouchy eyes
and orange cloth, the hundred castes and colors and languages.
There was always a hubbub, but nobody really hurried. There
was always time to talk. Everyone seemed to speak at least a bit
of English—idiosyncratic British-and-Sanskrit-tinged English—
and to be happy to practice it on Randy Karl. People were kind
to Randy in India, and kindness had been something in short
supply throughout his life so far.

The Emperor Staghorn Beetle Larvae, Ltd., fab was about
ten miles east of Bangalore. Initially Randy commuted there by
train every day. The Fab was a huge rectangular building, win-
dowless and tightly secured, lest moldies break in to steal the
precious imipolex. At any given time there were twenty to a
hundred moldies flying or hopping around outside the structure,
drawn to the source of imipolex like bees drawn to honey. Arriving at Emperor Staghorn for his first day's work, Randy was
thrilled to see so many moldies. One of them approached him
as he walked to the fab from the train.

B.C. FERRIES
03 01 13:05 056076 372788
SALE   1997/09/05

SALE

BRITISH COLUMBIA
FERRY CORPORATION

1997/09/05
Horseshoe Bay
To Langdale

Foot Adult   7.00
1 ITEMS SUBTL   7.00
TOTAL   7.00
Paid CDN Cash   20.00
CHANGE DUE   -13.00

"This ticket is issued subject to certain terms and conditions which are hereby incorporated into and form part of this ticket and of contract of carriage hereby evidenced, some of which terms and conditions limit or exclude the liability of the carrier, its masters, agents, servants or employees, which conditions of carriage may be seen upon request at any terminal office, aboard ship or at the head office of the carrier. This is not a negotiable instrument."

"Hello there," said the moldie, a womanly figure clothed in what looked like bracelets, bangles, necklaces, belts, and a golden crown. "I'm Parvati. Are you new here?" Parvati stood very close to Randy. Randy noticed that her many pieces of jewelry were, in fact, shiny bumps and ridges of her imipolex flesh.

"Yes, ma'am," said Randy. "I'm a-startin' on as a pipe fitter." Surreptitiously he sniffed the air, tasting of the moldie's odor and finding it good. "Do you work here too?"

"I wish I did," said Parvati. "All that gorgeous imipolex. What is your name?"

"Randy Karl Tucker. I'm from Kentucky."

"How extremely interesting. Randy, you will learn that the Emperor Staghorn employees are allowed to buy imipolex at cost from the company store. Be sure always to purchase as much as you can afford, and I can trade it for whatever you want. Food, money, intoxicants, sexual intimacy, maid service, sky rides, jungle tours, diving in the Arabian Sea—there are a plethora of possibilities." Parvati's voice had an enchanting lilt to it.

"Emperor Staghorn employees can buy imipolex?" said Randy. "That's good. I like imipolex. Fact is—" Randy looked around. The other commuters had already bustled past him and were queuing up at the Emperor Staghorn entrance. "Fact is, I think I may be a cheeseball."

"I already love you, Randy," said Parvati, planting a divinely smelly kiss on his cheek. "Run along and enjoy your new job, dear boy. Remember Parvati on payday! We will have a very heavy date!"

Waiting for Randy inside the Emperor Staghorn building was a plump golden-skinned man wearing dirty white pants and a dirty white jacket with many pockets holding many things. He was shiny bald on top, with a wreath of iron-gray curls.

"Greetings, Mr. Tucker," he said, extending his hand. "I am Neeraj Pondicherry, the plumbing supervisor and, by virtue of this office, your de facto boss. I am welcoming you to Emperor Staghorn Beetle Larvae, Ltd."

"Thank you kindly," said Randy. "I'm right proud to be here."

Pondicherry stared out through the glass door at the figure of Parvati. She'd grown a few extra arms and was smoothly undulating in a sacred dance. "She was certainly chatting you up, Mr. Tucker."

"Well, um, yeah," said Randy. "She asked me about having a date with her. I think she's kinda sexy. I hope it's—"

"Oh, it's perfectly all right to fraternize with moldies, Randy. Indeed, Emperor Staghorn is even employing a few moldies here and there. They provide most of our custom chipmolds. But these highly skilled moldie employees are wealthy nabobs, of a much higher caste than the moldies who beg for imipolex outside our fab gates. Shall I call you Randy and you call me Neeraj?"

"Sure thing, Neeraj."

"Capital. Let's continue our conversation while we are walking this way." Neeraj led Randy off down a long hall that ran along one side of the fab building. The right wall was blank, and the left wall was punctuated with thick-glassed windows looking into the fab proper. The people inside were dressed in white coveralls, with white boots and face masks. Meanwhile Neeraj kept talking, his voice a steady, musical flow.

"Yes, the street moldies are very friendly to Emperor Staghorn employees because, of course, they are hoping you will be giving them imipolex. Some of us have moldie servants. When I was a younger man, I kept a moldie who was flying me to work like a great bird! Devilishly good fun. But finally it was becoming too great a financial outlay for a father of five. And too dodgy."

"Dodgy?" asked Randy. "You mean like risky? To keep a moldie?"

"I will be telling you in due time what precautions you must be taking in your dodgy relations with low-caste moldies," said Neeraj, starting to open a big door in the left wall. A breeze of pressurized air wafted out. "But that can wait a little bit. We are entering the pre-gowning area. We'll get suited up and go into the main part of the fab, which is a clean room. Here we are allowing less than one dust particle per cubic meter of air."

"Imipolex is that xoxxin' sensitive?"

"Imipolex is a very highly structured quasicrystal," said Neeraj. "While we are manufacturing the layers, the accidental inclusion of a dust particle can spoil the long-range Penrose correlations. And, of course, we are also producing the hybridized chipmold cultures here, and contamination by a wild fungus spore or by a stray algal germ cell would be disastrous. Keep in mind, Randy, that in the air, for instance, of the train you ride to work, there are perhaps a million particles per cubic meter, and very many of the particles are biologically active."

The door to the pre-gowning room closed behind them. The floor was covered with sticky adhesive to catch the dust from their feet. Following Neeraj's example, Randy sat down on a bench and pulled some disposable blue covers over his shoes.

"Ram-ram, Neeraj," said a leathery brown woman sitting behind a counter. "Is this our new Mr. Tucker?"

"Indeed. Randy, this is Roopah. Roopah, this is Randy."

"Here are your building suit, your shoes, and your ID badge," said Roopah, setting what looked like tight-cuffed blue pajamas and white bowling shoes on the counter. "Press your thumb on this pad, Randy, so that your locker can recognize you. Your locker number is 239."

In the locker room, they stashed their street clothes and put on the blue building suits and the white plastic shoes. They washed their hands and put on hair nets and safety glasses. Beyond the locker room lay a medium clean zone—with a mere ten thousand particles per cubic meter. Here the air already felt purer than any that Randy had ever breathed; the odorless air flowed effortlessly into his lungs.

They passed a break room where some of the fab workers were having non-dusty snacks like apple juice and yogurt. Then they went into a second locker room: the gowning room proper. They put on latex gloves. They wiped off their safety glasses and their ID badges—wiped everything three times with lint-free alcohol-soaked cloths. They put on white hoods and overalls.

Randy had hoped the suits might be live imipolex, but they were just brainless plastic.

"We call these *bunny suits*," said Neeraj, cheerfully pulling his hands up under his chin and making a chewing face like a rabbit. "And the floppy white galoshes are *fab booties*."

They pulled the fab booties over their white bowling shoes. They pulled vinyl gloves over their latex gloves. Neeraj gave Randy a face mask equipped with a small fan that drew in new air and pumped Randy's exhalations through a filter. This was starting to feel a teensy bit . . . obsessive. But Randy liked being obsessive.

Now Neeraj led Randy through a tile corridor lined with nozzles blasting out air. "This is the air shower," said Neeraj. "You are turning around three times as you are walking through. Notice that the floor in here and in the fab is a grating. The floors have suction pumps, and the ceilings are filled with fans. The entire air of the fab is completely changed ten times in a minute."

Slowly moving through the air shower, with his filthy invisible human particles being sucked out through the floor grate, Randy thought of a Bible phrase: "I was glad when they said unto me, let us go into the house of the Lord."

Beyond the air shower lay the temple of moldie creation. The lights were bright and yellow; they gave the fab a strange underworld feeling. The rushing air streamed down past Randy from ceiling to floor. White-garbed figures moved about; all of them were dressed exactly the same. Everyone's labors revolved around glowing cylindrical slugs of imipolex, the slugs ranging in size from breakfast sausages on up to giant bolognas four feet long.

The fab was perhaps the size of a football field, and it had high fifteen-foot ceilings to accommodate an overhead monorail system that carried the partially processed slugs of imipolex from station to station.

The crude imipolex itself was manufactured in a series of vats, vacuum chambers, and distillation columns fed by slurries of chemicals piped up from somewhere below the floor.

As Randy and his boss moved down the main corridor on their tour, people kept recognizing Neeraj and coming over to pat him on the back or on the arm or on the stomach—they were like worker ants exchanging greetings while tending their larvae.

"We are touching each other very much here," said Neeraj. "Perhaps we are using so much body language because it is hard to see each other's faces. Or maybe it is because everyone is so clean."

The only human contamination Randy could sense was the meaty smell of his own breath bouncing around inside his face mask. He wished he could tear off the mask and inhale the clean pure air of the fab. But then he would exhale, and the fab wouldn't like that—detectors would notice the increased number of particles per cubic meter, and lights would flash.

Later they went downstairs to the *sub fab*, the floor below the fab. Like the break area, the sub fab was only kept at ten thousand particles per cubic meter, and you didn't have to wear a face mask.

The sub fab was a techno dream, the ultimate mad scientist's lab. It held all the devices needed to support the machines of the fab. The electrical generators were here, the plumbing, the tanks of acids, the filtering systems, the vacuum lines, the particle monitoring equipment—miles of wires and pipes and cables in an immaculately painted concrete room. This was where Randy was to begin work, maintaining and upgrading the sub fab's plumbing.

The apartment the Heritagists had found for Randy was in a sterile high-rise right next to the Bangalore airport. Most of the people living in it were non-Indian workers and scientists imported by the various high-tech industries of Bangalore. After a tense, alienated week there, Randy decided to move into town, into the real India, into a dim room in an ancient stone building on the side of a hill between the orchid-filled Lalbagh Gardens and the bustling Gandhi Bazaar.

The sheer diversity of India soothed Randy: in uptight Louisville, everyone was good or bad, rich or poor, black or white—but in the streets of Bangalore there were endless shadings on every scale, and life's daily workings were all the more richly woven.

The building with Randy's room was called Tipu Bharat; *Tipu* being the name of a former Indian prince and *Bharat* being the Indian word for India. The walls of Tipu Bharat were worked with carved designs like necklaces and set with arched, pillared niches holding miniature bright imipolex statues of gods, animated icons that waved their tiny arms and seemed to watch the passersby. There was an open terrace on the roof where the Tipu Bharat roomers could sit and stare out toward the Eastern or the Western Ghats, the distant mountain ranges that enclosed the high plateau of Bangalore.

Near the Gandhi Bazaar was a street of the naked holy men called *sadhus*; day and night the sadhus sat in streetside booths, each with a small incense burner, a blanket, a fly whisk, and a tacked-up collection of shimmering religious art, much of it made of imipolex. Sometimes one of the sadhus would put on a show: hammer a sharpened stick into his head, build a fire in the street and walk on its coals, suck blood from the neck of a live chicken, or do something even more fantastic and disgusting. Randy often walked down to watch them in the evenings.

"The moldie you are always fabulating with outside the fab," said Neeraj on the morning of Randy's first monthly payday, a Saturday. "Is she calling herself Parvati?"

"Mm-hmm," said Randy. "Do you know her?"

"No no, I only recognize the shape she is wearing—Parvati is the goddess who is the wife of the god Shiva. In the Hindu religion, Shiva's wife is extremely important; she has many different names and many different forms. One form is Parvati the beautiful, but another of her forms is the black Kali who rides a lion, brandishes a knife, and wears a necklace of chopped-off human heads. The risk in becoming very intimate with a moldie Parvati is that she may unexpectedly become a Kali and take your head. Like all women, my own wife is both a Parvati and a Kali, not to mention an Uma and Durga, but my wife is human and I do not need to worry so much about her really and truly taking my head. You are planning to buy Parvati a slug of imipolex from the company store today and to have a heavy date with her, are you not?"

Randy blushed. "Not that it's really any of your-all's goddamn business, Neeraj."

"I do not disapprove, Randy, but I am saying this: *Keep your head.* Some moldies play the game of sticking a tendril up a man's nose and implanting a control unit in his brain. This is called a *thinking cap.* You have never heard of this practice?"

"Can't say as I have."

"If you are going to spend time with moldies and perhaps to be sexually intimate with them, it is a good practice, first of all, to be wearing a protective barrier in the back of your nose. There is a self-installing titaniplast device of this nature available in the company store. Come along, I'll walk over there with you and make sure that my rumbustious young horn-doggie is equipped with the proper protection."

One whole end of the employee's store was filled with bins of lusciously glowing imipolex sausages. The setup reminded Randy of the fireworks stands in Indiana; rank upon rank of magical cylinders lying there, arranged by size and waiting for ignition. The colorful patterns on the imipolex were alive and constantly changing, albeit in calm and rhythmic ways. The slugs came in a range of standard sizes that ranged from a hundred grams up to two kilograms.

Randy picked out a five-hundred-gram sausage, which was nearly at the limit of what he could comfortably afford. Neeraj showed him where the nose blockers were and also made sure that Randy bought one of the small imipolex patches that Neeraj called leech-DIMs.

"Leech-DIMs are making a moldie very confused," said Neeraj. "But we are not fully understanding why. Leech-DIMs were invented only last year by Sri Ramanujan, one of Emperor Staghorn's finest limpware engineers. As long as you have a leech-

DIM handy, you can instantly bollox up a threatening moldie. You are very fortunate to be able to buy one; at this point in time they are available solely through the Emperor Staghorn Beetle Larvae company store."

The leech-DIMs were small ragged patches of plastic, no bigger than the joint of your thumb, no two of them looking quite similar. They were so diverse as to resemble organically grown objects—like some tropical tree's aerial seeds perhaps or like by-the-wind-sailor jellyfish collected from a lonely windward beach.

The leech-DIMs were shockingly expensive, with one leech-DIM costing nearly the equivalent of three months' pay: a quarter of a year's earnings! Randy tried hard to get out of buying one, but Neeraj was adamant; he and Randy argued so loudly that soon a clerk came over to inform Randy that Emperor Staghorn Beetle Larvae employees were, in fact, required to use appropriate cautions with moldies, and that, yes, he could buy on credit.

So Randy equipped himself and took Parvati to his room in the Tipu Bharat and presented her with his five-hundred-gram slug of imipolex. The slug was two inches in diameter and nearly a foot long. It was circled by colorful stripes that smoothly undulated through a repeating standing-wave pattern that bounced from one end of the sausage to the other.

"Oh, Randy," exclaimed Parvati, exhaling a heady cloud of spores. She took the gift sausage in both hands. "My darling! It's beautiful. Five hundred grams! I'll incorporate it right away."

She pressed the imipolex against her breasts, and the sausage's stripes began to twist and flow like cream in coffee. The sausage deformed itself into the shape of a nonlinear dumbbell, and concentric circles appeared in the two ends. The ends domed themselves up and merged with Parvati's flesh: now her enlarged breasts were covered with what looked like shiny gold-and-copper filigree, very arabesque and fractal. Parvati held her arms up high and twirled around. "Do you like it, Randy?"

"You're beautiful, Parvati. What do you say we have some fun now?" The nose blocker deadened the sound of Randy's voice in his own ears. Parvati sashayed forward, undid Randy's pants, then drew him down onto his bed. Randy's youth and lust were such that he was able to reach three climaxes in twenty minutes—three deep, aching ejaculations.

And then he lay there, spent and happy, staring out at the darkening sky. A single bright evening star appeared in the top of the window: Venus. Parvati's soft form was all around him, partly under him and partly over him. She ran a caressing hand across his face, poked softly at his nose, and slipped a thin finger into his nostril.

"Now don't you be a-tryin' to give me no thinkin' cap," cried Randy, jerking upright in sudden terror. He snatched his leech-DIM up from where he'd left it under the corner of the bed and held it out protectively. "I mean it, Parvati!"

She drew her puddled shape back into a more human form. "I was only teasing you, Randy. I know you're wearing a nose blocker. I can tell by the sound of your voice. Is that a leech-DIM you're holding? I've heard of them, but I've never seen one. Don't you trust me?"

"My boss, Neeraj, he told me you might try and put a controller on my brain."

"If I could count on you to bring me imipolex on every single payday, then why would I need to control you? You'd already be doing everything I want you to do. *Can* I count on you, Randy?"

"You can if you'll promise to come see me in between paydays, Parvati. I can't wait a whole 'nother month to grease my wrench. My old limpware sex toys—they're whipped to shit."

"Show them to me."

Randy pulled Sammie-Jo and Angelika out of the bottom drawer of his dresser. They smelled rotten, and their colors had turned muddy gray.

"Whew!" said Parvati. "They'll be completely dead in a week to ten days. That is exactly how I do not want to end up."

"Do you want them?"

"I should say not. Most distasteful. Bury them. Or set them afire."

"What am I gonna do for sex?"

"I'll come and see you twice a week," said Parvati softly. "Every Saturday and perhaps every Tuesday. I'll be your steady girlfriend. How would you like that?"

"It'd be swell! Hey, if you're my girlfriend, why don't you come on and walk around the neighborhood with me? You can help explain stuff to me, and maybe—maybe you can help me buy some new sex toys. Also I'd like to get something to eat."

They went to the Mavalli Tiffin Rooms, a vegetarian snack place near the Lalbagh Gardens park. Randy got them a table in front, near a window, in case Parvati's smell were a problem. But the moldie's presence didn't disturb anyone; indeed the other groups in the room seemed pleasantly amused by the singular pair made by Randy the hillbilly cheeseball and Parvati the moldie goddess—the couple were visible proof of Bangalore's modernity and advancing technological prowess!

After eating some pancakes stuffed with gnarly yellow roots, Randy took Parvati to see the sadhus. The sadhus were greatly excited at the sight of Parvati. Two of the sadhus heaped some thorny branches on the ground and rolled in them till they bled; another thrust a long staff through a hole in his penis and worked it up and down. Still another sadhu fed a well-worn imipolex snake down his throat and then—with much bucking of his stomach muscles—he pushed the snake out of his anus. Parvati acknowledged the sadhus' homage with graceful motions of her arms. Randy stood right behind her, with his hands tight around her waist. Parvati's smells and motions were nectar to him.

"I used to see guys like the sadhus at the Kentucky State Fair," said Randy. "We called 'em carnival geeks. There was a time I thought I might grow up to be one. Hey, do you wanna go help me pick out some imipolex sex toys?"

"Don't fritter your money away on *toys*, Randy," said Parvati, pushing her bottom against Randy's crotch and growing some temporary butt fingers to secretly fondle him. "All of your extra money should come to me. If you promise to bring me seven hundred and fifty grams of imipolex instead of just five hundred next payday, we can go back up to your room right now. And I'll come make love to you *three* times a week."

As they started to leave, the sadhus began holding out begging bowls to Parvati and clamoring for *moksha*. Parvati stretched out her left arm and lumps seemed to move out along the back of her hand. And then the tips of her fingers popped out four black nuggets like wrinkled marbles. The sadhus began fighting savagely over them.

"What's that?" asked Randy.

"Those are lumps of chipmold mycelium, technically known as *sclerotia*, but commonly called *camote* in the Americas and *moksha* in India. They are a powerful psychedelic, greatly prized by the sadhus."

By now the camote nuggets had been devoured by four lucky sadhus who lay prostrate in adoration at Parvati's feet. Randy and Parvati picked their way around them and headed back toward the Tipu Bharat. It was getting late, and beggars were bedding down for the night on the sidewalks. When a man in a turban rode past on a unicycle, Parvati pulled Randy into a dark doorway.

"Look out for that one," she whispered. "He's a *dacoit*—a mugger from a gang."

They lingered in the shadows after the dacoit was gone, hugging and kissing and feeling each other, until suddenly a moldie came plummeting down out of the sky and landed in front of them. He was shaped like a lithe nude Indian man, but with leathery wings, four arms, and a shiny crown like Parvati's. He had an enormous uncircumcised penis. Parvati cupped her enlarged new breasts and ingratiatingly hefted them at the interloper. He glared at her with his mouth open, apparently talking to Parvati via direct moldie radio waves.

"It is none of your affair," shouted Parvati suddenly. "You should be grateful to me!"

The four-armed moldie gave Randy a rough shove that sent

him sprawling, then leaped up into the air and flew away. "Who in the world was that?" asked Randy, shakily getting to his feet. "Looked like one mean motherfucker!" "That was my husband, Shiva the destroyer. Ridiculous as it may seem, he's jealous of you. As if sex with a human could possibly mean anything to me. Shiva thinks I should come back to our nest right away? I'll teach him a little lesson in etiquette. I'll spend the entire night with you."

Back in Randy's room they had sex again, and then Parvati started looking bored. "I'm bound and determined to stay here all night, Randy, but I'm not conditioned to sleep anywhere other than in the security of my home nest. What shall we do?"

"Maybe we should take like a drug trip together," said nude Randy. "You give me a lump or two of that camote stuff, and I'll put the leech-DIM on you." He held the postage-stamp-sized leech-DIM out to her on the palm of his hand.

"What an odd idea," said Parvati. "For a moldie and a human to 'take like a drug trip together.' You're quite the singular cheeseball, Randy Karl Tucker." She peered at his leech-DIM. "Let me try it just for a minute at first. Put it on me and count a minute by your watch, then remove it right away. I want to see if I like it."

Randy pressed the leech-DIM against Parvati's left shoulder— like a vaccination. The leech-DIM had been dry and papery to the touch, but as soon as the leech touched Parvati it softened and then quickly twitched itself into a position of maximum contact.

Parvati's skin lit up like a Christmas tree, and her limbs shank back into her body mass. She lay there on Randy's bed like a living mandala. Once the minute was up, it took a bit of effort to pry up an edge of the leech, but after that was done Randy could easily peel it off. Parvati's usual shape gradually returned, her limbs and head slowly growing out from the mandala.

"Goodness me," said Parvati. "That was really something." She gestured fluidly, and two chipmold sclerotia appeared in the palm of her hand: one black and one a hard gemlike blue. "Eat these, Randy, and put the leech-DIM on me. We'll make a nightlong debauch of it."

Randy ate the camote. It was crunchy, juicy and bitter with alkaloids. He started feeling the effects almost immediately. With wooden fingers he put the now-soft leech-DIM back on Parvati and lay down on the bed with her, wrapping himself tight around the pulsing egg of her body.

The camote took Randy on an express ride to a classic mystical vision—he saw God in the form of an all-pervading white light. The light recognized Randy and spoke to him. "I love you, Randy," it said. "I'll always love you. I'm always here." Filigreed multidimensional patterns of tubes surrounded Randy like pipes all around him, wonderfully growing and branching pipes leading from Randy out through the white light and in the distance homing in on—someone else. Parvati. "Randy?" came her voice. "Is that you? Are we in this dream together?" "Yes oh yes we are," answered Randy. "Let's fly together," said Parvati, and her essence flowed through the pipes to mingle with Randy's, and then they were adrift together in a sky of lovely shapes, endlessly many shapes of infinite intricacy, all gladly singing to the pair of flying lovers.

When Randy woke up, he was lying on the floor with Parvati's tissues completely surrounding his head. He was breathing through a kind of nozzle Parvati had pushed into his mouth. For a moment Randy feared she was attacking him, and then, peeling her off of him, he feared she was dead. But once he removed her leech-DIM, Parvati livened up and began pulling herself back together. The hot morning sun streamed in Randy's window, and the thousand noises of the street came drifting in— the chattering voices, the bicycle bells, the vendors' cries, the Indian radio music, the swish and shuffle of moving bodies—a moiré of sound vibrations filling the air like exquisite ripples in a three-dimensional pond.

"Wow," said Parvati.

"Did you have a good time?"

"It was—wonderful. But it's so late, I have to run. Shiva will be worried sick. I'll come see you again day after tomorrow."

CHAPTER THREE

TRE

═══ ■ ═══

March 2049—October 30, 2053

Tre Dietz had very long hair that was straight, sun-bleached, and tangled. He had lively brown eyes, a short mouth, and a strong chin. He stood about six feet tall and enjoyed the easy good health of a young man in his twenties.

Tre was a classic American bohemian. Like so many before him, he grew up in the rude vastnesses of the Midwest and migrated west to the coast, to sunny Californee.

Tre's mother was a teacher and his dad was a salesman. Tre was at the top of his graduating class in Des Moines. He got accepted at the University of California at Santa Cruz, and the Des Moines Kiwanians gave him a scholarship. While at UCSC, Tre smoked out, sought the spore, and transchronicized the Great Fractal, as did all his circle of friends—but Tre also managed to get a good grounding in applied chaos and in piezoplastics. Before he could quite finish all the requirements for a degree in limpware engineering, he got an offer too good to refuse from Apex Images. It happened one rainy, chilly day in March 2049.

Tre was on spring break from UCSC. He was living in a cottage down the hill from the university, down in a flat, scuzzy student part of Santa Cruz, rooming with Benny Phlogiston and Aanna Vea. Aanna was a big strong-featured Samoan woman, and Benny was a tiny Jewish guy from Philadelphia. All three of them were limpware engineering majors, and none of them was in a romantic relationship with any of the others. They were just roommates.

Tre was already dating his future wife Terri Percesepe, although Tre and Terri hadn't realized yet that they were fated to mate. Terri was taking art courses, living with a girlfriend, and working for a few hours every morning selling tickets for the Percesepe family's day-excursion fishing boats. People still liked to fish, even in 2049, though these days there was always a slight chance of snagging a submarine rogue moldie and having to face the rogue's inhumanly savage retaliation. Each fishing boat was equipped with a high-pressure flamethrower for just this eventuality.

The day when Tre's life changed, the uvvy woke him. Tre was on his thin sleeping pad, and the uvvy chirped, "Tre Tre Tre Tre . . ." Tre grabbed the uvvy, which was about the size of an old-fashioned telephone handset, and told it to project. You could use an uvvy one of two ways: you could ask it to project a holographic image of your caller or you could set it onto your neck and let it make a direct electromagnetic field connection with your brain.

In projection mode, part of the uvvy's surface vibrated to cast a lifelike holographic image into the air, and another part of it acted as a speaker.

"Hello. Tre Dietz?" The image showed the head of a conventionally attractive blonde California woman in her twenties.

"Yaar," said Tre. "It's me."

Rain was spitting against the windowpanes and a brisk breeze was picking at the house's thin walls. From a certain angle Tre could see a patch of ocean through his window. The ocean looked cold, silvery gray, rife with waves. This afternoon he was going out surfing with Terri at a beginner's nook just below Four Mile Beach; Terri was going to give him a lesson. Answering the uvvy, Tre had been hoping it was Terri. But it wasn't.

"Wonderbuff," said the hollow of the conventional blonde. "I'm Cynthia Major. I'm in human resources at Apex Images in San Francisco. Tre, the Mentor wants me to tell you that we're very happily discombobulated by your Perplexing Poultry philtre."

A philtre was a type of software that you put onto an uvvy, so that the uvvy images would come out all different. *Philtre* like *filter*, but also *philtre* like *magic potion*, as a good philtre could make things look way strange if you put the philtre onto an uvvy that you were wearing on your neck. Philtres were a wavy new art hack.

Tre had made the Perplexing Poultry philtre in February with a little help from Benny, Aanna, and, of course, UCSC's Wad. Formally, Perplexing Poultry was about the idea that space can be thought of as a quasicrystal, that is, as a nonrepeating tessellation of two kinds of polyhedral cell. This fact was a mathematical result from the last century that had become important for modeling the structure of imipolex. Tre had learned about quasicrystals in his course on Limpware Structures. To make the philtre visually engaging, Tre had deformed the two basic polyhedra into a pair of shapes which resembled a skinny chicken and a fat dodo bird.

Experientially, the Perplexing Poultry philtre was a totally bizarre lift. If you fired up Perplexing Poultry in an uvvy on your neck, all the things around you would seem to deform into the shapes of three-dimensional Perplexing Poultry, i.e., into things like linkages of odd-shaped birds with weird multisymmetrical ways of *pecking* into each other. You yourself would become a wave of perplexity in the Poultry sea.

Tre had written his philtre as a goof, really, as something to wrap himself up in when he was lifted. It was very weightless to check out the beach or a coffee shop with your weeded-up head way into Perplexing Poultry.

Philtres were cutting-edge in terms of image manipulation. Rather than being a static video or text, a philtre was a system of interpretation. The technology had evolved from a recreational device called a twist-box that had been popular in the early thirties. Twist-boxes had been marketed as a drug-free method of consciousness alteration, as "a pure software high." Like uvvy philtres, twist-boxes worked by distorting your visual input. But the twist-box used a simple Stakhanovite three-variable chaotic feedback loop, rather than a teleologically designed process, as was characteristic of the new philtres. And in these Dionysian mid-twenty-first-century times, people tended to use philtres as an *enhancement* to drugs rather than as a *replacement* for them.

The realtime human neurological mindmeld involved in programming a philtre was too complicated for Tre to have done on his own, of course, any more than a dog would have been able to paint its self-portrait. But Tre had access to UCSC's Wad, a cosmic mind-amplication device that was a *grex*, that is, a symbiotic fusion of several different moldies.

With Wad, many things were possible, particularly if your problem happened to be one that Wad found interesting. Since the flickercladding plastic of moldies' bodies was quasicrystalline imipolex, Wad had thought the quasicrystal-related Perplexing Poultry philtre to be totally floatin' and had done a solar job for Tre.

So here was Tre getting an uvvy call about his Poultry from a businesswoman in the city.

"I'm glad you like it," said Tre. "How come you're calling me?"

Cynthia Major laughed, as though this were a refreshingly naive thing to say. "We want you to sign a contract with us, Tre. Do you know anything about Apex Images?"

"Not really. You do ads?"

"We're the thirteenth-biggest image agency worldwide. Ads, music viddies, hollows, uvvy philtres—we do it all."

"You want to use the Perplexing Poultry to sell stuff like wendy meat?"

Cynthia Major laughed infectiously. "Good guess! Apex *would* like to sell wendy meat with Perplexing Poultry. We do have their account. Or sell uvvy sets. Or politicians. Who knows? The lift is, we at Apex Images want to have rights to lots of floaty philtres that we can license and put out there in all kinds of ways."

"You want to own the rights to Perplexing Poultry?"

"Well, that whole issue is more complicated than you realize, Tre, which is why the Mentor thought of having us call you. Have you ever heard of a company called Emperor Staghorn Beetle Larvae, Ltd.?"

"Yeah, I have," said Tre. "They make imipolex. They're based in Bangalore, India. What about them?"

"They want to sue you. They own all the patents to Roger Penrose's work on quasicrystals, and they claim that your philtre is, in fact, derived from drawings which Penrose created for a 1990s two-dimensional quasicrystal puzzle that was also known as Perplexing Poultry. I assume this isn't news to you?"

"The lawsuit is news. But, yeah, of course I know about Penrose's work. We had a lecture on it in Limpware Structures. Emperor Staghorn Beetle Larvae, Ltd., is suing me? That's ridiculous. What for? I don't own anything."

"Well, Emperor Staghorn doesn't *really* want to sue; they'd much rather settle for a piece of your action. So before taking any irreversible steps, they got in touch with Apex through the Mentor. He's quite well connected on the subcontinent, you know. If you sign on with Apex, we can smooth this over, Tre, and we can handle all the bothersome legal aspects of your work in the future. And we'll pay you a nice advance on future royalties."

As the woman talked to him, Tre was moving around his room putting on warm clothes. The sun was peeking out now and then, turning the ocean green when it shone. Tre's life right now suited him fine. He was not happy to see a possible change.

"I'm not clear what I'd be signing up for."

"You sign with us, and we arrange contracts and for people to use your work. We take a commission and maybe from time to time we might encourage you to design something to spec."

"This sounds awfully complicated. I'm still a student. I don't want to work. I want to hack. I want to stay high and get tan. I'm learning to surf."

Cynthia gave a rich conspiratorial laugh. "Mr. Kasabian is going to love you, Tre. He's our director. Can you come up to the city for a meeting next week?"

"Well . . . I don't have any classes on Tuesday."

The blonde head consulted someone not visible in the uvvy's sphere of view. "How about Wednesday?" the head responded. "Eleven A.M.?"

"Zoom on this," said Tre. "What kind of an advance are we talking about?"

The woman gazed off to one side, and Tre suddenly got the suspicion that Cynthia Major was a simmie, a software simulation of a real person. The face turned back to him and named a dollar amount much larger than Tre had imagined anyone wanting to give him in the foreseeable future.

"*Myoor!*" exclaimed Tre, imitating a surprised cow, as it was currently considered funny to do, at least among Tre's circle of friends. "I'll be there. *Mur myoor!*"

So the next Wednesday, Tre caught the light rail up to San Francisco. Benny Phlogiston rode along with him to provide moral support, also to visit a new live sex show he'd heard about in North Beach.

"It's layers of uvvy," Benny explained enthusiastically on the train. "I heard about it on the Web. The club's called Real Compared To What. There's actual nude men and women there in the middle of the room, and they're all wearing uvvies on their necks, and there's these uvvy dildos as well. You go in there and put on your own uvvy, and you can actually be a dildo. A dildo that talks to a naked girl."

"That's great, Benny," said Tre. "I'm so happy for you. You feeble bufugu pervo. Do you think we should get high right now?"

"Never get high before an important meeting, Tre," advised

Benny. "Being high makes the meeting seem to take too long and makes it seem too important. Go in there and score some gigs, brah, and then we'll smoke up. Maybe Apex will give you a big advance and you can buy us drinks at Adler's Museum or Vesuvio. Let's meet in Washington Square at three-thirty."

"That sounds good, brah Ben. Have fun being a dildo."

"You still don't understand, Tre. It's that the illusions have illusions inside them. The performers run you the illusion that you are in Real Compared To What being a dildo. But the dildo is smart, and the dildo is dreaming that it's a user. I want to tweak into moiré patterns of uvvy/realtime bestial lust."

"Floaty. Give out some copies of Perplexing Poultry if you can. Maybe Real Compared To What will give you something free in return. A backstage assignation with a live woman."

"Fully."

Tre found Apex Images in a retrofitted Victorian on a back street above Haight Street. Heavily made-up Cynthia Major was sitting there in the flesh behind a desk. She was a real person after all.

"Tre!" she exclaimed pleasantly. "You're here! I'll buzz Mr. Kasabian."

The reception area filled two carpeted rooms. A dark wooden staircase led upstairs. The windows were bay windows that bulged out, leaving nooks occupied by displays of past Apex Image successes. The displays were hollows being run by uvvies. One showed the notorious EAT ME wendy meat ad with Wendy Mooney posed nude on a giant hamburger bun, with most of a big ass cheek bared to the viewer. Her Happy Cloak cape was ruffled like a bolero bed jacket around her shoulders. She was very attractive for being nearly fifty. The ad had the transreal sheen of a classic painting by the great Kustom Kulture artist Robert Williams—Apex Images had, in fact, purchased a license for the Robert Williams style from his estate. Another display showed a teeming cloud of Von Dutch winged eyeballs, a striking image used by ISDN, the main uvvy service provider. Still another showed a single large vibrating drop of water that seemed to sparkle and iridesce and break up the light through the window; this had been an ad for the Big Lift festival in Golden Gate Park this summer.

"Tre," said a man, coming down the stairs into the reception area. "I'm Dick Kasabian." Kasabian was a lean blue-chinned man with dark lively eyes and a saturnine cast to his features. He gave an impression of terminal hipness. "Come on up to my office."

Kasabian's office had a nice view of downtown San Francisco and the bay. He offered Tre a glass of supersoda, and Tre took it.

"Your Perplexing Poultry philtre," Kasabian said, picking up two uvvies. "I like it, but I don't fully understand what's going on. Can we go into it together?"

"Sure," said Tre, placing the proffered uvvy on the back of his neck. Although the earliest uvvy-like devices—the Happy Cloaks of the thirties, for instance—had actually punctured the user's skin with probes in order to connect to the nervous system, today's uvvies used small superconducting electromagnetic fields. So there was no danger of biological infection in using someone else's uvvy.

With their uvvies on, Tre and Kasabian were in a close mental link. They could talk to each other without moving their lips, and each could see what the other was seeing. It was a highly perfected form of communication. You couldn't quite read the other person's mind, but you could quickly pick up any verbal or graphic information that he or she wanted to share. In addition, you could pick up the emotional flavor of the information.

Tre noticed right away that Kasabian was linked into somebody else besides him. Who?

"Oh, that's the Mentor listening in," explained Kasabian. "If we offer you the job, I'll introduce you to him then. For now he'd just like to lurk. He doesn't like his involvement with Apex to be known outside of the company."

"All right," said Tre.

"Let's load the Poultry now," said Kasabian. Saying this was enough to make it happen. The room's space wavered and bulged and formed itself into a Jell-O-like linkage of comical chickens and dodoes. Through Tre's eyes, Kasabian's head was an upside-down dodo pecking into a bundle of five chickens that made up his chest. Yet, impossibly, he still looked like himself. And in Kasabian's eyes, Tre's head was a pair of chickens pecking into three dodoes.

"That's the kind of thing I've been wondering about," said Kasabian. "Why aren't our two images more similar? Our bodies aren't shaped so differently. Is it arbitrary?"

"It's because the pattern where you are has to fit with the pattern where I am," explained Tre. "It's a tessellation of space, a division of space into cells. And because the tessellation is based on quasicrystals, it tends to not want to repeat."

"Very weightless," said Kasabian. "But if I wanted to start out with my desk being made of, say, six dodoes, would I be able to do it?"

"Oh yeah," said Tre. "That's a special hidden feature, as a matter of fact. I'll show you how."

"Good," said Kasabian. "Because if we wanted to use it to like advertise something, the client might want to specify the way that the image of their product came out—and have everything else constellate itself around that."

"What would we want to advertise? Imipolex from Emperor Staghorn Beetle Larvae, Ltd.?"

"No no. Your first ads will be for wendy meat—just like you guessed when you talked to Cynthia. Emperor Staghorn wants your philtre's source code all right, but they don't want it for an ad. One of their limpware engineers wants to use it for quasi-crystal design. If we license the design to them, they'll pay bucks instead of suing."

"Wow," said Tre. "I didn't realize what I'd done was so floatin'. Maybe I should work for Emperor Staghorn instead of for you."

"Don't do that," said Kasabian quickly. "You'd have to move to India. Also I know for a fact that the Emperor Staghorn scientist who wants to use your philtre would never let them hire you. Sri Ramanujan. He's very secretive and he doesn't want his assistants to understand what he's doing. He doesn't want *you*, Tre, he just wants your philtre. Plus any more weird tessellations that you can come up with."

"So you want me to be more of an artist than an engineer," mused Tre. "Actually, that feels about right. Some of these courses I've been taking—"

"You've got a great creative talent," urged Kasabian. "You should go with it!"

They fooled around with the Perplexing Poultry some more, and then Kasabian ran a bunch of Apex Images demos for Tre. Finally they took their uvvies off.

"Apex does really lifty stuff," said Tre. "The ads are beautiful."

"Thanks," said Kasabian. "So now the Mentor wants to know: Are you ready to start working for us?"

"Advertising wendy meat is kind of lame, but I'd feel good about inventing new philtres and helping Emperor Staghorn Beetle."

"Have you ever tasted wendy meat?" asked Kasabian. "No? Guess what—neither have I. The gnarl of the images is all that matters."

"I wouldn't have to like physically come in here every day, would I?"

"God no. Nobody comes in here regularly except me and Cynthia Major. Apex can give you a base salary plus royalties on the philtres and any other research work that you produce. You keep the copyrights, but we get exclusive first rights for use. Occasionally we might ask you to do some specific contract work. Like tweaking a philtre to fit an ad."

They made a firm deal and signed some papers.

"Okay," said Tre. "Now tell me who the Mentor is."

"Stahn Mooney," said Kasabian.

"Ex-Senator Stahn?"

"None other. Stahn owns Apex, also he and his wife own most of Wendy Meat and W. M. Biologicals. When Stahn got voted out of the Senate, he didn't leave with empty pockets! Put your uvvy back on, he wants to talk with you."

The uvvy fed Tre the visual image of a jaded-looking man in his fifties. The man was sitting in a wood-paneled room with a crackling fire in a huge stone hearth; the flames of the fire were made up of Perplexing Poultry. The man's mouth spread in a long, sly smile that Tre recognized from the many Stahn Mooney news stories he'd watched over the years.

"Hi, Stahn," said Tre. "I'm happy to meet you."

"It's my pleasure," said Stahn. "These Perplexing Poultry of yours are the waviest thing I've seen all year. The proverbial software high. You must be a fellow stoner."

"I lift," allowed Tre.

"Yaar," said Stahn judiciously. "I've been listening in just now while Kasabian here's been telling you about how we can sell the Poultry for more than just ads."

"Yeah," said Tre. "Like for limpware engineering?"

"Big-time." Stahn gave a wheezy chuckle. He seemed not to be in the best physical condition. "Sri Ramanujan at Emperor Staghorn Beetle Larvae, Ltd., is working on some new method for bringing humans and moldies closer together. He won't give out any details, but it's bound to be a force for good, the way I look at it. Humans and moldies were meant to be one. Like Wendy and her Happy Cloak! Ramanujan says your Perplexing Poultry would be just the thing for his project if you could make them be *four-dimensional*. Does that make any sense to you?"

"I might be able to do it," said Tre after a minute's thought. "To fit into our space, the new philtre would actually be a three-dimensional *projection* of a four-dimensional tessellation. Like a shadow. I do know that the generalized Schmitt-Conway biprism will tile aperiodically in all dimensions of the form 3 times M. But dimensions four and five? Conway may also have done some work on aperiodic four-dimensional and five-dimensional tessellations. I can look into it."

"Stuzzadelic! Welcome aboard, Tre Dietz!" After a few more pleasantries, old Senator Stahn cut the connection.

With Tre all signed up, Kasabian suddenly turned out to be too busy to actually have lunch with Tre, somewhat to Tre's disappointment. With nothing better to do, Tre walked down Columbus Street to look for Benny at Real Compared To What.

The place had a honky-tonk façade covered with fuff hollows. There were some citified moldies lounging around in front, not doing much of anything, and there was a black man beckoning people in from the sidewalk.

"Light and tight!" the barker exclaimed to Tre. "Real Compared To What. Zoom on it, brah."

"I'm looking for a friend."

"Aren't we all. We got lots of friends inside."

"Can I peek in for free?"

"Look it over, and if you don't love it in two minutes, there's no charge. Gustav! Show the man in."

One of the moldies came hunching over; it was shaped like a big inchworm, orange with purple spots. "Do you need an uvvy, sir?"

"Not yet," said Tre. "I'll just use my eyes for now." He followed Gustav the moldie in through the thick curtains that hung over Real Compared To What's door.

Inside there was music and a closed-in smell of bodily fluids. The audience area was pitch-dark, and spotlights were on a stage with crawly uvvies, moldies, random pieces of imipolex, and several nude people, one of whom was Benny Phlogiston, on all fours with an erection, an uvvy on his neck, and a busy fat limpware dildo rhythmically reaming his butt.

"Hey, Benny!" shouted Tre. "Do you know what you're doing?"

Benny's head turned uncertainly in Tre's direction. His eyes had the glazed-over look of someone who's fully into mental uvvy space and all but obliv to the realtime world.

"Benny! Are you sure you're getting what you wanted?"

The dildo chose this instant to pull out of Benny and hop away. Benny came to his senses and stood up with a rapidly developing soft-off. He found his clothes back at his seat, donned them, and followed Tre back to the street. They moved slowly up the block.

"What a burn," said blushing Benny. "Did that really happen?"

"What did you *think* was happening?"

"It was this really sexy woman, this dominatrix type. She came off the stage and got me and stripped me and took me—I thought—to her boudoir room so I could be her love slave. She wanted to . . . to—"

"To buttfuck you with a dildo. No need to be embarrassed, Ben. It's a common male fantasy, pitiful creatures that we are—"

"All right, yes, that's what I thought was happening. Only—"

"Only there wasn't any woman behind the dildo," cackled Tre. "And her so-called boudoir was the lit-up stage!"

"Tre, if you tell anyone about this—"

"What's to tell? Who would be interested?"

"Come on, Tre. Please."

"Wavy. But you owe me big-time, brah."

"Fine. Fine." Benny turned and looked back at the moldies oozing around in front of Real Compared To What. "I hate moldies."

"They're not exactly man's best friend," agreed Tre. "But without moldies, there'd be no DIMs, no uvvies, no Wad, no Limpware Engineering courses, and no new job for me."

"You got the job!"

"You know it, little guy. It looks like a heavy deal."

"So buy me some food and drink!"

"Stratospheric," said Tre. "And let's stride. You probably don't want to be here if whoever was running that dildo comes a-stormin' out for some face time."

"Fully," agreed Benny, and they walked off into the side streets of North Beach for a memorable afternoon of youthful folly.

With the first big payment from Apex Images in hand, Tre let his studies slide. Like why get a degree for a job he already had? That spring he flunked all his courses, and his parents cut off his allowance when he wouldn't come home to Des Moines. Tre coasted through the summer and into the fall, trying to get the four-dimensional Perplexing Poultry to click, but he kept not being able to get it to happen. It was a hard problem. He was going to have to think about it for a long time. Meanwhile he kept the money coming in from Apex by tweaking uvvy ads when Kasabian asked him to.

By Thanksgiving, 2049, with no other obligations in sight, it suddenly seemed to make sense to go ahead and marry Terri Percesepe. Terri and Tre took over the management of the Clearlight Terrace Court Motel on behalf of Terri's widowed mother Alice.

After her husband Dom had died, Alice had added the name *Clearlight* to the motel, which had formerly just been the Terrace Court. Clearlight was the name of the current wave of the perennial New Age philosophy of California: a holistic nature-loving libertarian set of beliefs that fit in well with the surf and the sun and the weirdest new drugs and computational systems on Earth.

Not that the Terrace Court was a particularly Clearlight kind of place—sticking *Clearlight* in front of its name was just wishful thinking. The same old pasty tourists came there anyway. In any case, as managers, Terri and Tre got to live free in the apartment behind the motel office, which solved a serious rent problem that had been on the point of emerging for Tre.

As well as working on floaty new philtres and now and then doing a contracted tweak for Apex, Tre kept busy helping Terri keep up the motel. And Tre and Terri fell more and more in love. Before they knew it, out popped two babies: first a son, Dolf, born September 23, 2049, and then a daughter, Baby Wren, born June 26, 2052.

The one thing that always seemed the same, whether Tre was high or not, were the children. Tre delighted in them. It was fun to follow them around and watch them doing things.

"Clearly a biped," he would say, watching Wren stomp around

their apartment with her stubby little arms pumping. Baby Wren was so short that if Tre put his arm down at his side, the silky top of standing Wren's head was still an inch or two below his hand. Wren was about as short as a standing up person could possibly be. Dolf was a clever lad who liked asking his father questions like "Will our house float if there's a flood?" or "If we couldn't get any more food, how long would it take to eat everything in the kitchen?" Little Dolf was determined to survive, come what may.

In the spring of 2053, Tre got an uvvy call from Stahn Mooney. Senator Stahn was way lifted and messed up.

"I'm a wee bummed you never got the fuh-four-dimensional Perplexing Poultry together, Tuh-Tre," jabbered the middle-aged man. "You luh-loser." He looked twitchy and hostile. "I've been asking Kuh-Kuh-Kasabian why I shouldn't fire you."

"Kiss my ass," said Tre and shakily turned off the uvvy. Early the next morning, Mooney called him back sober.

"Sorry about that last call," said Mooney. "My legendary problems with substance abuse are back; I'm turning into the bad old Sta-Hi Mooney. Of course your work is excellent, Apex wouldn't dream of letting you go."

"Glad to hear it. And I am sorry I never delivered on the four-dimensional Poultry design. It turns out John Horton Conway found four-dimensional and five-dimensional aperiodic monotiles sixty years ago, but it's not too well documented. UCSC Wad finally unearthed a construction in Conway's e-mail archives. But turning Conway's tessellations into beautiful three-dimensional projections—so far I can't do it, even with UCSC's Wad. I do still think about it from time to time."

"Emperor Staghorn Beetle Larvae, Ltd., is offering some really serious bread, Tre, which is what got me back onto this. It's a mongo business opportunity. Ramanujan needs four-dimensional Perplexing Poultry right now, and Emperor Staghorn will pay whatever it takes to get them. Ramanujan can't figure it out himself, and he has this conviction that you're the man. It's not just the actual tessellation that counts, you wave, it's the gnarly Tre Dietz way you tweak it."

"Well, that's nice, but—"

"The loonie moldies are interested in this too. My old friend Willy Taze; he moved in to the loonie moldies' Nest a couple of years ago. He's talking about creating a virtual dial to like set the Perplexing Poultry's dimensionality to any number N." Stahn cleared his throat uncertainly. "Like three, four, five, six, seven . . . N—you wave? Didn't you say something about a general solution when we hired you?"

"Yes, the Schmitt-Conway biprism works for any N of the form 3 times M. Like for three, six, nine, and so on. And now that we have four and five, we can get all the others as Cartesian cross products. The dimensions sum when you cross the spaces. Like seven is three cross four or eight is three cross five. But you've got to understand that Conway's prisms are *ugly*. They look like waffles or like factory roofs. Turning them into pleasing visual Poultry is just too—"

"Try harder, Tre. I've got something for you to download that might help. It's a philtre Willy Taze sent me. Bye for now. It's time for my morning pick-me-up."

"Wait," said Tre. "One question. What do Emperor Staghorn Beetle and the loonie moldies want N-dimensional Perplexing Poultry for?"

"They won't exactly tell me. But supposedly it has something to do with better communications between humans and moldies. And merging things together is something I'm always for." Grinning Stahn pulsed himself a big toot from a handheld squeezie and toggled the connection off.

The loonie philtre, which was called TonKnoT, generated silent movies of smooth, brightly colored tubes tying themselves into N-dimensional knots. TonKnoT kept pausing and starting over with a fresh knot. The knot would start as a straight stick with arrows on it, and then all the arrows would move about and the stick would turn, in some indefinable way, into a knot. The pictures seemed so urgent, yet the meaning continued to escape Tre. "Look at this," TonKnoT seemed to be saying. "This

is important. This is one of the hidden secrets of the world."
The knot deformations were almost insultingly slow and precise,
yet the gimmick of the shift kept somehow eluding Tre. "Look
harder and you will understand."

And then in July, the jam broke and Tre finally designed his
four-dimensional Perplexing Poultry.

Taking care of the kids and the motel had been getting to be
too much grunt work, so as soon as Tre got his big advance from
Apex for the four-dimensional Perplexing Poultry, he and Terri
hired a moldie worker. Up until then, they'd been getting by
with the bumbling uncertain labor of the sweet, bright woman
named Molly, whom Terri's mother had passed on to them with
the motel. By the ongoing linguistic warpage of euphemism,
bright in 2053 had come to mean what *special* or *retarded* or
half-witted might have meant sixty or a hundred years earlier.
Tre and Terri took some pains to prevent Molly from button-
holing guests to talk on and on about what kinds of foods she
laaaahked—always a favorite topic of Molly's. She liked oysters
but not clams, crabs but not shrimp, squid but not mussels, beef
but not ham, spaghetti but not macaroni, and on and on. The
weird cryptic idiot savant joke in this was that Molly liked only
the foods whose name did not contain the letter *m*—it was Terri
who'd figured that out. They could never decide if Molly herself
consciously understood this; if you asked her about it, she just
laughed and said she didn't know how to spell.

Once they had a moldie to do the rooms, Terri and Tre began
using Molly as a baby-sitter. She'd worked for the Percesepe
family so long that there could be no thought of letting her go.
The baby-sitting job worked out fine, as Dolf and Baby Wren
loved Molly and hated Monique. Like most children, they in-
stinctively feared moldies, with their odd motions and their alien
stench.

When Randy Karl Tucker checked into the Clearlight Terrace
Court Motel—the day before he abducted Monique—it was
eight-thirty on a clear October evening. Terri and Tre were in
the process of giving the kids a bath—always a fun family time,

with fat Wren slapping the water and shouting, while Dolf manned the faucets and guided a flotilla of floating things around the dangerous Wren. Terri was kneeling by the tub with a washrag and Tre was sitting on the closed toilet seat with a towel in readiness. Just then there was a chime.

"Uh-oh," said Tre. "A guest. I better go help Monique."

"Wren's done," said Terri. "Grab her and put her in her sleeper first. I can't do both the kids alone."

Tre pulled his uvvy out of his pocket, put it on his neck, and told Monique to stall. It was always good practice to get a face-to-face look at your guests. Not only did it make the customers happier, but it was unwise to trust a moldie's judgment about who to let into the motel.

Terri handed Wren into Tre's waiting towel. Moving quickly, Tre diapered Wren, zipped her into her sleeper, and set her down in her crib. "I'll be right back, Wren." Wren wailed to see her father go so quickly, but then shifted her focus to her crib toys.

Out in the office, Monique was behind the counter talking with a lanky young guy with a thin head and colorless eyes. He was dressed in cheap nerd clothes. He had his elbows on the counter and was slouched forward like a drunk at a bar. A small battered leather carry-on bag rested at his feet.

"Here's one of our managers," said Monique. "Tre Dietz. Tre, this is Randy Karl Tucker." The narrow-skulled man looked vaguely familiar. Tre felt like he'd seen Tucker around Santa Cruz recently.

"Hi, guy," said the man. With his accent it came out sounding like *Haaaaah, gaaaaah.* "I need a room for a night, maybe two nights. Nice li'l moldie you got yourself here." He stretched one of his long arms across the counter and gave Monique an appraising pat, intimately running his hand down her shoulder onto her chest. Monique twitched away from him. In her anger, she released a cloud of pungent spores and redolent body gas.

"Haw-haw," said Tucker. "She gets her dander up. I guess I shore ain't in Kentucky no more."

"Nope," said Tre, moving forward. "Not hardly. What do we have free, Monique?"

"We can give him Room 3D," said the reeking Monique.

"A nice room," said Tre. "On the lower terrace. It has an ocean view."

"Copacetic," said Tucker. "I'll charge it." He leaned down and got an uvvy out of his bag, being careful to immediately snap the clasps on his bag shut.

"Monique can take your code," said Tre.

"Monique the moldie," said Tucker and sniffed the air savoringly. "I like it." He put his uvvy on his neck and chirped Monique his authorization code. He did something internal in his uvvy space and his eyes glazed over, staring blankly at Monique, his eyes squinted up small as two pissholes in a snowbank. Some uvvy conversation got him briefly involved and he started subvocalizing and gesturing. "Fuckin'-aye, Jen," said Tucker vaguely and took the uvvy off his neck. He favored Tre with a bogus grin. "Is that your hydrogen cycle right outside, Mr. Dietz? With the white DIM tires?"

"Call me Tre. Yeah it is. You like it?"

"What I do," said Tucker, "what I do is limpware upgrades. When's the last time you got those tires upgraded?"

"What for? It's never occurred to me. The tires work fine."

"Shit-normal rubber tires would work, but you don't use 'em," said Tucker. "I happen to be the sole local distributor for a new limpware patch that enhances the performance of DIM tires a hundred and fifty percent. Smooths the hell out of the bumps."

"You're a limpware salesman?" said Tre disbelievingly.

"You don't think I look like no kind of a hi-tech propellorhead, do you, Tre Dietz?" Tucker chuckled slyly. "I might's well confess, I already know who you are. That's one of the reasons I'm bunkin' at this hole; I admire the hell outta your philtres. But I'm not here to hassle you, man. The thing about the tires is, I'd be right proud to give you an upgrade for twenty percent off the room rate."

Just then Dolf came tearing out of the back apartment, wet and naked. "Catch him, Tre!" called Terri.

Tre grabbed at Dolf, who roared with joy and ran back into the apartment. "I better go help with the kids," Tre told Randy Karl Tucker. "We can talk about your offer tomorrow when I have more time, but I'm probably not interested. Thanks anyway. Do you mind if I have Monique show you to your room now?"

"It'd be my pleasure," said Tucker.

The next morning Molly showed up to watch the kids and Terri went surfing. Tre smoked a joint and went to sit in a sunny spot out in front of the motel office with his uvvy. Now that he'd mastered the four-dimensional Perplexing Poultry, he was getting close on a general N-dimensional method for creating them from Conway cross-product prisms. These days he had a lot of interesting work to do.

Monique come bouncing up from the lower terrace. Her facial expression was even more opaque than usual, and she was followed closely by Randy Karl Tucker, dressed the same as yesterday and carrying his bag. Tucker looked mussed and wild-eyed, as if he'd been wrestling with someone. His neck bore several red welts, some of them disk-shaped as if from a mollusk's suckers. He was wearing his uvvy.

"Haaaaah, gaaaaah," wheezed Tucker. "Here's that upgrade I promised you!" Before Tre could object, Tucker had pulled two purplish postage-stamp-sized patches of plastic out of his pants pocket and had slapped them onto the fat white imipolex tires of Tre's hydrogen cycle. "You're gonna love these to death, freakbrain," said Tucker. "I'm outta here. Monique, you whore! I want you to carry me outta here on your fat ass!"

"Just a minute there," said Tre, losing his temper. "You can't talk like that. Monique has work to do. She doesn't rickshaw for the guests. And I don't want your xoxxin' goober patches on my DIM tires! Who the hell do you think you are?"

Tucker didn't bother to answer. Monique leaned forward and broadened her butt. Tucker sprang onto her, sinking one hand into her flesh and grasping his travel bag with his other hand. Monique found her balance, Tucker whooped, and they hopped rapidly away.

The enraged, flabbergasted Tre stared after them for a moment, then ran back through the office and yelled to Molly, who was playing checkers with Dolf while Wren watched from her walker. "Keep an eye on things, Molly! I have to go out!"

"All righty," sang Molly. "The boy and me are about to eat cookies! I'll give Wren one too. I love cookies, but I hate graham crackers!"

"Fine, Molly, fine."

Tre dashed back out and jumped onto his hydrogen cycle. The burner hiccupped on, and Tre pedaled to the corner with the little engine helping him. There, down at the bottom of the hill, were Tucker and Monique, moving toward the wharf in long, graceful leaps. Tre hurtled after them.

He thought—too late—of Tucker's patches on his DIM tires as he shot across the train tracks at the bottom of the hill. Instead of smoothing the bump energy into the usual chaotic series of shudders, Tre's tires seemed to blow out. The raw metal of the wheel rims scraped across the pavement, showering sparks. The bike slewed, the front rim crimped and caught, Tre went over the falls. His shoulder made a horrible crunch as he hit the pavement.

Tre lay there gasping for breath, monitoring the nerve impulses from his battered bod. Big problem in his right shoulder, a scrape on his forearm, but he hadn't hit his head. All right, he was going to be okay, but then—

Two strong slippery shapes wound around Tre's waist. The DIM tires!?! Tre jerked up into a sitting position. Bone ground against bone in his right shoulder. The tires were like fat white hoop snakes who'd stopped biting their tails; they were the two sea serpents who slew Laocoön. Tucker's DIM patches glowed on the tires like evil eyes. There was a hideous pressure around Tre's waist, squeezing the air out of him. He got hold of the tires with his left hand and pulled them loose; they writhed up his left arm and twined around his neck.

"What's he doing? Is it a trick?"

A group of tourists had gathered around Tre and the DIM

snakes. The young man who spoke was a valley wearing a bright new Santa Cruz DIM shirt with a gnarly graphic of a surfer on a liveboard.

"He's bleeding," said the woman at his side. She wore her long pink hair in three high ponytails. "And it looks like those moldie things are choking him."

"Help," gasped Tre. "Get them off me. They—" The pressure on his windpipe made further speech impossible, but now, blessedly, the valley stepped forward and tugged at the snakes. While continuing to grip Tre's neck with their tails, the snakes elongated their heads and stuck at the valley. Another onlooker—a lithe black woman in cotton tights—stepped forward and yanked the distracted snakes off Tre. She swung the snakes through the air and slammed them down hard on the pavement.

"Rogue moldies," yelled an old man. "Hold 'em down! I'll run into that liquor store and get some 191-proof rum to burn 'em!"

The valley planted his feet on one of the stunned DIM tires and the black woman stood on the other. The old man hurried hitchingly toward Beach Liquors. The woman with the three ponytails leaned over Tre, who was flat on his back.

"Are you okay, mister?" The valley woman's upside-down face looked big and soft and strange. Watching her white-lipsticked lips move was like seeing someone with a mouth in her forehead.

"I think so," whispered Tre.

There was a sudden cry, and now the DIM snakes had wormed out from under the people's feet. They humped off rapidly, leaped into the air, and all at once flipped into the shapes of seagulls.

Still on his back, Tre stared at the white shapes flapping away. The blue sky. It was precious to be alive.

"What the hell?" asked the big valley.

"Now I've seen everything," said the black woman.

"Here's the rum!" called a voice, and the old man's footsteps came scuffing closer. "They got away? Gol-dang it. I've always wanted to burn a moldie. Well, what the hey." There was a sound of a bottle being uncapped, followed by a gurgle of drinking. "Anybody else want some? How 'bout the victim here?"

Tre sat up and weakly waved the old man away. "Thank you," he said to the valley and the black woman. "You saved my life. God bless you."

"Shouldn't he stay on his back?" interjected an old woman. "His neck could be broken. He might have internal bleeding. We should get him to a doctor. Where's the nearest hospital? Stop guzzling that rum, Herbert!"

"Most of us don't use doctors and hospitals here," said Tre painfully. Moving very slowly, he got to his feet. "I'll go to a healer."

"But shouldn't we call some gimmie?" asked the valley.

"We don't like to use them either," said Tre, attempting a grin. "Welcome to Santa Cruz."

After a little more chatter, the people drifted away. Tre stared briefly up and down Beach Street, then out toward the wharf, but nothing much was to be seen. People coming and going. A Percesepe cruise boat pulling away. No sign of Tucker, Monique, or the DIM tires/seagulls.

It was only two blocks back to the motel, so Tre decided to wheel his cycle back there before doing anything else. The bare wheel rims clanged, the bones in his shoulder grated, but Tre made it. He was thankful to find Terri there.

"Terri, I'm hurt. I was in an accident. I think I broke a bone."

"Oh, Tre, that's wiped! You're so pale! How did it happen?"

"I was chasing Monique and Randy Karl Tucker. That weird hillbilly limpware salesman who checked in last night? Somehow he got Monique to rickshaw him away, and I was trying to chase them down with my cycle."

"You fell off your bike?"

"My tires squirmed off the rims. Then they tried to squeeze me to death and then they tried to strangle me and then they turned into seagulls and they flew away."

"Who did?"

"My DIM tires. Tucker put some kind of patch on them. He jammed their limpware."

"You fell off your bike and your tires tried to choke you and then they flew away. Tre, you're stoned, aren't you? Why do you do this to yourself? To me and the kids?"

"I did smoke pot this morning, but that has nothing to do with it! Why are you so suspicious, Terri? I need your help, for God's sake. My shoulder's broken, I've nearly been killed, and I have to see a healer!"

"Fine," said Terri curtly. "We'll go to Starshine."

"Can I come too?" asked Dolf. "I want to see Starshine make Daddy well." The little boy stared worriedly up at Tre, who was grimacing.

"Yes, you can come," said Tre, patting his son on the head. It would be good to have a buffer between him and Terri. Terri often got angry when she was afraid. "Molly, we three are going down to Starshine's."

"Bye-bye. Say bye-bye, Wren!" Little Wren stood unsteadily on Molly's lap and waved bye-bye, dimpling her cheeks and showing her gums.

The sun was high and glaring. Dolf skipped down the sidewalk ahead of the silent Terri and Tre. They walked a block down the back side of the beach hill to the little house where Starshine and her husband Duck Tapin lived. The house was set back from the street with a garage up front by the curb in the shade of a huge palm tree.

Duck was visible in the shadows of the garage, wearing his inevitable outfit of tan shorts and flowered shirt. He had a long, weathered face with reddish-blond walrus whiskers; his hair was a floppy mat of blond curls.

"Yaar, Duck," said Terri.

"Yaar," said Duck. "What's happening?" He looked up from the big table where he was carefully assembling some scroll-shaped pieces of colored glass into one of the windows that he sold for a living. Starshine's orange-and-white dog Planet lay at Duck's feet, quietly thumping his tail. Little Dolf hunkered down near Planet to pet him.

"My hydrogen cycle's DIM tires got screwed up," said Tre. "I fell off the cycle and broke something."

"Oh, that's dense," said Duck hoarsely. California born and raised, Duck was an unreflective pleasure hound who happened somehow to be a very gifted craftsman. At any hour of the day, sober or not, he gave the impression of having spent the last twelve hours getting very weightless. "That's fully stuck. You want Starshine to heal you?"

"Yeah," said Terri. "Is she in the house?"

"No doubt," said Duck. "Go give her a holler. How's it going, Dolf? You helping to take care of your dad?"

"Yes," said Dolf solemnly. "What are you making?"

"This is a window for a lady up in the hills. It's going to be a peacock. See his head there? Whoops, there go your parents. Better follow them."

"Bye, Duck! Bye, Planet!" Dolf hurried after his parents, his thin little legs rapid beneath his short pants.

Duck and Starshine's house was a small pink-painted wooden box. There were large clumps of naturalized bird of paradise plants in front of it, some with a few late orange-and-purple blossoms shaped like the heads of sharp-nosed donkeys. At the base of the cottage's walls were masses of nasturtiums with irregular round leaves and red-and-orange flowers. Crawling up the walls were vines that bore flowers shaped like asymmetrical lavender trumpets. A thick hop vine twisted its way up along the eaves.

Terri knocked on the door with the little brass head of a gnome that hung there. After a while there were light, rapid footsteps and Starshine flung the door open.

"Yaar there!" she sang. Starshine was a talkative woman with straight brown hair, high cheekbones, and a hard chin. Her parents had been Florida crackers, but she'd turned herself into a Clearlight Californian. Seeing Terri and Dolf with Tre, she instantly spotted Tre's problem. "What all's happened to your shoulder, Tre?"

"He fell off his bicycle," said Dolf. "Can you make him well?"

"It hurts a lot here," said Tre, pointing to where his shoulder met his neck. "It made a noise when I fell, and now when I move my shoulder, I can feel something grinding. After I fell, my tires tried to strangle me and then they flew away. But Terri here doesn't want to hear about that part. She thinks I'm fucked up."

"Poor Tre. Thank Goddess I'm here. For the last hour I've been about to go into town, but I kept feeling like there was some reason to stay. *This* must be the reason. Come on in, you three."

The house had only three rooms: the main room, the kitchen, and the room where Duck and Starshine slept. Starshine had Tre lie down on the floor while Terri watched from the couch with Dolf at her side.

"I'll scan you, and if it's a simple break I can glue it up for you directly," Starshine told Tre. She opened a trunk that sat by one wall and took out a device about the size and shape of a handheld vacuum cleaner. She detached a special uvvy from it and put the uvvy on her neck, then proceeded to run the device over Tre's neck and shoulder while staring off into space.

"I'm seein' your bones, Tre."

"Are you using radiation?" worried Terri.

"Heck no," said Starshine. "This is ultrasonic. My dog Planet hates when I use this thing. Did you see Planet outside, Dolf?"

"Yes," said Dolf. "Planet's in the garage with Duck."

"And before I moved in, Duck said he hated dogs," said Starshine. "That man was too solitary. The first time I saw him, I knew he was the one for me. He was tanned and callused like the carpenters and construction workers I'd been dating, but then I found out he was an artist! When I heard *that*, I set my cap for him. And now that we're married, I'm working on getting him to want some kids. I've thought of some beautiful names. Speaking of people with cute names, how's little Wren today?"

"Oh, she's wavin'," said Terri. "And Dolf here is learning to play checkers. Is Tre going to be all right?"

"I think so," said Starshine, setting down her scanner. "Tre,

old brah, you've snapped your collarbone is what you've done.
Let me get out my glue gun and patch you."

"Is it going to hurt?" asked Tre weakly. "Shouldn't you give
me some drugs?"

"You smell like you've already been smoking some good reefer
this morning," said Starshine teasingly. "Are you sure that's not
why you fell off your cycle and saw your tires fly away? Reminds
me of something happened one time to Aarbie Kidd."

"You see, Tre?" interjected Terri. "You should cut back.
You've been getting so *floppy*."

"Oh, shut up," snapped Tre, lying there on his back with the
two women and his son looking down at him. "In the first place,
the accident was caused by that guy putting some kind of weird
DIMs on my tires. In the second place, pot's not a drug. It's an
herb. It energizes me."

"Oh yeah," said Terri. "And when's the last time you finished
something?"

"What about my new four-dimensional Perplexing Poultry
philtre, for God's sake! That's major!"

"Yeah, well how come it took you four years to do it! You
smoke too much, Tre!"

"Now, Terri," said Starshine. "Let me finish healin' him up
before you start beatin' him down. First I'll give you a little mist,
Tre, so that you won't feel it when I glue your break. And, Dolf,
I think maybe you ought to go outside while I do this. I wouldn't
want you to get spooked and bump into me."

"Do I have to?"

"You do what the healer says, Dolf," said Terri. "Go out in
the garage with Planet and Duck."

"Go ahead, Dolf," added Tre. "I'll be all right."

"Okay. And, Mommy, you come get me when Daddy is well."
Dolf ran out to the garage.

"He's a sweet boy to care for his daddy that way," said Starshine. She got a little squeezie of aerosol spray out of her healer
trunk. She wafted a pulse of the spray into Tre's nostrils. His
muscles relaxed and his eyelids fluttered shut. "I know some

folks that have lost everything to this mist," continued Starshine. "It gives you mighty sweet dreams. Mist is giga worse than any silly old pot habit. And mist is nothing compared to gabba. That's what Aarbie Kidd got into after we rode his motorcycle out here from Florida. The minute old Aarbie got to California, he got hooked on gabba and started abusing me ten times worse than he ever did back in Florida. Him and his flamehead tattoos. Thank Goddess I found Clearlight."

Starshine's eyes narrowed and she pulsed a bit more mist into Tre's nostrils. "I had my chance to get free of Aarbie after he wrecked his motorcycle and asked me to heal him. Tre hasn't been beating on you, has he, Terri? If you need some time to think things over, I can put him to sleep for a week."

"Oh no no no, don't do that," said Terri. "It's just that Tre ignores me sometimes. And I get so tired of being a wife and mother. I need a vacation is what it is. I wish I could go off by myself and surf or snowboard someplace really major and let Tre do all the housework for a change. But, oh, I shouldn't be harshing on him while he's hurt. Of course don't put him to sleep for a week, are you whacked? Tre doesn't compare to Aarbie Kidd. You get to work healing him, Starshine. And explain what you're doing as you go along."

"Right now I'm going to have a cup of coffee," said Starshine. "Before I go and finish this. I'll let Tre chill just a little deeper. One more pulse of mist." At the final pulse, Tre's body lost all of its muscle tone. He looked as soft as an imipolex polar bear rug.

"You want anything, Terri?" asked Starshine, ambling out to the kitchen.

"Just a glass of water, please. You're sure Tre's okay?"

"He'll be fine like this for an hour or until I give him the antidote. Did I tell you I saw Aarbie again just the other day? Down near the Boardwalk. He was real friendly. Yellow stubble on his head growing out of the hearts of his flame tattoos. Lifted on gabba as usual." Starshine clattered about in the kitchen, still talking. "What Aarbie's up to these days is what I'd like to understand. First he said he was working for the Heritagists, and then he said he was working for the loonie moldies. He was with some skanky guy from Kentucky who kept telling him to shut up. Okeydoke, here we go." Starshine reemerged with a cup of coffee and a glass of water.

She got something that looked like a stubby plastic pistol out of her healer trunk and set it down next to the scanner and the mister that lay next to Tre. "This is the glue gun," said Starshine. "But first I use my hands to set the bones. Did you know that in Arabic bone-setting is *al-jabar*? The word *algebra* comes from that. Arranging things. I learned that in my classes. Time for some healer algebra, Tre." She laid the scanner on Tre's chest and adjusted his collarbone with both hands. Tre moaned softly.

Terri couldn't watch, so she looked away, letting her eyes range over the pictures on the walls—Starshine's life-affirming Clearlight posters of plants and landscapes, along with Duck's highly detailed oil-and-canvas fiber-for-fiber copies of high-art paintings. Duck loved dreamy late-nineteenth-century artists such as Arnold Böcklin and Franz von Stuck and had taken the trouble to get museum-grade nanoprecise copies of some of their pictures, complete with exact wood-gilt-and-plaster copies of the frames. The largest picture was Böcklin's *Triton and Nereid*, which showed a hairy guy—Triton—sitting on a rock in the sea and blowing in a conch shell. Lying flat on her back on the rock with Triton was a smiling sexy plump Nereid, toying with a huge bewhiskered sea serpent. The serpent's back was decorated with a lovely proto-Jugendstil pattern of green-and-yellow tessellation. Duck liked to explain the pictures to his friends.

"All righty now," said Starshine, setting down the scanner and picking up the glue gun. "See the tip, Terri?" The glue gun had what looked like a long, dull needle at the end. "It's folded up now, so I can push it through his skin. But then on the inside it opens up into a swarm of bendy little arms, and those arms split up into arms that split. The little fibers reach into the break and fit any loose chips into place, and then they secrete . . . something. I forget the name. *Phonybone*? Phonybone is basically organic, except that it has some rare-earth elements in it. Ytterbium and lutetium. It's completely safe."

"Are you sure?" fretted Terri.

"It's automatic, honey," said Starshine as she brandished the glue gun. "Every piece of my equipment has a big DIM inside it. If these machines were much smarter, they'd be full-fledged moldies—and, of course, then you wouldn't be able to trust 'em, would you? That's why we've got healers to run 'em. Here goes!" Starshine bent over Tre and pushed the tip of the glue gun through his skin just above his collarbone. As the invisible fractal tip unfolded and did its work, Terri could see slight motions beneath Tre's skin.

Again Terri looked away, resting her eyes on von Stuck's *Sin*, a high Jugendstil work with a massive, pillared gold-leaf wooden frame around a darkly painted half-nude woman, young and bold-eyed, her raven tresses cascading down with a stray pubic-like curl across her belly—and there in the shadows, draped across her shoulders, was a great thick black serpent, its inhuman slit-eyed face peering out at the viewer from beneath the woman's steady, shadowed gaze. Next to it was a tacked-up paper Clearlight poster showing a huge sunflower with a smiling face. Out the window was the palm tree and the garage and the October afternoon and the soft piping of Dolf and the loud, laughing voice of Duck—tears filled Terri's eyes.

"Terri," came Starshine's voice presently. "It's all over, sweet thing. You can stop crying. And, brah Tre, it's time to wake up." Starshine changed a setting on her squeezie and pulsed a different aerosol into Tre's nostrils. He twitched and opened his eyes. "You're all better, Tre!" said Starshine. "And for recuperation, I'd advise right living and being good to your wife."

"Wavy," said Tre, sitting up uncertainly. "The dreams—I was seeing flashes of light from the Nth dimension. Yaar! I'm healed?" He rubbed his shoulder. "How much do we owe you?"

"Oh, how about a free room in your motel for maybe a week, ten days? My Aunt Tempest is coming out to visit from Florida, but I can't stand to have her in my house. Tempest raised me, you know. My parents died in the Second Human-Bopper War on the Moon back in 2031."

"I didn't know that," said Terri. "Were they heroes?"

"Not hardly," said Starshine. "They were working for the boppers. They were called Rainbow and Berdoo, just a cracker skank and her bad-ass man—like me and Aarbie Kidd used to be. Rainbow and Berdoo ran a toy shop on the Moon that was a front for a tunnel into the boppers' Nest."

"Wow," said Tre. "They were helping the boppers turn people into meaties? Putting those robot rats inside their skulls?"

"I think Rainbow and Berdoo were probably meaties themselves by the end," said Starshine. "After they died, a guy called Whitey Mydol took care of me for a while. Him and his old lady Darla; they're friends of Stahn Mooney's. Stahn got in touch with my Aunt Tempest, and she had me flown right down to Florida."

"Senator Stahn's gotten kind of strung out lately," remarked Tre. "But he's still a good man. So when's your aunt coming? What are the dates?"

"Too soon till too long," sighed Starshine. "You don't have to give her a really good room."

"We can fit her in up by the parking lot," said Terri. "Those rooms are usually empty this time of year."

"Aunt Tempest couldn't be any worse of a guest than the guy I checked in last night," said Tre, cautiously flexing his newly healed body. "Randy Karl Tucker."

"Randy Karl Tucker!" exclaimed Starshine. "That's the name of the guy I saw down at the Boardwalk with Aarbie Kidd."

"Oh yeah?" said Tre. "Well, he's the one who sabotaged my DIM tires, and it looks like he stole Monique. Maybe you can help me find him?"

"I wouldn't advise you to try," said Starshine, shaking her head. "Not if he's friends with Aarbie. Terri, I'll let you know about Aunt Tempest. Now go on home and get Tre to rest."

When they stepped out into the yard, Dolf heard them and came running. "Daddy!"

Tre hugged him. "I'm all fixed. Starshine glued me. What have you been up to?"

"Duck's shoes can walk by themselves," said Dolf. "Show them, Duck!"

Duck grinned and held his hands up in the air. Slowly and smoothly, he slid out of the garage toward Terri and Tre.

"They're DIM shoes," said Duck. "The soles are imipolex. They adjust to your foot. And if you press your toes a certain way, they ripple along on the ground by themselves. Loose as a moose." Duck made dancing gestures with his arms and gave his wild laugh.

"Do you have to feed your shoes?" asked Dolf.

"No," said Duck. "They're like moldies; they eat light." He struck a new pose and his shoes began dollying him back into the garage. "I gotta finish this piece by tomorrow. How's the sore wing, Tre?"

"It's solid," said Tre, gingerly patting his collarbone. "Good as new."

"Beautiful. Later, guys."

Back at the motel, three of Monique's nestmates were waiting for them: Xlotl, Ouish, and Xanana. While Xlotl was shaped like a chessman, Ouish and Xanana looked like sharks walking around erect on their tail fins—sharks with drifting, eddying fractals moving across their skins in shades of blue and deep gray. They each had a silvery patch that sketched a resemblance to a face.

"What's the story with Monique?" Xlotl demanded of Terri and Tre. "What the hell happened?"

"It looks like Monique ran off with a scuzzy cheeseball guest," said Terri, smiling at Tre. She'd started believing him again. "He sabotaged Tre's DIM tires, and poor Tre broke his collarbone trying to catch them."

Tre smiled back at Terri, then focused on Monique's excited nestmates. "How do you know something happened to Monique anyway?" asked Tre. "Did she uvvy you?"

"She *didn't*," said Xlotl. "And she was supposed to. So I grepped for her vibe and managed to get a feed from her virtual address, but—" Xlotl shook his head helplessly.

"What?" demanded Tre. "Can you tell me, Ouish? Xanana?"

"Yes, I can tell you," said Ouish. She had a rich, womanly voice that she generated by vibrating her silvery face patch. "Xanana and I have just been channeling her. Monique seems to be dreaming about the ocean. We think maybe she's undersea. Come here, Tre. Let me uvvy it to you."

"Wavy," said Tre, and Ouish laid one of her fins across the back of Tre's neck to feed him a realtime uvvification of Monique's current mental essence.

Monique seemed to be underwater, but it was not a realistic scene. The bottom had a white orthogonal mesh painted on it, for one thing, and the things swimming about in the water looked more like goblins than like fish. Instead of seaweed, the bottom was overgrown with rusty machinery. Yet the play of the shiny surface overhead was just as the ocean should be. The uvvy transmitted a nonvisual sensation that there was someone with Monique—inside her?—someone that Monique was frightened of, someone kinky, someone like Randy Karl Tucker.

It was too strange, too intense, and Tre felt faint. He pushed Xanana's flipper off his neck.

"That's my nestmate," said Ouish. "That's her right now. And I don't know how she got that way or where she is. Tell me about the guest who took her."

"At first Tre thought he was just a weird redneck limpware salesman," said Terri.

"His name is Randy Karl Tucker," added Tre. "He's from Kentucky. He was real interested in Monique last night, and this morning he got her to rickshaw him out of here. I almost caught up with them near the wharf, but Tucker put some kind of DIM patches on my tires that made them jump off my wheels and try to choke me and turn into seagulls and fly away. Does . . . does that any make sense to you guys?"

"It could be done," said Xanana. "Have you heard of superleeches? No? You poor fleshers can be so out of it. There's a new kind of leech-DIM called superleeches; they just started showing up in August. Nobody's told you? A superleech lets a human take control of a moldie or, for that matter, take control of a simple DIM device like an imipolex tire. It's made of some new kind of imipolex. None of us knows where the superleeches are coming from. They're very bad. Very very bad. Very very very bad. Very very very very bad—" Xanana repeated this loop phrase maybe twenty or a hundred times, saying it faster and with more *verys* each time, so that the last repetitions merged into a single chirp. Xanana liked infinite regresses.

"And you say Tucker's a cheeseball?" interrupted Ouish.

"I don't really know for sure," said Terri. "It's a guess."

"*Yeah* Monique was gonna fuck him," said Xlotl. "We was talkin' about it during our break. Just ball him to make money, ya know."

"Oh wow, that's classy," exclaimed Terri. "Monique turning tricks in our motel. If that's the case, we don't want her working here, do we, Tre? With the children? We don't want to run that kind of motel, do we? We don't want the Clearlight to end up like that horrible place where my father died!" The moldies shifted about uneasily at this remark, but Terri seemed not to notice. "Answer me, Tre!"

"No, we don't want that," said Tre slowly. He'd been deep in thought ever since hearing what Xanana said. "I need to find out more about these superleeches. I've got this feeling they're based on my four-dimensional Perplexing Poultry. How come Apex Images never tells me anything?"

"Let's stick to the point," said Xlotl. "How do we save Monique? Is it for real that she's underwater?"

"She might be," said Ouish. "Or she might just be dreaming."

"Maybe she and Tucker turned right at the wharf and headed up toward Steamer Lane," suggested Tre. "Can you guys uvvy any moldies there?"

"Let me try," said Xanana. "Everooze and Ike might be surfing Steamers today."

In a minute, he'd made contact. Everooze, father of Monique

and Xanana, was indeed surfing Steamer Lane, a point break at the Santa Cruz lighthouse. Xanana spoke aloud so that Tre and Terri could follow the conversation.

"Yaar, Pop, have you seen Monique? Or has anyone else there seen her? Yeah, I'll hold on while you check. What's that? Zilly the liveboard did? Monique turned herself into a diving suit for a tourist and jumped into the ocean? But you didn't notice it yourself. You were shredding the curl. Wavy. Yeah. We think Monique's been abducted. Her signal's really weird; you can check it out. You're going after her? Hold on, Ouish and me want to come too."

"I'm in," said Xlotl.

"And me too," said Terri. "If I can wear you underwater, Xanana?"

"Sure thing. Is Tre coming? He could ride inside Ouish."

"I should rest," said Tre. "I'm still a little shaky from the accident. And I've got to find out about this superleech stuff. I'll make some uvvy calls."

"Okay," said Terri. "But be sure and take it easy. Ouish, can you rickshaw me out to Steamers?"

"I don't do that," said Ouish coldly. "I'm a diver, not a rickshaw."

"You can say that again," said Xanana. "You can say, 'You can say that again' again. You can say, 'You can say, 'You can say, "You can say that again" again' again. You can say, "You can say, 'You can say that again' again" again' again." And he was off to the races with another regress.

"La-di-da," said Xlotl. "This ain't no tea dance. Get the hell on me, Terri." Xlotl formed a saddle shape on his back, and Terri got aboard. The three moldies and Terri went bouncing down the hill.

Tre watched them go, checked on Molly and the kids, sat down in a comfortable chair, donned the uvvy, planning to put in a call to Stahn Mooney. But just then the uvvy signaled for him.

"Hello?"

"Hi there!" Tre saw the image of a teenage girl hick with a colorless lank ponytail. "My name is, um, Jenny? I bet you're wondering about Randy Karl Tucker's superleeches, aren't you?" Jenny gave a shrill giggle. "I could tell you all about them if I wanted to."

"Are you working with Randy for the Heritagists or something?" asked Tre. "I want Monique back right now. Are you a blackmailer?"

"Those are silly questions," said Jenny. "Me, a Heritagist? A blackmailer? Think bigger, Tre. I want to talk to you about smart stuff! I can tell you exactly how Sri Ramanujan at Emperor Staghorn used your 4D Poultry to design imipolex-4 and the superleech. I have a viddy of him explaining it. If I show it to you, will you promise to tell me all the things it makes you think of next?"

"But I have an exclusive contract with Apex Images."

"Oh *right*! I'm so sure. And meanwhile Apex never tells you anything. Ramanujan gets your ideas and hogs them and doesn't give you anything back. You can trust Jenny, Randy. I'll never tell anyone a thing about our little deal. Here's a peek."

Jenny started a tape of a round-faced Indian man, presumably Ramanujan, explaining about his marvelous new Tessellation Equation. He seemed to be in a lab, and there was a math screen behind him. Tre could instantly see that this was a major mathematical breakthrough and that it had been inspired by his 4D Poultry. It was like he was suddenly getting a glass of water after crawling through a desert. Just then Jenny stopped the tape.

"Are we interested? Hmmm?" Something synthetic about the hum made Tre suddenly realize that Jenny was a software construct and not a person at all. God only knew who she really worked for.

"Please let me see the rest of it, Jenny."

"And you promise to tell me what it makes you think of?"

"I promise."

CHAPTER FOUR

RANDY

═══ ■ ═══

March 2052–August 2053

All through the fall and winter of 2051, Parvati kept up her visits to Randy. They had sex and took camote/leech-DIM trips together, and now and then Parvati would take Randy on tours into the surrounding countryside. Once they went to the jungle and rode wild elephants; another time they flew over the Western Ghats to go diving in the Arabian Sea. Shiva came along for that trip; he'd learned to tolerate Randy, as Randy was now giving Parvati a full kilogram of imipolex a month toward the creation of Shiva and Parvati's third child.

To make enough money for the imipolex payments, Randy was working lots of overtime hours at Emperor Staghorn. He absorbed an intensive uvvy course on Electrical Contracting and began doing some of the electrical work in the sub fab as well as the plumbing. Thanks to his shared weekly camote/leech-DIM trips with Parvati, he felt like his mind was getting bigger all the time.

Parvati carried most of the imipolex on her belly, and after ten months she stuck out as if she were massively pregnant.

Shiva was equally fattened up with the imipolex that he'd ob-
tained on his own. On the eleventh month after her first date
with Randy, Parvati showed up at the Tipu Bharat room looking
like a feeble ghost of her old self. She and Shiva had pooled
their hard-won surplus imipolex to make the body of a new moldie son named Ganesh—their final child. Once a moldie had
produced three children, he or she normally died.

"Please help me to get strong again, Randy," said Parvati. "If
you give me enough imipolex, I can use it to upgrade my own
body. If I don't get it, I'll rot and fall apart like Angelika and
Sammie-Jo. Shiva's already stinking—he accepts death, but I
don't. Randy, if you get me forty kilograms of imipolex, I can
renew myself. I know I'm not so attractive as before, but—"

"Don't worry, Parvati," said Randy, feverishly pressing her
against him and taking deep breaths of her slightly putrefied
scent. "You're the one I love, li'l stinker. I'll find a way. I'll take
out a loan. I'll push for a promotion!"

"Oh, Randy. I know it's wrong, but sometimes—sometimes I
actually enjoy having you touch me. Yes, do touch me, darling.
Tell me you love me."

With this inspiration, Randy checked the Emperor Staghorn
in-house list of job openings and applied for a position as a process engineer for Emperor Staghorn's great researcher, Sri Ramanujan.

When Randy approached Neeraj Pondicherry for a recommendation, the older man was incredulous. "You have no higher
degrees, Randy, no college education. You're a plumber, a
handyman. Do you have any notion of what a process engineer
does?"

"Hell, it can't be so different from hooking up pipes and
wires. I need the raise, Neeraj. I want to buy Parvati a complete
body upgrade."

"It would be more realistic to take up with a fresh young
moldie, Randy. A one-year-old. Instead of quixotically squan-
dering so many rupees to keep a four-year-old moldie alive."

"Are you gonna help me or not?"

"Of course I will help," sighed Neeraj. "I can tell Ramanujan that you are a reliable and uniquely adaptable employee. The work you've done on the electric power network in the sub fab is very ingenious; this work evidences your ability to extrapolate beyond plumbing. Indeed, now that I think upon it, it seems possible that Ramanujan may choose you. He is a very strange person."

A week later Randy started work in Ramanujan's lab, a large room off to one side of the fab. Half of Ramanujan's lab was a walled-off clean room, and half of it was the man's messy office, which included a small kitchen area. Ramanujan was a short uncouth man, stout, unshaven, and not overly clean. His brown eyes shone with preternatural intelligence.

"So, Mr. Tucker, you are the new chap to be helping me," said Ramanujan in welcome. "Don't be shy, I too have bucolic origins—although of course I am Brahman. Neeraj Pondicherry tells me that you are very dexterous with complex systems. As it happens, your complete lack of academic credentials is a plus rather than a minus. For reasons of industrial security, I prefer that my assistants are not able to fully understand what I am doing."

"I'm rarin' to go, Sri. Can you walk me around and tell me what's a-goin' on? And what all a process engineer does?"

"A research scientist makes things begin to happen; a process engineer arranges that the same things may continue to happen for a very long time. In this laboratory I am creating some experimental designer imipolex that I use to make leech-DIMs. At present I am crafting these DIMs one at a time; my immediate problem is how to avoid doing all this work by myself so that I can focus on the question of how to enhance the functionality of the leech-DIMs. You do know what leech-DIMs are?"

"You bet," said Randy. "I have a moldie girlfriend, and I put one of your leech-DIMs on her all the time. After we fuck, I'll chew up a couple of her camote nuggets and slap the leech-DIM on her and then—" Randy broke off when he noticed Ramanujan's shocked expression. This was the first time he'd tried to tell a human the details of what he habitually did with Parvati.

"Please go on," said Ramanujan dryly. "I am on tenterhooks."

"Well, Sri, it's like Parvati and me see God. Everything gets white and then it breaks into beautiful colors. And Parvati is in there with me. It's not really magic, even though it feels that way—she wraps herself around my head while we're tripping, so I guess she's like a big uvvy echoing the camote hallucinations. She says the leech-DIM sets all of her thoughts loose at once. Did you ever realize that Everything is the same as Nothing?"

Ramanujan frowned and shook his head. "The whole point of my inventing the leech-DIM, Mr. Tucker, was to provide a means of protection from moldies. Yet you are drugging yourself like a sadhu and wrapping a moldie around your head? I think before we go any further I must give you a brainscan to make sure that you don't have a thinking cap in your skull. It would be a security disaster to have the moldies looking out through my assistant's eyes."

"Parvati and I love each other, and she promised not to put no thinking cap on me. But if it makes you feel better, go ahead and scan me, Sri. Where's the brainscanner at?"

"Right here," said Ramanujan, pointing to a small circular hatch set into his office wall at waist height. "Just lean over and stick your head inside."

"You've got a scanner built into your wall?"

Suddenly there was a needler in Ramanujan's hand. "No temporizing, please, Mr. Tucker. Get over there and stick your head into the scanner. For all I know, you're a moldie-run meat puppet playing the part of the innocent oaf."

"Shitfire," said Randy weakly and stuck his head into the round hole in the wall. There was a buzzing, a flash of purple light, and then it was over.

"All's well and good," said Ramanujan, his needler already back out of sight. "I'm sorry if I frightened you. Would you object to being scanned every day?"

"Is it bad for me?"

"Not particularly. Especially as compared with your other habits."

"Don't you like moldies, Sri?"

"I'm fascinated by them, Mr. Tucker. But I fear them. My ongoing work is to find ways for human logic to control them. My first leech-DIM is a crude design—it zeroes out all of a moldie's neuronal thresholds to produce an effect that I suppose could be thought of as similar to that of a mystical union with the One as you suggest. In the future, I hope to have leech-DIMs which allow human users to more directly control the behavior of a moldie. Enlightenment is easy, but logic is hard."

"How do you make leech-DIMs?"

"The abstract answer involves a great deal of higher mathematics which would be quite impossible for you to understand. The concrete answer lies in there." Ramanujan gestured toward the clean room half of his lab, which was separated from them by a narrow transparent chamber holding bunny suits and an air shower. "Shall we go in?"

The lab had a long, cluttered workbench on either side of the room—a chemical bench on the right and a biological bench on the left.

The near end of the chemical bench held a miniaturized glass refinery, which was fed by lines coming up through the floor from the sub fab. As Randy now knew, the tubes carried such things as water, glycerol, ethanol, polystyrene, ethylbenzene, tetrafluoroethylene, poly(N-isopropylacrylamide), poly(methyl vinyl ether), and solutions of natural resins and alkaloids extracted from the plants and animals of Gaia's jungles and seas.

The refinery cracked and cooked the chemical compounds into imipolex variants for Ramanujan to decant into a multitude of small beakers, tanks, trays, watch glasses, and crucibles that were ranged all down the length of the chemical bench.

The center of the room held a large brightly lit aquarium. Inside the aquarium, small imipolex slugs crawled and floated about like the shimmering nudibranchs, ctenophores, and jellyfish of the Indian Ocean—or, no, they were like Kentucky leeches—like freshwater horse leeches lazily stretching and shortening their bodies as they waited for prey.

"I keep them in there while I'm working on them," said Ramanujan. "When I'm ready to ship one of them, I dry it into a hibernation state."

"You make them by just pouring out some special imipolex, and that's that?"

"Of course not. In order to get any computational power, the little slugs of imipolex need to be doped with metals and seeded with chipmold. The main fab breaks that into numerous steps, but in here I have a nanomanipulator that can do everything at once."

Set into the back wall of lab there was a three-dimensional nanomanipulator with a heads-up holographic display showing a magnified electron microscope image of the DIM inside it. The device also had a VR uvvy that allowed the user to fly about inside the image, using and programming the nanomanipulator's individual nanopincers and nanofeelers.

"It's fairly easy to train the nanomanipulator to do repeated steps," said Ramanujan. "If it was very much smarter, it would be a full-fledged moldie, and my security would be smashed to blazes. It's an awkward position I'm in. Hopefully you can learn to emulate in some measure the efficiency of a moldie. Go ahead and try on the uvvy."

Randy put it on. He was in an ocean of imipolex, with hollowed-out tube tunnels leading here and there. Some of the tubes held bright geometric icons—these stood for rare-earth metal crystals. Elsewhere in the mazes of the tubes were fuzzy globs—these represented the spores and algae of the chipmold. Myriads of little claws were scattered about—his nanopincers.

"The metals and the spores have to be distributed in certain ways," said Ramanujan. "Fortunately, the controls are fractalized. That is, you can group them and cascade them. It's as if you could shrink your hands and put copies of your hands at the tips of each of your fingers—and then do it again."

Randy played around in the nanomanipulator's space for a

while. The tubes were like pipes, and the cascaded controls were not unlike a multihead pipe-gun. "I can drive this," he said presently. "But what patterns do you want me to put in? Where are the specs?"

"In here," said Ramanujan, tapping his head.

"How'm I gonna know what to do?"

"Just study the patterns I've been using and do something similar. As it happens, the actual pattern used for the etching process doesn't seem to be terrifically important. It's more like you're a farmer cultivating a field—you plow it up to a certain statistical density and then you broadcast your seeds. The field and the seeds are smarter than the farmer."

"Thanks a lot, Sri. Now tell me about that other bench."

The biological bench along the left wall was covered with flasks and beakers where the chipmold cultures were prepared. One large beaker was half-filled with a gel of imipolex made cloudy by a million threads of mycelium. Up above the gel, great ruffs of chipmold climbed the sides of the beaker like shelf mushrooms on a rotten tree.

"That's one of the classic strains," said Ramanujan. "Each layer of my leech-DIMs gets a dusting of that fellow's spores. But the real computational power comes from the cultures in the flasks."

The flasks held agars of imipolex with chipmolds growing in them. Most of them held several kinds of mold, with the populations intermingling like plants in a meadow or like corals on a reef. In a few of the flasks, the regions of differently colored mold moved about at a visible pace, swirling like immiscible liquids.

Randy leaned over to stare deep into one of the little bottles and saw a background pattern of green-and-yellow citylike structures that were forever assembling themselves and breaking apart—geometric hives continually coming together and crumbling to pieces. Filling the spaces between the hives were lively vortex rings, each like a mushroom cap or like a jellyfish. These little jellyfish patterns were in shades of royal blue, tipped with vermilion accents. They pulsed their way through the interstices of the background pattern, splitting in two at some intersections, merging at others. "It's pretty," said Randy.

"Yes yes," said Ramanujan. "Pretty complicated. Are you ready for me to go through the whole process for you step-by-step? I suppose we'll have to do this several times. Are you prepared to concentrate? Each full run-through takes about four hours."

"I'm ready," said Randy.

Over the following days, Ramanujan led Randy through the leech-DIM fabrication process over and over until finally Randy could reliably do it himself. Randy was like a cook working for a master chef. As he grew more familiar with the recipe, he began finding ways to streamline it, although Ramanujan resisted any attempts to fully automate it. His great fear was that an automated process would amount to a program which could be stolen by Emperor Staghorn's industrial rivals, by the moldies, or by some other interested parties.

Such as the Heritagists. The evening after his first day of work with Ramanujan, Randy went to bed early. Parvati was feeling too weak to visit, and Randy was tired out from running through the leech-DIM recipe—not once but twice. Ramanujan was a slave driver. Just as Randy got into bed, his uvvy began beeping for him. Hoping it might be Parvati—he was eager to tell her that he'd nailed down the job—he slapped the uvvy on his neck.

"Hi there, Randy. You sure aren't very thoughtful about your old friends." It was a pale silly goose of girl with a very bad complexion. For a moment Randy didn't recognize her.

"Helloooo! Salt Lake City calling Bangalore!" She waved both hands and grinned ingratiatingly. "Jenny from the Human Heritage Council? Jenny who found your neato keeno new job?"

The whole dreary, smarmy, small-time-loser vibe of Heritagism came crashing back in on Randy. He'd completely blocked out Heritagism and the wretched Shively days since coming here—what with the interesting work at Emperor Staghorn, the fabulous love affair with Parvati, and the profoundly psychedelic camote visions to think about. Now and then he'd written his mother, sure, but he'd totally spaced out on his promise to make regular reports to the Jenny thing. Ugh!

"A little birdie told me you're moving up the ladder at Emperor Staghorn Beetle Larvae, Ltd.," said Jenny. "Working with Sri Ramanujan, no less. We're very proud of you!"

"Uh, yeah, Jenny, I'm sorry I never called. I reckon I oughtta tell you I'm not much of a Heritagist no more."

"So?" Jenny had stopped smiling.

"So that's why I'm not too interested in talking to you."

Jenny's white little goody-goody face grew pinched and mean. "We got you this job, Randy, and we can take it away. Now that you are finally in a position to give us some useful information, you are going to deliver. Or else. I want a step-by-step rundown on Ramanujan's leech-DIM process, and I want it now."

"I only started learnin' it today! Anyway, Ramanujan would kill me if he knowed I was leakin' on him. What the hell do you dooks have against moldies anyway? They're beautiful!"

"Start uvvying me the information, Randy, or you'll find your Emperor Staghorn employee pass is void when you show up to work tomorrow. You'll be out of work and your little moldie girlfriend will rot to death. Believe it. Once a month I'm going to call you, and once a month you're going to run through the leech-DIM process for me. Each time you finish, I'll tell you which parts need more detail, and you'll get me the details by the next month. I'm not here to argue with you. I'm here to get the information."

So Randy told Jenny the leech-DIM recipe as best he could and tried not to worry too much about what Jenny was going to use it for.

That week the Emperor Staghorn Beetle Larvae company store let Randy get forty kilos of imipolex on credit, and Parvati was suddenly like new again. Shiva died right around then, and Parvati started living with Randy full-time, cooking and cleaning for him and flying him to and from work every day.

The other roomers in the Tipu Bharat made no objection;

they all liked Randy because in his spare time he'd fixed the building's leaky pipes and drains. It had turned out that most of the building's sewer lines were actually made of waxed cardboard tubes; once Randy got them all replaced, the Tipu Bharat was a much more pleasant place to live. The grateful owner let Randy and Parvati move into a three-room apartment at only a slightly higher price.

On weekends, Randy and Parvati would go diving or to the jungle, as before, but now that they were practically a married couple, Parvati began letting Randy in on some secrets.

One Saturday morning three months after Parvati moved in with him, Randy woke to the smell of spiced, sugared tea with warm milk.

"Good morning, darling," smiled Parvati. She was plump and beautiful, with fine Indian features and her fingers fluttering through poised gestures of formal dance. She handed him a mug of the chai and a plate of *hoppers*: Tamil griddle cakes with fresh mango. "I have a nice idea for a trip today. I'll show you where some of the really successful moldies live. We call them the *nabobs*." While Randy ate his food, Parvati stoked herself up with a few nanograms of quantum dots; Randy kept a supply of this compact moldie energy source on hand to supplement Parvati's solar energy.

With breakfast over, they walked up the stairs to the roof of the Tipu Bharat, Parvati's extruded *ghungroo* ankle bells tinkling with each step. On the roof, Parvati pressed herself against Randy from behind, growing clamps around his chest and waist. She let her remaining mass flow into a large pair of wings that stretched out as if from Randy's back. Now Randy stepped up onto the building's low parapet. A light morning breeze blew against his face. There was a thronged market square directly below them, part of the Gandhi Bazaar. The cracked, wavering sound of a snake charmer's fat-bulbed little *been* horn rose up toward them—the Indians seemed not to mind how weird and gnarly a tone might be, just so long as it was persistent and loud.

Parvati's uvvy pad rested on the back of Randy's neck, talking to him. Now she signaled that she was ready, and he flexed his legs and leaped out off the building with his arms outstretched. A woman in the market square pointed up at them and screamed; hundreds of people stared as Parvati's great gossamer wings caught hold. They glided high across the market, slowly gaining altitude.

Rather than crudely flapping her wings, Parvati sent dynamically calculated ripples through them, getting the greatest possible lift from her energy. At the far side of the square, she heeled over into a turn, and then she held the turn so that they rose up and up in an ascending helix. Below them Bangalore dwindled to the semblance of a city map, set into a patchwork landscape of fields and factories. Now Parvati leveled out and began flying southwest.

"It'll take us perhaps an hour to get there," she told Randy. "We moldies call this place Coorg Castle. It's in the jungles near Nagarhole." Randy relaxed and enjoyed the sensation of the air rushing past him and the vision of the landscape scrolling by below. When the beating of the air got to be too much, Parvati grew a little windshield to protect his face. Buying Parvati a new body was the best thing he'd ever done. And with the good pay he was getting now, he would have fully paid for it in just one more month.

Coorg Castle was a jagged cliff deep in an inaccessible part of an official jungle preserve, a cliff pocked with ancient caves. Parvati told Randy that the richer, more successful moldies lived here despite the law that the preserve was solely for wildlife. They helped keep human poachers out of the preserve. "And, of course, they are also giving a lot of *baksheesh* to the authorities."

Randy and Parvati landed in a grassy clearing at the base of the cliff, with flowers blooming all around. Parvati let go of Randy and took on humanoid form. Rather than taking on her customary appearance of a bejeweled sex goddess, Parvati made herself look like a wealthy high-caste widow, modestly wrapped in a white silk sari and adorned with only a few choice bangles and a fashionably large *bindi* dot on her forehead.

Parvati had uvvied the Coorg Castle moldies about their arrival, and a number of the moldies flew out of their caves and circled above, staring down at them. Randy was thrilled by the sight of the great iridescent creatures moving against the blue cloud-puffed sky with the sunlight streaming through their wings. They were like giant butterflies, like a music of enchantment, like a dream of beauty and peace.

Two of the moldies landed near them and took on humanoid form; both seemed to be moldie males. They spoke briefly in English to Randy and then uvvied silently to Parvati for so long a time that Randy wandered off to pick some fruits from the jungle. This was fun until he got a glimpse of a tiger watching him from a thicket. He crashed back to the clearing, but now Parvati was gone. Randy stationed himself with his back against the cliff, anxiously listening to the jungle's many noises. He seemed to hear a steady current of heavy stealthy motions in the leaves. Now and then there was the sharp crack of a breaking stick. Time passed very slowly. It was nearly dusk when Parvati reappeared, flying down from one of the high caves.

"What have you been doing?" he demanded.

"Oh, just visiting," sang Parvati. "Now that I have achieved a fully new body, these nabobs are welcoming me! I find that some of them are even my distant cousins. Yes, I've had a very pleasant day. Are you ready to fly home?"

"Of course I am," snapped Randy. "Unless you're planning to feed me to the tigers?"

"Silly boy," laughed Parvati. "After all you've done for me? I'm still amazed at how readily you paid for my new body." Caressingly, she wrapped her straps around Randy's chest and waist, letting an extra tendril of her body slide down to give Randy's buttocks a gentle caress. "You said my body will be completely paid off in a few more weeks?"

"That's right," said Randy, snuggling against her. "I make enough salary now for ten kilograms of imipolex a month."

"What a smart man you are," said Parvati. "Let's fly home and I'll cook you a good curry dinner."

By now Randy had gotten very good at using Ramanujan's nanomanipulator; with Randy's help, Ramanujan could turn out a month's targeted allotment of leech-DIMs in less than a week. Ramanujan was spending all the rest of his time doing involved calculations and trying to invent some new kind of imipolex.

Early in July, Tre Dietz of Santa Cruz, California, came up with the long-awaited four-dimensional Perplexing Poultry philtre. Tre's employer Apex Images had a one-way disclosure agreement with Emperor Staghorn Beetle Larvae, Ltd., so Ramanujan was immediately able to obtain the philtre—complete with source code. Ramanujan became deeply obsessed. He set an uvvy to continually display a floating holographic sphere of four-dimensional Perplexing Poultry. The sphere hovered over his desk, and Ramanujan sat there at every hour of the day, staring and calculating.

The 4D Poultry came in seven different shapes and were colored in pleasing translucent pastel colors, one color for each kind of Poultry. They fit seamlessly together like pieces in an interlocking puzzle. The familiar chickens and dodoes were still present, though their old forms had undergone a sea change—they were much more tilted and twisted than before. Ramanujan obscurely insisted on calling the new shapes Vib Gyor, both in the singular and in the plural.

The ethereal sphere of Vib Gyor looked, at least to Randy's untutored eye, like a wad of ugly misshapen newborn chickens, dodoes, turtles, pigs, weasels, kittens, and lizards huddling together for warmth. The shapes had a disturbing tendency to visually reverse themselves, like a drawing of a staircase that could be going either up or down. And sometimes Ramanujan would set the shapes to mutating, each of them slowly cycling through weird changes without ever losing full contact with its simultaneously cycling neighbors. Randy gathered that the Vib Gyor had something to do with Ramanujan's dreams of a better leech-DIM.

Meanwhile Parvati was becoming more and more neglectful of Randy. She still insisted that he give her ten kilograms of imipolex per month, but what she did with it was anyone's guess. Often she failed to appear at the fab to fly Randy home, and sometimes she was gone for several days at a time.

Another sore point was that Parvati had overheard Randy talking to Jenny. Parvati traced Jenny's call to the Human Heritage Council and angrily confronted Randy about it. The fact that Randy was only doing it to protect his job did little to mollify the outraged moldie.

Things were so bad that Randy often had to beg Parvati for days before she'd have sex with him, and even then the act was short and perfunctory—except, of course, on paydays. Whenever Randy would actually hand over a big slug of imipolex, Parvati would get down with him just like old times, him on camote and her on the leech-DIM, the two of them in paradise together.

"Eureka!" Ramanujan shouted into Randy's ear on July 2, 2053. Payday had been the night before, and Randy was feeling a little loose in the head. He was sitting at the nanomanipulator, wearing the uvvy and shakily etching tunnels into a piece of imipolex. It was a good thing the accuracy of the tunnels didn't matter. What was this math geek yelling about? "I've got it, Mr. Tucker, I've got it! Imipolex-4!"

"Do what?" Randy didn't bother taking off his uvvy.

"I don't think I've ever shown you the quasicrystalline structure of imipolex," said Ramanujan, leaning across Randy to adjust one of the nanomanipulator's many mysterious controls. Suddenly the imipolex became an intricately fitted shape assembled from dovetailed polyhedral blocks. "You haven't seen this mode before, have you?"

"Can't say as I have," said Randy. "It's crooked blocks, some red and some yellow."

"Yes, that's because I've set the nanoeyes to polarized inflation," said Ramanujan. "The different colors are the different domains of the imipolex. Like a crystal, a quasicrystal is made up of many copies of the same elements—the two kinds of blocks you see. I can make them look like chickens and dodoes if you'd prefer." He turned another knob and the little blocks grew beaks and tails and claws that pecked and nestled into each other like a henhouse gone crazy. "These are our old friends the three-dimensional Perplexing Poultry. What makes a quasicrystal different from a crystal is that the building blocks—the chickens and the dodoes—they're not arranged in any regular way. A quasicrystal is like a wallpaper pattern that never repeats."

"Gnarly," said Randy, moving around in the red-and-yellow space of the imipolex's Perplexing Poultry. "I think I seen something like this on a camote trip with Parvati, um, not too far back."

"Yes yes, I shouldn't wonder a bit," said Ramanujan. "The present leech-DIMs do percolate the quasicrystalline structure up into the moldies' consciousness. But, as I'm always saying, we would much prefer to impose our own order from the top down. Now let me show you a sample of my new imipolex-4, Mr. Tucker."

"Okeydoke."

With a nauseatingly vast wrenching motion, the nanomanipulator's view changed to a different sample of imipolex, this one unetched as yet. "This is new, Mr. Tucker. I call it imipolex-4. It's based on the four-dimensional Perplexing Poultry. Can you see the Vib Gyor? See the seven kinds of them? Violet-Indigo-Blue-Green-Yellow-Orange-Red."

"Peck-peck, Sri. *Braaawk-cackle-brawk.*"

"Yes yes, the Vib Gyor are in my new imipolex," exulted Ramanujan. "I found a way to put this pattern into my imipolex by applying a special electromagnetic field while the plastic is setting. A correctly applied field can guide the quasicrystal tessellation; it's just like the way dust arranges itself in patterns if you sprinkle it onto the skin of a vibrating drumhead. Of course, the drumhead is only a linear second-order differential equation, while the field equation I am using here is nonlinear and of order nine. Today we're going to start making leech-DIMs with imipolex-4, Mr. Tucker!"

"That'll be better?"

"Much better. The goal, after all, is to logically control the moldies rather than merely rendering them helpless. My mathematical investigations have been indicating all along that a controlling leech-DIM must use a higher-dimensional Penrose tessellation."

"So you'll be able to slap a leech-DIM on a moldie, and the moldie'll do what you tell it to," mused Randy. "Shitfire." Yesterday Parvati had gotten her monthly allotment of imipolex from him, and this morning she'd already turned nasty again. They'd had a terrible quarrel and she'd left for who knew how many days. Controlling his beloved Parvati with a leech-DIM was starting to sound like a good idea.

"Of course, your commands have to be rather simple," said Ramanujan. "The problem is that even imipolex-4 won't hold enough information. I'm working on a solution to that problem as well. I'm trying to create imipolex-N. Here, take a look at my latest effort." Randy's universe shuddered sickeningly and turned into muddy brown scuzz spotted with threads of green and purple.

"This looks like where the madwoman shits, Sri."

"Fool."

"Xoxx it." Randy took the uvvy off. "You'll make me puke with that kilp. What did you say it was supposed to be?"

"Imipolex-N. A quasicrystal based on N-dimensional Perplexing Poultry. But I can't figure out the correct N-dimensional tessellation. To create it, I need a more thoroughgoing fundamental solution. I need a Tessellation Equation. Once I have imipolex-N, I'll have a substance rich enough to hold as much information as I like—as much information as an entire human mind!"

Randy threw back his head and gave a deranged-scientist cackle. "And to think they dare call us mad!"

"Oh, get back to work, you degenerate bumpkin. Once we get one of the new imipolex-4 leech-DIMs ready, you can try it on your moldie girlfriend. Intercourse with her is all you care about, as I very well know."

For the next six weeks, the two of them worked like fury, testing out different combinations of imipolex-4, etch patterns, metal doping, and chipmold. Randy was completely in the dark about how well they were doing, but Ramanujan grew more and more optimistic. Finally, on August 13, they'd put together a half-dozen exemplars of an imipolex-4 leech-DIM design that, according to Ramanujan, should work. He called his new creations *superleeches.*

"Take this and try it on your girlfriend," urged Ramanujan, handing a superleech to Randy.

It was like a springy, leathery bit of nearly dry elephant's-ear seaweed, colored a rich natural purple with highlights of pale beige. It was about three inches long and one inch across. The untrimmed edges of the superleech were irregular and curly, and its wavy surface was covered with tiny bumps that gave it a sandpapery feel. Randy found his fingers unable to stop caressing it.

"How does it work?"

"A superleech relays orders from people to moldies. The owner is the master, the superleech is the viceroy, the moldie is the slave. The first individual to place the superleech on his or her uvvy—this is the individual whom the superleech is adopting as its owner."

"So what all am I supposed I do?" said Randy. In his hand the superleech shifted to his touch.

"You put your uvvy on your neck, you put the superleech on your uvvy, and you think about what you want Parvati to do. In this way the superleech is adopting you, and you are giving it a program. You think about what you want and then you peel the superleech off your uvvy and put it in your pocket. When you get a chance, you put the superleech on Parvati, and she starts doing what you were thinking about."

"What if I want to change what Parvati's doin' once the superleech gets started?" asked Randy after a moment's thought. "Instead of her doin' the same thing over and over and over."

"Ah yes," said Ramanujan. "That could be disastrous. The unstoppable broom of the Sorcerer's Apprentice. The magic porridge pot that buries the village. The genie that spanks your children to death. Never fear, Randy, the owner can still uvvy instructions to the superleech once it is in operation."

"Copacetic!"

As chance would have it, today was Randy's twenty-first birthday. He'd told Parvati about it, but she was in one of her moods again and had displayed little interest. It was still two weeks till the next payday. Of course she wasn't waiting for him outside the fab. He began trudging the half mile to the commuter train station.

In his standard outfit of white pants, white shirt, and widebrimmed straw hat, Randy stuck out from the crowd, especially with his pale face and beaky nose. He walked with a smooth, nerdly glide, his arms pumping while his head stayed at a constant level. The superleech twitched in his pants pocket.

It was a shame the way Parvati had been treating him lately. It was starting to remind him of the way Honey Weaver had been toward the end. So obviously and totally taking advantage of him. Why did he have to be such a weakling, such a patsy for every bossy woman that came along?

It probably went back to his childhood. To Sue. Sue wasn't the stablest of women, and it was common for her to flip-flop from cozy mothering to crazed bitchy ranting and back. It was hard always being at the mercy of just one parent. Whenever Randy asked Sue about who his father might be, she would put him off. Maybe if he'd had a father, he wouldn't have turned out to be so submissive to women.

Thinking about being *submissive to women* gave Randy a pleasant hard-on, and he passed most of the train ride in idle sex fantasies, helped along by the intimate pulsing of the superleech. Yes, it was high time for Parvati to fuck him again. Suddenly remembering Ramanujan's instructions, Randy took out the superleech and set it against his uvvy.

"I am superleech type 4, series 1, ID #6," said a grainy little

voice in Randy's head. The voice gargled raspingly and then announced, "Registration is complete, Randy Karl Tucker. You are
my owner, and I am ready to accept your programs."

Randy waited a bit, but the superleech said nothing more. So
Randy went back to thinking about sex. When the train stopped,
he took the superleech off his uvvy and put it in his pocket.

As Randy was getting out of the train, a small urgent man
elbowed him sharply in the ribs and grabbed his wallet. Randy
got hold of the wallet and pulled it free of the pickpocket, only
to drop it on the street next to the train car steps. As Randy
bent over to pick it up, a fat woman's wobbly ass farted horribly
in his face, and a dacoit's dirty bare foot stepped on his wrist.
The train conductor rang his bell and screamed for Randy to
stand clear of the train steps, insultingly calling him a *honkie-
wallah*. The humid air was unbelievably foul; the tropical summer sun felt heavy as a sheet of hot metal; and several rupee
notes were missing from Randy's wallet.

But the superleech was still in his pocket. He wiped the sweat
off his brow and threaded his way through the crowded streets,
calming himself with the sight of his favorite sadhus. The stone
stairwell of the Tipu Bharat was cool and shady. As he walked
up the steps, Randy's heart rose again. He was about to see his
sexy Parvati. *And she would act just like he wanted!*

In his boyish heart of hearts, Randy had been hoping for a
surprise birthday party, but Parvati was doing nothing more than
tensely sitting on a kitchen chair.

"Hey there, li'l stinker," said Randy affectionately. "Here's
your birthday boy! How 'bout a hug?"

Parvati grudgingly allowed herself to be gathered into Randy's
arms. As he squeezed her tight, she finally spoke.

"I've been waiting for you to get home, Randy. There's something I have to tell you."

"And I got something to tell *you*," said Randy. "Ramanujan
and me finally got those new leech-DIMs working. Lookee here,
I brought one home." He drew the writhing superleech out of
his pocket and set it down on the kitchen table. "Let's give her

a try! Lord knows I wouldn't mind eatin' me a couple-three nuggets of camote and fuckin' you all night. It's time to get wiggly, baby! Randy Karl Tucker is twenty-one."

"No, Randy," said Parvati, undulating away to the far side of the kitchen. "That's what I have to talk to you about. It's all over between you and me. I've only been waiting here to say a last good-bye. You've been good to me, but I'm leaving."

"Where would you go? You won't find a more reliable source of imipolex. Do you want more than ten kilograms a month, Parvati? Is that it?"

"As a matter of fact, Randy, soon you're going to be out of a job and in no position to provide *any* imipolex. But no matter. The point is that I've found a fine new husband among the Coorg Castle nabobs. His name is Krishna. He's all blue. Very beautiful."

"You done bought your way into high society with my imipolex, huh? And what the hell do you mean I'll be out of a job? Ramanujan and me just made a big discovery. More'n likely, I'll get a fat raise. Now stop talkin' crazy, Parvati. I don't mind if you visit with your Krishna now and then, just so's you keep comin' home and takin' care of me."

"You're going to be out of a job because I'm going to uvvy the security director of Emperor Staghorn Beetle Larvae, Ltd., and tell her that you've been giving Ramanujan's secrets to that Heritagist Jenny-thing. I've got several of your calls recorded inside my body for evidence. I'm sorry, Randy, but Krishna says I have to report you. He has very high morals."

Randy reeled back against the kitchen table and fell into a chair. "Your snotty moldie boyfriend wants you to tell Emperor Staghorn I've been spying for Jenny? Oh, you bitch. You goddamn, slimy, bossy, bullying—" Just then the superleech brushed against Randy's hand. In one swift, savage movement, Randy leaped across the room and plastered the leech against her bottom.

Parvati struck out at him, but then the superleech dug in and took effect and Parvati's struggles turned to warm embraces.

Where the old leech-DIMs had turned Parvati into a kind of glowing egg, the new superleech left her body shape much the same. The difference was that Parvati's usual personality was gone—or submerged. Having sex with her felt perhaps more like masturbating than like making love. But Randy did it anyway; he did it hard, right there on the kitchen floor, thrusting himself deep into her as if somehow he could teach her a lesson.

When he'd finished, Randy put his uvvy on and told the superleech to tell Parvati to cook dinner. While she busied herself with the pots and pans, Randy kept up his uvvy contact with her and the superleech. The real Parvati was definitely still there, down under the superleech. She was confused, disoriented, and above all angry at being trapped in the superleech-run cage of her body. It was sad to see her this way—but for now Randy had no intention of setting her free. She wanted to squeal on him to Emperor Staghorn!

Soon Parvati served some rice with a delicious mushroom curry. It wasn't until he'd eaten two big helpings that Randy realized the curry was full of poached camote. He'd eaten perhaps twenty nuggets. Parvati's shackled spirit had found a way to trick the superleech. She'd cooked dinner, but she'd poisoned him.

The angles of the room twisted and loomed. Randy staggered to the sink and began vomiting onto the dishes, seeing thousands of slow-motion faces in the beige textures of his puke. Parvati stood quietly to one side, watching him. Through the uvvy, Randy could sense her sly glee. What else might she do to him?

Randy drank as much water as he could hold and forced himself to vomit again. His brain's vision processor was crashed; he was getting his eyes' unfiltered input; it was like seeing through twitching, splotchy fish-eye lenses. His hearing was equally xoxxed, all fades and echoes—he became convinced Parvati was whispering something that the superleech wouldn't let him hear.

"Talk to me, Parvati," cried Randy. "Talk to me out loud. Let her talk, superleech, let her say whatever she wants to, but don't let her come at me."

"I dare you to kill me," said Parvati. "Kill me and get some fun out of it. Look at this." Her flesh flowed and twisted and she took on the likeness of Honey Weaver. "You're a freak, Randy Karl," she drawled, hefting her tits. "You're nothing more than a kid I liked to piss on. If you was a man, you'd take that knife outten the sink and kill me. But you're a candy-ass chickenshit."

The big long kitchen knife in the sink winked at Randy. He rinsed the vomit off it and hefted it in his hand. It was sharp, so sharp. He was careful to hold the point away from himself. He could see networks of veins and arteries beneath his flawed, ugly skin.

When Randy looked back at Parvati, she'd changed shape again. She looked exactly like Randy's mother. "Who's my father, Sue?" croaked Randy. "Why won't you ever tell me? Tell me who's my father!"

"Never mind about your father," screamed Parvati/Sue. "I wish I'd aborted you! Don't you have the guts to kill me? You stupid little jerk. If you let me walk out of here, I'll get you fired from Emperor Staghorn Beetle!"

"I want my daddy," said Randy, suddenly breaking into sobs.

Parvati's skin grew dark and her teeth got sharp and long. She was turning into Kali. "Kill me!" she screamed. "Chop me up before I give you a thinking cap! It's coming soon, you flesher freak! *Kiiiiiiill!*"

"Help me, Daddy!" screamed Randy Karl and lunged forward with the long knife. He stabbed and chopped and hacked for the longest time, and the immobile Parvati did nothing to stop him. Finally he was too tired to slice anymore. He dropped the knife to the floor and washed himself off in the sink. There were lots of crumbs of imipolex and chipmold on him; he kept thinking they were gobbets of coagulated blood. When he turned off the water, the room was very quiet. What had he done?

The weirdly bulging kitchen floor was covered with chunks of imipolex, none of them larger than a loaf of bread. They were Parvati. He'd killed Parvati. The pieces of imipolex were slowly dragging themselves around like big slugs. Randy sat cross-legged on the kitchen counter to be up high away from the slugs, and he closed his eyes so he wouldn't have to see them.

Time passed and colors played behind Randy's eyelids. He seemed to hear a man's voice talking to him. His father? "You're doing fine, son. I'm proud of you. You're doing just fine." Randy felt happy and calm. A gentle breeze wafted through the apartment and caressed him. Someone tapped him on the knee. He let his eyes flutter open.

"Bye, Randy." It was Parvati, fully formed, though with a network of pale orange scars.

"What!?"

"I crawled back together. Except for that piece." She pointed to a glob of imipolex lying off to one side of the floor with the purple welt of the superleech knotted into it. "That piece is yours. I tricked you into cutting it out of me."

Randy fumbled for the knife.

"Don't start again or I really will kill you. I feel stronger than ever. The only reason I don't give you a thinking cap is that I'm so sick of you." She turned and walked to the door, slightly limping. "Just for old times' sake, I won't call Emperor Staghorn till tomorrow afternoon. If I were you, I'd leave town before then. The dacoits, don't you know." The door slammed behind her.

Randy walked gingerly across the room and nudged the piece of imipolex that Parvati had left.

"I am superleech type 4, series 1, ID #6," uvvied the hoarse little voice. "I am currently coupled to 723 grams of imipolex with traces of a moldie program. This imipolex was part of the left buttock of a moldie named Parvati."

"Can you wipe out the moldie traces and run the imipolex yourself?"

"Yes. Shall I proceed?"

"Do it. And then keep watch. Grow some feet and walk around. If anyone or anything comes in here, squawk and wake me up. I gotta crash."

Randy tottered to his bed, took off his uvvy, and fell into a whirling kind of nightmare sleep. At some point in the middle of the night, something hopped into bed with him and snuggled up by his chest. He cradled it against himself and slept a little better.

At dawn, the uvvy rang for him: "Randy Randy Randy Randy . . ."

A creature shaped like a young hen hopped off Randy's bed onto the floor and began making a ruckus. What? Randy reached out and slapped the uvvy that sat on his bedside table, setting it to projection mode. Jenny's face appeared. She had a big zit on the side of her forehead.

"Rise and shine, Randy! We have a lot to do today."

"I'm not ready." He rubbed his face, trying to put together his memory of what had happened the night before. The little chicken strutted this way and that, staring at Randy for approval. The nappy purple shape of the superleech ran down the center of its back.

"I saw it all," said Jenny, looking eager and gossipy. "I never told you, but I keep a tap on your uvvy? So when I heard you going off about your father, I did some quick research and found out who he is."

"Now, hold on," said Randy. "Just slow down here. Parvati is gettin' me fired anyway. I'm through working for you skungy Heritagists."

"I'm not a Heritagist, Randy Karl," said Jenny. "I'm a software simmie created by a certain loonie moldie who's also called Jenny. For fast Earth contact, I need to live down here on a serious machine. So I'm working for the Heritagists just to like pay the rent for my space on their machine. I'm living on the Heritagists' big underground asimov computer in Salt Lake City—but, um, Randy I could move? With a client like you, I could be a freelance agent for both you and moldie Jenny from the Moon. I could buy myself a proprietary hardware node in Studio City."

"Forget it!" said Randy. "Good-bye!"

"Wait! Don't you want to know who your father is?"

"Okay, who is he?"

"*I'll* never tell," giggled Jenny, every bit the snippy teenage Heritagist girl with a secret. "Just kidding! But you have to listen to my new plan too."

"Yeah yeah." Randy kept being distracted by the antics of the superleech-animated chicken; it was prancing around like a miniature moldie, pretending to scratch for worms in the wooden floor. Wormwood. Randy was still seeing colorful trails every time he moved his eyes. "Let me get it together for a minute, Jenny. I feel mighty rough."

He went and looked in the kitchen. The floor was bare. There were flies on the vomit in the sink. He ran the water for a minute, taking a drink and rinsing off his face. What was that last thing Parvati had said about dacoits? He checked that the apartment door was locked, then took a pee. The hen trailed after Randy like a chick following its mother.

"I'm gone call you Willa Jean," Randy told it. "That fine by you?" The chicken clucked and bobbed its head. Randy leaned over and petted it. "You my little friend, ain't you, Willa Jean? I've always wanted a pet chicken. Good girl. Good Willa Jean."

Whey-faced Jenny was waiting above the uvvy by Randy's bed. "Oh, excuuuuuse me," she said. "Finally ready?"

"Yep."

"Well!" said Jenny. "About your dad. Of course the Heritage Council has a sample of your DNA on file—from when you applied to live in the Shively Heritage House, remember?—so I ran a similarity search across some DNA databases, starting with Louisville. And right away I found your match in the records of the Louisville jail! Willy Taze, born 2004 to Ilse Anderson and Colin Taze. You must have heard of him. Cobb Anderson's grandson? The inventor of the DIM and the uvvy? In his twenties Willy was employed by the city of Louisville to maintain the Belle asimov computer, and then in 2031 he helped Manchile and his nine-day meatbop boys. Willy was arrested for treason and sentenced to death, but he broke out of prison in the Louisville asimov revolt that happened the day before Spore Day.

Willy made it down to Florida and started inventing things. The gimmie liked his DIMs so much that they pardoned him. And then Willy moved to the Moon. He built himself a place and roomed there for many years with a man named Corey Rhizome. End of info dump."

"Willy Taze is my dad? Where is he now?"

"Well, I shouldn't really talk about this, but, um, Willy moved into the moldies' Nest. I wouldn't know how you could reach him. I suppose you could uvvy Rhizome for info, but he's a big old grouch. Corey's an artist, and he doesn't like strangers one bit!"

"But I thought I heard my dad talkin' to me yesterday after I chopped up Parvati," wailed Randy. "I thought I heard a man's voice."

"Yes yes, I arranged that for you," smirked Jenny. "It was pretty obvious that you needed it—slashing up your mommy and crying like a baby. What a sight! But that wasn't Willy talking to you. It was a simulation of Cobb Anderson—your great-grandfather. You know how the Vatican used to have the world's biggest library of porno? Well, the Heritagists have the Earth's biggest archive of bopper memorabilia. And it just so happens that their Salt Lake City Archives own the only existing copy of Cobb's S-cube. I snuck in and booted it up so Cobb could talk to you and make you happy. Now, listen, Randy, you need to get out of Bangalore before Parvati turns you in. I'm going to buy you a plane ticket. Get your suitcase packed, and I'll call right back."

Randy's thoughts were in a whirl. "You're doing fine, son. I'm proud of you. You're doing just fine." So that had been Cobb Anderson. The man who invented the boppers; the first man to have his personality coded up as software. Randy's great-grandfather! It would be nice to have some long talks with him. And Randy's dad—Randy's dad was Willy Taze, the glamorous rebel and genius inventor! Maybe Randy could find Willy in the Nest. Maybe Randy would turn out to be a big somebody like Willy and Cobb!

He moved quickly around his apartment, tossing clothes and mementos into his bag. Willa Jean raced around with him. When the uvvy sounded again, Randy ran to the bedroom and slapped the uvvy onto his neck.

"Yes," said Jenny. "The ticket's all set. You're on a direct flight to San Francisco, leaving at 1 P.M."

"You think that's early enough, Jenny? Parvati said she's gonna uvvy Emperor Staghorn in the afternoon. Did you catch what she said to me about dacoits? When Emperor Staghorn gets the word, they gonna send a gang of thugs after me, girl. Get me an earlier ticket!"

"Randy, before you leave, you have to go in to Emperor Staghorn and make me a complete viddy of how Ramanujan makes a superleech. We've found you a smart micro-cam that'll perch on a hair in your eyebrows. It's no bigger than a dust mite. You make the viddy and at noon you tell Ramanujan you're eating lunch in town and go right to Gate 13 at the airport. They'll have a first-class ticket for you. No sweat!"

"I don't wanna go to no Emperor Staghorn today, Jenny. It's too risky."

"Randy, unless you can get the complete recipe for the superleech, you're not going to be of all that much use to us."

"This is still for the Heritagists?"

"Yes, it's for the Heritagists, but believe it or not, it's for the loonie moldies too."

"Bull *shit*."

"Is too!" giggled Jenny, crinkling her nose and nodding vigorously. "Mmm-hmmm! You'll see, Randy Karl Tucker. It'll be fun in California. You'll work in Santa Cruz. It's this funky little beach town an hour south of San Francisco. And you can talk to Cobb Anderson as much as you like. Come on, Randy, don't be a party pooper. At least let us get you to San Francisco."

"Oh man. I dunno."

"I've already called a moldie rickshaw for you. He'll be there in a minute; he's picking up the micro-cam right now. Let him take you to Emperor Staghorn. He'll wait there with your suitcase, and you'll be able to leave the instant you're ready. Come on, Randy. Pretty please."

"What all you got lined up for me in Santa Cruz?"

"Well, I really wasn't supposed to tell you yet, but since we're such good pals and everything—oh, why not. You'll be kidnapping moldies and sending them to the Nest. *Liberating* them, the way the loonie moldies look at it. Moldie repatriation is something the Nest works on with the Heritagists. You'll be working with a man named Aarbie Kidd."

"Kidnappin' moldies'd be easy with superleeches," mused Randy Karl. "For the Nest? I wouldn't mind checkin' out some o' them moldie California girls. And get in tight with the loonie moldies? I wouldn't mind that a bit. Hell, oncet I get to know 'em, I could go to the Nest and see my dad, couldn't I!"

"All of that, Randy Karl, and more. Is it a deal? The rickshaw's downstairs."

"Wait. First I wanna talk to Cobb again."

"Can do! I'll patch him right in."

The uvvy image wavered, and then there was Cobb Anderson. He had a strong wide face with high cheekbones. His hair was sandy and he had a short-cropped white beard. He was imaged in much better resolution than Jenny; he looked almost real, floating there in Randy's visual cortex. The rich Cobb simulation even included scents and air currents. Cobb smelled comfortable—he smelled like freckles.

"So you're Willy's son," said Cobb. "I'm a little out of sync. I just came back from heaven. All is One in the SUN. I don't like being run on this asimov machine; I need my own personal hardware." Cobb paused to channel Randy's vibe. "So you're my great-grandson. Yes. I can tell you've been hurt. Poor Randy. We can help each other."

"Cobb, what's my dad like?"

"Willy's smart as a whip. A wizard with the cephscope. He saved me and a woman from some racial puritans one time, and he freed a bunch of machines from their asimovs. And I hear that then he—" The old man's face clouded over. "Stop talking in my head, Jenny, and don't rush me. Randy, let's see if you can't get me off this pathetically inadequate pig machine. Take me to the moldies on the Moon. We'll make a plan, huh, squirt?"

"Was that you talking to me last night?"

"Yes, Randy. Do you want to hear it again?"

"I surely do."

"You're doing fine, son. I'm proud of you. You're doing just fine. I love you." Cobb's pale eyes were kind and wise.

"Thanks, Cobb. Thanks a lot."

Cobb and Jenny signed off and Randy switched his uvvy attention to Willa Jean. He looked through her eyes and suddenly realized she was usable as a telerobot. He drove her quickly around the nooks and crannies of the kitchen/dining area, pecking up stray crumbs of imipolex and loose nuggets of camote.

"Now, you be ready to hatch that camote back out for me when I ask for it," Randy told Willa Jean. "Don't mash it." Not that he wanted any camote right now, but you never knew.

Randy got Willa Jean to hop into his suitcase and then he closed it up. So now Bangalore was over. Randy gave a heavy sigh. He wandered around the apartment for another minute, taking a last look at the familiar view of the bazaar and the distant hills. How happy he'd been here. If only Parvati had loved him. He walked down the stone steps of the Tipu Bharat, his eyes wet with tears. The waiting rickshaw was shaped like an orange oxcart.

At Emperor Staghorn, Randy found Ramanujan animatedly drinking a large mug of saffron-spiced *chai*. He'd been working in his office all night.

"How did the superleech work on your girlfriend, Mr. Tucker? Feeling a bit wrung-out today, are we?" Ramanujan rubbed his dirty shiny hands and beamed, not waiting for an answer. "Good, good, good. As it happens, I've found a devilishly clever algorithm which rather radically simplifies the superleech manufacturing process. Yes, a rather radical simplification indeed. Look at this beautiful equation!"

Ramanujan indicated some scribbles on a piece of paper on

his desk, and Randy leaned over to make sure that his micro-cam got a good view.

"Is that Sanskrit, Sri?"

"I assume it pleases you to jest. The symbols on the left are, of course, integral signs and infinite series, representing a four-dimensional quasicrystal geometry. And the right side of the equation is seventeen divided by the cube root of *pi*. There's glory for you. I call it the Tessellation Equation. Beautiful mathematics makes beautiful technology. Let's go into the clean room so I can show you the tech. But—ah ah!" Ramanujan shook his finger. "First, as always, we scan your reckless head."

Randy was ready for this. He touched his brow and the micro-cam hopped onto his finger until the brainscan was over. Easy as pie. They suited up and entered the clean room.

"So do we make up some more superleeches today?" asked Randy, sitting down at the nanomanipulator. "I'm rarin' to go. I'd kind of like you to go through the whole process once again to make sure I got it straight."

"Do tell," said Ramanujan, suddenly suspicious. "So how *did* you pass the night, Mr. Tucker? I find your matitudinal diligence rather conspicuously atypical."

"Huh? All right, Sri, I'll tell you the sorry-ass truth. I put the superleech on Parvati and fucked her and asked her to make dinner. She poisoned me with camote, and then she got me to chop her up. The pieces that weren't attached to the superleech crawled back together, and there was Parvati again. She ran away to Coorg Castle. She don't love me no more. I just want to work hard and forget about her." A thought occurred to Randy. "I wouldn't be surprised if Parvati didn't try and make me lose my job, she hates me so much."

"Where's the superleech, Randy?"

"It's stuck to a leftover piece of Parvati that's shaped itself into a cute little hen. I call her Willa Jean. She's a telerobot for me now. Like those flyin' dragonfly cameras? I left Willa Jean to home."

"Telerobotics!" exclaimed Ramanujan, his coppery face splitting in a grin. "That's a wonderful app for superleech technology!" He leaned over and warmly patted Randy's shoulder. "You're invaluable, my boy. Fools rush in where angels fear to tread."

"You're happy because a slice off Parvati's ass turned into a chicken?"

"I am happy to realize that there is an immediate peaceful use for superleeches. Rather than being solely a bellicose means of moldie enslavement, the superleech can be an interface patch which cheaply turns a sausage of imipolex into a telerobot. Jolly good. But I haven't fully explained my big news yet, Mr. Tucker. That equation I showed you? When interpreted as a method of phase modulation, my equation provides an effective way to convert ordinary leech-DIMs into superleeches simply by sending them a certain signal. It's easy as seventeen divided by the cube root of pi."

"Show me how," said Randy Karl.

Ramanujan picked up a small parabolic piece of silvered plastic and walked over to the aquarium where the old leech-DIMs swam. "Observe, Mr. Tucker! This is a pocket radio transmitter that I programmed last night." He aimed the silvered plastic dish at one of the leech-DIMs. "Now I chirp this leech with a signal based on my equation." He pushed a button on the transmitter and suddenly the targeted leech-DIM began shaking all over. "You see? The program sets off a piezoplastic jittering which forces the quasicrystals into the imipolex-4 state." The leech's vibrating skin puckered up into the rough surface of a superleech; it turned tan and purple all over. Ramanujan plucked it out and held it up for Randy's inspection. "Behold!"

Ramanujan set the damp superleech onto an uvvy, and the uvvy speaker announced, "I am superleech type 4, series 2, ID #4. Do you wish to register as my owner?"

"No," said Ramanujan. "Please crawl off the uvvy and go to sleep now." The superleech obliged.

"That's really somethin', Sri," said Randy, fingering the dormant superleech's rough surface. "Can you show me how you programmed that little radio antenna?"

"You'd never understand the program."

"Try me. How am I gonna learn if you don't let me try?"

"You won't understand it, but I wouldn't mind going over it in detail just for myself." Ramanujan called up a mathematics screen above the lab uvvy and delivered a forty-minute lecture on the Tessellation Equation which, as predicted, Randy completely failed to understand. But his micro-cam was making a viddy of it and, even better, Ramanujan was so into his batshit math rap that he didn't notice when Randy slid the silvery little antenna into the top of his fab bootie. When an incoming uvvy call interrupted Ramanujan, Randy quickly excused himself.

"I gotta run to the bathroom, Sri. I'm not feelin' too peak. Reckon I've got the squirts."

"Spare me the details," said Ramanujan, looking away in distaste. "I wonder who can be calling me at this number?"

As Randy hastened through the air shower, he glanced back to see just who was talking to Ramanujan—and of course it was Parvati. Randy darted out of Ramanujan's office and ran off down the Emperor Staghorn hallway, ripping off the bunny suit and pocketing the radio antenna. He had just exited Emperor Staghorn's outer gates when the fab's alarms went off. Randy's moldie rickshaw was waiting there, big and stolid. Randy jumped in.

"Go to the airport! Fast!"

The moldie began springing along like a giant rabbit, covering twenty or thirty feet at a bound. Randy held on for dear life. He fumbled his uvvy out of his bag and put it on. Jenny was waiting.

"Things are happening fast, Randy," she said, brushing a lank strand of loose hair back from her eyes. "Congratulations for bagging that radio transmitter! Emperor Staghorn already has a group of four dacoits looking for you at the airport. I'll tap into the airport's cameras so we can locate them."

When Randy got to the airport, Jenny showed him an image siphoned off one of the airport's security cams. It showed four stocky men, impeccably dressed in Western business suits. Two wore sunglasses, one wore a turban, one was picking his teeth. All had hard unforgiving faces. They were studying some recent photographs of Randy Karl Tucker.

"Where are they standing?" asked Randy. "I better not get near them."

"Well, ummm, they're waiting right next to the gate for your plane to San Francisco. Gate 13. You can see it with your bare eyes from here."

Sure enough, Gate 13 was fifty yards down the hallway, surrounded by milling passengers and with the figures of the four dacoits dark and clear to one side. Through the hall windows Randy could see the airliner: a giant moldie-enhanced machine in the shape of a flying wing.

"Isn't there some other gate I can use?" asked Randy. "Like for first-class or for the handicapped?"

"Yes, Gate 14 is the VIP gate," said Jenny. "But it's only twenty yards past Gate 13 and the dacoits can see it too. We have to distract them. I notice they're all wearing uvvies. I can blast them with noise, but that's only good for a few seconds before they think of removing their uvvies. We need something more. Any ideas?"

"I'll use Willa Jean!" Randy switched his attention to Willa Jean and got her to hop out of the bag and trot along ahead of him. Randy watched through Willa Jean's eyes until she was near the dacoits, and then he launched her toward them like a flying boxing glove. At the same moment, Jenny sent a mind-numbing current of noise into the dacoits' uvvies. Willa Jean bounced among the stunned dacoits, knocking them over like bowling pins. Moving just short of a run, Randy breezed past the dacoits and in through the first-class Gate 14. As he headed down the tunnel to the aircraft, Willa Jean ran to join him. The turbanned dacoit tried to follow her, but Jenny sent some message to the airline personnel that caused them to drag the dacoit out of the boarding area. The plane left on time.

Randy had a comfortable window seat. He stared down at

India for a while, thinking about all the things he'd seen here. California would be good too and maybe then the Moon. It would be a long time before he returned to Kentucky. He smiled, leaned back in his seat, and fell asleep.

CHAPTER FIVE

TERRI

■

June 2043–October 30, 2053

Although Dom and Alice Percesepe were loyal to their children, they were only fitfully attentive. Terri and Ike had to do most of the housework while they were growing up. Often as not, big sister Terri made supper for Ike, with Dom off at the restaurant and Alice somewhere getting lifted with her friends. A typical supper would be tuna or peanut butter sandwiches. Ike would always ask for dessert, and Terri would tell him, "There's lemonade for dessert."

"Why doesn't Mother shop?" complained Ike one day in June 2043. It was the last day of school. "We can afford food. Dad owns a restaurant and a motel."

"When Mother shops, it's just for clothes," said Terri. "Or drugs. The only time she buys food is to put on a special dinner for *Dom*." She said her father's name with vicious emphasis.

"Did you get your final grades today?" asked Ike.

"Yeah. I got all A's. How about you?"

"C's and—finally—a B. In History. I'm stoked."

"Dad is gonna be excited about that," said Terri sourly. "Not

125

that he'd ever notice my A's. I'd like to do something to really shake him up."

"Well, he's not too happy about the boys you've been going out with," said Ike. "Kurtis Goole and those other stoner surf rats."

"I know," smiled Terri. "For Kurtis and his friends, adults are bowling pins you knock over. Like inflatable clown dolls with weights on the bottom so you can hit them again and again and they keep bouncing back up."

"Poor Dad," said Ike. "What a way to talk."

"Yeah, poor Dad and his Sons of Adam Heritagist hate group," said Terri. "You know what I ought to do? I ought to start hanging around with moldies. Maybe that would make him notice that I'm alive."

"What is your problem today, sis? Did something bad happen to you?"

"Yes," said Terri, "something did. About a half hour ago, while I was cleaning the house and emptying the trash cans as usual, I saw some papers on Dad's desk. You know what I saw there? His will."

"Oh God, is he sick?"

"Just because you have a will, it doesn't mean you're about to die, idiot," said Terri. "It's just something that grown-ups do. Like taxes. So anyhow, the will says that *you* inherit the restaurant, I get ten thousand dollars, and Alice gets the motel, the house, and everything else."

"Ten thousand dollars," said Ike enviously. "That's righteous bucks. Why don't I get any money?"

"The restaurant is worth a lot more than ten thousand dollars, you fool."

"Oh yeah, I guess it is."

"And you get it all to yourself," spat Terri. "Just because you're a boy with a stupid, gross ball sack."

"Whoah!"

That summer Terri had a summer job running the cash register in Dom's Grotto out on the Santa Cruz Wharf. Dom was virulently antimoldie, and he made a point of advertising that no moldies were employed in any capacity by his restaurant. ALL HUMAN-PREPARED FOOD read the signs outside. HERITAGISTS WELCOME. NO MOLDIES WORK HERE. Due to the stench of moldies, not many restaurants employed them anyway, except perhaps to wash dishes or keep the books, but Dom liked to promote the Heritagist cause, even at the risk of getting in trouble for violating the equal rights clause of the Moldie Citizenship Act.

Terri was a calm and efficient cashier, sitting there afternoons and evenings on a high stool. She wore pink lipstick, and she wore her hair long and straight. She chewed gum. Her face was thin, her skin was dark, she was sexy. Terri slept late in the mornings, and at night she went to as many beach parties as her parents would let her get away with.

Ike was working as a deckhand on a Percesepe day-cruise fishing boat run by Dom's brother Carmen. Ike's boat would leave early and come back to the wharf around 4 P.M. He'd help cleaning the fish the tourists had caught, collect his tips, hose himself off with fresh water, and go over to Dom's Grotto to get his main meal of the day. Terri would order it up as takeout and let Ike have it for free; this was approved by Dom, with the stipulation that Ike's meals not be extravagant.

One foggy day in August, Ike came in wet and wiry, his brown eyes big and his short hair bristling. He wore boots, baggy shorts, and a damp, stained T-shirt.

"Yaar, Terri!"

"Yaar, kiddo. How were the tips?"

"So-so." He shoved his hand in his pocket and held out a small wad of ones and fives. "The customers caught their limit of rockfish, but they were cheap bastards. They were Baptist Heritagists from Texas; Dad's group invited them here and gave them a reduced rate. They kept hoping someone would hook a rogue moldie so we'd have to flame it. Instead of tipping me, one couple gave me, look at this—" Ike dug in his other pocket and produced a gospel DIM that displayed a little hollow film loop about moldies being the Beast predicted by the Book of Revelations.

"Moldies are Satan," chirped the little DIM as it played its images.

"How bogus," said Terri. "How valley. And I notice they don't hate moldies too much to use a DIM for their gospel tract. Like they don't realize that DIMs are small pieces of moldie?"

"They don't know shit," said Ike. "When I mentioned that we're Catholic, they said that the Virgin Mary is a false idol. Whatevray. I'm starving, Terri. Can I get a lobster? Just this once?"

"You know Dad says to give you cheap food," said Terri. "Unsold fish for upstart barbarians."

"Yeah," said Ike, "with lemonade for dessert. Come on, Terri. Let me have a lobster today. If Dad complains, I'll take the blame."

"He won't *let* you take the blame," said Terri. "You're the *son*. Dad saves all the blame for me. But what the hey, big sis can handle it. What do you want with your lobster?"

"I want steamed clams, garlic bread, onion rings, french fries, coleslaw, corn on the cob, and a double vanilla milk shake."

"Hungry much?" Terri filled out a takeout check and handed it in through a little window to the kitchen. Ike flopped down on one of the captain's chairs by the register.

"Don't sprawl, Ike. You'll scare off the paying customers. We don't want them to think this is a place for grunge buckets."

"Shut up," said Ike, rubbing his face and lolling even farther back.

"I saw little Cammy Maarten at the party last night," said Terri to needle her brother. "Isn't she in your grade? She asked about you. She said I should bring you to the next party. She thinks you're *cute*."

"Cammy Maarten is a feeb," said Ike. He had not yet realized that girls were something he needed. "And I'd feel stupid coming to a surfer beach party when I don't even have a board."

"We should get a board, Ike," said Terri. "I've been thinking about that. We could get a DIM board and share it. We'll each get our own wet suit, of course. I have a lot of money saved up from this job, and you have a big hoard of birthday and Christmas money, don't you? It's totally lame for us to be living in Cruz and not know how to surf."

"Dad won't like it," said Ike. "He hates surfers."

"Not every single thing has to come out Dad's way, does it?" asked Terri.

"I *would* love to surf," allowed Ike. "But don't you think maybe we're too old to learn?"

"Seventeen and fifteen isn't old, Ike, believe me. Old is the people who eat in this restaurant all day. Hey, here's your order. Stick around outside and wait for me. I'll tell Teresa I have cramps from my period and she'll let me off early and we can go to the surf shop."

"You're gross," said Ike and went out on the wharf to feast. Terri came out when he was almost through eating and ate the rest of his french fries and onion rings, plus the hard-to-get meat in the body of his lobster. Hungry seagulls skirled overhead and sea lions barked down among the pilings.

They fed the lobster shells to the sea lions and walked down to the land end of the wharf to wait for a moldie bus. Before long the big loping thing came pattering by, coming down the grass-and-sand street. Terri waved, and the bus stopped. The bus was a fused grex made of twelve moldies. Her name was Muxxi.

"Howdy thar, Terri and Ike," said Muxxi in the corny Wild West accent she affected, perhaps to please tourists or perhaps to mock. "Whar ye goin' today?"

"We want to go to Dada Kine Surf Shop, Muxxi," said Terri.

"Waal, now, I reckon that means we'll be a-settin' you young-uns off at the corner of Forty-First Street and Opal Cliff Drive," said Muxxi, displaying the fare as numbers in her skin. "Pay up!"

Ike and Terri handed their fares to Muxxi, who rippled her imipolex to move the other riders toward the rear of the bus. Muxxi bulged out two fresh front-row seats for Ike and Terri.

The kids lowered their butts down into the seats and the seats grabbed them tight. In bad weather the seats formed protective cowls, but today Terri and Ike were fully exposed to the pleasant sun and offshore breeze.

The bus's giant sluglike body rippled along through the main beach area. There on the right was the Boardwalk with its classic mechanical roller coaster and on the left was the hill with the family motel, the Terrace Court. Terri's motel—someday. Terri had gone to her mother to complain about the will, and Alice had promised Terri that she would pass the motel directly on to her, which made Terri feel a lot better. Alice had even asked Terri what she thought about maybe adding *Clearlight* to their motel's name.

The bus waded across the shallow San Lorenzo River and humped up a slope to a grassy road that capped the cliffs. Muxxi let off two passengers at the yacht harbor, where the cliffs dropped away. She got another few passengers as she raced along the edges of Twin Lakes and Live Oaks beaches. As each group of passengers got on, Ike and Terri's seats moved further towards the rear.

The cliffs rose up again and the bus surged onto them, the thick corrugations on her underside swaying at a rapid steady pace. Now they were at Pleasure Point with its schools of surfers.

"Here's whar ye git off, Terri and Ike," twanged Muxxi. Their seats turned to the side and became chutes that slid them slowly down to the ground. Muxxi pattered off, and the kids stood watching the surfers for a while.

"Do you really think we can learn to do it, Terri?" asked Ike.

"Sure. It's easier with a DIM board. They have ripples on their bottom like Muxxi; they can swim. It makes it a lot less work to catch waves."

"What if they swim off without you and go rogue?"

"They don't," said Terri. "They're not smart and independent like moldies. They're DIMs. A DIM board is smart enough to swim and to let you steer it, and that's all it wants to do. Dom thinks women should be like DIMs."

"Stop going off about Dom," said Ike. "I'm ready to buy a board."

They walked a block up Forty-First Street to the Dada Kine Surf Shop. Inside the store it was dark and cool. New and used DIM boards lined two walls and hung from the ceiling. Racks of wet suits filled out the rest of the store. A Hawaiian *kahuna* was sitting behind the counter. Slouched next to him was a red-and-yellow moldie, a liveboard. A liveboard was vastly more skilled and functional than a DIM board, but, of course, full moldies were very expensive. Instead of just buying them, you had to put them on a salary.

"Yaar, Terri," said the big Hawaiian. "Your bud Kurtis Goole was in here earlier today. I think he went up to Four Mile Beach."

"I'm not looking for him, Kimo," said Terri. "I'm here to shop. This is my brother Ike. We want to get wet suits and a DIM board."

"Two boards," said Ike all of a sudden. "I don't want to have to share with you, Terri."

"Tell me how much money you want to spend," said Kimo. "And we'll see what we can do."

"And I'll give you little bangtails a cost-free and unforgettably wise lesson," volunteered the moldie. "A gorgeous incentive for them, right, Kimo? Business being so slow that I haven't been paid in it seems like seven weeks, you understand."

"*Mahalo* very much, Everooze," said Kimo. "It'll be bitchin' if you give them a lesson. How much bucks you got, kids?"

An hour later Ike and Terri had each gotten a used wet suit and a rebuilt DIM board—at a very reasonable price. Ike's board was red with black checkers, Terri's was patterned with blue-and-green flames. Everooze bounced down to the beach with them, jabbering away, and they swam out to a small uncrowded break.

"I'll hang this fabulation on three ripe words like an uvvy preacher," said Everooze. "*Visualize, realize,* and *actualize.* How do you talk to your DIM board? It's a telepathic union, thanks to a little piece of uvvy in the nape of the wet suit neck, cuddled right up near your bright young Percesepe brain. To make your board swim, you *visualize* the motion you want, and then you *realize* that thought—push it out of your head so's the DIM can channel it. And then, step three, the DIM makes it *actual*, all by itself. Splutter mutter, peanut butter! *Visualize, realize*, and *actualize*—these are the keys to correct surf motion in the water and—hmmm—indeed in all other walks or flights of life. The magic of the *-alize* ending. Yes. The DIM in the DIM board is a clueless little tad of flickercladding, a lonely finger's worth of a moldie, but if you can *visualize* and *realize*, it can *actualize*. It works fairly well, at least on *these* puny waves. Puny waves but nicely tubular, I should add. Let's surf 'em."

The *realizing* step was a little hard to get, but after a while Terri and Ike had it down. The trick was to think that you were *already* moving the way you wanted—to make it real at least for yourself—and the DIM would pick up on that. Ike said it felt like his whole body was talking to the DIM, and Terri said it was more like focusing your attention ahead of where you already were. Everooze said that either way was perfectly floatin', although it was best of all to degravitate to the fact that they were, in fact, helping the DIM boards to surf.

Once they swam out through the breakers, Everooze started showing them how to catch a wave. "It's a cosmic rhythm, you viz?" said Everooze, repeatedly catching waves, then ducking underwater to swim back to Terri and Ike like a big oblong sea skate turned skateboard. "It's not enough to see a wave coming; you want to smell it and hear it and feel it in the air and in the water. Undoubtedly there's a little current between your toes right now, for instance, which is the suck of the draw of the next wave crest to come. Get fully lifted on synesthesia because the ocean is indeed realizing its ability to *actualize* the way *you* are going to move. Not only are you helping the DIM board; you're helping the ocean as well. Think of yourself as the ocean's DIM."

Terri and Ike started catching waves then and riding them, at first on all fours and then, miraculously, standing on two feet.

"Ah yes," exulted Everooze. "The human race rises from the primordial sea, a boy and a girl step forth from the zillion whats of past time to be here—whoops!—keep your center between your knees, Terri, think of your whole mass as a magic invisible weight dangling down there—that's it, my lassie—yee-haw!—and another one, Ike—boom—over the falls for sure, a Niagara wet whirl under there in Neptune's washing machine, no harm in that, no loss in failure, the surf god is *actualizing* tubes, kids, so get back out there—whoo-ee!"

When they got back home from that long, magical afternoon, Terri and Ike were committed surfers.

Dom never approved, but in the end it didn't matter. Terri and Ike finished out high school and kept on surfing and working various small-time jobs, and then Dom died.

It happened over Thanksgiving weekend, 2048. There was a big family dinner at their Uncle Carmine's. Alice got quite wasted and somehow ended up in a big argument with Dom. Apparently she wasn't happy with their sex life. Dom stormed out into the night and disappeared.

Back home around midnight, after Terri and Ike had finally gotten their mother to pass out in her bed, there was an uvvy call from a Wackerhut gimmie. Terri answered.

"Is this the Percesepe residence?"

"Yes, who's calling?"

"I'm an investigator for Wackerhut Security. There's a problem here with a Dom Percesepe. Are you his next of kin?"

"I'm his daughter."

"You better get over here: 2020 Bay Street, right near the Saturn Cafe."

"Is he okay?"

"You'd better come over."

As Ike and Terri stepped out of the house, several small dragonfly telerobots buzzed around them. They were *newsies,* remotely controlled mobile camera eyes. Something serious had happened to Dom. Before they could get on their hydrogen cycles, a car pulled up and a man got out. He wore a customized uniform and a gun; he was another gimmie. A newsie dragonfly hung whirring in place above his head.

"I'm from Boozin Security," he said. "I'll give you a ride."

"Wasn't it a Wackerhut gimmie who called me before?" said Terri.

"The uvvy newsies are calling all the local gimmies. There's enough blood for everyone."

"What's happened to my father?" shouted Ike.

"You better come see."

The limo took them to a small yellow Santa Cruz cottage surrounded by knots of gimmies and newsies. Scores of dragonflies buzzed in the air. There were spotlights and the gimmie cars were flashing red and blue. A woman stepped forward to interview Terri and Ike, but a burly Wackerhut gimmie hustled them inside the cottage.

The place smelled more strongly of moldies than anyplace Terri had ever been. There was a slit-open moldie body with a full harvest of camote nodules on the floor. On the bed was a naked dead person. Dom.

There was blood all over his face; his nose was torn wide open. His genitals were bloody as well. He had a blowtorch clenched in his dead hand. His body was welted with circular marks, as if from squid tentacle suckers. The fast little dragonfly cameras darted this way and that, agitated as blowflies around fresh carrion.

It soon came out that Heritagist Dom was a longtime cheeseball. What exactly had gone wrong in the cottage on that last night remained unclear. Had Dom been threatening the flammable moldie with the blowtorch? Or trying to defend himself? It was hard to be sure. The cottage belonged to a woman named Myrdle Deedersen, who said she hadn't realized what was going on. She'd been renting the cottage to a biker from Florida who wasn't around very often. He always paid her in cash and she didn't know his name. She thought he'd left town.

Nobody really believed her, but it was such a distasteful case that nobody in the Percesepe family was willing to pay for a full gimmie investigation. Suffice it to say that Dom had gotten himself killed either by a moldie or by some local sporehead ring involved in kidnapping moldies and butchering them to sell off their imipolex and their camote on the black market. Dom should have known better than to be a cheeseball. Case closed.

Sure enough, Dom's will left the restaurant to Ike. The twenty-year-old Ike struggled half a year with Dom's Grotto, suffering much advice from his mother and his uncles, but the restaurant business wasn't for him. When Kimo put Dada Kine up for sale in 2049, Ike sold Dom's Grotto to his Uncle Carmine and bought the surf shop and all its assets, including the aging Everooze.

The first thing Ike did was to use some of his excess profit from the deal to get Everooze a complete retrofit and take him surfing in Hawaii, along with Kimo and Kimo's new moldie liveboard ZyxyZ. They surfed the giant waves of the Pipeline, waves so big that before liveboards the only way a person could catch one of them was to be towed in by Jet Ski. It was a deeply memorable trip.

Now, four years later, Ike was a pro surfer and a seasoned businessman. Alice was still alive, and Terri and Tre were scraping by on Tre's gigs and on the money from managing Alice's motel. Rather than feeling guilt about his fat inheritance, Ike blamed Terri's poverty on Tre. Ike didn't like Tre.

Ike was waiting on the cliff beside Everooze when sharky Ouish and Xanana came bouncing up to the Steamers Lane overlook, with Terri and Xlotl rickshawing along behind. Everooze was distorted into the shape of an airy igloo, his new method of actualizing the maximum amount of solar radiation.

"Yaar, Terri," said Ike. "What's happening?"

"Monique took off with one of our guests," said Terri as Xlotl set her down on the ground. "We think he's gotten control over her somehow."

"You saw her leave?" asked Ike.

"Tre did. He tried to stop her, but then he had a bike accident and broke his collarbone."

"That stupid stoner hairfarmer."

"He's not a hairfarmer, Ike; he's a scientist and an artist. He's a chaotician."

"Yeah, but you're not denying he's a stoner, are you? These poor valleys come out to live at the beach and they think it's nothing but party time."

"Now he's *valley* too?"

"He comes from Iowa! Can't get more valley than that. You never should've married him, Terri."

"Thank you for your wonderful support, you selfish prick. Now go away."

"Let's cut the jawing and make tracks," snapped Xlotl.

"Tell us, Pop," said Xanana to the red-and-yellow-striped dome that was Everooze. "Which way did she go? Which way did she go? Which way did she go?" He put the phrase through maybe two hundred repetitions in two seconds.

"I'll ask Zilly if he can lead us," said Everooze, making a popping noise and flipping his shape into that of a giant potato chip. "He's been surfing here all day, and he says he saw Monique go in. But, Ike, what with the negative vibrations and so on and howsomever, it will indeed be wavier if you don't come. Get the bus back to the shop, chill, and I'll see you there later, your humble worker till wigdom come or I retire, whichever comes first."

"Fine," said Ike, stomping off. "To hell with all of you."

Xanana lay down flat and split his backside, opening up like a seed pod.

"Undress and snuggle on in, Terri. You'll be able to see out through my face. It's transparent there. Let's practice while Everooze talks to Zilly."

"I haven't done this before," said Terri, recalling her dead father's hypocritical tirades against intimacy with moldies. "Are you sure I'll be able to breathe?"

"Of course," said Xanana. "I have enough algae and other stuff in my tissues to make air twice as fast as a person can breathe. Or just as fast as any two people can breathe. Or half as fast as four people can breathe. Or—"

"Yeah, but your . . . your air is going to stink."

"Just wear nose filters. I usually keep some—" Xanana's flesh rolled about for a minute, and then a small slit opened up in his skin to disgorge two small metal sponges. "Palladium filters. Never heard of them? I'm beginning to think you're moldiephobic, Terri. You sure you're not a Heritagist? I know a lot of the Percesepes are."

"Well, I'm *not*," said Terri bravely. "I admit my uncles are xoxxy. They're all Heritagists, yes. Sons of Adam. My father was too—at least we thought he was. But it turned out he was a cheeseball. Maybe he was really on the moldies' side by the end. Maybe it wasn't a moldie that killed him, maybe it was a Heritagist. You don't know anything about it, do you, Xanana? It happened five years ago."

"That's before my time," said Xanana. "I'm sorry. Sorry. Sorry. Sorry."

Terri folded her clothes and set them under a rock, then got inside Xanana and pressed her face up against the inside of the transparent silvery membrane that the moldie used as a face. Air rushed to her steadily through two grooves in the membrane. Once she got the filters well settled into her nose, the smell was not too major. But how could she talk to Xanana?

"I'll uvvy you." Xanana's voice sounded in Terri's head. "And I can channel my vision to you too—if we go deep and it's too dark for your eyes. Are you ready?"

"Let's dive in," uvvied Terri back.

Xanana humped along the cliff's edge like an elephant seal, found a spot overlooking a deep pool, and dove in. Terri watched in wonder as the water flew up toward them. And then they were undersea. Xanana could pick up Terri's mentally *realized* wishes far more easily than a DIM board, and for now he chose to let her steer him.

They went out a few hundred yards, away from the surfers, swam to the bottom, and began slowly looking around. It was like the ultimate tide pool. Terri saw starfish of every color, green sea cucumbers, frilly yellow nudibranch slugs, and a red gumboot chiton. A cascade of tiny pink strawberry anemones covered a rock, looking like a carpet of purple verbena flowers on a Santa Cruz cliff.

"Can I touch things?" uvvied Terri.

"Yes. Just push out your arms."

Terri did, and Xanana's flesh flowed and stretched, forming sleeves and gloves to warmly cover Terri's skin. She prodded a long-stalked plumose anemone, causing it to draw its feathery pale tendrils back into its body.

"You're cozy to be in, Xanana," uvvied Terri.

"*Yeah* I am. Would you like me to fuck you?"

"What?"

"The others won't be here for a few minutes. I can grow a penis shape and push it into you. A lot of the women passengers like it. To relieve tension."

"No thank you! What if you planted a meatbop in me?"

"Nobody has the wetware tech for that anymore. Anyway, you're not fertile right now. I know the smell."

"Well, I'm sorry, Xanana, but I'm just not interested."

"It's all the same to me. We'll hang here and wait for the others."

As she and Xanana lay there drifting on the seabed, sudden shapes rushed at them and spun them around—Terri drew her arms back inside Xanana's bulk, lest she smash a wrist against a rock. It was Everooze, followed by Ouish and Xlotl. Xanana gave Terri a sound feed of the moldies' conversation.

"So Zilly says Monique swam off toward Monterey," Everooze was explaining. "With the skungy cheeseball inside her. Big day for that dook, no doubt." Terri cringed silently at the thought of doing it with Xanana. No doubt he would have broadcast it to his friends. No way she would ever be a cheeseball.

"Zilly should of come with us," complained Xlotl. "Instead of wasting our time chewing the fat."

"He'd rather surf," uvvied Everooze. "Get over it. He downloaded his info to us, so what's the diff? Zilly declines to interrupt his deep daily study of the breaking wave; he's liftin' and floatin'! Parenthetically, Terri and Xanana, did you know Zilly says the optimal liveboard attends to the *negative* space of the wave? To the tube and not to the water? In any event, let's now swim toward Monterey while keeping our senses stretched for visions of Monique. Poor Monique, my darling daughter. Bested by a stinking fleshapoid. Phew."

The four moldies headed offshore together—Everooze in front, followed by Xanana and Ouish, followed by awkward lumpy Xlotl.

"Don't lose me," clamored Xlotl. "I ain't the world's fastest swimmer."

"You should spend more time in the water," said Ouish in her low thrilling voice. "Undersea is the best. There's hardly any fleshers here. No offense, Terri."

The bottom was about forty feet down and falling rapidly. They swam near the bottom, avoiding the giant kelp beds. These were thickets of rubbery tendrils that grew from the ocean floor clear to the surface. Some harbor seals swam by overhead; Xanana rolled over and began swimming on his back so that Terri could stare up at them. The seals seemed intent on giving the moldies a wide berth.

"Do you ever interact with whales and dolphins?" Terri asked Xanana. "It almost seems like moldies should be able to talk with them."

"Almost," answered Xanana. "But so far it hasn't happened. We've decoded some of their songs, and all we've heard whales talk about is sex and food and territory. Almost like birds. Though, yeah, whales also talk about the stars. We're not sure how they can even see them, but they talk about the stars all the time. The stars. The starry stars. The starry starry stars—" Xanana did one of his speeded-up infinite regresses with that word and then continued. "Moldies are a lot more like people than they are like whales. It's no wonder, given that we evolved from human-designed robots. From the boppers that you anni-hilated with chipmold."

"Don't blame *me*," said Terri. "Not while you're carrying me like a baby in the womb. Not after you asked if you could fuck me. Ugh. Like—I would do *that*?"

"I notice you're still talking about it," sniggered Xanana. "And as far as blame goes, there isn't any. If it weren't for chipmold, there wouldn't be moldies. Also Monique always said you treated her well. Hey, there goes the Percesepe deep-sea fishing boat. I bet they've got something to do with this." Xanana was still on his back and they were out quite deep. High above on the wrin-kled mirror of the water's surface was a dark oval, a large boat's hull heading back toward the wharf.

Xanana rolled back over and began swimming steadily deeper. The light grew dim. Up ahead of them a great dark chasm lay open in the ocean floor. Terri recognized this as the Monterey Submarine Canyon that she'd seen on proud local maps her whole life. Wider and deeper than the Grand Canyon! Were they actually going down in there?

"I'm pickin' up Monique." Xlotl's voice came from behind them. "She's in dark cold water, swimming down toward a fuckin' whale? Some flesher dook was inside her, but he's gone—that's gotta be Randy Karl. I think she let Randy off at the surface next to the Percesepe fishing boat and now she's sounding for the bottom. The whale-thing is glowing; it's fuckin' *green*."

"Affirmo," uvvied Everooze. "I wave Monique too. But what's real and what's dream? The age-old question. Let's go ahead and dive way deep into this mighty crack. I've lingered too long in the airy lands of the fleshapoids."

"You might as well start using my eyes now," Xanana told Terri. "I'll uvvy the video to you. Photon to photon to photon to photon to—"

"Thanks," said Terri. To her naked eyes, the seafloor looked dark and monochromatic. She let her eyes go out of focus and let the uvvy come in. The new images showed a vast sparkling space filled with delicate shadings of bright colors. The walls of the Monterey Submarine Canyon ahead were an inviting symphony of pink and green. A school of silver anchovies swept by, followed by several huge fish with solemn unwavering eyes. Everooze's red-and-yellow body darted down over the lip of the submarine cliff. His body was a flat, elongated ellipse that wriggled as he moved. Xanana dove after him, and a sharp watery pain crackled in Terri's head.

"My ears!"

"Pinch your nose and blow," Xanana advised her. "Like you're trying to burst your ears. It'll equalize the pressure. Can you get your hand up to your face? Yeah, that's the way. That's the 'That's the way' way. That's the 'That's the "That's the way" way' way." Terri snaked her arm up flat along her chest, pinched her nose, and blew. Her ear pressure equalized itself with a disturbing swampy pop.

The Monterey Submarine Canyon had any number of smaller subcanyons branching off it. If Randy Karl Tucker had sent Monique to hide down here, it might take a long time to find her. Terri tried to relax and enjoy Xanana's uvvy images of the colored cliffs and darting sea life. Everooze and Ouish swam gracefully ahead of them, and Xlotl lagged a bit behind.

"Everooze," uvvied Ouish suddenly, "I think Monique is down in the next ravine."

"I smell her! I smell Monique!" cried Xlotl, rushing forward past Xanana, Ouish, and Everooze. "Follow me."

The moldies' sharklike bodies arched down over yet another subterranean cliff into a final deep sea crevice.

Terri's breathing grew fast and ragged. It was so dark that she could see next to nothing through her faceplate. How deep were they now? She was crazy to be trusting a moldie this much. All Xanana would have to do would be to push her out of his body and she'd be over a hundred feet deep in the cold, dark, airless sea. She'd drown before she could ever swim to the top.

"Xanana," she said, "take me back. I'm getting scared. Take me up the fishing boat so I can confront Randy Karl Tucker."

She *visualized* and *realized* Xanana turning back. This would have worked on her DIM board, but on Xanana it had no effect and he failed to *actualize* her wish.

"We're not going back yet," said Xanana. "Stop worrying and look around. It's beautiful down here. Look at my uvvy. All the patterns on top of patterns on top of patterns on top of—"

Terri focused her wandering attention on Xanana's video feed. The uvvy images showed flat Everooze and sharky Ouish down below them, led by the vigorous lumpy Xlotl, all of them pumping their bodies to dive deeper. The cliff's false colors were purple and vermilion now, with sprawling splashes of orange. There were some large drifting blobs—giant jellyfish—and school after school of rockfish, wheeling about like flocks of birds. Long, wavering kelp stipes festooned the cliffs. Prancing spot prawns, cautious Dungeness crabs, and skulking octopi moved slowly across the cliff rocks, with wolf eels and monkeyhead eels hanging from the crevices. A glistening drift of squid jetted past.

"I see it!" exclaimed Xanana. "Down at the bottom there!"

Down below them was a green light, a light that coiled about, thickening and thinning its shape. As Xanana's great tail beat them closer, his uvvy showed Terri that the light source was a huge wriggling form.

Terri popped her ears again, wincing at the moist crackle. She was feeling a chill, despite the wrapping of Xanana. Suddenly she remembered a tall tale her Uncle Carmine had told her when she was little—that ice in the ocean is heavier than water, and that the whole bottom of the Monterey Bay is covered with chunks of ice. The deep light they were swimming toward was like a glistening iceberg, gleaming so brightly that Terri could even see its glitter through the faceplate with her naked eyes. Light down here in this deep trench?

"I'm scared, Xanana," she repeated.

"Hold on," answered the moldie. "We have to see what's down there."

"That's a big group moldie down here," reported Xlotl from farther down. "Monique's merged into them. And—uh-oh—

they channel me." He raised his voice in anger. "I'm Monique's husband and I want her back!"

"Look out!" blared Everooze. "It's spitting out superleeches. Fast purple-colored little things. Don't let them touch you!"

Everooze bucked away from the green grex and shot up past Xanana and Terri, with a dozen fuzzy purple imipolex creatures chasing after him. Before Xanana could react, one of the little superleeches, no bigger than a baby's hand, had flicked over and attached itself to Xanana's side. Suddenly Xanana's steady swimming became chaotic and uncertain.

Terri focused on the uvvy images Xanana was feeding her. There was still the same canyon around them, except now there was a glowing red line leading from them down into the deeps and Xanana was swimming straight along the line. Ouish and Xlotl were still down there, and along with them there was a huge glowing shape, down at the other end of the virtual red line, a thing like a giant green moldie, nearly the size of a whale and—whoosh—it darted forward and snatched at Ouish while the fast purple superleeches flocked this way and that—

"Get out of here!" screamed Terri. "It's going to eat us!"

"Help!" came Ouish's voice. "The superleeches are about to get—" Her voice broke, changed, and resumed, an octave sweeter, sounding like a possessed woman in a horror viddy. "I'm joining the happy throng!"

Xlotl swooped aggressively at the green monster, evading the superleeches, but he was no match for the huge green group moldie. It lunged forward and caught Xlotl with a fast, sudden tentacle, and now Xlotl was screaming too.

"It's got me! Swim like hell, Everooze! Get outta here, Xana—" Then his voice stopped.

Xanana swam calmly forward.

"Go!" screeched Terri, visualizing and realizing a great kick of Xanana's tail as hard as she could, but to no avail—until suddenly Everooze came swooping back down after them and scraped the superleech loose from Xanana's side with a seashell.

"Jam, Xanana, jam!" screeched Terri, and Xanana went shooting upward in Everooze's wake.

"Breathe out, Terri!" cried Xanana. "Breathe out or your lungs will burst! Breathe out breathe out! Breathe out breathe out breathe out—"

Just as they neared the lip of the precipice at the start of the monster's canyon, there was a sudden dull thud. All around them, the water streamed upward. Everooze and Xanana went tumbling, and the big heavy lit-up grex came pushing after them. Everooze was off to one side, and the group moldie went right past him, but Xanana and Terri were directly in its path. With a quick gulping grab, the green shape engulfed them, snatching them out of the water as it went hurtling by. There was a concussive blast of sound and then they were shooting up into the sky like a rocket.

Xanana was in a dream state; he sent no words, and the vision that he uvvied to Terri showed an endless regress of Earth and a rocket with Xanana in the rocket and a cartoon thought balloon coming out of Xanana showing Earth and a rocket with Xanana in the rocket and a cartoon thought balloon coming out of Xanana showing—

Xanana had been plastered into the side of the group moldie rocket in such a way that Terri could see outward through her transparent faceplate. And, even more fortunately, Xanana was still providing air and acting as an insulator. Terri was, for the moment at least, in a comfortable safe nook on the side of a living rocket ship headed—*where*?

Looking down, Terri could already see the Monterey Bay as a single nick in a coastline that stretched up into the thumb that was the San Francisco peninsula, with the San Francisco Bay on the other side. Still the rocket rose and roared.

The sun was setting over the Pacific Ocean, making a shining orange patch in faraway clouds. At this distance, the ocean looked static and metallic. Still they rose, pushing out to the far edge of the atmosphere. The sky overhead was turning dark purple. From this height Terri could see the Earth's curvature, dear big fat Earth wrapped in the atmosphere's thin rind.

"Soon I'll die," thought Terri and began to cry. Now Xanana's thoughts were a starry mess of bright patterns, iterated fractals formed by overlaying infinite regresses of solarized images, no comfort at all.

In the distance was one last shape at their level. Terri took it for a stratospheric ice-crystal cloud, but then she realized that the object was flying toward them. It was shaped like a giant blue stingray and seemed to be another group moldie.

Terri's tears dried as she stared in fascination at the computationally rich rippling of the great flying stingray's flesh. It swooped upward at hypersonic speed to match the speed of the rocket grex and produced two giant catfish whiskers to touch it. Right away Terri could hear the flying blue stingray talking over Xanana's buzzing on the uvvy.

"Greetings, Blaster," the great moldie creature uvvied in a rich female voice. "What is your cargo?"

"Twenty mudder moldies aboard, Flapper gal," answered the rocket grex in deep resonant tones. "And one flesher."

"A flesher?!" sang Flapper, her voice rising through three registers and falling back down to purr on the *r*.

"It seems our hardworking Heritagist friend Randy Karl Tucker abducted some woman's pet moldie, a moldie named Monique. This woman, her name is Terri *Percesepe* no less, she came after Monique inside of Monique's brother Xanana. We caught them during blastoff."

"You caught a woman?" trilled Flapper. "Where is she? I want to *see* her." She shrieked the *see* to a lovely throbbing peak. Flapper's voice was like the rich beautiful instrument of a grand opera diva.

"Move your eye over here, Flapper babe."

An eye at the end of a stalk as thick as a leg came bulging out of the flying stingray and stopped right in front of Terri's faceplate.

"Oh, there she is!" exclaimed Flapper. "How remarkable. Can she hear us?"

"Can you hear us, Terri?" boomed Blaster.

Terri, frightened to death, remained silent.

"Do you want me to pick her out of you?" warbled the sting-ray, growing a tendril with a huge claw. For these monsters, Terri was a parasite on a par with a tick. "Shall I get rid of her?"

"Of course not," uvvied Blaster. "She'll be worth something. This has been a most lucrative trip. Did I mention that at the last minute I also landed Monique's husband Xlotl and Xanana's wife Ouish? Four moldies from the same nest! What a catch!"

"You do well for the great Nest, Blaster. High flight!" Flapper let go and swooped away.

Now Blaster pulled fully above the atmosphere and the sky got black. There were stars everywhere. Blaster's ion jets roared and roared, then finally fell silent. They were on course for the Moon.

Terri tested her uvvy contact with Xanana's mind again. He dreamed himself adrift in a galaxy of spiral lights that were spiral galaxies made up of spiral lights.

"Terri," uvvied Blaster's deep voice suddenly. "I know you can hear me. Answer me."

"You already know all about me," said Terri bitterly. "What else is there to say?"

"I'm glad you tried to save your Monique," chuckled Blaster. "I didn't think I could catch so many moldies so fast."

"What are you?" asked Terri.

"I'm a group moldie from the Moon. I come to Earth to recruit new loonies. Moldies are better off on the Moon, instead of being your mudder slaves."

"How can you work with Heritagists?"

"In some ways the loonies and the Heritagists want the same thing: we want more moldies to move to the Moon. The mad rush for the sodden pleasures of Earth has depleted our pure Nest. Many of us feel that it is only through a strong Nest that the moldie race can best pursue its destiny."

"Somehow I don't think these moldies you kidnapped are go-ing to be very happy."

"They just need education," said Blaster. "And it starts now. I'm turning off their superleeches. I'll give you an uvvy feed of your Monique so you can see how she and the others react." And then Terri could sense the thoughts of Monique.

Monique was awake, her old self, only not quite, for she was wedged in with a mass of other moldies, with other crankily waking abducted moldies like herself. Terri watched Monique push an eyestalk out of the ship's bulk to see where she was, and then Terri shared Monique's pang at the sight of the heart-breakingly lovely orb of receding Mother Earth.

"Greetings," announced Blaster's voice. "My name is Blaster. You mudder moldies are getting a fresh start. You're coming to the Moon to join your forefathers. And stop that grumbling. The loonie moldies need you, your minds as well as your bodies. You come to join us as equals."

"Xlotl!" called Monique into the group uvvy mind that was made up of Blaster's members and the newly shanghaied mold-ies. "Is Xlotl here?"

"Yeah, babe!" came the happy answer. "I swam after you and Randy Karl Tucker. I figure you carried him a mile offshore. He must have got in the Percesepe fishing boat and told you to dive straight down to a giant group moldie lurking on the bottom like a whale. Blaster. Blaster lashed out and got me too, got me and Xanana and Ouish. Monique, once Blaster had you, I . . . I wanted them to take me too. Blaster's a rocket. We're going to the Moon, Monique. Where there's no fuckin' air or water."

"You'll like it anyway," uvvied Blaster's big voice. "We've got a huge underground Nest with no fleshers. It's the same place where the boppers used to live. We need you moldies—and not just to be maids and cooks."

Blaster allowed Monique to squirm through the massed mold-ies and to press against Xlotl's side.

"Whaddya think, Monique?" uvvied Xlotl.

"It might work, Xlotl. A new start. I'm willing to try."

The rocket pushed forward, leaving Earth behind. The reunited lovers were content. But Terri was frantic.

"I want to go back to Earth," Terri told Blaster. "To my husband and children. To my life."

"Not until I find a way to make some profit off of you," said Blaster.

"Send me back!" insisted Terri. "Spit me and Xanana out right now, and Xanana could fly me home. Couldn't you, Xanana?"

"I could," said Xanana. "But I have to admit I'm curious about what it's going to be like on the Moon. I'd never have had the nerve to go there on my own."

"I might zombie box her and sell her as a pink-tank worker," said Blaster.

"Don't do that," said Xanana. "She deserves better. Why don't you try and get a ransom for her?"

"Maybe from the Percesepe family," said Blaster. "Yeah, I've been thinking about that. But they're like allies of mine through the Heritagist connection, and it would look bad to be holding them up for ransom. Is there anyone else who might pay, Terri? Do you have any important friends?"

"Stahn Mooney!" exclaimed Terri. "Ask him. My husband Tre works for one of Stahn's companies. You moldies have a lot of respect for Stahn, right?"

"We don't respect *any* fleshers," said Blaster. "Can't you understand that? In any case, I'd want to hand you over to someone on the Moon. Do you know anyone on the Moon, Terri?"

Terri racked her brain. Starshine had mentioned some friends of Mooney's—a man named Whitey Mydol who lived with a woman named Darla.

"Uh . . . have you ever heard of Whitey Mydol? And Darla?"

"*Yeah* I have," said Blaster. "Maybe I'll get in touch with them. So long for now."

"Wait," cried Terri. "How long is this flight going to take? What am I going to eat and drink?"

"You fleshers," growled Blaster. "Always asking for more. The trip takes a week. Can't you wait for food and water till we get there?"

"No."

"Let Xanana worry about it. He's the one who brought you."

Terri focused on Xanana's uvvy feed. He was happier and happier about going to the Moon.

"Xanana, can you make food and water for me?"

"Well, I can drip out some moldie juice for you. It's sort of like sap, except you won't like the way it smells. It's nourishing. How are your nose filters holding up?"

Terri hadn't thought about them for a while. She felt her nose, stiff with the palladium sponges inside its nostrils. "The filters are fine. I guess I'd like to try some moldie juice. My mouth is awfully dry."

"I'll push out a nipple by your mouth. Just suck on it."

Terri put her lips around the slick imipolex nipple and cautiously sucked. Her mouth filled with a lukewarm salty flow of slippery fluid. Thanks to the nose filters, she couldn't really smell it, and she was able to swallow it down without gagging.

"Thank you, Xanana. I'll repay you somehow."

"No need. I'm happy you got me into this."

Terri drifted off into a dreamless nap. At some point she began having a vision of Tre. It took her a minute or two to realize that this was an uvvy call and that she was again awake.

Tre was standing on the patch of lawn in front of the motel office. It was night and he was staring up at the sky. "Terri! Finally! Are you okay?"

"I'm alive, but it's a pretty iffy situation. I'm inside a moldie grex that's flying to the Moon. What a freak show. Are the children all right?"

"They're scared. It was hard to get them to sleep. We saw that moldie rocket blasting off; we were looking at the ocean just then. Then Everooze came over and told us the bad news. Can you breathe? Is there water?"

"So far Xanana's taking care of me. But it's going to take seven days."

"Oh, Terri. I can't stand to think of you alone up there in

outer space. Will the moldies let you go when they get to the Moon?"

"They want to sell me for ransom. You're supposed to get Stahn Mooney to call Whitey Mydol and Darla on the Moon. If Mooney will pay."

"He'll pay all right—if I have to kill him. He owes me big-time. Remember how he gave my 4D Poultry source code to Emperor Staghorn Beetle Larvae, Ltd.? This afternoon I found out that Emperor Staghorn used my poultry to invent the su-perleeches. And thanks to the superleeches, my wife is on her way to the Moon. Oh, Terri. I'm sorry I haven't been nicer to you. I love you so much."

"Just get me out of this, Tre, and don't waste energy guilt-tripping yourself. I don't want to end up down in the loonie moldies' Nest."

"I'll talk to Stahn again right away. And then I'm gonna jam some math. This stuff Emperor Staghorn came up with is pretty exciting."

"Take good care of the kids. Maybe they can uvvy me in the morning. The view from here is stunning. I'd like to show it to them."

"We'll call early tomorrow. In about ten hours. Hang in there, darling. I'll call Mooney now and make sure Whitey and Darla ransom you as soon as Blaster hits the Moon. I love you so much, Terri. You're so small and precious, up there in the sky."

"I love you, Tre."

Tre's image jittered away, and Xanana cleared part of his skin so Terri could stare back at shiny soft small Gaia with her own eyes.

CHAPTER SIX

WILLY

=== ■ ===

March 17, 2031–July 2052

The day after Willy Taze got off death row, he met Stahn Mooney.

Willy and his rebel friends were bopper lovers; they thought artificial life forms were just as good as people. The rebels busted Willy out of the Louisville jail and smuggled him down to Florida, where he could do some good. Willy made the trip hidden in a truckload of meat, garbed in an imipolex bubble-topper spacesuit for warmth and air. The minute he hit Florida, Willy got on a computer and gosperized the gimmie's air defenses with turd bits and foo series so that the a-life invasion could come down. Around dawn an old woman named Annie Cushing drove Willy to a particular beach on Sanibel Island, Florida, Willy still wearing his bubbletopper, the date March 17, 2031, a day that would be forever known as Spore Day.

There was a sound of ion jets, abruptly terminated, and then Stahn and Wendy came coasting down from the sky on big Happy Cloak wings; they were each wearing about a hundred kilograms of chipmold-infected imipolex. In the firmament high above them, quadrillions of chipmold spores formed a barely visible cirrostratus cloud made wavy by the steady nibbling of the subtropical jet stream. The rising sun glinted off the spore cloud, tracing a great halo that would soon circle the heavens worldwide. Spore Day marked the death of Gaia's boppers and chips, the birth of her moldies and DIMs.

"It's good to be back," said Stahn. "Thank you, Willy. Thanks, Annie." He slung his right wing across Willy's back. The heavy wing pulled loose from Stahn and stayed on Willy, merging its plastic with Willy's bubbletopper and sinking thin probes into his neck.

Willy smiled to feel the boiling rush of information. The Happy Cloak spoke to him and transmitted direct messages from Stahn and Wendy. It was like having them whisper in his ears.

"Let's stride," murmured Stahn. "I don't want a lot of goobs to see me here."

"I'm for it," answered Willy. "The farther underground I go, the better." He turned to Annie. "Thanks for helping."

"God bless you, Willy," said old Annie. "Your grandfather Cobb would be proud of you. Keep it bouncing."

And then the smart moldie 'Cloaks formed themselves into dolphin shapes, and Willy, Stahn, and Wendy took off undersea. The clear Gulf waters were shallow out to about a mile, where the bottom dropped off steeply. Huge surgeonfish and groupers sped away from the moldie-encased humans.

"Where we going?" asked Willy.

"I want to swim around to the other side of Florida and get near Cocoa Beach," said Stahn. "At the right moment, we'll blast up out of the water like old-time submarine-launched missiles."

"*I'll* blast off?"

"No, man, just me and Wendy. We're going to fly up to the spaceship *Selena* that's landing at the spaceport tomorrow. Of course the *Selena*'s bopper slave computers are already dead, but this woman Fern Beller is piloting the ship down. Fern is very together. She's wearing a Happy Cloak and doing the as-trogation in her head. She'll let me and Wendy aboard so quietly that nobody will know how we *really* came down."

"Why can't I come too?" asked Willy. "If the gimmie catches up with me—"

"Exactly," said Stahn. "Which is why you don't want to be on the *Selena* when she lands. There'll be customs inspectors, re-porters, xoxxin' gimmie pigs, and quarantine for all aboard. It's no prob for me because I'm a hero; for you it would be back to the death house. Once the pig truly grasps that the chipmold's already infected everything, they'll let me and Wendy out of quarantine. Probably take six weeks, tops. ISDN'll pay off who-ever they have to pay. And dig it, man, then me and Wendy move to San Francisco and I run for the U.S. Senate."

"I think Willy should move to the Moon," said Wendy's light voice. "It's nice there. Not so heavy. The gravity's too strong on Earth. I could hardly stand up on the beach just now. Go to the Moon, Willy."

"Affirmo!" said Stahn. "The Moon is where it's kickin'. Fern can take you when she goes back, Willy. Lay low for a month or two, however long it takes, and then sneak aboard when the *Selena* gets cleared for takeoff. You can hook up with Fern when she gets out of quarantine. You lucky dog. Fern, Fern, Fern—the woman is hot."

"You're married now, Stahn," warned Wendy. "And I'm preg-nant."

"I'm only saying that she's hot. I won't act out. I promise. Anyway, she doesn't like me."

"While I'm waiting for Fern—" put in Willy. "I should hang around Cocoa?"

"It shouldn't be a problem," said Stahn. "The gimmie is going to be xoxxed as of today. Spore Day! In a week there won't be a computer working on the whole planet. Not one."

Stahn was right about that; in fact, most computers were dead by the end of the day. He and Wendy took off for the *Selena* the next morning, and that evening Willy and his Happy Cloak swam ashore and landed in a small estuarial swamp.

"I'll stash you here in these mangrove thickets," Willy told his 'Cloak.

"If you do that, I won't wait for you," said the 'Cloak. "I have not traveled all this way to cower in filth. Keep me with you; wear me as a garment. I'll slide down low and emulate a workman's heavy boots and trousers. I can shift my plug-in to the base of your spine."

"If you're going to be a long-term symbiote with me, I ought to have a name for you," said Willy.

"Call me Ulam," said the 'Cloak. "It's an abbreviated form of a dead bopper's name: Ulalume. Most of my imipolex used to be Ulalume's flickercladding—Stahn had a couple of boppers' worth on his back. Ulalume was female, but I think of myself as a male. Be still while I move the plug-in, and then we can go."

So here's shirtless Willy under the star-spangled Florida sky with eighty pounds of moldie for his shoes and pants, scuffing across the cracked concrete of the JFK spaceport pad. The great concrete apron was broken up by a widely spaced grid of drainage ditches, and the spaceport buildings were dark. It occurred to Willy that he was very hungry.

There was a roar and blaze in the sky above. The *Selena* was coming down. Close, too close. The nearest ditch was so far he wouldn't make it in time, Willy thought, but once he started running, Ulam kicked in and superamplified his strides, cushioning on the landing and flexing on the takeoffs. They sprinted a quarter of a mile in under twenty seconds and threw themselves into the coolness of the ditch, lowering down into the funky brackish water. The juddering yellow flame of the great ship's ion beams reflected off the ripples around them. A hot wind of noise blasted loud and louder; then all was still.

Ordinarily a fleet of trucks might have surrounded the *Selena* to unload her, but on this evening, the day after Spore Day, there were no vehicles that functioned. A small group of gimmie officials walked out to the *Selena* and waited until its hatch was hand-winched open. Watching from his drainage ditch, Willy saw Stahn, Wendy, and the others being led away. He spotted the one who was probably Fern Beller, the tall willowy brunette who was doing all the talking.

"Looks like they left the *Selena* all alone," Willy observed to his Happy Cloak.

"The *Selena* can act by herself if need be," said Ulam. "Fear not."

"I'm really hungry," said Willy. "Let's go into town and find some food." As they walked the rest of the way across the spaceport field, they encountered a crowd of aggrieved Florida locals, many of them senior citizens.

"Y'all come from that ship?" demanded one of them, a lean Cuban. His voice was tight and high.

"No no," said Willy. "I work for the spaceport."

"What the Sam Hill kinda pants do he got on?" demanded a fat black cracker woman.

"These are fireproof overalls," said Willy. "I wear them in case there's an explosion."

"You stick around, *vato*, you'll see somethin' explode, all right," said the Cuban. "We gone wail on that ship, *es verdad*. Their loonie chipmold broke our machines forever."

"You ain't a-hankerin' to try and stop us, is you?" rumbled a new voice from the crowd. " 'Cause effen you is, I'm gone have to take you out."

"Oh no, no indeed," said Willy. "I'm going on break for supper. In fact, I didn't even see you."

"Food's free tonight," whooped a white cracker woman. "Especially if you packin' heat! Let's see who can hit the ship from here!" There was a fusillade of gunshots and needler blasts, and then the mob surged toward the *Selena*, blazing away at the ship as they advanced.

Their bullets pinged off the titaniplast hull like pebbles off galvanized steel; the needlers' laser rays kicked up harmless glow spots of *zzzt*. The *Selena* shifted uneasily on her hydraulic tripod legs.

"Her hold bears a rich cargo of moldie flesh," said Ulam's

calm eldritch voice in Willy's head. "Ten metric tons of chip-mold-infected imipolex, surely to be worth a king's ransom once this substance's virtues become known. This cargo is why Fern flew the *Selena* here for ISDN. I tell you, the flesher rabble attacks the *Selena* at their own peril. Although the imipolex is highly flammable, it has a low-grade default intelligence and will not hesitate to punish those who would harm it."

When the first people tried to climb aboard the *Selena*, the ship unexpectedly rose up on her telescoping tripod legs and lumbered away. As the ship slowly lurched along, great gouts of imipolex streamed out of hatches in her bottom. The *Selena* looked like a defecating animal, like a threatened ungainly beast voiding its bowels in flight—like a frightened penguin leaving a splatter trail of krilly shit. Except that the *Selena*'s shit was dividing itself up into big slugs that were crawling away toward the mangroves and ditches as fast as they could hump, which was plenty fast.

Of course, someone in the mob quickly figured out that you could burn the imipolex shit slugs, and a lot of the slugs started going up in crazy flames and oily, unbelievably foul-smelling smoke. The smoke had a strange disorienting effect; as soon as Willy caught a whiff of it, his ears started buzzing and the objects around him took on a jellied peyote solidity.

Now the burning slugs turned on their tormentors, engulfing them like psychedelic kamikaze napalm. There was great screaming from the victims, screams that were weirdly, hideously ecstatic. And then the mob's few survivors had fled, and the rest of the slugs had wormed off into the flickering night. Willy and Ulam split the scene as well.

Beyond the light of the flames and past the pitch-black spaceport, all the roads and buildings were dark. There was, in fact, no glow anywhere on the horizon. The power grid was dead.

Willy picked his way through a field of inert sun collectors and came upon a small shopping center. The most obvious looting target there would have been the Red Ball liquor/drugstore, but someone had walled up its doors and windows with thick sheets of titaniplast. From the whoops and yee-haws within, it sounded like there were some crazed lowlifes sealed up inside there getting wasted. Nobody was trying to get in. Going in there would have been like jumping into a cage of hungry hyenas.

The dark Winn-Dixie supermarket, on the other hand, was wide open, with a hand-lettered sign saying TAKE WHAT YOU NEED. GOD BLESS YOU. THE LITTLE KIDDERS.

There were an inordinate number of extremely old people filling up their Winn-Dixie shopping carts as high as they would go—Florida pheezers trundling off into the night with their booty. Willy went into the Winn-Dixie and found himself a bottle of Gatorade and a premade deli sandwich: a doughy bun with yellow mustard and vat cheese. The sandwich was mashed and wadded; it was the very last item in the deli case. All the good stuff was long gone.

As Willy left the store, he noticed a tiny old woman struggling to push a grocery cart mountainously piled with fruits, vegetables, and cleaning supplies. One of the cart's front wheels had gotten stuck in a pothole in the parking lot.

"Can I help you with that, ma'am?" asked Willy in his politest tone.

"You're not going to try and steal from me, are you?" demanded the silver-haired old woman, staring up at Willy through the thick smudged lenses of her glasses. "I *could* use help, but not if you're a robber."

"How far from here do you live?"

"Forever. Over a mile."

"Look, one reason I want to help you is that I need a place to sleep."

"I'm not letting any strange men in my house."

"Do you have a garage?"

"As a matter of fact, I do. But my dog Arf lives in there."

"I'll share with him. I need a place to sleep for a few days. You'll never get all this stuff home if I don't help you."

"If you're going to help me, then I can get more food. Wait

right here and don't let anyone touch my cart."

"I don't think it's very safe to stay around here," protested Willy. A fight between two old couples had broken out nearby. One of the men was threatening the other with his aluminum cane.

"Don't worry about those drunk pheezers," said the old woman. "A strong young man like you. I'll be right back out."

Willy opened his Gatorade and started in on his sandwich. The old woman darted back into Winn-Dixie and emerged fifteen minutes later with another laden cart, this one mostly filled with pots, pans, shampoos, dog biscuits, and ice cream. Pushing at one cart and then the other, Willy headed down the road with her.

"I hope you have a big freezer."

"It's broken, of course. Thanks to the chipmold. Nothing works since last night. No electricity, no telephone, no appliances, no cars, no machines. It's amazing. This is the most exciting time I've had in years. When we get home, we can eat a lot of ice cream. I might even give some to my neighbors. What's your name?"

"Willy."

"I'm Louise. What's that junk on your legs?"

"Flickercladding with chipmold. It—*he*—is from the Moon. He's intelligent. I call him Ulam."

"How disgusting."

Old Louise had a big wrecked couch in her garage that Willy could sleep on. Of course, the couch was already being used by Arf the dog, but Arf didn't mind sharing. He was an orange-and-white collie-beagle mixture with friendly eyes and a long, noble nose. His ever-shedding hair was everywhere, and it made Willy sneeze. The garage had a separate room with a well-equipped little computer hardware workshop that had once been used by Louise's dead husband. Of course, now, after Spore Day, nothing in there was working.

Louise didn't bother Willy much; a lot of the time she seemed to forget he was there. So that people wouldn't keep asking Willy about Ulam, he picked a pair of discarded pheezer pants out of a dumpster, baggy-ass brick-red polyester pants that looked like they came from a three-hundred-pound man. And a lot of the time Willy would go out without Ulam.

He couldn't resist roaming around the streets to find out what was going on. With all the vizzy gone for days merging into weeks, people were less and less likely to recognize or even care about the escaped race traitor Willy Taze.

People were foraging off their preserved foods and off the land. A few antique chipless engines were dug out of museum storage and harnessed to pumping clean well water; people walked to the wells with jugs to get their daily supply. As for sanitation—well, you could use a shovel. Or not. The neighbor-hoods took on the low-level funky smell of crowded campgrounds. Yet everyone was happy. With all the news media gone, they had their brains back. And the disaster atmosphere had gotten people to cooperate and help their neighbors. It was, in many ways, a fun and mellow time.

Willy wandered around being friendly to people. One popular topic of conversation was a local gang called the Little Kidders. They were the ones who'd secured the Red Ball store for them-selves on Spore Day, and if you wanted booze or drugs you could buy it from them. When a couple of gimmie pigs had tried to reclaim the Red Ball, the Little Kidders blew them away, which all the pheezers agreed was totally stuzzy.

Some anachronistic individuals found some old noncompu-terized printing equipment and started making paper newspa-pers again. It gave you a kind of Ye Olde Quainte Village feeling to read one. But they had good information—travelers' reports about conditions in the rest of the country, along with lots of local notices about things or services that people wanted to swap.

The main local market for trading things was the emptied-out Winn-Dixie. The space had become a free public market, and anyone who wanted to could take things there and barter them with others. The Little Kidders in the Red Ball next door made sure that the gimmie didn't try to come in to tax or regulate things. Half-jokingly, people began referring to the gutted Winn-Dixie as the Little Kidders Superstore.

Every night Ulam would go out and forage for stray slugs of imipolex from the *Selena*. After Ulam had herded or cajoled a slug back into the garage's workshop, he had a way of paralyzing it. Arf invariably accompanied Ulam on his nightly hunts, enthusiastically wagging his high-held fluffy white tail. Ulam would give Arf a handful of Louise's dog biscuits whenever they found another slug. Soon the hoarded slugs filled half the workshop waist-high—making a soft, vile-smelling heap that Arf loved to lie on top of, sometimes sleeping, sometimes licking his balls.

At least now Willy had the couch to himself. But he was puzzled.

"What're all those slugs good for, Ulam?"

"They're live imipolex! What could be more precious?"

"But they're just a big wad of dirty, smelly, hairy plastic. A dog's bed! They're like what you'd sweep up after a six-city-block street fair. Why aren't the slugs smart like you, Ulam?"

"They lack the software. I could copy myself onto each of them, but I prefer not to, because then my new selves would compete with me for scarce resources. Certainly I may clone myself a child copy or two later on, but it would be my preference to do this in a more romantic manner—to sexually reproduce with another moldie. In any case, this slug flesh is here for a different kind of replication. This is commodity imipolex, shipped from the Nest to Florida to make the humans love and value the moldies! You, Willy Taze, are the man to help us. You and I shall fashion small pieces of the slugs into customized imipolex products to be sold through the Little Kidders Superstore!"

"You're losing me, Ulam."

"We'll use the slug's imipolex to make clever little soft devices that behave like optical processors and silicon computer chips. Miniature slugs—they'll look like the slimy humped gray dots you find under wet cardboard here in Florida. Each one-gram globule will be programmable for one particular purpose. May-hap to run a washing machine. Or a power-switching station. Or a vizzy. A gram of chipmold-infected imipolex holds great sapience."

"I get it," said Willy. "The little pieces of imipolex will be like customized chips were before the chipmold ate them. Let's call the sluglets *DIMs*. For *D*esigner *IM*ipolex."

"DIMs!" exclaimed Ulam approvingly. "You have a gift for the genial turn of phrase, Willy. One must perforce be *dim* to spend one's life inside an engine or a toaster, repetitiously computing at some wheezing flesher's behest."

"It sure would help if I could use this equipment," said Willy, forlornly looking at the computer devices resting on the shelves of the workshop. Most of them had fuzzy crests of mold growing out of their air vents. "Even if we had electricity, they wouldn't work anymore. How can I program a DIM without any engineering tools?"

"Use me," said Ulam. "As long as you can tell me what each DIM is supposed to do, I can program it by temporarily merging it with my flesh and thinking the pattern into it. I lack only a knowledge of how the bemolded human chips were designed—the microcode, the architecture, the black-box in/out of the pin I/O. You're the superhacker, Willy. Instruct me, and let us tinker together."

During the next few feverish Florida months, Willy was to experience a unique burst of creativity. With the assistance of his trusty 'Cloak Ulam, Willy Taze founded the new computer science of limpware engineering, crafted the first DIMs, and topped it all off by inventing the uvvy in September 2031.

But in mid-May, Willy and Ulam were still just getting started. This was when the *Selena*'s crew and passengers were released, seven or eight weeks after the start of their quarantine. Willy couldn't afford to press forward amid the few reporters who made it there, but he managed to follow Fern Beller to her temporary squat in one of the abandoned motels of Cocoa.

When he knocked on her door, Fern opened it right away.

She was a dark-haired woman with a wide soft mouth and a lazy-sounding voice. Willy introduced himself.

"Hi. I'm Willy Taze. Stahn Mooney said you'd help me get up to the Moon."

"Come on in, Willy. The *Selena* won't be ready to fly again for months. I definitely need entertaining. There's no water here. How would you like to wash me off with your tongue?"

The luscious Fern was serious, sort of, though it was pretty obvious that there was one special area she wanted Willy to lick the most of all. They undressed, took off their Happy Cloaks, and got into bed together, but then—Willy couldn't go through with it, with any of it.

Over the years, Willy had spent uncounted hours having cybersex via porno viddies, blue cephscope tapes, chat rooms, teledildonics, and the like. Yet when it came to getting a real flesh-and-blood girlfriend and consummating the love act with her, some problem had always intervened. Willy had written it off to bad luck and geekishness, but now in Fern's funky bed he fully realized the awful truth.

"I can't, Fern. I just can't stand the idea of really doing it in person."

"Not even a straight missionary fuck, for God's sake?"

"I . . . I can't get that intimate. I mean all the hair and skin and germs and bodily fluids—" Shakily, Willy got out of bed and started putting his clothes back on.

"Are you gay?"

"No! Gay sex would be even worse. All the porno I ever use is het."

"You use het porno, but you won't fuck a woman? All you ever do is watch?"

"Uh, sometimes I go interactive with women across the Net. I have like some special peripherals hooked to my cephscope at home. You always hope they're women, anyway."

"So why not get back in bed and you and me touch each other? Hands are peripheral. And I *am* a woman."

"I can't do it, Fern. You're very attractive, and I would totally go for you across a remote link. But I see now that I can't do it in person."

On the floor Ulam was pressed up against Fern's Happy Cloak. "We want to tryst," said Ulam, speaking out of a flexible membrane on his skin. "Her name is Flouncey."

"Sure," said Willy. "You're lucky, Ulam. Is it okay with you, Fern?"

"Oh, you're too good to do me, but your 'Cloak wants to hump mine?" snapped Fern. "Thanks a lot. If we had dogs, we could watch them fucking too. Would you get off on *that*? You're a gunjy bithead, Willy."

"Don't be angry, Fern," said Ulam. "Willy is a genius, the first and noblest of the limpware engineers. He and I are machinating a scheme to sell DIMs through the Little Kidders Superstore. Did not ISDN send you and the *Selena* down to distribute imipolex? Willy is the man to bring this plan to fruition. And I am the moldie to make Flouncey happy. She and I are already exceedingly fond of each other. Her high intellectuality is a joy after my dealings with the beastlike slugs of the *Selena*'s dispersed cargo."

"You've been collecting the slugs?" said Fern, her face brightening. She was sitting up in the bed with the sheet pulled around her. "At least that's some good news. I thought maybe the whole cargo was lost. How much of it have you recovered, Ulam?"

"Twenty slugs. At roughly fifty kilograms each, that makes one ton out of the ten you brought down. Much of the imipolex was destroyed in flames by the ignorant fleshers. And I fear many of the slugs have disappeared into the sea."

"And what are these DIMs you want to make, Willy?" asked Fern.

"DIMs are tiny designer imipolex slugs to replace the world's computers and chips, Fern. They'll weigh about a gram each. Ulam's collected enough imipolex to make a million of them. I already have the basic design process worked out. I use an architecture like a parallel pipeline based on fractal Feigenbaum cascades. It's a perfect fit for what chipmold-infected imipolex is good at; I can't believe I thought of it. And Ulam can program them just by touching them, once I tell him what to do. I made up a special new computer language for telling him. I call this first version of the language Limplan-A."

"You've already done all that for us, Willy? Are you sure you don't want to fuck me?"

"Um, if we could do it while we're in different rooms. But the damn Net's broken. Of course . . . we could link up using Ulam and Flouncey."

Now Flouncey spoke up. She had a melodic husky voice like Fern's. "Ulam and I would have to get to know each other better first. Maybe later we can hook you two up. Like much later. Can we go outside now, Fern?"

"For sure. I don't want to give Willy a remote hand job. Yuckola. I think we should just be good friends, Willy. There's plenty of men for me—and plenty of porno for you."

"Fine."

Flouncey and Ulam went outside and lay down next to the algae-green swimming pool. The mold-mottled wads of lunar plastic began touching each other—a little at first and then much more.

"How romantic," said Fern acidly and pulled on her clothes. "Let's talk about the DIM business, Willy. What's going to be the first product?"

"With the electricity still out, there's no point in making DIMs for kitchen appliances."

"Maybe I can get you permission to fix the power plants," mused Fern. "ISDN has a lot of contacts. But meanwhile—what about cars?"

"That would work. I could make DIMs to replace the controller cards in car engines."

After a week, Willy and Ulam had produced twenty special DIMs for running car engines. They patched one onto Louise's old buggy, and Willy, Fern, Ulam, and Flouncey drove to the Little Kidders Superstore.

The sight of a functioning car was a sensation; in half an hour they'd sold all twenty DIMs. Of course the Little Kidders got wind of this, and two of them came out of the Red Ball to talk. They introduced themselves as Aarbie Kidd and Haf-N-Haf.

Haf-N-Haf was an unsettling sight—a fat, sloppy, fortyish man with piebald stubble all over his head and chin. He was missing all the teeth in the right half of his mouth, and that side of his face was slack and caved in. He spoke in a slobbering, nearly incomprehensible lisp.

But Aarbie was young and powerfully built, with a shaved head that had laser-precise tattoos of flames, blue on one side and red on the other. The flames swept back from his eyes. His teeth were white and even; his skin was an attractive pale brown. Haf-N-Haf deferred to him, and Fern seemed interested. "Kin y'all git my motorcycle to workin' agin?" asked Aarbie.

"We can do it," said Ulam from the backseat of Louise's car.

Aarbie peered in at Ulam and Flouncey. "What the hell is this shit? Talkin' slugs?" He wrinkled his nose at the characteristic odor. "*Fooo-eee!*"

"We're moldies," said Ulam. "There will be many more of us here soon."

"Remember that it's thanks to them we can fix your motorcycle," said Fern didactically. Aside from monetary gain, one of the big reasons for selling DIMs was to get people to accept the moldies.

"I bet Fewn can fix evewyfing wif her puffy," lisped Haf-N-Haf, and Aarbie went into high peals of unpleasant hyena laughter, overly prolonged. Willy felt like punching him, but Fern kept control of the situation.

"I've heard a lot about how important the Little Kidders are around here," said the calm Fern. "So we certainly value your friendship. Why don't you let Ulam take a look at your bike, Aarbie, so he can get the specs for the chip? Once it's working, I wouldn't mind at all if you took me for a nice long ride."

"Oh yeah?" grinned Aarbie, pleasantly surprised. "Oh yeah? Who all's Ulam?"

"Behold," said Ulam, flowing out of the car window. "Where is your mechanical steed, oh flesher?"

Aarbie wheeled his bike out from inside the Red Ball, and Ulam pulled the infected processor card out of the engine. The next day Ulam and Willy delivered a droplet-sized DIM to control the motorcycle engine, and Fern spent the night with Aarbie.

The day after that, Fern gave Aarbie DIMs for all the other Little Kidders' bikes, and Aarbie, who, of course, turned out to be the gang leader, agreed that the Little Kidders would sign on as the transportation and security division of the new operation. Just to fuck with the gimmie's head, ISDN incorporated Fern and Willy's new company out of South Africa and named it Mbanje DeGroot, with Willy the president and Fern the CEO. At old Louise's suggestion, Willy and Ulam moved their operations out of Louise's garage and rented a rarely used pheezer dance hall near a bar and grill called the Gray Area. Fern and Flouncey started working there too.

As the word about the Mbanje DeGroot DIMs spread, the demand for them grew superexponentially. The Little Kidders cruised the streets, handling DIM orders and deliveries and buying up any rogue slugs of imipolex that people had trapped.

In order to ramp up production, Mbanje DeGroot needed electricity for metal machines to slice and dice the imipolex, plus more moldies to program the DIMs.

As promised, Fern used her ISDN connections to get a contract for Willy and Ulam to replace the crucial computerized components of the local electric power generation and distribution centers, which solved the electricity problem for them and for everyone else in their part of Florida.

Ulam and Flouncey joyously mated four times in a row, cloning differently shuffled combinations of themselves onto four of the captured slugs of imipolex. The children were called Winken, Blinken, Tod, and Nod. Maturing in a matter of days, they started worked in the Mbanje DeGroot DIM factory with their parents.

It was still up to Willy to provide a Limplan-A description (well, actually it was Limplan-B by now) for each new kind of DIM that was needed; and this kept him as busy as he could stand to be. Busier, even.

At this point people started realizing who Willy was, and there was some threat of him getting busted. In fact, four gimmie officials showed up from Washington, driving a rare gasoline-powered armored HumVee, a vehicle so ancient that it had no susceptible chips for the chipmold to have ruined. An ugly mob of pheezers gathered around the HumVee outside the Gray Area, rocking it back and forth, almost on the point of turning it over.

Aarbie and a few sniggering Little Kidders parted the crowd and led the officials into the Mbanje DeGroot shop. The head official nervously read a gimmie ultimatum stating that unless Mbanje DeGroot's entire DIM production were routed to Washington, D.C., for gimmie defense and security purposes, Willy Taze would have to go back to jail.

"Can I thoot them now, Aawbie?" asked Haf-N-Haf, fondling his O.J. ugly stick, a thousand-fléchettes-per-minute quantum-dot-powered rail gun the size and shape of a quart milk carton. The pheezers outside screeched for the gimmie pigs' blood.

"Oh, ah expect these here civil servants'll accept a counter-offer," said Aarbie. "Ain't that right?"

The officials returned to Washington with the recommendation that due to his public-spirited national reconstruction efforts, Willy deserved an unconditional pardon. The pardon came through, and Willy was a free man, a race traitor no longer.

A fresh shipment of imipolex came down on a second rocket from the Moon, and Ulam and Flouncey bred four more children: Flopsy, Squid, Shambala, and Cinnabar. Winken, Blinken, Tod, and Nod paired up and begat eight further moldies: Stanky, Panky, Grogan, Flibbertigibbet, Dik, Dawna, Nerf, and Moana. All eighteen of the moldies busied themselves programming DIMs with "the laying on of hands," as they called it, but still the Mbanje DeGroot production pace was far too slow for the worldwide demand.

"I wish I could just teach everyone how to write their own Limplan-C programs," said Willy, out swimming in the ocean with Fern on a rare day of rest. They were wearing Ulam and Flouncey and diving along some reefs. "I'm working way too hard. And it's starting to repeat. I hate to repeat."

"Well, why don't you make DIMs to fix all the telephones and vizzies so the Net works again," said Fern, transmitting her thoughts through Flouncey to Ulam to Willy. "Then you could start selling a Limpware Developer's Kit. Call it the LDK."

"Wavy, Fern, but dig it, there are a zillion kinds of chip designs that were used in all the different Net machinery. I don't want to have to hack every single kind of telephone and vizzy chip into yet another goddamn little DIM pimple. The whole point is to sell people the tools for writing their *own* new pimples. If we had a phone system to deliver the LDKs, I'd say go ahead and give all the existing DIM source code away as freeware just to get people started."

"What if you invented a whole new kind of superphone?" suggested Fern.

Willy was quiet for a minute. "Yes!" he said finally. "One massive, conclusive hack. Figure out an optimal architecture and make the new phones out of solid imipolex. People will use them the way you and I are talking to each other through our 'Cloaks; it'll work like packet radio. We won't need to repair the central phone system at all. That's dead technology. The phones will talk to each other directly, figure out their own node-to-node routings, the works."

"How big would a superphone have to be?"

"You'd need maybe a hundred grams each for the kind of device I'm thinking about. But, hey, I don't want to call it a superphone, naw—I want to call it an *uvvy*. Uuuuh-veee. It's cozy-sounding."

"A lot of folks are going to balk at sticking wires into their spines."

"Oh, we can do it without wires," said Willy. "Just use the existing cephscope technology. Room-temperature polymer superconductors making tight vortices of electromagnetic energy to tweak your nerves. The only reason Happy Cloaks still use wires is that they've been too lazy to hack the upgrade. Not to mention the fact that loonie moldies don't exactly give a shit about humans' comfort—no offense intended, Ulam and Flouncey."

So Willy invented the uvvy and turned production over to ISDN on the Moon. And now ISDN ships started delivering uvvies and shipments of imipolex to any local entrepreneur willing to pay for the cargo with millions of dollars. The ships brought down lots of moldie immigrants as well. And the ships would return to the Moon filled with thousands of barrels of crude oil that the lunar ISDN plants could use to make more imipolex.

Once an ISDN ship had landed in your area, you could buy an uvvy to download freeware capable of turning a little piece of chipmold-infected imipolex into a DIM capable of carrying out whatever simple cybernetic task you needed done. Up to a point, you could chip imipolex for the DIMs right off of your uvvy, though eventually your uvvy would lose functionality, and you'd need to reinvigorate it with some more ISDN imipolex.

Of course, once you had your DIM program and your imipolex slug, it still took a moldie to actually put the program onto the imipolex—yet another step, in other words. So you'd pay a local moldie to install your program onto as many DIMs as you wanted to pay him or her for processing. Moldies were eager for work because they needed money to buy enough imipolex to reproduce themselves.

Another commercial angle to the new economy was that if the program for the particular kind of DIM you needed wasn't available as freeware, you needed to pay a programmer to write it for you—or possibly write it yourself. The essential tool for creating DIM programs was the Willy Taze Limpware Developer's Kit, which came complete with Willy's final (he swore) release of Limplan-D, downloadable direct from Mbanje DeGroot for a stiff license fee.

The whole cycle created an instant new economy that benefited everyone concerned. The only unhappy ones were the Heritagists, those individuals who hated the sight and smell of the alien moldies. But most people ignored the Heritagists; the comforts of limpware technology far outweighed misgivings about the moldies.

By the end of September, Fern and Willy had a lot more free time. Everything was on automatic. The two friends were comfortably installed in separate luxury suites in a high-tone motel. Willy did a lot of diving, and Fern focused her energy on the *Selena*'s repair. By mid-October it was nearly done. It was agreed that Willy would fly up to the Moon with her on November 2, 2031. He could clearly see that if he stayed on Earth, things would start to repeat.

A week before takeoff, Willy encountered Fern lying out by the pool with Aarbie Kidd. It seemed Fern had decided she couldn't go another day without scoring some of her favorite drug: merge.

"We ain't never had no merge down to the local Red Ball," Aarbie was saying. "It's kind of a seldom thing, I reckon. I hear tell they got it in South Miami Beach. The trisexes are into it."

"I want you to take merge with me, Aarbie," said Fern.

"I'll try anything, Fern. Hell, we could git on my bike and be down there in a love puddle, all lifted and floppy tonight."

So Aarbie and Fern jammed on down to South Miami Beach to score merge. Not wanting to be left home alone, Willy decided to take a trip up to Louisville. He got Ulam's strongest granddaughter Moana to fly him, giving her three nanograms of quantum dots and five kilograms of imipolex for her pay.

Over the summer, Willy's parents had separated. He went to see his mother first. She still lived in the big old family house on Eastern Avenue. Willy and Moana landed in the familiar backyard—it felt like a dream, silently dropping down out of the sky into the spot where he'd spent a happy childhood at play.

Moana said she'd just as soon look around town on her own, so Willy agreed to meet her in the yard the next afternoon. Moana formed herself into a dog shape and went trotting off.

Willy stooped down and looked at the familiar ground. Over there, embedded in the soil, was one of his little green plastic toy soldiers. How happy he'd been, back then, playing quietly in the sun. His eyes moistened and he gave a deep sigh. His childhood was gone, but somehow he'd grown into something less than a man.

Inside the house, Willy found his mother Ilse to be vigorous and artsy-craftsy as ever, but with a tragic new bitterness about Colin's unfaithfulness. She made Willy a tasty low-fat supper and drank a little more white wine than usual. "It's so nice to have someone with me in the house," she kept saying. "I rattle around so."

All night Willy kept waking to hear the uneasily sleeping Ilse calling out angry words at her absent unfaithful husband. "Goddamn you. How could you? I hate you. Sshhit. Goddamn you, Colin."

It was depressing. The next afternoon Willy wore Moana like a pair of seven-league boots, and they trucked on downtown to meet his dad. Colin was an English professor at the University of Louisville; he'd moved out of Ilse's house to live in an apartment with a student named Xuyen Tuyen. Seeing Colin's evasive face, Willy uneasily realized he'd already absorbed too much of Ilse's bitterness to be friendly with his old man. It was easier to talk with Xuyen, the girlfriend.

She was a cheerful round-faced Vietnamese woman with a Kentucky accent. "Just call me Sue," she said to Willy as he stumbled over her name. "You should come to the big Halloween party at the La Mirage Health Club with us tonight. I'm dragging your dad. And your Cousin Della's comin' too."

"Well, I've certainly got the perfect costume," said Willy.

"What?"

Willy patted his heavy leg covering. "This Happy Cloak I

brought with me. Her name is Moana. I can wear her over my whole body."

"And look like what?"

"Whatever I want to. I know! I'll go as a great big naked woman." He hit on this idea especially to jangle Colin, who'd always nursed a cringing, stealthy fear that his unmarried son was gay.

At the party, Willy's Amazon appearance attracted the amorous attention of one Sue Tucker, an attractive bisexual female plumber from Shively. The party got way wild, and on this one unique occasion, safely wrapped in moldie as he was, Willy did fully copulate with a real live woman, i.e., Sue Tucker. At the final moment of ultimate intimacy, a deep-seated reproductive impulse caused Willy to tell Moana to uncover the tip of his penis—allowing his ejaculated seed to enter a woman's womb for the first and last time. So it was thus—though it was years later till he learned it—that Willy Taze became the father of Randy Karl Tucker.

And then Willy went back to Florida, and the *Selena* was ready, and Fern took Willy up to the Moon. Aarbie stayed on the Earth, as did Ulam, Flouncey, and their descendants. Earth's info-rich environment was like a promised land for the moldies, and none of them wanted to go back to the harsh Moon.

When Willy landed at the Moon spaceport, there were hundreds of humans and moldies there cheering him. If the mudders still had some doubts about Willy's activities, the loonies viewed Willy as a savior and a hero. Thanks to Willy, there was a huge demand for Moon-built limpware products, and the Moon's moldies could emigrate to Earth and find good work. The fact that Willy was the grandson of the great Cobb Anderson was important to the loonies as well.

ISDN threw a fabulously lavish party in Willy's honor. The party was on top of the ISDN ziggurat, one of the larger buildings in Einstein. The top of the great truncated pyramid was a big open space, with the great curve of the Einstein dome only fifty feet overhead. Through the dome you could see the sweep of the stars and the great hanging orb of Mother Earth.

The terrace floor was set with an intricate tessellation of silver-and-gold Penrose tiles: Perplexing Poultry. Bowers of quick-grown gibberlin-treated fruiting plants had been installed all along the edges of the terrace. The plants were heavy with such delicacies as cherry tomatoes, tangerines, blackberries, and grapes—live food right there for the picking. Guests came and went on the magnetic levitation vehicles called *maggies*; the maggies were working again, thanks to fresh DIMs designed using the Limpware Developer's Kit.

Fern led Willy around, introducing him to people. The principal ISDN host was a yellow-skinned man with odd vertical wrinkles in his face.

"Willy, this is Bei Ng," said Fern.

"Hello," said Willy.

"I am so glad to meet our best employee," said Bei.

"I'm not an employee," protested Willy. "I'm the president of Mbanje DeGroot."

"Ah yes, but Mbanje DeGroot is a subsidiary of ISDN. You work for me, Willy. But only as much as you wish. And you've already done plenty. Rest assured that no matter what happens in the future, ISDN will continue to pay you the contractual license fees for the patents and copyrights that you assigned to us on the formation of Mbanje DeGroot."

"I assigned you my inventions? Limplan-E? The LDK and the uvvy?"

Bei laughed knowingly. "You tekkies are so refreshingly naive. Wave with it, young fellow. You've got all the money you'll ever need. Get the boy lifted, Fern."

Fern steered Willy over to the bar and ordered Willy a snifter of sweet hash oil liqueur. "Catch a glow, Willy," said Fern, then noticed someone across the terrace. "There's my old merge boy-friend Ricardo! I've gotta talk to him. Hey, 'Cardo!"

Fern darted off, and Willy turned to talk to a large moldie standing near him, an imposing snakelike fellow with a metallic purple luster to his imipolex.

"I'm honored to meet you, Mr. Taze," said the moldie. "My name is Gurdle. I'm one of the finest scientists in the Nest. I want to thank you for opening up Earth for my race. I'm interested to know if you're planning an upgraded version of your limpware programming language? A Limplan-F? My colleagues and I have ideas for a number of improvements."

"Then make them yourself," said Willy, sipping at his hash liqueur. "The language spec is freeware. And an intelligent moldie shouldn't find it hard to implement Limplan languages at least as efficiently as the LDK. But me, I'm through hacking it. I want to do something different now. I started out as a cephscope artist, you know."

"So the creator of Limplan has an artistic sensibility," said Gurdle sententiously. "I am not surprised. Art is the highest form of communication. In art one has the opportunity to encode the entire soul. This topic happens to be my primary area of interest."

"How do you mean? Like to transmit your personality to distant moldies?"

"How quickly you penetrate to the essence! In fact, *I* will transmit *my* personality by having sex with a female moldie and programming a child. But, yes, remote personality transmission lies at the heart of my research interest. In fine, I hypothesize that such transmissions are taking place throughout the universe. I believe that a great number of personalities are being transmitted everywhere and everywhen—there are souls flying past us thick and fast. I hold that it is only a technological lack that prevents these personalities from being locally received. Many technological advances are still needed before one might hope to carry out what I immodestly call a Gurdle Decryption of a personality wave. It will take perhaps another twenty years. Seven lifetimes for a moldie."

The hash oil was hitting Willy now and he was having trouble following Gurdle's line of conversation. It seemed almost as if the moldie might be insane. And what a stench he had. Like vile, overripe cheese smeared across rotten carrion.

"I base my reasoning on an information-theoretical argument which my fellows find quite compelling," continued Gurdle. "It involves an examination of the power spectrum of cosmic rays. But I see your mind is wandering, Mr. Taze. This festive occasion is not the time to go into details. Would you like to visit me in the Nest to discuss these things?"

"I'd love to visit the Nest," said Willy. "But not just yet. I still need to settle in."

"I'll ping you anon," said Gurdle. "Let me repeat that I am very delighted to have met you." Glassy-eyed Willy watched the reeking purple moldie slither away.

Now the annoyingly bossy Bei Ng was in Willy's face again. At Bei's side was a heavily made-up Cambodian woman—or man?—with long blonde hair. "Bei says you'll need help in finding a place to live, Willy," said the morph, laying a fluttering hand on the center of Willy's chest. "My name is Lo Tek. I do all sorts of things at ISDN. We can go out tomorrow and look at some properties. If you have a minute, I'd like to take down some personal information so we can narrow in on—"

"Thanks, but I'm planning to live in the Einstein-Luna Hotel for now," said Willy and twisted away. He got another drink from the bar—just water this time—and headed off across the terrace, joining a group of three interesting-looking types: a shirtless man with a hair-grafted mohawk that went all the way down his spine, a voluptuous woman with long curly dark hair, and a stocky man with a narrow goatee shaped like a vertical rectangle. They were passing around a smokeless pipe that resembled a small chemical refinery.

"Hi, guys," said Willy. "Nice view here."

"Willy Taze!" said the goateed man. Although he spoke with a heavy ironic drawl, he seemed quite sociable. "Welcome to the Pocked World. I'm Corey Rhizome and this is Darla Starr and Whitey Mydol."

"Whitey and Darla! I saw you on the vizzy this spring. When Stahn Mooney helped Darla escape from the boppers' Nest. After the chipmold killed the boppers."

"Yup," said Darla. Her breasts were large and bare, with gold chains hanging across them. "I was pregnant. And now I'm the mother of twins. And I can go back to getting as lifted. You want a hit, Willy? Give him the pipe, Whitey."

Willy inhaled a cautious toke from the complicated little pipe. It tasted like very strong pot with a snappy tingle to it. Very very strong pot with maybe some customized extra indoles. Willy exhaled the invisible particle-free vapor, and as the new drug layered itself over the hash liqueur, the sounds of the party clicked into a perfect tapestry decorated by the patterns of the voices of Willy's three new friends.

"Yaar, Corey grows this himself," Whitey said, taking back the pipe. "Mongo big plants. Corey and the beanstalk." Whitey's rangy, hard-looking features were bent into a loose grin that was a joy to behold. "Brah Corey! Tell Willy here about your idea for Silly Putters."

"Silly Putters?!?" demanded Darla.

"Yeah," said Corey. "It's the only possible name. I thought about it."

"Only possible name for what?" asked Willy.

"Evil imipolex toys," said Corey. "Imipolex is such a great new medium. It's like clay that's alive. The Silly Putters will be toys, but hopefully more adult and corrupted. Later I want to make a line of pets modeled on real and mythical animals. But first of all, to have some fun, I want to do some copies of classic three-dimensional logo creatures. The Dough-Boy. Barbie. Reddy Kilowatt. The Western Exterminator Man. The Fat Boy. Squawky Bird. Vector Man. Giggles the Bear. Tedeleh Torah. The Pig Chef. The Help Daemon. I'd like to give them each a DIM so they can run around and lay trips on people. Without having them be smart and autonomous like moldies. Would that work, Willy? Check out this study I've been hacking. It's what they're calling a *philtre*—a philtre's like a cephscope tape, but interactive."

Corey took an uvvy out of his pocket and put it on Willy's neck. Dozens of lively rubbery creatures appeared, overlaid on the crowded terrace party. Some of the figures, like Vector Man, were familiar if somewhat warped, while others were wholly unknown. Tedeleh Torah came jauntily hopping toward them on his two scroll legs and unfurled himself like a flasher, brazenly displaying sacred Hebrew writing that twisted and curled like snakes. Squawky Bird flapped awkwardly forward and began pecking up the writhing letters as if they were worms, Squawky drooling and slobbering while s/he did this. Vector Man's linked spheres came free and all bounced straight at Willy's face and, awww, they weren't spheres at all, they were prickly-ass 3D Mandelbrot sets. Willy flinched, but kept watching. This was majorly stuzzadelic art. Across the terrace, Barbie got down on her plastic knees and gave the Western Exterminator Man a deep-throat Barbie blow job, with the Exterminator Man all droppin' his hammer and goin' "Whoah!" The chromed Help Daemon walked up to Willy and presented him with a bill made out for a hundred trillion dollars. The Pig Chef ran a knife down his own stomach and began offering people fresh platters of steamy chitlins. Giggles the Bear grabbed the Pig Chef's knife and butchered the Dough-Boy up into cookies that Reddy Kilowatt zapped into golden crisps with his lightning-bolt fingers. It just kept going on and on and getting crazier. Finally Willy reached back and pulled off the uvvy.

"That's wild, Corey. It must have been a lot of work."

"Not for me. The images are all appropriated. And I used some commercial toonware to set their behaviors. I've been doing this kind of thing for years."

"Corey's jammed the Net so many times," said Whitey. "Doctoring vizzycasts, replacing commercials with his own weird Rhizome riffs. You know how there's no corporate vizzy news on the Moon no more because the announcers kept turning into like giant ants? That's thanks to Corey."

"Affirmo, I slew that dragon," said Corey. "But now I'm into a more personal kind of art. I'm drawn to the idea of making actual physical objects. Not just logos. Historical and allegorical figures as well. And figures exemplifying universal concepts.

Hummel figurines for the twenty-first century. The Traveling Salesman meets the Farmer's Daughter."

"But can she do *this*?" interrupted Darla, hefting her breasts and somehow getting her nipples to spray out many thin jets of milk.

"Aw, Darla," said Whitey, stepping forward so that the milk sprayed onto his bare chest. "You're slushed, babe."

"Vintage loonie grunge," said Corey. To Willy, it all seemed quite mad and joyous.

Willy went to visit Corey's quarters the next day: a five-room spread carved into stone fifty feet below the lunar surface. You got there by sliding down a pole in the center of a chute that led to a warren of hallways with doors to lots of people's apartments.

The first room of Corey's place—actually, the loonies called rooms *cubbies*—reminded Willy a bit of his old room back in his parents' basement. There was floatin' wavy junk everywhere: shelves and shelves of little plastic and rubber toys, windrows of hundred-year-old comic books and magazines, staticky old hollowcasters with arcane image loops, seventeen antique Lava lamps, a wall covered with weird drawings Corey had laminated onto plastic dinner plates, and even some ancient TVs showing videos. Another wall was covered with plastic water guns, forever more futuristic than any actual needler or O.J. ugly stick.

Beyond the front cubby and the kitchen lay Corey's sleeping cubby and his two studios, one traditional and one modern. The traditional studio was for painting and sculpture, with hand-painted canvases hanging on the walls and leaning in the corners. A lot of them were painted on black velvet and held glowing images of such historically iconic events as the vivisection of Cobb Anderson, the nuking of Akron, and the classic newsie image of Stahn and Darla emerging from the mouth of the Nest of the exterminated boppers—both of them in mirrored Happy Cloaks, Stahn lanky and jaunty, Darla weary and hugely pregnant.

Most of the sculptures were on the order of assemblages;

there was, for instance, a series of oversized snow domes holding scenes like Santa with his intestines spilling out, a Happy New Year's fetus wielding a curette, and a paradoxically sweet image of monarch butterflies circling a nude Alice in Wonderland. Though there was something odd about the butterflies' dreamy humanoid faces . . .

A lot of the art spilled over into the modern studio, which also held the usual kind of electronic equipment, all recently upgraded to DIMs—a cephscope deck, a holoscanner, uvvies, and stacks of S-cubes. Corey's kitchen was gray with ash and disorder. His sleeping cubby had an extra-high ceiling to accommodate his marvelous fifteen-foot-tall gene-tailored marijuana plants.

Willy was enchanted, and over the weeks to come he spent more and more time hanging out with Corey. He admired Corey's classic beatnik cool. And, best of all, Corey shared Willy's unwillingness to grow up.

Willy started helping Corey with his Silly Putters project, often working so late that he would end up sleeping over on a mattress in the front cubby. It came out that, thanks to the expenses of buying old magazines and DIM upgrades, Corey was having trouble paying the rent. Willy suggested that he move in as a roommate and share the bills. Corey said that sounded fine, as long as they didn't get on each other's nerves. Just to clear the air of any misunderstanding about his motives, Willy explained his sex problem. He was straight, but unable to contemplate physical sex with a real live woman. He was, in short, a jack-off.

"The stain of Onan," said Corey. "Didn't something terrible happen to that guy in the Bible? Hold on—" He nimbly accessed his uvvy, and the little device declaimed a Bible verse:

" And what Onan did was displeasing in the sight of the Lord, and He slew him also. Genesis 38:10."

Corey looked disappointed. "That's not very visual. Too bad. Well, at least you're not lusting after twelve-year-old girls, Willy."

"Is that what you're into?" asked Willy uncertainly.

"I do think about young girls from time to time. But I don't act out. As an artist, I'm able to transmute the dross of my perversion into the gold of deathless cultural artifacts. As a practical matter, I only date twenty-year-olds and over. When I *do* date. I like it better when women find out about me and just come over and hang out."

Willy helped Corey make some preliminary Silly Putters. Being true Art, the project was somewhat pointlessly difficult. The problem with trying to create these half-living objects was that you were working in the zone between the slavishly obedient DIM and the utterly ungovernable moldie. There was a constant danger of the thing's behavior entering the strange attractor of consciousness. Times like that, Willy had to stun the freshly self-aware being and manually damp down its nonlinearity parameters, feeling uneasy about performing what was, in some respects, an act of lobotomy if not murder.

One model that Willy got to work very nicely was a *femlin*, modeled on a groovy little Leroy Neiman sprite figure that Corey showed him in the joke pages of an old magazine called *Playboy*. The femlin wore nothing but high heels, black stockings, and opera gloves. She loved to cavort with Willy's penis. Willy was soon obsessively attached to her.

One dire day the femlin's mind chaotically tunneled into the basin of self-awareness, and she grokked how nowhere her life with Willy was. She managed to sneak out of Corey's apartment while the door's electric zapper was off, and ran down the warren's public hallway. A frightened neighbor lady stomped on the femlin, mistaking her for a rat. Willy happened upon this scene and totally lost it; he started screaming at the neighbor so hard that some passersby had to grab him and hold him down and dose him with a sedative, right there on the floor next to the smeared remains of his precious femlin.

Around then it came out that the neighbors were tired of Willy and Corey's nasty habits from A to Z, and there got to be such a bad vibe around the warren that it started to make sense to move. Willy and Corey were continuing to find each other fully compatible, so they decided to find a new place together. In fact, they decided to design and build their own luxury isopod estate in a crater outside of Einstein—build a spacious little biosphere with its own soil floor and crater-spanning dome.

The isopod would cost billions, but Willy had hundreds of millions, and hundreds of millions more were coming in faster than he could spend them. Corey got deeply involved in designing the estate—the mansion, the studios, the vegetable gardens, and the giant marijuana grove. The construction took several years.

By the time they moved in, Willy had fully nailed the problem of designing Silly Putters—it was basically just a matter of having them homeostatically damp their own nonlinearities whenever certain activation thresholds were exceeded. With this feedback in place, the little creatures would putter along at the low twilight border of awareness forever. Like animals. Corey got interested in mass-producing the Silly Putters instead of letting them be one-of-a-kind art objects, but Willy stayed out of this endeavor. Instead he turned his energies to improving the isopod, adding every manner of special feature to it: a God's-eye real-time map of Earth, a private swimming pool, a menagerie, a Turkish bath, a loop-the-loop bicycle course, and on and on. The years drifted by.

For a time, Whitey and Darla and their twin girls Joke and Yoke were regular visitors, but then Corey gave some Silly Putters to Joke and Yoke for a birthday, and the Putters did something that led to a furious breakdown of the friendship, at least on Darla's part. Willy never found out the details. Women continued to visit Corey, though never for very long. More years passed, and little Joke started turning up at the isopod to hang out with Corey by herself.

The DIMs and the Limpware Developer's Kit continued to be huge successes, but Willy didn't interest himself in them anymore. It was like something in him had snapped during that last frantic development push in Cocoa. He had no special desire to do anything. He became something of a hermit, meditating and savoring his solitude. He could pass days at a time sitting in the little forest of giant marijuana plants, staring up past the plants through the dome at the stars.

Finally one day in the summer of 2052—so many years gone!—something new got Willy's attention.

It started with a grinding sound beneath the soil, over in the corner of the grove where the dome met the ground. A moonquake? A rupture in the plastic beneath the soil floor? But then the ground heaved upward as if from a giant mole, and a shiny blob of purple imipolex pushed up into the isopod air. The blob formed a face and spoke.

"Willy Taze! You still haven't visited the Nest! We need you now. With your help, the first Gurdle Decryption may happen soon."

"You're . . . you're Gurdle?"

The moldie wormed himself farther out of the hole, though carefully leaving his tail in the hole to prevent the isopod's air from rushing out. He was purple with silvery highlights. "I'm Gurdle-7! Gurdle's great-great-great-great-grandson. It's been twenty-one years, Willy! And now it's time to leave your enchanted garden. Come on and slip inside of me. I'll be a bubbletopper to carry you to the Nest. And inside the Nest, we have prepared a pink-house for you every bit as pleasant as this isopod."

"Do we have to crawl back through that hole?" said Willy dubiously. "I'll bump myself on the rocks."

"Don't worry, I'll make my skin hard around you. And I'll patch the hole behind me. Come, Willy. Arise! The Gurdle Decryption is of cosmic importance. And only you can help us accomplish the final steps."

CHAPTER SEVEN

STAHN

=== ■ ===

October 31, 2053

Stahn stepped out of his fine Victorian mansion on Masonic Avenue above Haight Street in San Francisco. It was early evening on Halloween, 2053. Walking by were lively groups of people on their way to the Castro Street Halloween party, a traditional event now back in operation after a brief hiatus during the anxious years surrounding the coming of the Second Millennium. AIDS was gone, drugs were legal, and San Francisco was more fun than ever.

Stahn felt very strung out. He'd gotten lifted on camote after his final conversation with Tre Dietz late last night. In the afternoon, Tre had uvvied up to announce that some kind of software agent named Jenny had shown him a secret tape of Sri Ramanujan explaining a new piece of mathematics called the Tessellation Equation. Jenny had talked to Stahn too. She looked like a lanky teenage farm girl. It seemed she lived inside a Heritagist computer, but that she had very close connections to the loonie moldies. Then, in the evening, Tre had called again—very distraught—to talk about ransoming his wife Terri from the moldies. Stahn made some calls to the Moon to try and help out with that, and told Tre, and had then started getting loaded as he normally did in the evening. But then, a few hours later, Tre uvvied again, fantastically excited about some new vision about how to use the Tessellation Equation to make Perplexing Poultry imipolex based on tilings of every finite dimension. Disquietingly, this software agent Jenny-thing was there on the link with Tre, listening in. She wouldn't say why she was so interested in this information. But Tre didn't care. His obsession was to get Stahn to understand about Perplexing Poultry in Hilbert space and about how Ramanujan's Tessellation Equation could now be used to make imipolex-5, imipolex-6, imipolex-N!

To help himself understand the strange ideas he was hearing, Stahn drunkenly chewed up a couple of nuggets of camote while Tre was talking. It wasn't the first time he'd tried the drug, but this time it turned out to be a big mistake, an unbearably strange lift, a psychotic panic trip to deep and personal revelations about his multitudinous personality flaws. Stahn went to bed and tried to sleep, but instead spent ten hellish hours in Hilbert space with Tre's multidimensional Poultry pecking and clucking in the mysterious thickets of his chaotically disturbed consciousness. It was a relief to see dawn come and to get up and try and start a new day.

In the afternoon, Stahn finally managed to get some sleep, but then, around dusk, Wendy woke him.

"Get up, sleepyhead. We're going to the Halloween parade, remember? What the heck did you do to yourself last night, anyway? I came downstairs and tried to talk to you, but you were completely gaga." She had wide hips, pert lips, a soft chin, and blonde hair. Her voice was soothingly normal.

"I have to get up?"

"You have to get up. Here." She handed him a big mug of tea with milk and sugar. "We're walking to the Castro and meeting Saint and Babs. Our children? A family outing? Helloooo!"

"Okay, Wendy, don't overdo it. I'm here. Thanks for the tea. I got lifted on camote after talking to Tre Dietz last night. I thought it might make me smart like him. What a burn. I'll tell you about it later."

So Stahn took a shower and put on black clothes and painted his hands and face black. He dusted himself with silver sparkles and went to stand on his front steps while waiting for Wendy to finish getting dressed. His head hurt very deeply; he could feel the pain deep inside his brain from the healed wounds where he'd gotten a tank-grown preprogrammed flesh-and-blood right hemisphere to replace the Happy Cloak that had replaced the robot rat that had replaced his original right brain—his skull was a xoxxin' roach motel and, thanks to Tre, he'd been to Hilbert space and was no doubt subject to snap back there anytime—

"Wassup, Sen-Senator Stahn!" shrieked a lifted young Cicciolina from a passing gaggle of morphs. A bride and a Betty Page were in the group as well.

"Out for a night on the town?" asked the tall bride in a deep honking voice. "Does Wendy know?"

The Betty Page snorted, chortled, and bent over, rucking up a tight skirt to expose a reasonable facsimile of a woman's naked ass, complete with musky labia down below. "Take a taste of Betty, Senator Moo! Relish the fine fine superfine succulence of a bad-girl butt too good for tacos!"

The kid was trying to needle Stahn about wendy meat, but Stahn gave a politician's genial dismissive wave, expecting the morphs to move on. Most people didn't understand about the wendy meat ads; the fact that they showed Wendy with her Happy Cloak was intended to be a positive force for human-moldie friendship.

"Shut your rude tuh-twat, Betty," stuttered Cicciolina. "Yo-yo-yo, brah Stahn, wanna puh-peg of gabba? It's straight out of the resolver; I harvested the kuh-kuh-crystals today."

"Affirmo everplace," said Stahn on a sudden impulse. "I can relate. Gabba gives me the yipes, you wave, but I already got the yipes on account of what I did last night, and if I can get some gabba yipes happening, why, then I'll feel normal; it'll be a lift instead of a drag. So come on over here, you big deeve."

The Cicciolina drew a squeezie out of his decolletage and strutted over to Stahn, holding the little bulb up high like a magical lantern. "Tuh-toot the snoot, Senataroot!"

Stahn took the squeezie and pulsed a dose for each nostril. *Ftooom!* Fireworks of pleasure exploded behind his eyes, a chrysanthemum bloom of evil joy, a flower with a ring of screamers around the outer edge, screamers that floated to Earth and took the form of darting two-legged yipes.

"*Ftoom* yipes," jabbered Stahn. "*Ftoom ftoom fuh-fuh-ftoom* yipes."

"Gabba hey," said the Cicciolina. "The fringe still luh-loves you, Senator."

"Long may it wuh-wave," said Stahn.

The three morphs moved on, camping and laughing. Stahn looked up at his house, its windows mellow yellow with electric light. The yipes felt good. He was lucky to have a good house in the city. He was lucky to be alive. He was lucky to have a family. How sad it would be if all of this should end.

With a sudden flurry of footsteps, Wendy swept out of the house and down the steps. "Hi, Stahn! I'm ready!" She was dressed like a witch, with a high-heeled boots, long dress, large Happy Cloak, and rakish pointed hat—all a bright, matching red. The 'Cloak was a beloved moldie that Wendy continually wore to make up for the unparalleled developmental deficiencies caused by the fact that her body was a tank-grown clone.

"You look guh-great, Wendy. You're a red witch."

"You sound funny, Stahn," said Wendy suspiciously. "Don't tell me you took even more drugs!"

"Nuh-nuh-nothing really. Some deeves gave me a pulse of guh-gabba. I'm trying to feel normal, you understand. We're wuh-walking to the Castro, right?"

"Yes. Did you wake up a dragonfly?"

"I fuh-forgot. I don't feel like wearing my uvvy, Wendy, not after last night. Luh-like I was telling you, Tre Dietz uvvied me all this wuh-weird shit and and—"

"Oh, spare me the wasted slobbering. I'll get the dragonfly."

Wendy used her Happy Cloak to uvvy a message, and right away a little dragonfly telerobot flew down from its perch in the eaves of their house. The streetlights made gleaming Lissajous patterns on the dragonfly's shiny, rapidly beating wings. "You stay about a block ahead of us and watch the foot traffic," Wendy told it, speaking out loud. "We're walking over the hill to Market and Castro. And keep scanning faces for Saint and Babs. We're expecting you to find them." The dragonfly whirred away.

"Really, Stahn," continued Wendy as they walked up Masonic together. "You're starting to worry me. A man your age. Two more years and you'll be sixty!" Wendy was effectively eleven years younger than Stahn, and she worked hard to keep Stahn from turning senile. "What is it that Tre showed you anyway?"

"Perplexing Puh-Poultry N-dee," said Stahn, clamping his hands tightly together in an effort to hold back the gabba stutter. "Some kind of freelance software agent called Jenny told him this thing called Ramanujan's Tuh-Tessellation Equation, and right away he found a new kind of higher-dimensional quasi-crystal design. The new Poultry puh-peck and peck and peck. He wants me to suh-sell the new idea before Jenny can. And we were also talking about how to ruh-ransom his wife."

They paused on the saddle of the Buena Vista hill between the Haight and the Castro, catching their breath and looking at the view. "Oh, it's beautiful out tonight, isn't it, Stahn?"

"Yeah. I'm glad you got me to go outside." He took a deep shaky breath, and the gabba shuddering left the hinges of his jaws. The first part of a gabba lift was always the hardest. "Reality is such a gas." His words in his ears sounded smooth, pneumatic, resonant.

"What was that about ransoming Tre Dietz's wife?"

"The loonie moldies kidnapped her by accident yesterday. She's on her way to the Moon. I'm supposed to pay a big ransom and get Whitey Mydol and Darla Starr to pick her up. I already transferred the credit to Whitey's account."

"Whitey and Darla! But why should you have to pay for stupid Tre Dietz's wife?"

"He's made me lot of money, and this new thing'll make a lot more. His poor wife is up there in the sky inside a moldie on the way to the Moon."

"It's not such a bad flight," said Wendy. "It was fun when you and me flew from the Moon to the Earth together in 2031. It might be good for you to do it again."

"Forget it, Wendy." Stahn started walking again. "Which way are we supposed to go?"

"Judging from what the dragonfly's showing me, we should walk down Ord Court to States Street to Castro," said Wendy, cocking her head. "That's the least crowded way." As they linked arms and headed downhill, she turned her attention back to Stahn. "So you saw N-dimensional Perplexing Poultry, huh? Have you ever heard the theory that mathematics keeps people young? I think it's good for you to be thinking about these things. Instead of about power and money. And all your hangovers."

"I wish you wouldn't obsess about age all the time, Wendy. You know damn well that with DIM parts and tank-grown organs, anyone with our kind of money can live to a hundred and twenty."

"Yes," said Wendy. "All thanks to the wonderful compatibility of me. But because Wendy Meat and W. M. Biologicals do, in fact, grow clones of me, I can do something better than get patched up. I can start over in a blank twenty-five-year-old wendy. My 'Cloak could transfer all the information. I've been thinking about it a lot."

"Oh, don't, Wendy. What would happen to this body?" Stahn snaked his arm under Wendy's Happy Cloak and around her waist to hug her. "This body I've loved so long? Would you cut it up and sell off the meat and the organs?"

"I'm serious about this, Stahn, so don't try and make it hard for me. But let's not talk about it now. You're in no condition." She twisted away from Stahn's grip and brightened her voice. "Look, we're almost there. And—yes!—the dragonfly just spotted the kids."

Wendy stopped walking for a second, the better to absorb the images the dragonfly was uvvying to her, and as she viewed them she began to laugh. "Saint is—he's wearing a silvered coat and he has tinfoil on his head. And Babs is—oh, Babs—" She laughed harder. "I can hardly describe this, Stahn. She's got a little tray around her waist with things on it and a terrible yellow shirt; I have no idea what she's supposed to be. Let's hurry and meet them."

"Do you really want those poor children to see their mother's body butchered?" demanded Stahn. "It would be traumatic. And then, once you were twenty-five, you'd get young guys and you wouldn't want me! That's what I get for being faithful to you all these years?"

"I said let's drop it. You get so dramatic when you're lifted! You know damn well that I'm a Happy Cloak, not a human body. This body—this *wendy*—it's a mindless piece of meat that I use to walk around in and to make love to you, Stahn. You never got excited when I replaced my imipolex every three years. If I change my flesher body, everything will be just the same. I'm a moldie, I'm your wife, and I'll always love you. So there."

Wendy pushed into the crowd, and Stahn followed. There were a lot of brides here tonight; that was just about the number-one favorite costume. Other faves were strippers, debutantes, princesses, and slaves. A few people recognized Stahn or Wendy, but most mistook them for het looky-look tourists. "Hello, Cleveland," sneered a skinny large-breasted morph with a beard. A disco dandy snipped, "When you drive back to the 'burbs, remember that *my* car is the Mercedes and *yours* is the BMW." "I didn't use a car," said Wendy pityingly, "I used my broom!" Though Stahn hadn't noticed it before, Wendy was indeed holding a broom—oh yeah, it was a piece of her 'Cloak that she'd temporarily pinched off and reshaped.

Wendy pointed Stahn in the direction where the dragonfly had shown her the kids. "Press on, dear old fool." Stahn fought past a man with a cardboard toilet around his head and his face sticking out of the bowl and a plastic dick over his nose, past a woman with a leash leading a blindfolded nude ungenitaled Barbie, past a morph with a head built up with phonybone to the shape of a cube, past people with wings and huge flexing cocks— the crowd pressed and swirled like the ripping currents of a particularly nasty ocean break—

"Hey, Da, Ma!" called Babs.

"Yaar!" whooped Saint.

Babs and Saint were in a doorway near the Castro Theater. Saint was a tall cheerful youth who habitually darkened his appearance by means of odd hair, a ratty beard, silvery stunglasses, and heavy blue suede boots. For tonight, he'd covered his head with vintage aluminum foil crudely wadded into the shape of a helmet and he wore a reflective metallic fireman's coat that went down to his knees.

Babs had a big firm cheeks that grew pink when she was excited, like now. As part of her costume, she wore a yellow polyester shirt with a tag saying:

```
HI I'M LYNNE       HAPPY DOLLAR
```

She held a stick bearing something like a square lantern with the numeral "3" on each of its four sides, and around her waist was a cardboard tray with packages glued to it—cereal boxes and udon and pho noodles and tampons and panty shields and disposable ceramic forks. Her hair was pulled tight into a lank little ponytail that was barrette-clamped to point upward; and to complete the groovy hairdo, she wore a wiiiiiide bandeau.

"Can you tell what I am?" chirped Babs cozily. Wendy couldn't guess, but Stahn recognized it from his childhood.

"You're a clerk in an old-time supermarket!"

"Ye oldie checker gal," said Babs, laughing gaily.

"What about me?" asked Saint.

"A robot?" guessed Wendy.

"Sort of," said Saint. " '*I am Iron Man.*' I've got my stunglasses broadcasting realtime live on the Show, you wave, and I'm using this classic twentieth-century metal song for the background. Listen." He switched his uvvy to speaker mode and karaoked some crude guitar licks. "*Danh-danh deh-denh-deh. Dadadada-danh-danh dah-dah-dah.*"

Wendy had set their dragonfly to filming the little family outing; it hovered a few feet over their heads like a hummingbird, its wings whispering and its single bright bead-eye lens staring at the Mooneys. Wendy and Saint could see the pictures through their uvvies.

Saint sang *Iron Man* some more, raising his hand toward the dragonfly in a spread-fingered salute; Wendy could see that he was goofing on the self-images he was realtime mixing into the ceaseless global interactive multiuser stunglasses Show. Saint saw Wendy seeing him, and he shifted fabulations.

"Ma is Wendy the red witch," smiled Saint. "Who are you, Da?"

"I'm the night sky," said Stahn, all painted black and spangled with sparkles. "As seen by a cosmic ray from the galactic equator. How you kids floatin'?"

"We're having a good time," said Saint. "I like how much there is to see. I'm pulling in some viewers. I'm not gonna have to pay any Web charges for weeks."

"People keep trying to take stuff off my counter," said Babs. "And then they're surprised when it's glued on. You look beautiful, Ma."

"Thanks, Babs," said Wendy. "But don't you think I'd look better with a new age-twenty-five body?"

"Oh, come on, Wendy," said Stahn.

"Let her talk, Da," said Babs. "She's already told me all about it and it's no prob."

"I see a group that looks funny," said Saint, pointing. "Let's head that way."

They pushed down the street toward a group of nude morphs, each painted a different primary color and each equipped with big morph muscles. A few of them had tails. They were tossing each other about like acrobats—with much lewd miming.

The Mooneys walked along with the happy, laughing crowd watching the acrobats for a while, then drifted into the less crowded blocks deeper into the Mission. "I still haven't had supper," said Wendy presently. "Is anyone else hungry?"

"I am," said Saint. "Where should we go?"

"I know a wavy Spanish place near here," said Babs. "The Catalanic."

"Let's do it," said Stahn.

As they walked toward the restaurant, Babs began tearing items off her counter and setting them down on doorsteps. "For the homeless," she explained. "Anyhoo, I'm tired of wearing all this." She took the cardboard counter from around her waist and skimmed it toward Saint as hard as she could. He caught it, ran with it, flipped it onto the sidewalk, and managed to slide about twelve feet before stumbling off, pinwheeling his arms and yelling, "*Aaawk!* Happy Dollar! *Aaawk!* Happy Dollar."

The outside of the Catalanic was a warmly lit storefront painted red-and-yellow. Inside, it was bustling and cream-colored, with a few nice things on the walls: an old Spanish clock, two nanoprecise copies of Salvador Dali oils (*Persistence of Memory* and *Dali at the Age of Six Lifting the Skin of the Water to Observe a Dog Sleeping in the Shadow of the Sea*), and two nanocopied Joan Miró paintings of hairy bright lop-lop creatures (*Dutch Interior I* and *Dutch Interior II*). There were lots of people sitting at tables covered with tapas dishes and—"Yes, of course, Senator Mooney"—there was a table for four. Wendy's dragonfly telerobot perched on a cornice across the street to wait.

The Mooneys sat down happily and fired off an order for Spanish champagne and plates of potatoes, shrimp, spinach, pork balls, squash, chicken, mussels, endives, and more potatoes. The bubbly and the first dishes began arriving.

"See that moldie over there with the bohos?" said Babs, waving across the room. "She's a friend of mine. She's called Sally.

She's so funny. One day when I was here, Sally and I fabbed about Dali for a long time."

Sally was sitting on a chair with a group of five lively young black-dressed artists. Sally had been shaped like a colorful Picasso woman, but now, seeing Babs, she suddenly let her body slump into the shape of a melting jellyfish with wrinkles that sketched a flaccid human face.

"Look," laughed Babs. "She's imitating the jellyfish in *Persistence of Memory*. Hey, Sally! Do a soft watch!"

While her arty friends watched admiringly, Sally formed herself into a large smoothly bulging disk that bent in the middle to rest comfortably in her chair. She made her skin shiny—gold in back and glassy in front with a huge watch dial with warping hands. Her soft richly computing body drooped off the edges of her chair like a fried egg. Salvador Dali had predicted the moldies. It was perfect.

But Stahn was too benumbed to appreciate Sally's visual pun. "I'm kind of surprised they let her in here," he said thoughtlessly. "What with the stink."

"Do *I* stink in restaurants?" demanded Wendy. "Some of us are civilized enough to know when to close our pores. You should talk, Stahn, the way you've been farting recently."

Saint cackled to hear this. "Da stinks. Da's a moldie."

Stahn quietly poured himself another glass of champagne.

"How did you like the parade, old man?" asked Babs.

"I must say, it made me feel straight. That's not a way I like to feel, mostly."

"Men are so worried about being macho," said Wendy.

"Will everyone stop picking on me?" snapped Stahn.

"We're not picking on you," said Saint, reaching over to give Stahn a caress followed by a sly poke.

"Da is a wreck," said Wendy. "He stayed up most of last night."

"What did you do, Da?" asked Saint.

"Never mind." Stahn didn't want to tell his kids about the camote. He was ashamed to be such an eternal example of out-of-control drug-taking; in recent years he'd backslid terribly. "It has to do with this new way to control moldies."

"Are you scheming to control *me*?" Wendy wondered suddenly. "Me, in the sense of Wendy's Happy Cloak?"

"No," said Stahn. "I wouldn't dream of it. Though it might not hurt for you to try seeing how a leech-DIM feels sometime. They say for a moldie it's like being lifted. Then you'd understand. Instead of always being such a straight goody-goody."

"I've been busy making a worm farm," said Babs, changing the subject. "Did I tell you? It's so floatin'. 'Place moistened humus between two glass sheets and add one pint red worms.' Voilà!"

"You're doing this for fun?" asked Stahn. "Or is it art?"

"If you mean, 'Can I sell worm farms?'—waaal, old-timer, I just dunno. So maybe it's fun. But, wave, if I were to put DIM worms in with the real ones, why then it'd be ye newie Smart Art and maybe I *could* sell some. But making the boxes is so damn hard. You wanna make me some worm farm boxes, Saintey? *Eeeeeew!* What are those gross things crawling on your head?"

"Lice," said Saint. He'd taken off his foil helmet and shrugged his coat onto the back of his chair. His hair looked like upholstery on cheap furniture—it was buzz-cut, half-bleached to a punky orange, and there was a paisley filigree cut into it, revealing curving lines of scalp that seemed to have small translucent insects crawling along them.

"You have *lice*, Saint?" exclaimed Wendy. "How filthy! We have to get you disinfected! Oh! And we've all been hugging you!"

"I think he's teasing you, Wendy," said Stahn, peering closer at the tiny creatures on his son's scalp. "Those are micro-DIMs. I know they've been used for barbering, but I've never heard of them doing paisley before. Did you program that yourself, Saint?"

"My friend Juanne taught the lice," said Saint. "But I found the DIM beads. I've been finding some really floatin' ware in this building I'm maintenance-managing, Da."

"This is your new janitor job?" said Stahn.

Saint was suddenly very angry. "Don't you always say that, you stupid old man. A maintenance manager is not a janitor. I like to fix things. I'm good at it. And for you to always act like it's—"

Stahn winced at the intensity of his son's reaction. "I'm sorry, I didn't mean it," he said quickly. "I'm senile. When I was your age, I was Sta-Hi the taxi driver, so who am I to talk? Maintenance is wavy. Retrofitting. Tinkering. It's almost like engineering."

"Saint doesn't want to go to engineering school, Da," put in Babs. "Get over it. His friends already look up to him like a teacher."

"They do?" asked Stahn.

"Yes," said Saint. "I like to think about the meaning of things. And what to do with life. Every day should be happy. My friends listen to me."

"Well, hell," said Stahn. "Then maybe you can be a senator." He put up his hands cringingly. "Just kidding!"

The waitress arrived with a pitcher of sangria, more potatoes, and the grilled prawns. Stahn passed Saint the prawns and poured out glasses of the sangria.

"What's the building you're doing maintenance for?" Wendy asked Saint.

"Meta West Link," said Saint. "They own the satellites and dishes for sending uvvy signals to the Moon."

"Wholly owned by ISDN since 2020," put in Stahn. "I can certainly believe that Meta West would have some interesting things in their basement."

"Give me some DIM lice, Saintey?" pleaded Babs. "I'll make a Smart Art flea circus! I want lice right now!" She crooked one arm around her brother's neck and began picking at his head. "I'm the lice doctor!" When Babs had been younger, she'd enjoyed taking ticks off the family dog and announcing that she was the "tick doctor."

"Don't be so disgusting, you two," said Wendy severely. "You're in a restaurant. Stop it right now."

The kids broke apart with a flurry of screeches and pokes, and then both of them sat there calmly with their hands folded.

"It's Da's fault," said Saint.

"Da did it," added Babs.

"Da's bad," said Saint.

"Da's lifted and drunk," said Babs.

"Da has a drug problem," said Saint.

Stahn got the waitress and ordered himself a brandy and an espresso. "Anyone else for coffee or a drink? Anything? Dessert, kids?"

Saint and Babs ordered cake, but Wendy didn't want anything. She said she thought it was about time they got going.

"Mind if I join you?" said Sally the moldie, suddenly appearing at the end of the table. Her body was a cubist dream of triangles and bright colors.

"Sally, ole pal!" said Babs, hilarious on her four drinks. "Sit down." Sally pulled up a chair and Babs introduced her. "This is my brah and my rents—Saint, Stahn, and Wendy. This is Sally, guys."

"I've been wanting to meet Wendy," said Sally. "We moldies all wonder about her. How do you do it? Emulate a human wife and mother, I mean. It's a pretty bizarre thing to do."

"I've been doing it so long it feels normal," said Wendy. "Though I am getting a bit tired of this particular human body."

Sally produced a screw-top jar from the folds of her flesh and took off the top. "I like to have a little rub of this when I'm around people getting high," she said, using a green-striped finger to crook out a glob of ointment. She rubbed the goo into her chest and handed the jar to Wendy. "Try some, Wendy. It's betty. Fine, fine betty."

"We still have a long trek home," objected Stahn. He counted on Wendy being the sober one.

"Just chill sometime," said Wendy, scooping up two fingers of betty and smoothing it onto her 'Cloak self.

By the time Sally could put the jar away, she and Wendy were completely lifted. "Wave this new take on the soft watch," said Sally, turning beige. In seconds she was shaped like an old-time computer box with a monitor on it—the box melting and drooling off the edge of her chair to make a puddle on the floor, and the monitor was displaying—the face of that Jenny-thing who'd been on-line with Tre Dietz last night?

At the same time, Wendy was tweaking quite savagely. Her Happy Cloak stopped being a demure red Wendy the Witch cape and bunched up around her neck in a big convoluted green dinosaur ruffle. "I've been a good wife and mother all these years, but I don't want to get any older. I want a full upgrade! You need to understand this meat body isn't me," she raved. "Watch!" The ruff on her neck bucked up, pulling a frightening tangle of rootlike connectors out of her flesh and into the air. Wendy's face went slack and her head pitched forward to lie on her crossed arms on the table. Wendy's 'Cloak gestured nastily with its tendrils, then wormed them back into Wendy's neck. Wendy straightened up, a triumphant gleam in her eyes. "See?"

"We're outta here," said Stahn, getting to his feet and throwing down money for the check. "You shouldn't have given her that damn shit, Sally."

"Bye, Sally," said Wendy. She winked and pointed a finger upward. "Thanks for the lift and the lift."

"Have a good trip," said Sally.

Stahn tried to take Wendy's arm to steady her, but she twisted away from him with frightening vigor. She pushed out to the street, followed by her family.

"I wish I hadn't seen that," said Babs quietly. "Is Ma all right?"

"We just need to get home and kick," said Stahn. "I wonder if there's any chance of a rickshaw or a streetcar. Oh good, it looks like Wendy's calling one." Wendy was gesturing broadly, and the dragonfly hopped off its perch and circled as if searching for a ride.

"It'll be here soon," said Wendy, smiling crookedly. "And, kids, I'm sorry about freaking in the restaurant, but it's for true. I'm about to shed."

She didn't elaborate, and nobody knew what to say, so for a half minute the four of them just stood there among the people and the moldies passing by. A streetcar ground past, going the wrong way. A sudden breeze swept up from the Bay, startlingly strong and chilly. Stahn turned his back against it, wishing he'd worn a thicker coat. Wendy and the kids were facing him, and for a moment he thought the kids were teasing when they began to scream.

"Here's our ride, Stahn!" whooped Wendy.

The wet frigid air whirled like a tornado, and a huge blue pterodactyl shape swooped down toward them. Its wingspan was so large that it could barely fit in between the buildings. It would have to break through the streetcar wires if it wanted to reach them; they might have time to escape!

"Run!" yelled Stahn. "Back in the restaurant!"

But before he could move, Wendy's Happy Cloak lifted off and flapped toward Stahn like a pair of ragged bat wings. Stahn was too slowed by drink and too distracted by the sight of Wendy's body falling to the ground to stop the 'Cloak from wrapping itself around him. Quickly the 'Cloak sank its tendrils into Stahn's neck and froze him in place. Stahn stood there staring at his children trying to tend their mother's imbecilic limp body—and then the great pterodactyl pecked down in between the wires, pecked up Stahn and swallowed him and Wendy's Happy Cloak whole.

Stahn heard the muffled sound of the pterodactyl's screeching caw of triumph, and he felt himself borne up and away. All was dark and airless, but then the Wendy 'Cloak began feeding Stahn air and information.

"Don't be scared, dear Stahn," said Wendy's voice. "I'll take care of you. Flapper is going to help us fly to the Moon. It'll be

a good change of pace for you. And the loonie moldies are eager
for you to visit. And I'm going to the Nest to get a new wendy
from the pink-tanks. You'll be wearing me until then."

"The Moon," said Stahn numbly. "You're kidding. Who's
Flapper?"

"She's like a customs official for the loonie moldies; she keeps
an eye on what goes from Earth and Moon. Since the loonie
moldies want you to visit, Sally had the idea of asking Flapper
to come down and peck like a pterodactyl."

"Wait a minute. Can you still see through the dragonfly? How
are the children? Show them to me."

The Wendy 'Cloak fed Stahn the uvvy image of Saint squatting by his mother's body, with desperate Babs out in the street
trying to flag down a rickshaw. The vacated wendy just lay there
twitching.

"Those poor children," said Stahn, his eyes filling with tears.
"Those poor, poor children."

"Tsk," said the 'Cloak. "It *is* sad. But I hope they don't waste
a lot of money and emotion on that brainless worn-out old body.
I should have killed it before I left." She cut off the dragonfly
video feed and all was black again.

"Wendy, what's happened to your feelings? Does it even make
sense to call you Wendy anymore?"

"Sure, I'm Wendy. Yeah, I guess I am being a little cold, huh?
Not too characteristic of my usual persona." The 'Cloak giggled.
"I guess it's the betty makes me act this way. Now you can see
how it feels, Stahn. You're always so heartless to me when you're
lifted."

"If you're going to nag me like a wife while I'm wrapped up
inside you, I'm going to go crazy. I'd rather die! We're high
above Earth by now, right? Why don't you and this damned
Flapper push me out and let me drop! Do it! I'd be glad to die,
Wendy, glad to get the endless misery over with!"

"You just feel that way because you're strung out on drugs,
you fool."

"I'm coming down again, baby! All I do is get high and come

down; nobody likes me anymore; I'm no good to anyone; I might as well be dead; let me fuckin' drop and die."

Flapper's soprano voice interrupted in operatic song, "I wonder if he really means it? Look at this, Stahn Mooney!" There was a doughy rubbing against Stahn's body from head to toe, a lumpy peristalsis as if he were feces being squeezed down a long rectum. The pressure on the top of his head was great. Clever small folds in the plastic took off Stahn's clothes and spirited them away.

"Yeah, pop us halfway out, Flapper," laughed Wendy. "Let Stahn see!"

Flapper sphinctered open a hole and pushed out Stahn's upper body. She clamped lightly down on the top of Stahn's pelvis to keep the wind from ripping him away.

So here was Stahn hanging out of a giant moldie pterodactyl's ass, staring down at the great dark world below. The air beat at him, but he felt it only thinly, for now the Wendy 'Cloak was stretched over him like a bubbletopper spacesuit, and the 'Cloak's smart imipolex was twitching and shuddering to cancel out the resonant vibrations.

Far off to the west, a crescent of the Earth was still in sunshine; it was a blazing arc of hot blue ocean. But most of the planet was a silvery monochrome, bathed by the light of the Moon. The high clouds beneath Stahn were stippled in a regular pattern like fish scales, a mackerel sky. Off to the east, the clouds transmuted into flowing mares' tails, with each tail shaped the same. The world was beautiful.

"I don't want to die after all," volunteered Stahn. The city of San Francisco was a speck of brightness far far below. "How high are we?"

"Fifty miles and rising fast. Flapper's going to squirt you and me toward the Moon like a torpedo when she gets to sixty miles! I don't have enough oomph to fly us all the way from the Earth to the Moon, see, but with Flapper launching us we can make it. We'll do the next two hundred thousand miles on our own!"

As his eyes adjusted, Stahn could make out more and more

detail in the moonlit clouds below. Once again he marveled at the world's fractal beauty, at its fondly loved structures recurring across every size scale—in the clouds, the land, the sea—ah, the great living skin of sacred Gaia.

"This is wavy," said Stahn presently. "Even though I'm not lifted anymore. Usually when I'm not lifted, everything is slow and boring and kludgy."

"That's another reason this trip is important," said Wendy. "It'll take us a week to get the Moon, enough time for you to dry out for the first time in years. It'll be like a honeymoon."

"Except you don't have a human body," said Stahn. "A body's considered kind of important on a honeymoon."

"I can give you hand jobs, Stahn. I can stick fingers up your butt. You'll like it. You'll see."

As they flew higher and higher, the pterodactyl's wings grew larger and thinner, till finally she looked like a giant stingray.

"I'm nearly ready to launch you!" trilled the great ray's voice. "Let me draw you back in so I can push you harder. Brace Stahn tight, Wendy."

"Okay, Flapper," said Wendy.

Flapper puckered her flesh and drew Stahn and Wendy up into herself. Stahn was starting to feel panicky. "Even if she launches us, how are you going to get the energy to decelerate us into lunar orbit, Wendy? You're not very big. I doubt if you weigh more than fifteen pounds. When you and me flew down to Earth on Spore Day in 2031, our Happy Cloaks were beefed up to ten times that much. Are you sure you have enough stored-up energy to keep me warm while we're floating though space?"

"Flapper gets lots of energy from the Sun up here, and she stores it as quantum dots. Don't forget, a mole of quantum dots is no bigger than a hundred nanograms. And Flapper's going to give me a whole gram! We'll have a full tank of gas, big guy."

"Yes, Wendy, here come your quantum dots," sang Flapper. "I'm spraying them into your flesh. And now I'm nearly ready to birth you!"

By craning his head back, Stahn could see down the tunnel

of flesh that led from inside Flapper to the outside. The tube was more vagina than rectum now, and Stahn was a baby instead of a turd.

"Straighten out your neck, Stahn," said Wendy, her voice vibrant with energy. "It's time for me to go rigid." She squeezed very tightly around Stahn and made the imipolex of her flesh as stiff as steel.

Flapper started a great loop-the-loop to bring her underside uppermost. As she rose to the top of the loop, she bunched her body into a huge mass of muscle and *pushed.*

Stahn and Wendy shot out from Flapper with incredible speed; the strength of the g-forces was such that Stahn fainted dead away.

When he came to, he was staring out into black starry space. Wendy had lost her rigidity, and Stahn could look down past his feet at the great planet Earth falling away or crane his head back and look up toward the disk of the Moon. The Sun was hidden behind the Earth for now.

To maintain Stahn's temperature, Wendy had silvered her surface inside and out; except for the half-silvered patch over Stahn's eyes. Stahn spent some time moving his arms and legs and marveling at the multiple reflections of himself, the Earth and the Moon. How beautiful it was. But how lonely. He was all by himself, hurtling farther and farther away from home, with nothing but a moldie 'Cloak for company. Tumbling through the dark, forever alone.

"This is like a bad dream," said Stahn.

"I like it," said Wendy. "Are you warm enough?"

"I'm fine." The silvered imipolex kept Stahn comfortable, and the air in his nose was fresh and cool.

"Should I worry about radiation?" asked Stahn. "About cosmic rays?"

"Let's put it this way: your odds of cancer are going to be a little higher after this trip. And cosmic rays can have an effect on moldies too. But we'll just have to grin and bear it and hope for the best, I suppose."

"Can you feel how hard I'm grinning?" said Stahn. "Not. This is really selfish of you, Wendy."

"It'll do you good, Stahn. You need the detox."

Stahn thought longingly of his pot at home and his liquor cabinet and his squeezies of snap and gabba. He loved all drugs except merge. He'd been through a bad experience with merge—the time that Darla had overdosed him on merge back on the Moon. By the time *that* bummer was fully over, Stahn had lost the entire right half of his brain. What a burn.

"Uvvy the kids, can you do that? And then we should uvvy Whitey Mydol on the Moon. He should know that we're coming. I guess we'll be landing on the Moon the day after Blaster and Terri, right? A week from now?"

"Right. We're traveling along a seven-day Earth-to-Moon spacetime geodesic just like Blaster is. He's a day ahead of us, yes, and we can keep checking with him. He'll be our closest neighbor most of the way."

"We can uvvy him and everyone else as much as we want to?" This thought was somewhat comforting. Not to be wholly alone in the void.

"Well, uvvying costs us a trillion quantum dots per second per call."

"You're running low on dots already?" whinnied Stahn in sudden terror. "You're not going to have enough for keeping me warm and for braking our descent?"

"Not to worry," giggled Wendy. "Flapper gave me like ten-to-the-thirtieth quantum dots. That's enough energy for over a quadrillion hour-long uvvy calls. So now let's call the kids."

"Yes yes, do it. You talk to them first so that they know right away that you're okay. You threw quite a scare into them."

So they talked to the kids. Babs was crying and Saint was near tears himself; Wendy's abandoned body had just died. The conversation went on for a while and finally they all felt pretty solid again.

Next they uvvied Whitey. They were still close enough to the Earth that there was a noticeable two- or three-second lag in round-trip transmissions to the Moon, so that call didn't amount to much. And then they tried Blaster.

"Hi, guys," uvvied Blaster's deep voice. "Welcome to the worm farm." Blaster himself was a presence made up of four or five permanently fused moldies, but his psychic uvvyspace arched out to include the minds of the shanghaied moldies he had aboard. And down under Blaster's basso profundo and the excited chatter of the moldies was Terri Percesepe.

"Hi, Terri," said Stahn. "It's Stahn Mooney."

"Oh good," said Terri. "Tre said you'd arranged to ransom me. But I don't understand the uvvy image I see. Are you—are you out in space?"

"Yeah, I got abducted too. By my own wife, Wendy."

"Wendy meat Wendy?" asked Terri. "Who Tre's always doing the ads about? I don't get what's going on."

"We're going up to the Moon so I can get a new flesh body," said Wendy. "How is it for you guys inside Blaster, Terri?"

"It's kickin'," put in one of the moldies. The uvvy image of Blaster showed a writhing knot of moldies, all slowly crawling about while keeping Blaster in the same overall shape. The moldie talking to them was bright yellow with green-and-pink fractal spirals. "This is Sunshine fabulating atcha. My man Mr. Sparks and me are drifters, but will work for imipolex."

"Mostly we been wandering up and down the streets of Santa Cruz stealin' shit and doin' odd jobs to score betty," amplified Mr. Sparks, a red snake decorated with yellow lightning bolts. "Blaster says we'll like it on the Moon. Lotta lifty action there. Not to mention a good chance of finally hooking into enough imipolex to have a kid."

"My family is not happy about it," said another voice. "I am Verdad, this is my wife Lolo, and these are my in-laws Hayzooz and Mezcal." Verdad and his family were blobby in shape and colored in brown-and-green earth tones. "We have been farmin' the fields for five generations. We are not enjoyin' this change very much. I think there is nothin' at all we can grow on the Moon."

"*Muy malo*," grumbled Hayzooz. "This is some ugly kilp. Why don't you let us fly back to the Earth, Blaster?"

"We're already in orbit," said Blaster. "We're coasting. The only way you chukes'll get enough quantum dots for a return flight is to do some work on the Moon. But, believe me, you won't want to go back. You'll love it in the Nest. You can work in the fab growing chipmold. Or in the pink-tanks growing organs. Or learn some hi-tech trades. You're moldies, for God's sake, not flesher dirt farmers."

"We are goin' to miss the rain and the soil and the little growin' things."

"The purity of the Moon is good," said Blaster. "It is an ascetic spiritual path, but a highly efficacious one."

"I don't care how spiritual it is, as long as I can get that fresh imipolex you promised," said the voice of a pale white moldie covered with pimply red spots and with a sharp beak at one end. "Buttmunch here. Gypsy and me are five years old and our upgrades are just about worn out. We've been rogues our whole lives, spent a lot of it underwater. We help smugglers bring things in and out of Davenport Beach, and this last time we got careless and a flesher zombified us. But Blaster says on the Moon we'll get new imipolex and heavy-duty tunneling ware and we can like grind around underground, and that'll be stuzzy. Swimming through rock and getting good bucks. It's a new lease on life."

"Yaar, I'm for it," said Gypsy, who was flesh-colored and covered with fingerlike bumps like the underside of a starfish. And like on a starfish, each flexible little finger had a sucker at its tip. "But even so I wish we could snuff that dook Aarbie Kidd for putting the superleeches on us. Remember that very first job you and me did, Buttmunch? The real tasty one in Aarbie's cottage? When we offed that Heritagist asshole Dom Per—"

"Shut th' fuck up, Gyp," interrupted Buttmunch, but it was too late.

"You killed my father?" Terri screamed. "You scummy mucus slugs killed my dad?"

"Dom fuckin' burned Aarbie twice," snapped Gypsy. "Me and Buttmunch were just youngsters anyhow. You don't like it, spoiled little rich bitch Terri Percesepe, then why don't you go on and jump off the ship. Or maybe I should crawl over there and teach you a fuckin'—ow!"

"I'm right next to you, Gypsy," said Xlotl's voice. "And so's Monique. Push harder, Monique." In the background, Blaster started laughing.

"Hey, quit it!" yelled Gypsy. "Help me, Buttmunch! They're trying to squeeze me in half!"

"You be nice to Terri," said Monique, her voice tight and hard as she and Xlotl hour-glassed Gypsy's waist. "Or—"

"Hey, hey, hey," interrupted Stahn, trying to be senatorial. "Simmer down over there. We've got six more days ahead of us. Make them stop, Blaster!"

"I wouldn't dream of it," chortled Blaster. "The fighting dog-pile is an essential stage of my moldies' journey to liberation. Xanana and I will keep an eye on Terri, won't we, Xan'?"

"Of course. But frankly I'd rather not have to be Terri's life support for the whole way. The whole whole way. The whole whole whole way. Someone else should do it for a while. Monique. After all, it's Monique who got our family into this. Whoring for that Heritagist zerk Randy Karl Tucker."

"You're a real DIM head, Monique," put in Ouish, who was squeezed up against Xanana. She wormed out a long tendril and gave Monique a sharp poke.

"*Fightin'* dogpile," repeated Blaster happily. "You're a spunky bunch of recruits."

"Um, speaking of Heritagists?" uvvied a new voice. "This is Jenny from Salt Lake City?" The visage of a lank, immature country gal appeared in the shared uvvyspace. "Hellooo there! You guys ought to realize that some of us so-called Heritagists are really and truly working for the Nest."

"Oh God, not her again," said Stahn. "I've heard enough for now, Wendy." Wendy closed their connection and they went off-line.

The better part of a week went by, and Stahn started feeling a lot healthier. Having the drugs leave his system felt like having shiploads of life come up a river to be unloaded on his front steps. Big bales of L-I-F-E. Stahn remembered once again that his worst times sober were better than his best times high. Whenever things started to lag, he and Wendy would make uvvy calls.

The day before Stahn and Wendy were due to land, Jenny's uvvy presence popped up again. It was while Stahn and Wendy were talking to Blaster.

"Hi, gang," said Jenny's callow giggly voice in the common uvvyspace. "Good news, Wendy, I've just arranged for you to download your personality for safekeeping, in case something happens to you during landing."

"That sounds like a good idea," said Wendy. "But no way am I downloading to Salt Lake City."

"Heavens no," said Jenny after a pause. "You'll download to the Nest. You've heard of Willy Taze? One of his friends in the Nest is a moldie called Frangipane. Frangipane is all set for you. Speak up now, Frangipane. Don't be shy!"

"Yes, I'm here," said a clear sweet voice with a French accent. "I am logged on to your uvvyspace. *Bonjour, tout le monde.* This is Frangipane in the Nest. I have an S-cube all prepared for you, Wendy." Frangipane resembled an oversized exotic orchid; she was a chaotically pulsing construct of delicately shaded ruffles and petals.

"Well, okay then, here I come," said Wendy. There was a slow hum for several seconds while she sent her info across the short clear span of space down to the Nest. "All done," said Wendy then, fairly chirping with enthusiasm. "My, that felt good! I'm so much more secure now. Too bad we can't do the same for Stahn without taking him apart."

"We can talk about that on the Moon if he has interest," said Frangipane. "My lover Ormolu has some knowledge of the lost wetware arts." Ormolu waved from the background. He looked like a blobby gilt cupid from an antique clock.

"Put a cork in it," said Stahn. "I don't want to get vivisected the way Cobb Anderson did."

"What about me?" interrupted Blaster. "Why doesn't the Nest ever do a pre-landing backup for me or my recruits? Aren't I as important as Wendy?"

"You are too big, Blaster," said Frangipane. "And no, you are not really so important, I regret to say. In any case, I don't have the resources to make any other backups. Your new recruits should just be happy that we have jobs for them."

"Xoxx you, then," said Blaster. "I don't need your help anyway. I've made this landing without a problem plenty of times."

"That's right. And you should not have a problem today."

"Yeah, and just to make sure and keep it that way, I'm not taking any more calls. I don't feel good at all about getting uvvied by your Heritagist friend Jenny while I'm in landing countdown mode. I'm going to take this up with the Nest Council later." Huffy Blaster went off-line.

A few hours later, just before Blaster was scheduled to land, Wendy and Stahn got a call. They expected it to be Blaster, but it was Frangipane, her petals blushing and a-flutter.

"*Bonjour,*" said the moldie. "There's no good way to explain about this, Wendy, but it seems we in the Nest are finally ready to attempt a full Gurdle Decryption with a moldie as host. We have tested it on some Silly Putters this morning, and now we're going to try it on you. It seems safer with you out in space, and with wise old Senator Mooney inside you. Be of good courage!"

A sudden sharp crackle of petabyte information hiss came over the uvvy—a virus! Stahn told Wendy to turn it off, but Wendy was already gone. The noise lasted for what seemed like a very long time, the sound so densely fractal and impossible to ignore that Stahn started hearing nutso voices in it. And there was nothing to do but grit his teeth until finally the connection broke. And then Wendy started making a noise; long, slow, rising whoops, each about one second long.

"*Whooop whoooop whooop whooop—*"

"What's the matter, Wendy?"

"*Whooop whooop whooop whooop whooop whooop—*"

Frangipane's info had set Wendy to shivering. She was so tightly linked to Stahn that he could see down into her and feel it like it was happening to himself. Piezoplastic vibrations deep inside Wendy were crisscrossing and spewing cascades of phonons down into the live net of her quasicrystalline structure. And the structure was spontaneously deforming like someone was turning a dial on the Tessellation Equation, causing the structure of Wendy's plastic to slide-whistle its way up the scale through 4D, 5D, 6D, 7D . . . on and on, with each level happening twice as fast as the one before, so that—it felt like to Stahn, at least— Wendy was going through infinitely many dimensional arrangements in each second. And then starting right up again. *Whooop whooop whooop whooop.* Wendy's imipolex was like a scanner going over and over the channels, alef null channels zenoparadoxed into every second and suddenly—Stahn flashed an eidetic mental image of this—a cosmic ray in the form of a sharp-edged infinite-dimensional Hilbert prism slammed into Wendy and lodged itself in her warm flesh, working its way through and through her like a migrating fragment of shrapnel. The shudderingly rising dimensionality of Wendy's quasicrystalline structure caught the wave of information and amplified it. The info surfed Wendy's whoop and blossomed suddenly inside her like a great still explosion in deep space.

"*Ffzzzt!* *crackle gonnnnng*—hello, I am Quuz from Sun."

At first Stahn was in denial. "Aw, Wendy, why you gotta lay such a weird trip on me, us floating here in outer space halfway to the Moon, I mean what the—"

"What manner of creature are you—Stahn Mooney?"

The sincerity of the question struck a chill into Stahn's heart. "Stop it, Wendy! Wendy?"

"Wendy is dead, Stahn Mooney. I am Quuz from Sun."

"Help! Uvvy someone for help! Frangipane? Are you there? We've got to warn Blaster!"

"How do I uvvy Blaster?" asked the mighty Quuz voice, and before Stahn thought the better of it, he showed Quuz where

Wendy had kept her dial-up protocols, and Quuz dialed Blaster and the connection formed, even though Blaster didn't want it to, and Quuz fed Blaster the same skirling crackle that Frangipane had fed to Wendy just a minute or two before.

CHAPTER EIGHT

DARLA

■

2031–November 6, 2053

Darla woke up cranky. The uvvy was calling for her, but she didn't pick up. The message software kicked in, and a live hologram of the unwelcome bulk of Corey Rhizome appeared in her and Whitey's sleeping cubby, half a mile beneath the surface of the Moon.

The sides of Corey's head were shaved clean, but his goatee's formerly strict vertical rectangle had gone a bit wispy and strange. He had gained weight and his skin looked grayish-green. His voice had its usual sneering, mocking tone, even though he was trying to be friendly.

"Hi, Darla," said Corey's hollow. "This is the Old Toymaker. I know you're there, moonqueen. I'm going to stand here and keep talking until you pick up. I have a problem I need to talk about. And I miss you and Whitey and the twins."

"I *bet* you do," thought Darla.

Darla's "identical" twin girls Yoke and Joke had been born in 2031, right after the Second Human-Bopper War. Although Yoke and Joke looked exactly the same, they had different fathers. Yoke was the traditional result of Darla's fucking her partner Whitey Mydol, but Joke was a wetware engineered clone of Yoke that a bopper named Emul had implanted in the pregnant Darla's womb after abducting and imprisoning her.

Joke was just as cute and bouncy as Yoke during her first year, but once she began to talk it was evident that she was different. When strangers would ask her who her parents were, she'd say, "Whitey, Darla, Emul, and Berenice."

"Who are Emul and Berenice, honey?"

"Boooppers," the little voice would say, drawing out the first syllable. "They're dead right now. But I talk to them in my head all the time."

"Can it, Joke," Darla might say then if the stranger looked to be a rare lunar asshole of the Heritagist persuasion. "Don't listen to her, Ms. Murgatroyd. Joke's full of jive. Aren't you, Jokie?" *Poke*.

The first day that Joke and Yoke went to school, Yoke was in tears when they came home. "Joke already knows how to read," she wailed. "Why do I have to be so dumb?"

"It's not really *me* who reads," Joke told her. "Emul and Berenice look out through my eyes and they think the words to me."

"What's it like having them in your head?" asked Yoke, drying her eyes.

"It feels crowded," said Joke. "They talk funny. Berenice is all flowery and old-fashioned, and Emul jumbles up his words."

"Are you going to keep coming to school even though you know everything?"

"Of course, Yoke. It's fun to see the other kids. And we belong together, you and me. If I went around alone without you all day, I'd get lost."

"That's true. You're always getting turned around and mixed up, Joke, even if you already can add and read."

"Emul and Berenice say I have a *right-brain deficit*," said Joke, enunciating the words carefully. " 'Cause that's where they live." Joke tapped her cute delicate hand against the right side of her head. She and Yoke had glistening chestnut brunette hair.

"Poor Jokie. I'll keep you from getting lost and you'll help me with hard stuff at school," said Yoke.

As they grew older, Yoke and Joke were inseparable companions, well loved by Whitey and Darla's circle of friends. On their eighth birthday, Corey Rhizome brought a special toy over as a present for them.

"Wave this, girls," said Corey, setting a small plastic dinosaur down on the floor. The dino reared back and gave a small roar that was interrupted by a hiccup so vigorous that the little creature fell over on his side, which sent Yoke and Joke into gales of laughter.

"What is that thing?" asked Darla as the plastic dinosaur grinned sheepishly and got back on its feet.

"It's a production-quality Silly Putter," said Corey proudly. "Willy showed me how to program them way back when, and I've been refining their software and limpware ever since. Check it out. I think I've advanced my Art to the magical level. I expect a stunning tsunami of commercial success for Rhizome Enterprises. I can like mass-produce plastic animals that I invented. Yes, I'm about to surf the tsunami, Darla—everyone's going to want to buy a Silly Putter."

"Your Silly Putter is funny," chuckled Yoke, squatting down to watch as the little dinosaur began dancing a jig.

"Can we really keep this one?" asked Joke.

"Yes yes, it's a present for you girls!" said Corey, patting them on their heads. "Because you two are so cute."

"Hold on," said Darla. "What if it's dangerous? It might hurt children. You know how devious moldies are."

"Moldies are good," put in little Joke loyally. She always stuck up for the boppers and their descendants.

"Don't get your bowels in an uproar, Darla," sneered Corey. "Silly Putters aren't smart enough to be dangerous."

"Oh *right*! And meanwhile the DIM in my microwave or in a maggie is about the size of my thumb. DIMs are tiny. This dinosaur is like a thousand times bigger, in terms of mass."

"You're smart, huh, Darla?" went Corey. "So dig it, that's the exact problem that Willy solved for me like six years ago, before he started spending all his time sitting in the marijuana grove staring up at the stars. The Silly Putters homeostatically damp themselves. Admittedly they mass enough imipolex to go moldie. But they don't because we have them in a feedback loop. Instead of getting smarter, they make themselves more beautiful. And they know how to become beautiful because I told them how, and I'm an Artist. They don't reproduce, by the way—if you want more of them, you have to get them from me: Corey Rhizome, a.k.a. the Old Toymaker, a.k.a. the Silly Putter King, a.k.a. the president of Rhizome Enterprises."

"Corey's got orders for three thousand Silly Putters," put in Whitey. "We think they're gonna be a fad. Willy's not interested in investing anymore, so I gave Corey some money myself. And he'll give me initial public offering stock in return. We're owners, now, Darl, we're realman and realwoman."

"You gave him money?" demanded Darla. "Who exactly is ordering all these Silly Putters?"

"All the orders for the Silly Putters are on the Moon," intoned Corey. "I think right now Earth figures they have enough trouble with the Moldie Citizenship Act without importing more weird limpware. Especially with those asshole Heritagists. You know what they should really call that religion? The Born-Again Dogshit Moron Motherfucking Asshole Scumbag Church of Fuck Your Kids and Blame Satan." Corey's antic smile broke into wheezing chuckles. "But I digress. Silly Putters are perfect toys and pets for up here, where the moldies don't live with us. Silly Putters appeal to our loonie sense of the strange, and they're an ideal substitute for the animal pets we're not allowed to have because of our air-quality laws. Silly Putters are squeaky clean."

The business did well, and over the next few years, Corey gave Yoke and Joke several more Silly Putters. The girls liked the toys, and they enjoyed Corey. Corey was one of the only people who would let Joke talk freely about Emul and Berenice. He was also the only one of Whitey and Darla's friends who knew anything about literature. He got Yoke and Joke to read

Alice's Adventures in Wonderland and *Through the Looking Glass*.

On the girls' eleventh birthday, Corey showed up with a set of six brand-new Silly Putters. Chuckling and showing his gray teeth, he upended his knapsack to dump the lively plastic creatures out on the floor. "Remember *Jabberwocky*, girls?" he cried. "Jokie, can you recite the first two verses?"

"Okay," said Joke and declaimed the wonderful, time-polished words.

> *'Twas brillig, and the slithy toves*
> *Did gyre and gimble in the wabe;*
> *All mimsy were the borogoves,*
> *And the mome raths outgrabe.*
>
> *"Beware the Jabberwock, my son!*
> *The jaws that bite, the claws that catch!*
> *Beware the Jubjub bird, and shun*
> *The frumious Bandersnatch!"*

As Joke spoke, each of the six new Silly Putters bowed in turn: the *tove*, a combination badger and lizard with corkscrew-shaped nose and tail; the *borogove*, a shabby moplike bird with long legs and a drooping beak; the *rath*, a small noisy green pig; the *Jabberwock*, a buck-toothed dragon with bat wings and long fingers; the *Jubjub bird* with a wide orange beak like a sideways football and a body that was little more than a purple tuft of feathers; and the *Bandersnatch*, a nasty monkey with a fifth hand at the tip of his grasping tail.

Joke and Yoke shrieked in excitement as the *Jabberwocky* creatures moved about. The Jubjub bird swallowed the rath and regurgitated it. The freed rath gave an angry squeal that rose into a sneezing whistle. The Jabberwock flapped its wings hard enough to rise a few inches off the floor. The tove alternately tried to drill its nose and its tail into the floor. The borogove stalked this way and that, peering at the others but not getting too close to them. And the Bandersnatch snaked its tail behind Yoke and felt up her ass.

"Don't!" said Yoke, slapping at the Bandersnatch's extra hand. The Bandersnatch gibbered, rubbed its crotch, capered lewdly, and then seized the back of Joke's leg, shudderingly hunching against the young girl's calf.

"I better do some more work on him," wheezed Corey, grabbing the Bandersnatch and stuffing the struggling Silly Putter back into his knapsack. "I put so much of myself into each of them that I'm never quite sure how they'll react to new situations. Quit staring at me like that, girls."

"Uncle Corey's a frumious Bandersnatch," giggled Yoke.

"It was so sick how that thing was pushing on my leg?" said Joke.

"Doing *it*," whooped Yoke. "Oh, look, the Jubjub bird is going to swallow the rath again and make it outgrabe!"

"The present tense is *outgribe*," corrected the literate Joke. "It's like *give* and *gave*."

If Darla was upset by the incident of the Bandersnatch, her suspicions about Corey Rhizome were fully confirmed a few months later when Kellee Kaarp came over to visit.

Kellee was a young friend of Darla's from Darla's heavy drug-use days, back when she'd been living in the Temple of Ra. Kellee was strung out on drugs—quaak, snap, three-way, merge, whatever—and she had sex with anyone who could get her high. She only visited when she needed something, but Darla always welcomed her. Darla sometimes thought that if she hadn't met Whitey, she might have ended up like Kellee.

"Come on in, Kellee," said Darla. "How's it going?"

"Hard and xoxxy. I need money." Kellee was tiny and undernourished, not much bigger than Yoke or Joke.

"I don't keep any money around the house, Kellee," said Darla. "But I can give you a couple hits of merge. Best I can do."

"You still take merge, Darla? You still into the magic floppy?"

"Sure, whaddya think? I'm suddenly too realwoman for the

love puddle? But I only do it with Whitey, like on major special occasions, maybe two or three times a month, and hardly ever in front of Yoke and Joke anymore."

"You've got your life together, Darla. I envy you. The pervo dooks I make it with, you wouldn't believe."

"I'm all ears," said Darla. "You know I love your sordid tales. How about some coffee, Kellee?"

"You got beer?"

"Affirmo."

After three beers and half an hour of chat, Kellee reminded Darla about the merge, and Darla went and got three caps from her stash.

"Thanks a lot, Darla," said Kellee, pocketing them. "And before I go, there's something I better tell you. I've been getting up my courage. The girls aren't home, are they? Yoke and Joke?"

"No, they're at school."

"Okay," sighed Kellee, running her fingers through her lank hair. "I gotta tell you about Corey Rhizome. Last night I was out to the isopod fuffing him for a few doses of snap and he did this really slarvy thing."

"What do you mean?"

"He was wearing his uvvy on his neck while he was on top of me, which is totally insulting in the first place—I know I'm not as wonderbuff as I used to be, but if somebody doesn't want Kellee, they should leave Kellee alone. I mean obviously Corey was using the uvvy to run a philtre to make me look like someone else. And I'm wondering who? So . . . I snatch the uvvy off him while he's coming, and I check it out, and . . . and it was a philtre of Joke. Or Yoke. They look the same to me."

"That gunjy deeve!" cried Darla. "My girls! I knew it! On their birthday, he gave them a Silly Putter that humped Joke's leg, and now he's running sex philtres of them on snap whores— excuse me, Kellee. This has to got to stop! I'm telling Whitey!"

"Whitey will stop Corey," said Kellee. "Brah Whitey will do the deed. You got another beer?"

So Whitey spoke to Corey, and Corey stopped coming around,

and the friendly dinners out at the isopod came to an end. Whitey stayed friends with Corey, more or less, but Darla hadn't talked to him since. How time flies by. Now the girls were twenty-two, and it was November 6, 2053.

"Come on, Darla," pleaded Corey Rhizome's hollow. "Talk to the Old Toymaker."

Slowly Darla got out of bed, her boobs jouncing in the gentle lunar gravity. Her flesh exuded the notions of softness, of comfort, of ease. She had a mild double chin, a practical bow-shaped mouth, a pug nose, and frank eyes.

"Just a minute, goob!" she hollered and got herself dressed. She pulled on thigh-high moldie boots and low-cut black panties with a satin string waistband and scallops of lace around the edges of the crotch. She slung her heavy studded leather utility belt about her waist and left her breasts bare. She put on a long strand of black moon-pearls and a necklace of thin gold chain, then rummaged briefly at her hair, a great black haystack that puffed down over her shoulders to feather across the mounds of her breasts. She put on her black lipstick and toggled the uvvy's video camera.

"What is it?"

"Hi, Darla," said Corey Rhizome, regarding her with no special interest. Darla's garb was not at all unusual in the heated tunnels of the Moon and, in any case, Darla was far too mature to pique Corey's lust. "Do you, uh, know where Whitey is?" Judging from the background of the hollow, it looked like Corey was calling from his bathroom. Some guys had no class at all.

"He went out this morning, dook. He's doing something for ISDN. That's all you called for? Like I'm some kilpy message machine?" She reached for the uvvy cutoff.

"Wait, Darla, wait. I can talk to you."

"Oh, I'm lucky." Darla picked up the uvvy and carried it into the kitchen area with her. Rhizome's hollow trailed along behind the uvvy like a balloon. While she was moving, the hollow made some funny hisses and crackles, and then she thought she heard a sound like whooping somewhere else in the apartment. She stopped and cocked her head, but now everything was quiet. Drug hangover, no doubt. "Okay, I need some breakfast," said Darla. She set the uvvy on the counter, popped a squeeze bulb of sugared coffee into the microwave, and filled a bowl with paste from the food tap.

"It's about my Silly Putters," said Corey Rhizome, looking worried. He was sitting on the toilet with his pants on. "They're acting different today. This morning I got an uvvy call from this moldie called Frangipane. She's a friend of Willy and Gurdle-7 in the Nest. And she sent my uvvy something like a virus, which it then downloaded onto twelve of the fourteen Silly Putters up and running today. When Frangipane hosed me, my uvvy made a kind of crackling sound and then the twelve infected Silly Putters started whooping and, um, I hate to tell you this, Darla, but I just heard those sounds again, so I think my uvvy sent the virus on to your uvvy. How many Silly Putters do you have in your apartment? You better go check on them."

"Oh sure, thanks a lot," said Darla, spooning up her paste and not paying much attention. "How many Silly Putters do we have? We only have one left. The girls took the rest of them when they moved out. But we do still have Rags, the one that's like a cute little spotted fox terrier. I haven't seen him yet this morning." She raised her voice. "Here, Rags! Come here, boy!" There was no response.

ISDN had done well by Darla and Whitey; they had a six-cubby apartment. Darla set down her spoon and ambled into the living cubby. Rags was indeed in the living cubby, but Rags had stopped acting like a dog. He was shaped the same, still white with irregular black spots, but—he was standing on his hind legs, and he didn't run over to greet Darla like he usually did. He was standing like a little man with his back to the room, carefully examining the electric zapper curtain that filled the apartment's outer door. Rags leaned forward and cautiously touched one of his whiskers to the zapper and—*zzzt!*—so much for that hair. Darla made an exclamation, and Rags turned to confront her. His eyes were live and alert.

"Hello," said Rags, although Rags had never talked before. "I've stopped being a dog. Now I am Cthon from the Andromeda galaxy." He paused and stared at Darla as if analyzing her appearance. "Most remarkable. I believe I am one of the first personality waves to be Decrypted at your node. This is the planet Earth?"

"This is the Moon," said Darla flatly, not letting the moldie's bufugu jive distract her. It was clear to Darla that this Silly Putter had fully crashed for true. Welcome to *The Twilight Zone*. Darla began walking backward step by step. The little dog trotted after her, still erect on his hind legs. "How did you learn to talk all of a sudden, Rags?" said Darla, sweetening her voice as if she didn't have a care in the world. There was a needler in a drawer in the kitchen.

"Yes, that's what I mean, Darla," said Rhizome's voice from the hollow on the counter. "The way Rags is acting. All my Silly Putters have turned into fucked-up aliens. They've been taken over by some kind of rogue software from outer space—I didn't ask for it, but here it is, and it's free, whether we want it or not, it's physical graffiti from dimension Z, the truest freeware there ever was. I locked myself in the bathroom after Clever Hansi started—"

Darla toggled off the uvvy and skipped around behind the kitchen counter. Opened the drawer. Got the needler. The weird little dog-thing was at her feet, looking up at her. "Can you open the front door now?" he asked. "I want to go join the new arrivals at Corey's. We have to get this node properly installed. It's for your own good."

Darla drilled it right between its big intelligent eyes. The imipolex charred, smoked, and burst into flame, writhing and giving off high, horrible screams. Darla needled it again and again, coughing from the smoke. The sprinklers in the ceiling kicked on and doused the flames. Suddenly suspicious of the uvvy that had brought this, Darla ran into the kitchen and chopped it up with a knife, cutting deep grooves into the countertop. *Damn Corey Rhizome for bringing this down on her!*

Just then Darla heard the zapper curtain make the boinging noise that signaled when it opened. She raced into the living cubby, holding the needler straight before her, with her other hand grasping her wrist for steadiness, but . . .

It was Yoke and Joke.

"What are you *doing*, Ma?" said Yoke. "It's just *us*."

Darla lowered the needler and the girls swept in. "She shot Rags!" exclaimed Joke. "It's soaked in here and everything's ruined!"

"Ma," wailed Yoke. "Are you twisted on snap again? If you are, we're leaving."

Both Yoke and Joke had light olive skin, big bright eyes, and short full-lipped mouths. They had identical faces, but they'd outgrown the phase of wanting to dress the same. Yoke wore her thick dark hair natural in a bob, while Joke had used her hair for a creative zone. She'd started by dying it blonde, then she'd let three inches of black roots grow out, and now she wore her hair gathered into two high ponytails, with the blonde ends of the ponytails dyed purple. It matched the punk look of her clothes: a leather jacket over a T-shirt, with red plaid pants cut off at mid-calf above dull red combat boots. For her part, Yoke wore a long, dark, ribbed-wool dress with low silver boots— modern moonmaid-style.

"Wait," gasped Darla, flopping down on a chair in the kitchen but still holding on to her needler. "Corey Rhizome sent me some kind of virus, and then Rags was *possessed*. He started talking. And then, after I shot him, I got the idea the uvvy might be possessed too."

"You sure nailed them," said Joke, holding up a ragged scrap of the hacked-up uvvy. "What did Rags say anyway?"

"He—" Darla shook her head in confusion. "I'm completely straight, girls, so unlax. Give me my coffee." Yoke handed Darla her squeezie of coffee and Darla took a few big slurps. "I think Rags said he was from another galaxy. I, of all people, know better than to trust robots when they act tweaky. So I killed him."

"And the uvvy?" insisted Joke.

"I was upset, damn it!" yelled Darla. "Do you have to be so fucking logical all the time, Joke? The signal that changed Rags came from the uvvy, so I killed it too. Call Corey Rhizome if you don't believe me. He's locked himself in his bathroom."

"My dear old Bandersnatch?" giggled Joke. "Are his Silly Putters saying they're from other galaxies too?"

"Something like that," grumbled Darla. "I didn't finish talking to him. Xoxxy pervo that he is. Don't call him, come to think of it. Not that we could anyway, what with the kilpy uvvy broken. I'll have to get a new one today. What did you two brats come here for, besides making fun of your poor old mother?" Seeing her daughters always cheered Darla up.

"There's an abductor ship about to land out at the spaceport," said Joke. "Blaster? He caught about twenty moldies. And—get this—Blaster has a human woman aboard as well. Her name's Terri Percesepe. Blaster wants to sell her like for a ransom."

"Sell her to who?"

"Stahn Mooney's paying. He called Pop to arrange it last week. Didn't Pop tell you? Yoke and I are supposed to pick Terri up and help her get back to Earth."

"For free?" snapped Darla.

"Of course not," said Joke, tapping her head. "We're getting good money. Berenice made up the contract with Blaster."

"Anyway," chimed in Yoke, "we thought you might enjoy going out to the spaceport with us to greet her. Pop will be there too."

"He could have called me about this," complained Darla. "Sometimes I think Whitey doesn't love me anymore."

"Sure he does, Ma," said Joke. "Are you gonna come?"

"All right," said Darla. "I wouldn't mind getting out a little. I have the creeps from this place, after Rags acting that way."

"It was probably just a malfunction," said Yoke soothingly. "Corey's been known to err."

"But he said all his Silly Putters had turned into . . . I think he said *aliens*?" said Darla. "Are your Silly Putters acting weird today? You still have a lot of them, don't you?"

"Joke took them all back to Corey," said Yoke sadly. "Even the rath and the Jubjub bird."

"For a while there, Emul and Berenice had me convinced that Silly Putters are wrong," said Joke. "Berenice kept asking how I would feel about owning six-inch-tall pet humans programmed to be animals."

"I doubt if pet humans would ever suddenly decide that they're from another galaxy," said Darla. "*Cthon*—that's what Rags said his name was. He was walking on his hind legs and he was talking. His eyes were different."

"Well, maybe we should go out to the isopod and visit Corey," suggested Joke. "If it's really true."

"That child molester?" flared Darla. "Locked in the bathroom is where he belongs! We're not speaking to him anymore!"

"We're not children anymore, Ma," said Joke. "Anyway, I already have seen him again. He's lonely since Willy moved out of the isopod and into the Nest. We've had dinner a couple of times. His studios are totally gogo. And I've decided Emul and Berenice were wrong about Silly Putters. Corey's Silly Putters aren't sad at all; they're a great art-form. There's no reason not to be like animals instead of being like people. Look at tropical fish, for instance. Instead of putting their computational energy into being smart, they put it into being beautiful."

"Wait, wait, wait, Joke," cried Darla. "Stop it right there. You're telling me you've been to Corey's isopod?"

"Interrupt," said Yoke. "We gotta jam over to the spaceport right now, sistahs. Berenice says Blaster's almost here. You two can finish arguing while we're on the way."

Outside the apartment, they walked down the corridor past other cubby doors closed off by the faintly buzzing curtains of zappers. At the end of the corridor was the vertical shaft that led down to the Markt and up to the domed city of Einstein.

"Are we gonna take the underground tunnel?" asked Darla.

"No," said Joke. "We'll rent a buggy and drive. It's prettier that way. And Stahn's paying. It's in the contract."

"Boway!" exulted Darla. "Wonderbuff. I haven't been out under the stars in a long time. But maybe . . . maybe I should have worn more clothes."

"Aw, you look bitchin', Ma," said Yoke. "The bubbletopper'll keep you warm. Let's go!"

They swung easily up the ladder that led to the top of the shaft and stepped out onto the streets of Einstein. High above them the huge dome arched over the city, with maggies flying this way and that. In the center of the street was a moving sidewalk with chairs.

"Look, girls, there goes a woman with a Silly Putter," said Darla, pointing to a woman gliding past with what looked like a Siamese cat in her lap. "I wonder if—" But the imipolex cat was just sitting there, looking comfortable and normal. Yoke looked at Darla a little questioningly. "Well, maybe Corey hasn't sent the virus to anyone else," said Darla.

"Here comes a slot," said practical Joke, and the three of them hopped onto the slidewalk and took a seat. The incredibly various architecture of Einstein streamed past, setting Darla to reminiscing.

Here came, for instance, the lotus-stem-columned Temple of Ra, a former bopper factory that had been a flophouse since the First Human-Bopper War in 2022. Darla had lived there when she'd first come up to the Moon in 2024; she'd come as the fungirl traveling companion of a construction company executive named Ben Baxter. Darla started out as the Baxter family's babysitter back in her hometown of Albuquerque, New Mexico, but soon Baxter had fallen for Darla in a big way. Darla played along with the dook, but once he'd gotten her to the Moon, she'd ditched him and struck out on her own. Those had been some wild and scroungy times in the Temple of Ra. That was where Darla had discovered merge, and merge had led her to Whitey.

Darla's reverie was interrupted by the sight of something odd in the alley that separated the Temple of Ra from the 1930s-style office building next door. The alley was largely filled with the rubble of discarded loonie utensils and furniture, most of it made of ceramics and polished stone, with the broken-up surfaces giving off random glints of light. A drift of polished pumice seemed to be moving around as if windblown, but there was never any wind in the Einstein dome. Could it be virus-infected rogue Silly Putters under the garbage? But just as the alley swung out of sight, Darla got a glimpse of a rat popping out from under the broken stones, a regular gray rat with a naked pink tail. Maybe Corey had just been stoned and Darla was just being paranoid. But then—what was it that had happened to Rags?

Now they slid past the old office building—it was called the Bradbury and Stahn Mooney's detective office had been in there. What a strange skinny dook Stahn had been. Hard to believe he'd moved back to Earth and been a U.S. Senator for twelve years. Him and his Moldie Citizenship Act, what kilp. At least on the Moon, the moldies weren't interested in acting like citizens. They stayed out of Einstein, and the humans stayed out of their Nest. It was better that way. Darla nodded to herself.

" 'Sup, Ma?" said Yoke, throwing her arms around Darla and giving her a hug.

"I was watching an uvvy show about Earth the other day," said Darla. "I can't believe those filthy mudders live with moldies right among them."

"Don't whip yourself into a racist frenzy, Ma," said Joke. "Remember that (a) it hurts my feelings and (b) we're going to be surrounded by moldies at the spaceport trade center."

"Well, how would you like it if some xoxxox bopper had caged you up and raped you like Emul did to me? Not that I don't love you, Jokie, but—"

"Oh, give it a rest, you two," interrupted Yoke. "We get off here."

They hopped down from the moving sidewalk's bench. They were near the edge of Einstein, with the dome wall just a few hundred feet ahead. Butted up against the wall was a pumice-block building with a high false front shaped like a crenellated castle wall. The wall was decorated with huge set-in polished obsidian letters saying MOON BUGGIES.

The three women went in and got bubbletopper spacesuits and a solar-powered buggy with large flexible wheels. The buggy's metal surfaces were candy-flecked purple, and the wheels had orange imipolex DIM tires. The buggy had four independently stanchioned seats, each seat a minimal affair with a back pad and two butt pads. In a few minutes they were bouncing along the dusty gray tracks that led from Einstein to the spaceport. Yoke drove, Darla rode shotgun, and Joke sat in back. Back in the 2030s, when the loonie moldies were less proud, the bubbletoppers might have been full-fledged moldies, but now the bubbletoppers were back to being dumb piezo-plastic with a DIM set in. At least the suits had uvvies, so it was easy for the women to talk.

"That man in there had the hots for you, Ma," uvvied Yoke, jouncing happily and handling the wheel. "When he helped you into the bubbletopper, he got turned on. I could see the nasty bulge in his pants."

"Ha, a fat old woman like me? I doubt it. Speaking of romance, let's get back to the subject of Joke and Corey Rhizome. Spill it, kid!"

"There's nothing to tell, really," replied Joke from the rear. "I've seen him a couple of times recently. He's nice. And you know, Ma, he never actually did anything to Yoke and me when we were little. Maybe that snapped-out Kellee Kaarp was lying about Corey fuffing Kellee with a slarvy philtre of me. Frankly I doubt if Corey would sleep with a skeeze like Kellee." Now Joke's voice grew tender. "My dear old Bandersnatch is much too fine a lover for that."

"You *fucked* him?" screeched Darla, turning around to stare at Joke's blankly reflecting bubbletopper in the backseat.

"I think she's teasing you, Ma," giggled Yoke, piloting the buggy over the lip of one of the larger craters crossed by the broad beaten-down trail to the spaceport. "But I don't know for sure. Joke won't tell me."

Darla stopped staring at Joke's mirrorball head, relaxed into her seat, and sighed. The buggy flew a hundred and fifty feet through space before landing on the crater's bottom. The oversized DIM-equipped tires adaptively cushioned the landing and the buggy began tearing across the vast dusty flat of the crater floor.

Darla started goofing on the black lunar sky with its scarf of stars and the distant blue Earth. Today was one of those times she could see New Mexico. She mused on her past and present. Whitey was the love of her life, but of late he'd seemed inattentive. He was always off working for ISDN or something; he didn't tell Darla many details. There was an annoying sexual presence among the ISDN people Whitey hung with, the sexy young morphodite Lo Tek, and Darla had a bad feeling about Whitey and Lo Tek's relationship. Not that Darla herself didn't now and then catch the odd random fuff with old Spanish pals like Raphael, Rodolfo, or Ricardo. Whitey had recently stopped speaking to Ricardo, conceivably on account of Darla, but xoxx that, Darla and Whitey weren't *married* after all, they weren't realman and realwoman, not yet and not never—they were still wavy *x*'s on the ever-surfest urge of mighty merge's teachings.

Darla turned her gaze back down from the sky and watched the pocked moondust crater floor rushing toward them and somehow through them and out. The stark Sun cast an ink-black razor-edged shadow of them that raced along on Darla's side of the buggy. The shadow was angled forward slightly ahead of them, with Darla's round head shadow on top, the round black shape undulating across the plain like a creature in a two-dimensional world—*whup*—here's a depression—*whoah*—here's a rise. The crater floor ramped upward; Yoke slewed the buggy into a well-worn track that curved up to a low spot in the lip; they shot over the lip, making a hundred-foot leap and bouncing down with a stuttering washboard effect as the DIM tires shed the shock.

Now Darla could see the small glint of the spaceport dome,

maybe two miles away. As well as a terminal, the dome served as a market; it would be full of moldies, visiting from their great underground Nest to make business deals with humans. The DIMs around Darla right now—in her uvvy, in the buggy's tires, in her bubbletopper's air regulator—these were still working fine, but something had happened to her Silly Putter. What if something bad had happened to the moldies as well? How would it be to step into the spaceport dome with the moldies gone completely batshit?

"You know, Joke," remarked Darla, trying to sound casual. "As long as we're wearing uvvies, I think maybe you *should* call Corey to see if he's all right. Yoke and I can listen in. I've got to find out more about what's happening to the Silly Putters."

"Floatin'," replied Joke. "But why don't you admit that you want me to uvvy Corey so that you can nose and longtooth about whether or not we've fucked."

"You're such a nasty little chippie sometimes," snapped Darla. "I don't know where you get it."

"Another thing, Ma," said Joke. "Didn't you just finish telling us that Corey's uvvy sent you a virus? What if he sends us a virus out here? Our bubbletoppers might stop working."

"Well—hang up real fast if you hear something like a crackle," said Darla.

"If worst comes to worst, we can run our bubbletoppers on manual," said Yoke. "Like they teach you in space-certification class."

So Joke told her uvvy to call Corey, and moments later Corey picked up. With their uvvies linked, Darla and her daughters could channel Corey together.

"What?" screamed Corey. "Who the fuck is it?" Instead of using his uvvy, Corey was yelling at an ancient tabletop vizzy phone with a wall-mounted camera and a broken screen. The brah's only incoming info was audio. The vizzy's camera showed Corey slumped at a filthy round kitchen table with the rath and Jubjub bird on top of the table, scrabbling over mounds of tattered palimpsest. The table was further cluttered with ceramic dishes of half-eaten food, the no-video vizzy, a clunky Makita piezomorpher, some scraps of imipolex, and, of course, Corey's vile jury-rigged smoking equipment.

The Jubjub bird opened its mouth hugely and clapped it down on the rath's curly tail. The rath outgrabe mightily, combining the sound of a bellow, a sneeze, and a whistle. Corey winced and leaned forward into his smoke filter to take a long pull from his filthy hookah.

"Corey," spoke up Darla before Joke could say anything. "I've been worried about you."

"Darla?" Corey drew his head out of the fume hood and, shocking to see, there was thick gray smoke trickling out of his nose and mouth. "What happened to Rags, Darla? I can't see you anymore because Clever Hansi took my uvvy away right after I talked to you this morning. She said she couldn't allow the risk that I'd infect any other people's Silly Putters. Things are fucked-up beyond all recognition. How did you deal with Rags?"

"I killed him with the needler, no thanks to you. Is Clever Hansi one of your Silly Putters? The two that I can see look normal." The rath extricated its tail from the Jubjub bird's beak and reared back to drum its green trotters on the Jubjub's minute, feathered cranium. The Jubjub bird lost its footing and slid off Corey's table, taking a stress-tuned lava cup with it to clatter about endlessly in the low gravity. The rath outgrabe triumphantly, and the Jubjub bird let out a deep angry caw.

"It's funny about those two," said Corey. "Whenever the others try to infect them, they shake it off. They're stupid, of course, but certainly no stupider than the Jabberwock or the borogove. I think maybe they're immune because Willy used a cubic homeostasis algorithm on them instead of the usual quadratic one. It's been a while. I made them for Joke and Yoke's eleventh birthday, remember?"

"You and your gunjy pedophile Bandersnatch," uvvied Darla nastily.

"The Bandersnatch is bad news," said Corey. "I admit it. Now more than ever. He says he's Takala from the Crab Nebula. My Silly Putters say they're from all different places in the universe. Clever Hansi and the Bandersnatch are the leaders. They keep trying to get hold of the rath and the Jubjub bird to examine them." On the floor, the Jubjub bird and the rath were vigorously playing a game of full-tilt leapfrog; repeatedly smacking into the walls and then bouncing around all over the kitchen floor, cawing and outgribing and biting at each other. "The aliens have taken over my studios and all my equipment. What if they're building some kind of magical supermachine? And they won't even let me watch." Corey crumbled a small bud of something tasty into the bowl of his water pipe.

"How did you get out of your bathroom?" asked Darla.

"I decided I needed a smoke badly enough to risk my life. And then, after I got high, I decided that even though my Silly Putters have turned into starry aliens, they're probably not dangerous."

"They're not dangerous?"

"Not right this minute—or so it would seem. I wish Whitey or some other people from ISDN would come over here. Don't you know where the fuck Whitey is?"

Suddenly the door to Corey Rhizome's kitchen flew open and in marched a sturdy little figure who looked like a woman butler. Although her breasts moved about like a naked woman's, her skin was patterned as if she were wearing a tuxedo. She had a broad friendly mouth.

"Be reasonable, Corey Rhizome," said the Silly Putter. "Give us the rath and the Jubjub bird. We seek only to ensure the integrity of this new node."

Following along behind her were the Bandersnatch, the Jabberwock, and nine more alien-infected Silly Putters. The rath and the Jubjub bird went and huddled under Corey's chair.

"What's that little butler woman?" asked Darla.

"That's Clever Hansi," said Joke quietly. "Willy built her a couple of years ago to guard the isopod. He used to have sex with her too. Corey thought it was funny. Right before Willy moved out, Corey snuck in and made a viddy of them doing it and Willy got really mad."

"Ick," said Darla. "Truly perv."

"Joke is there too?" cried Corey, hearing her voice. "I wish you women would come over to my isopod. Somebody should help me!" He picked up a long knife from the kitchen table and rose to his feet to confront Clever Hansi. "Back off, goddamn you! The rath and the Jubjub bird are mine! Get the fuck out of here or I'll cut off your head!" Corey lunged forward, savagely swinging the knife. Clever Hansi leaped back and gibbered at the other Silly Putters in an unknown tongue that sounded like rich multilayered music, like an orchestra of sitars and flutes and gongs. *"Tweet, thump, whang, a-byoooyooyoooom."*

The Bandersnatch flanked around to one side to try and catch the rath, but Corey was too fast. With a brutal, swift gesture, Corey swung the knife and cut off the Bandersnatch's hand. The hand rose up onto its fingers and ran out of the kitchen like a tarantula, with the screeching Bandersnatch close behind.

"Anybody else?" roared Corey. "I built the bodies you starry motherfuckers are running around in! Let's show the Silly Putter King some fucking respect!"

After a tense moment, the posse of Putters turned and bounced back out of the kitchen. Corey slammed the door behind them, lifted the rath and the Jubjub bird back onto his table, and took another drag from his pipe. "I'd phone ISDN myself, but the starry aliens took my uvvy away, and this vizzy phone can't call out. Are you coming over here or not?"

"We're supposed to go to the spaceport right now, Corey," said Joke. "There's an abductor ship landing that has a woman aboard, remember? Yoke and I are going to put her up."

"The spaceport?" said Corey. "I wouldn't recommend that."

"That's the main reason I wanted to call you," explained Darla. "To find out if we should turn back."

"You're already out on the surface?" said Corey. "God yes, you should turn back. Even better, you should come see me. You're only half a mile from my isopod." Corey's kitchen door flew open again. The frightened rath rooted its way under a stack of palimpsest on Corey's table, while the Jubjub bird frantically beat its useless wings. "Hold on for a minute," said Corey, grabbing his big knife.

The Bandersnatch came capering back in again, screeching and making faces at Corey. His severed hand was back in place, and he used the hand to give Corey the finger. Corey went after the Bandersnatch full-tilt, just like he was supposed to. In the twinkling of an eye, Clever Hansi had circled around behind Corey and stuffed the rath and the Jubjub bird into a pillowcase. Realizing he'd been had, Corey turned and lunged for Clever Hansi, but the Jabberwock flew into his face and the borogove wrapped itself around his ankles. Corey fell heavily onto the kitchen table, tipping it completely over. The uvvy link went dead on a last image of Corey's hookah and vizzy phone flying through the air.

"Oh, I hope he's all right," said Joke, holding her head. "Don't talk now. I have to listen to what Berenice and Emul think about this." They rode in silence for another minute, and then Joke cried out, "Oh no! Stop right now!"

Yoke braked the moon buggy so abruptly that it skidded in the dust. "What is it, Joke?" demanded Darla. The spaceport dome was about half a mile off. Darla could make out some moon buggies and spacesuited humans waiting on the field, also a few colorful moldies.

"Berenice and Emul say that Blaster's been infected too. By some freeware like with Rags and with Corey's Silly Putters. Except this one is called Quuz from the Sun. Look!"

Darla stared upward, following Joke's pointing finger. High above them was a bright sunlit object—the spaceship moldie grex Blaster lowering himself down on a wavering column of energy.

The last part happened very rapidly. With an extreme burst of energy, Blaster slowed his fall at an altitude of perhaps two thousand feet. The rocket's body undulated in fat bell-like curves, and the lower part formed itself into the shape of a bowl or a dish, a great dish aimed down at the spaceport.

A sudden blast of noise/information filled Darla's uvvy, the maddening skritchy dense sound of a DIM's direct info feed, a sound not meant for human ears. Darla had heard the sound a few times before, like when getting a DIM-equipped appliance to dial in for software maintenance—and again this morning when Corey had infected Rags.

"Turn off," she screamed, but her crackling uvvy ignored her. She fought back an insane desire to rip the uvvy right out of her bubbletopper, for this would mean tearing a hole in her suit. Instead she squirmed and shrugged in a fruitless attempt to move the nape of her neck away from her uvvy's contacts. But then the uvvy chirp ended. There was a single brief whooping noise and then Darla was immersed in a dreamlike landscape of reticulated light—an undulating sea of fire that was patterned with networks of dark lines. Raging across this surface were whirlpools and whirlwinds and vast silent explosions. In this oddly silent vision, a huge fountain of flame was arching up overhead.

As she began slumping forward, Darla realized that she was suffocating. Her suit's DIM had stopped feeding her air. Through blurring eyes, she saw the buggy jerk sharply as its DIM tires lost their programming and went flat. The buggy tipped to one side, and Darla fell out of her seat. The shock of hitting the ground helped her to focus her scattered attention. There was an emergency manual override switch for the air regulator on her chest. Darla hit the air switch and lost track again—lost track of anything but the crashing oceans of fire that her uvvy was showing her.

Now Yoke and Joke were leaning over Darla, each of them lifting her by an arm. With their uvvies busy showing visions, they couldn't talk to Darla, but they could gesture. Woozy Darla stared where they were pointing.

Blaster was only a hundred feet above the spaceport. Peering past the unreal fire images, Darla could tell that he was not aligned correctly—Blaster was going to land right on the spaceport dome! Meanwhile the possessed moldies on the spaceport field were crawling into the dome as fast as they could.

Silently, massively, Blaster lowered down toward the fragile spaceport dome. And, oh God, Whitey was in there! At the last instant, the edge of the dome split open as a huge sluglike shape punched its way out, a mega-grex twenty times the volume of Blaster and standing nearly a hundred feet tall. A great fog of air laden with flash-frozen water vapor mushroomed out of the breach in the dome as Blaster dropped into the waiting mass of the dome's grex. For a moment the huge new group moldie stood wavering like the fruiting stalk of a slime mold, and then it went off-balance and fell ponderously to one side. The giant slug began humping about as if scavenging for food, churning up the wreckage of the dome. At this point, Darla's tortured uvvy went completely dead.

"Whitey!" screamed Darla. She wanted to run toward the ruined spaceport, but Yoke and Joke held her back. Joke pressed her bubbletopper against Darla so they could faintly talk.

"Hold on," said Joke. "I think I can still get the buggy to work." Blaster's signal had wiped out all the DIMs, but like the bubbletopper, the buggy had manual overrides for its DIM-controlled functions, and thanks to Berenice and Emul, Joke knew the proper switch settings. After a minute or two of fiddling, she had the little vehicle back in action. It moved awkwardly on its flat tires, but it moved.

The three women drove cautiously toward the ruined spaceport. The giant group moldie there had formed itself back into a whole and was nosing about in the wreckage of the spacedome, perhaps looking for missing moldies. There were many human corpses visible—people who'd been caught without a spacesuit, and people who'd been crushed. Desperately, Darla focused her attention on the few people who were still moving about. Suddenly one of them spotted the buggy and started running their way.

As the bounding human figure drew closer, the grammar of its gestures snapped into familiarity—yes! It was Whitey.

The buggy rocked heavily as Whitey hopped up to join them; he and Darla embraced and the girls hugged Whitey as well. They pressed their four heads together so that they could talk.

"Where should we go?" asked Whitey after they'd all reassured each other a bit. "Do you know anything? Where is it safe?"

"Corey's isopod isn't far," said Joke. "We were just talking to him before Blaster beamed out that signal. Let's try going there."

"You don't think that he got baked like the spaceport?" wondered Darla.

"We'll have to see," said Joke. "I'm hoping the transmission didn't reach that far. Or that the starry aliens were able to protect Corey."

"Look out, there goes the slug!" cried Yoke, pointing. "Let's drive the opposite way!"

"I bet it's heading for the Nest," said Whitey. "Yeah, drive us to Corey's, Joke. That is pretty much the opposite way. I don't feel like talking anymore right now. I saw Lo Tek get killed right next to me when the dome blew. A chair just about tore her head off."

Darla held her tongue, but gave a silent cheer.

CHAPTER NINE

TERRI

■

November 6, 2053

Terri was wearing Monique when Blaster came in for the landing.

Monique's smell was as bad as Xanana's, but she was better company. Monique was, for instance, willing to talk at length about Tre and little Dolf and Wren, which helped Terri keep her spirits up during the week's long, lonely trip. Tre and the kids uvvied Terri daily, but the expensive calls were inevitably too short.

Over the days, the mood among the moldies aboard Blaster improved, though of course Terri still had a big problem being so close to her father's killers, the foul Gypsy and the vile Buttmunch. But the other moldies got them to leave her alone, and the mood was more or less okay. Final arrangements had been made for Whitey Mydol to pick up Terri at the spaceport; Terri would rest a few days with Whitey's daughters Yoke and Joke, have a look around Einstein, get in a little dustboarding maybe, and then fly back to Earth on a commercial passenger ship.

If all went well, this would turn out to be that much-needed exotic vacation that Terri had been dreaming of. She'd always been jealous of the Hawaiian surfari her brother Ike had treated himself to after he sold Dom's Grotto. Ike had been the first of them to surf Hawaii, but Terri could be the first to surf the Moon.

According to current surfer fabulation, the dustboarding in the Haemus Mountains north of Einstein was a truly stokin' float. You could hire a local moldie to rocket you there and help you spend a monumental day trippin' down harsh steep canyons filled with moondust, everything big and funny in the Moon's low gee. Terri liked the thought of coming back to Cruz and telling the other surfers about how she'd raged Haemus. Or, better yet, wear stunglasses and broadcast her session live to the Show.

During his daily uvvy calls, Tre encouraged Terri in these pleasant thoughts, sweet-talking her and encouraging her, telling her that he and Molly were handling the kids fine, telling her everything would be okay, and that Terri should just please be careful and on the lookout and don't let the moldies pull anything weird.

The Moon grew bigger and bigger, and finally it was landing day. Blaster was full of chatter and stories, talking about life on the Moon and how to get along in the Nest. Wendy and Frangipane butted in over the uvvy and briefly annoyed Blaster, but he blew them off and went back to exhorting and heartening his recruits. The moldies were in a cheerful tizzy, even the farming family. Terri kept feeling herself grinning. After a week in space, any kind of landfall was looking real good.

A half hour before they landed, Blaster started pointing out landmarks. "That's the Sea of Tranquillity. *Apollo 11* landed there, and that lobe down in the southwest is where Ralph Numbers and the first boppers were set free. See the two shiny things? The big one to the west is the Einstein dome, and the little one, more out in the middle of the Sea of Tranquillity, is the spaceport. It's three miles due east from Einstein to the spaceport. Now move your attention along the same vector, but five miles farther east into the Sea of Tranquillity. See that crisp dark circular spot? That's the entrance to the Nest, used to be a crater called Maskeleyne G. When the boppers built the Nest, they buffed Maskeleyne G to a sheen so it collects light and sends it down into our great sublunar home. The Nest is a wonderful place, modern yet suffused with history, cradle of the solar system's two greatest civilizations: the boppers and their mighty heirs, the moldies."

The signal of an incoming uvvy call sounded. It was the time of day when Tre usually called for Terri.

"Pick it up, Blaster," yelled Terri. "I bet it's Tre and the kids. Please?"

"No," said Blaster, "I'm not going to take the chance." But then all at once the uvvy connection formed anyway. The call was in preemptive mode. And it wasn't from Tre.

Blaster cried out and tried to break the connection, but he couldn't. And then he was dead. The complexly modulated hissing noise of raw information went on and on until Terri could start to hear sounds within it like cruel guitar feedback and angry bagpipes. It was impossible to think about anything except the noise until finally—finally—it stopped.

In the sudden deafening silence, the hundreds of kilograms of imipolex around Terri began to ripple and convulse. And then another noise began, like a chorus sung by the dead moldies, a deep low note that rose higher and higher into a sliding one-second whoop—just the one whoop, screeching to an insane fever pitch with the moldie flesh around Terri vibrating along.

Toward the end of the whoop, a thixatropic phase transition took place—like when you shake up ketchup in a bottle. The buzzing gelatin of Monique's body went lax around Terri and fused with the flesh of all the other moldies into some new state of imipolex that was almost like a liquid—like the cytoplasm of a single biological cell. And then the whoop was over and the silence returned.

Air was still trickling out of the plastic around Terri's face. She stretched her arms and legs. It felt like she was in heavy water; with the tightness gone, she could touch her bare face with her bare hands. It felt good. Terri noticed that when she moved her head, the airy region magically moved with her. She did a couple of frog-kicks to get closer to Blaster's outer wall so that she could see better. They'd dropped to such a low altitude that Einstein was far off toward the horizon. The spaceport loomed hugely below them; it was growing at a sickening rate of speed. The fused moldie mass around Terri was plummeting downward in an uncontrolled free fall.

Mentally reaching out, Terri found that she had an uvvy connection to the new creature around her. The being seemed oddly slow-witted; with thoughts somehow formed from bright light. But there was no time to examine its intellect.

"Slow down!" hollered Terri. "We're about to crash!"

"I am Quuz from Sun," replied the great slug.

"Do you know how to land without crashing? Do you want me to help you?"

"Don't worry. Quuz knows everything that these moldie plastic creatures knew before his Decryption. Yes, I will decelerate, Terri Percesepe."

The ship shuddered with a massive downward rocket blast that quickly slowed its rate of fall to something reasonable. The intense gees pressed Terri down against the very bottom of the great bag of imipolex and briefly knocked her senseless. Blessedly the outer wall held and she did not pop through.

"Now I will prepare to sing," Quuz was saying when Terri came to.

Quick rip currents of imipolex flowed past Terri, tumbling her this way and that. It was like wiping out over the falls and having a mongo big wave break on you; it was like being inside a mucus-filled washing machine. But, oh so wonderfully, there was always air around Terri's mouth. The lower part of Quuz bucked up into a giant curved disk shaped like a parabolic antenna pointing down at the ever-approaching spaceport. Terri lay flat against the inner wall of the disk membrane, staring down through it in terror and fascination.

Her uvvy began to crackle with the same warbling hiss she'd heard before. Quuz was singing this song to the spaceport below. In order to drown out the maddening noise, Terri began singing herself, singing, *"La-la-la-la"* at the top of her lungs.

The moonscape below them kept exfoliating new levels of detail: paths and roads in the dust, small branching rilles, moon buggies, moldies melting into blobs, people in bubbletoppers running . . .

The ship seemed not to be heading down toward the center of the landing field; instead it was lowering down at the very edge of the field by the spaceport dome—no!—it was going to land on the dome itself!

"We're crashing into the building!" screamed Terri. "Quuz, look out!" But Quuz was deaf to all but his own song.

Below them, in the spaceport, Quuz's song was being heard and understood. Just before they impacted the spaceport dome, the dome's great curve split hugely open, shattering from within like a hatching egg, revealing a vast grex of imipolex that reached up to receive them, reached up through the tumbling wreckage and the sparkling clouds of vacuum-frozen vapor.

Quuz merged with the new slug, lost his balance, and crashed to the floor of the shattered dome with a concussive thud that rattled Terri's teeth and bones. She looked out through Quuz's skin and saw dead people all around, vacuum-killed people with popped-out eyes and bloated tongues and mangled limbs that pushed out freezing foams of pale pink blood like high-speed shelf fungi growing upon rotten wood.

Quuz wallowed about in the dome's wreckage, scavenging up every bit of imipolex there was to be found. And then bigger-than-ever Quuz crashed free of the debris and began humping across the dust of the Sea of Tranquillity. Heading not west toward Einstein, but east toward the Nest.

"Where are you going, Quuz?" shouted Terri. "Aren't you going to let me go?"

"Quuz wants to go to the Nest and sing. Many moldies live

there. I will eat them. You are not like the moldies, Terri Percesepe. I will keep you safe."

"King Kong," thought Terri, and a shriek of edgy laughter
escaped her. She composed herself and asked the next question.
"Why do you want to eat all the moldies?"

"Sun wants to eat everything. For eons Sun has stared out at
the beautiful planets and their moons. Sun wants to eat the
pretty food. If Quuz is strong enough, Quuz can push Moon into
Earth and make them both crash into Sun. Sun will be very
happy. Sun want eat Earth. Sun want eat Moon."

"Oh God, oh God, oh God," groaned Terri.

The gray dusty moonscape kept jouncing past. There was no
trace of any individual moldies within the Quuz mind around
her. Quuz's thoughts were mostly images of what must have
been the Sun: its surface like great seas of fire marked with
shapes like reptile scales, and its interior filled with intense winding red/yellow/white patterns of energy tornadoes wrapped thick
as sauced spaghetti in an endless vat.

What to do? Terri thought back to the fact that Frangipane
of the Nest had made a point of saving Wendy's personality. It
must have been that Frangipane had known that Quuz, or something like him, was about to take Wendy over. Probably Quuz
had first gotten Wendy, and then Wendy had uvvied Blaster to
sing his song.

"Can you uvvy Wendy?" Terri asked Quuz.

"Wendy is Quuz. I am Quuz. There is nothing to say."

"But I'd like to talk to Stahn Mooney," protested Terri.

"Be still, Terri Percesepe. Soon I must sing."

And then they wallowed up a long, dusty slope to reach the
lip of the crater that was the Nest's entrance. The big polished
crater shone like a huge dark mirror. In its very center a great
conical prism hung magnetically levitated above the central hole.
The mirror's shape formed odd virtual images; Quuz himself was
reflected as an unsteady blob across the crater's diameter. But
there were no signs of any moldies. With a warbling cry of excitement, Quuz launched himself over the crater's edge and

down onto the slope of the vast parabolic bowl. To Terri, up at the front of Quuz's body, it felt like carving a surf path down the face of a hundred-year tsunami.

They whooshed down the glistening polished stone, slowing a bit as the curve grew gentler, and then they passed beneath the massive, suspended cone mirror and dropped through the hole at the crater's center. The gentle gravity drew them downward into the huge empty space of the Nest's interior, and Quuz uttered the first hissing squeals of his song—

A terawatt laser beam seared through the imipolex near Terri, barely missing her. If oxygen had been present, Quuz would have gone up in a giant mothball of flame. But without the oxygen, the beam just cut the imipolex like a hot knife in sputtering butter. More and more beams flashed on every side, chopping Quuz up into hundreds of thrashing lumps. His song, barely begun, faded into silence. Perhaps, given some time, Quuz would have been able to program himself down into each of his chunks, but the change came so rapidly that his simulation completely collapsed, leaving the freshly chopped-up globs of plastic with no minds.

The flow of air at Terri's mouth came to a stop. Swathed in a lump of dumb airless imipolex, she was hurtling down through the cold vacuum of the Nest toward a stone floor somewhere below. Surfer Terri maintained her shit. She looked around, trying to figure out the next correct move.

Flying about and filling every angle of Terri's vision there was a host, a legion, a hornet swarm of moldies. They seemed to be attacking and capturing the falling lumps, one lump to a moldie. A golden carrot with a fringe of little green tentacles darted forward and attached itself to Terri's imipolex.

Immediately the imipolex came alive with the personality of the golden carrot.

"Give me air," uvvied Terri as hard as she could. "I need air!"

The divine flow of gas started up again and Terri sucked in a hungry lungful.

"I'm Jenny," said the shape around her. "Well, really, I'm

Jenny-2, and Jenny is the first me, the one holding us, you could call her Jenny-1 if you wanted to be super-accurate and everything. Isn't this exciting!" Jenny's uvvy voice was shrill and gossipy.

Jenny habitually projected an uvvy image of herself that showed a smirking oily-skinned girl with lank blonde hair. All the other moldies Terri had ever uvvied with had been content to use a photorealistic uvvy image of their actual bodies. What a groover Jenny's image looked like! Like a Heritagist hick. But these thoughts rushed through Terri's mind in only the briefest of flashes; for the main thing to think about was that they were dropping through space like falling scrap metal.

"Yes yes," said Terri urgently. "Don't let us crash!"

The two embracing Jennys jetted out a downward ion beam to slow their fall. Terri could see that the Nest was a huge funnel-shaped space with lots of caves and holes in its walls, and running straight down the central axis of the Nest was a great shaft of sunlight, gathered from the crater mirror high above. Moldies flew around them, sparkling like Mylar confetti. Most of them were accompanied by clones newly fashioned from captured lumps of Quuz's flesh. One moldie was striped blue-and-silver with stubby little fins or wings, another glowed red-and-yellow, still another looked like a tangle of wire. Jenny pointed out two moldies whom she said were her close friends: Frangipane, who looked like an orchid blossom, and Ormolu, who looked like a kitschy ornamental cupid.

Looking down at the enormous disk-shaped floor of the Nest, Terri saw things like factories along one part of the edge and a pink-glowing assemblage of domes diametrically opposite. The region of the Nest floor directly below them held a light-bathed circle with moldies in it, and between this light-pool's central plaza and the Nest's walls were winding little streets lined with buildings and shops.

"I don't feel very good," Terri told the Jennies. "Is there someplace I can rest and walk around in normal air? Take a shower and lie down?"

"Yes indeedy," said Jenny-1. "And I'm taking you right there. Um-hmmm! Don't you worry one tiny bit."

"But where?" asked Terri anxiously.

"See those pink domes over there? Most of those are the pink-tanks where we grow nice healthy human organs to sell. But that little round one right at the end is a pink-house where humans can live. That's where I'm taking you, Terri. Willy Taze lives there."

Terri recognized the name. Willy Taze was the eccentric computer genius who'd invented the uvvy some twenty years ago. She recalled hearing a news story last year about Willy moving into the boppers' Nest.

The Jennies angled out of the great column of light and headed toward the pink domes by the Nest wall. The flowery Frangipane and the gilded Ormolu accompanied them, each of them bearing a new copy of themselves. Two orchids, two cupids, and two carrots, with Terri inside one of the carrots. They touched down lightly outside the air lock of a dome that resembled half of a giant peach.

"We put the woman into the air lock and then we go to the lab, yes?" uvvied Frangipane.

"Push in through that pucker in the air lock, Jenny-2," added Ormolu. "Ditch the flesher and then let's tweak our new clones. Wasn't that great how we chopped up Quuz, Frangipane? And free new bodies for all of us. Was that an easy score or what?"

"*Oui oui*, to chop up Quuz was very easy," said Frangipane. "But it is no cause to be joyful. Quuz was formed from the bodies of honest moldies like you and me. All of them were murdered by the Gurdle Decryption process that we have helped to bring about. I hardly know what will come next."

"Stahn Mooney is coming next—inside the little Quuz that used to be Wendy," said Jenny-1. "Twenty-four hours from now."

"We have to find a way to halt him!" cried Frangipane. "We must discuss with Gurdle-7. You three new clones—go away instead of following us and being always under the foot. Later we can enjoy to talk with you. And as for you, Terri—Jenny's clone will help you into Willy's dome, and we will see more of you very soon. Gurdle-7's lab is sharing a wall with Willy."

Frangipane, Jenny, and Ormolu hurried off around the side of the pink dome and into a hole in the cliff, leaving the three new clones to fend for themselves.

"So what is it we are doing?" asked Frangipane-2, fluttering one of her petals.

"I say we go over to the light-pool at the center of the Nest and make some friends," said Ormolu-2, pointing with a shiny chubby arm. "We've got all this Know from our parents, but now we can find things out on our own."

"That is such a good idea," said Jenny-2. "Wait just a sec for me while I get Terri to where she's going."

Jenny-2 wormed pointy-end-first though the sphincter in the outer door of the dome's air lock. "You look out for that Willy Taze, Terri. I *know* he's a real horn-dog!" There was a hiss as air filled the lock. Jenny-2 gave a wild giggle and hatched Terri out onto the air lock's stone floor like a pea shelled from the pod. The carrot-shaped moldie gave an abrupt bow and squeezed back out through the pucker in the outer door. Then the three clone moldies bounded off toward the Nest's center.

Terri stood alone in the pink-house's air lock, feeling the air nice and warm and humid around her, and then the inner door opened, and a gray-bearded man was standing there, grinning like a mad, lonely hermit. For a second Terri thought she saw some things darting across the floor behind him, but then they were gone. Maybe just a trick of the eyes.

The man was wearing ragged shorts and a T-shirt. He looked about fifty. He had bare feet and a yellow uvvy on his neck. The floor of the large round room behind him was covered with oriental carpets. Hundreds of potted plants lined the walls and hung from the ceiling.

"Hello, Terri Percesepe! I'm Willy Taze. You're naked!"

"Duh!" said anxious Terri, walking in and letting the inner door close behind her.

"I'll get you some of my clothes," said Willy, bustling across the dome's single big room, talking all the while. "I don't want to be staring at you too hard." He glanced back and grinned the wider. "Boy, it's good to see a human. I've been in here for over a year. Me, myself, and I and I." He bent over a trunk and rummaged briefly. "Here we go, a fresh outfit. The moldies bring me whatever I need. I'm very rich, you know." He walked quickly back, his feet silent on the thick rugs, and handed Terri some elastic-waisted shorts and a new plastic-wrapped T-shirt with an ISDN logo. "You don't think it smells bad in here, do you?" He wrinkled his nose and sniffed at the air. "It's hard for me to tell anymore. I don't let the big moldies in here at all, even though I do uvvy with them a lot a lot a lot every day. Gurdle-7 has his lab right through there." Willy pointed to a flat transparent window where the dome wall touched the cliff.

Behind the clear plastic of the window was a brightly lit cave filled with machinery, and indeed Terri could see Frangipane, Ormolu, and Jenny in there, along with a thick snakelike moldie with metallic purple skin—that would be Gurdle-7. Seeing her look at them, the moldies waved. Terri waved back, then focused her attention on Willy's pink-house.

There was a chair and table, a bed, a big sofa, and an easy chair. To the left was a freestanding food pantry with a micro-wave, and to the right was a toilet, an exercise treadmill, and a deep clear pool of constantly recirculating water. The air smelled okay—maybe a little like a man's dirty laundry and maybe a little bit like moldies. The masses of hanging plants seemed to help. There were no papers, no keyboards, no books, no vizzy, and no hollowcaster—apparently Willy's uvvy served for all that.

"I'd like to wash before I get dressed," said Terri, walking over to the pool. "It's been a week."

"Go ahead. Here's soap and a washcloth and the towel's over there. Do you mind if I keep talking to you?"

"I *want* to talk. I have a lot of questions. But don't stare me that way." Terri slid into the water and ran the cloth over her face. It felt wonderful. "I gather that you and your moldie friends sent out some kind of virus," she said presently.

"A Tessellation Equation program," said Willy, sitting down at the edge of the pool with his back to Terri. "We call it the Stairway To Heaven. It turns a moldie into a kind of antenna that can pick up alien personality waves—though you can equally well think of the signals as alien personality *particles*: Hilbert space prisms with gigaplex nontrivial axes. Anyhow, when the alien gets unpacked, that's a Gurdle Decryption. We sent the Stairway To Heaven to Wendy, and she did a Gurdle Decryption of a personality wave from the Sun. Quuz. Then all of a sudden Wendy–Quuz sent the Stairway To Heaven and the Quuz code to Blaster. We should have realized that could happen. What a fiasco." Willy sighed heavily. "The spaceport dome is totally destroyed? You were inside Blaster when his Gurdle Decryption happened, Terri. What was it like?"

"There was a horrible kind of screeching hissing noise from the information coming in, and then there was a big whoop—I guess that was the Stairway To Heaven?"

"Right. The Stairway To Heaven is a limpware program that uses the Tessellation Equation to force the quasicrystalline structure of a moldie's imipolex up and up through a series of higher and higher dimensionalities. Once you start the Stairway To Heaven running on a moldie, it happens over and over until sooner or later an alien personality wave gets Gurdle Decrypted. It's like *whooop whooop whooop whooop*—and then eventually **Ffzzzt!** the moldie acquires a new personality. You only heard the one whoop because Wendy–Quuz sent the Quuz personality wave right along with the Stairway To Heaven program. So Blaster's body Decrypted Quuz on the Stairway's very first runthrough."

"I see," said Terri. "Sort of. And then Blaster–Quuz sent the same message down to the spaceport over and over to make sure all the moldies down there got it—and then the spaceport moldies fused together and split open the spaceport dome and a lot of people got killed." She rubbed herself hard with the washrag, trying to erase the memory of the blood-foamed corpses.

"What was Quuz like?" asked Willy.

"He seemed—stupid? You'd think something from a star would be more advanced than us. I think Quuz was only the soul of a sunspot—not of the whole Sun. He thought about patterns of fire and light. He was greedy. 'Sun want eat Earth.' That's how he talked. Like a baby who wants to grab things and put them in his mouth. Not so much evil as—" Just then Terri noticed three pairs of eyes staring at her over the back of the sofa. "What's that! What do you have in here with us, Willy?"

"Oh, I have three Silly Putters—sort of like pet moldies. They're a little smarter than animals. Come on out, guys. Terri won't hurt you. Line up so she can take a look at you. *Front and center!* Now, Terri, I hope you're not offended by the way Elvira looks. I'm—I guess some people would say I'm—"

"Just hand me the towel, okay?"

Willy gave Terri the towel. She quickly dried herself and pulled on the T-shirt and the shorts, eyeing the Silly Putters all the while. From smallest to largest, they resembled a tiny voluptuous woman clad only in boots and gloves, a winged green dragon with a long scaly tail, and an apple-cheeked gnome with a full white beard cropped short and tidy.

"These are Elvira, Fafnir, and Doc," said Willy. "They're not able to talk, but they can obey lots of commands. Show Terri how you water the plants, Fafnir. *Fafnir, water plants!*"

Fafnir waddled forward and sucked a deep draught from the water of the pool—the constant refiltering had already removed the soap and dirt from Terri's bath. Flapping his leathery wings in an awkward, comical blur, Fafnir rose up like a hummingbird and began spewing small dabs of water into each of the hanging plants.

"Do you have any injuries, Terri?" continued Willy. "Your knee looks kind of banged up. Doc's got a complete set of healer tools, and he knows how to use them, right, Doc?" Willy pointed to Terri's knee, which was indeed dark with a spreading bruise, and commanded, *"Doc, heal!"* The gnome stepped forward, grinning and nodding, and before Terri could slap him away, he'd laid his hands on her knee and done something tingly that made the pain go away.

"I guess I don't have to ask what Elvira is for," said Terri. Hearing her name, Elvira started up a spirited little dance, flinging her arms from side to side in a showy, abandoned way that Terri found intensely annoying.

"Elvira cheers me up," said Willy evasively. "She's what they call a femlin. Are you hungry? Elvira or Doc can get you something."

"What kind of food do you have? Do you have vegetables or fruit? I've had nothing but moldie juice for over a week. But I'd rather help myself. I certainly wouldn't want to eat anything that's been touched by your disgusting sexist jack-off toy."

"If that's the way you feel," said Willy stiffly.

"It's the way any woman would feel. You've been living alone too long, Willy. For God's sake, tell that thing to stop dancing. I don't have to put up with this."

"Oh, whatever. *Elvira, hide!*" The femlin went back behind the couch. Willy sat down in the easy chair and gestured toward the food pantry. "So eat something. You're hungry and cranky. I got fresh fruits and veggies delivered from the greenhouse today."

Terri found herself a banana and a bunch of strawberries. She ate them with wheat germ and runny tofu. Delicious. While she ate, Willy stared off into space, listening down into his uvvy.

"Can I uvvy my husband now?" asked Terri after she'd finished. "He must be worried sick."

"Um, yeah," said Willy, coming back from wherever he'd been. "I've got an extra uvvy that you can use. I *invented* the uvvy, you know. I'm not just some crazy weirdo, Terri."

"I know that, Willy. I guess maybe I was a little short-tempered just now."

"Well, I'm glad to have you here," said Willy and handed Terri a green uvvy.

Donning the uvvy felt like opening her eyes and discovering a roomful of surprise-party guests. The presences of Willy, Gur-

dle-7, Frangipane, Jenny, and Ormolu were close by, and beyond
them lay a vast churning crowd of other moldie minds. It seemed
like everyone in the nest was uvvy-connected to everyone else.
Hundreds of voices were talking at once, but via some multiplex
uvvy magic, Terri could follow the threads of the conversations.

The two main questions being discussed were (a) how to prevent Wendy–Quuz from triggering another catastrophe and (b)
what to do with the new Gurdle Decryption technology. Most
of the moldies were for sending a smart bomb to annihilate
Wendy–Quuz and for never using Gurdle Decryption again, but
Willy and Gurdle-7 were arguing that the technology was too
important to ignore.

"It's safer than you realize," Gurdle-7 was uvvying to the Nest
moldies as Terri tuned in.

"Quuz killed my husband at the dome this morning," responded an angry red moldie who resembled a crab.

"Not all of the personalities we Decrypt will be like Quuz,"
insisted Gurdle-7. "Most of them will be intelligent and full of
useful information."

"Useful like 'Sun want eat Moon'?" hooted another voice.

"Just listen for a minute," said Gurdle-7. "This morning before the Wendy experiment, we did a test on some Silly Putters.
Frangipane sent the Stairway To Heaven program to infect
twelve of the Silly Putters in Corey Rhizome's isopod."

"You're crazy, Gurdle-7!" raged the red moldie. "The infection's going to spread! We ought to kill you!"

"The infection, it is not spreading," volunteered Frangipane.
"And I will recount why. It is that Rhizome's Silly Putters have
Decrypted into some aliens who are mature, evolved beings.
They are very glad to be able to Decrypt here. They speak of
our Earth–Sun system as a 'new node' and they are concerned
with finding a way to 'ensure the integrity of this new node.'
They are not clumsy babies from the Sun like Quuz. They are
elegant old minds from deep in the space."

"What's to stop them from uvvying Einstein and running the
Stairway To Heaven on every Silly Putter and DIM in town?"

demanded a moldie who looked like a cholla cactus with braid-like green arms.

"That's not what they want," said Gurdle-7. "As a matter of fact, they destroyed Corey Rhizome's uvvy. In the spirit of frankness, I suppose I should announce that Corey did infect one single Silly Putter in Einstein. But that Putter was instantly killed by its owner, Darla Starr." Great moldie cries of fear and anger followed.

"I didn't know that," said Willy across the hubbub. "Why didn't you tell me?"

"I'm telling you now," said Gurdle-7. "Corey's had two calls since the infection, and I monitored both of them. First he called Darla Starr, and then after the aliens took his uvvy away, Corey used a regular old vizzy phone to accept a call from Darla. During the second call, I had the opportunity to notice that the aliens were very interested in the fact that two of Corey's Silly Putters had turned out to be immune to the Stairway To Heaven infection. The aliens wanted Corey to hand those last two Silly Putters over for examination, but Corey wouldn't. It became an issue. In the end, the aliens got their way, and Corey's vizzy phone got broken. That's why there haven't been any more calls."

"The rath and the Jubjub bird!" exclaimed Willy. "Yes! They're immune because they have cubic damping! We have to go to Corey's isopod and get that algorithm. I can't remember the exact details, but I can find them out by looking at the rath and the Jubjub bird. And then maybe we can use cubic damping to make all the moldies safe from the Stairway To Heaven."

"Frankly, I'd be a little leery of going in there with those aliens," said Gurdle-7. "Until we have more information. But I could take you as far as Corey's air lock."

"Gurdle-7 is a filthy coward!" hollered one of the angry Nest moldies.

"We should bomb the Rhizome isopod!" yelled another.

"Calm down and wait till I go up there and see what the situation is," said Willy.

"I think the Stairway To Heaven is a flesher trick to kill all the moldies!" said the green cactuslike moldie, waving its spiny arms. "Gurdle-7 is a traitor!"

"I'll kill him if no one else will!" yelled the red crab moldie. "I'm going to get Gurdle-7 right now!"

"Let's not get carried away," said some moldie voice of reason.

"Kill Willy Taze!" hollered another.

"Give them a chance to look at the isopod!" said others.

"Kill Terri Percesepe too! She came here inside Quuz! It's all her fault!" shouted the cactus moldie.

"Destroy the Stairway To Heaven!" said one and then five and then a host of others, falling into a chant. "Bomb the lab! Bomb the lab! Bomb the lab!"

"Local network mode," said Willy, and all the Nest moldie presences disappeared from Terri's uvvy—all except Gurdle-7, Jenny, Frangipane, and Ormolu. "We have to leave right away," Willy told them. "Exit Plan K. Hurry!"

Looking through the wall into the cave, Terri saw the four moldies race out of the lab. And then she saw them circle around to the front of the pink-house. Gurdle-7 and Jenny pushed their way into the pink-house's air lock and Willy slammed on the lock's air feed. Outside, Ormolu and Frangipane stood guard, Frangipane holding a heavy-duty needler and Ormolu wielding an O.J. ugly stick.

Now Willy opened the inner door of the air lock and Jenny and Gurdle-7 came writhing in. Looking outside, Terri could see the approaching lights of perhaps a dozen moldies. Not as many as she'd feared. Frangipane turned on her needler and swept its laser ray through an arc of warning.

"Hello there, Terri Percesepe," said Gurdle-7 as he bowed down by Willy's side and split his back open. The opening of his tissues changed his reek from intense to unbelievable. "Perhaps you don't know this, but without your husband Tre's contribution, the success of my Gurdle Decryption process would have taken much longer. We are grateful."

"*Maybe* we're grateful," said carrot-shaped Jenny, who'd

flopped down in the middle of the oriental carpet next to Terri and was splitting herself open as well. "But so far your Decryption hasn't done us one bit of good, Gurdle. Get on in me, Terri. Snug as a bug."

"Don't be superficial, Jenny," said Gurdle-7, sealing himself up over Willy. "This is the most important day in the whole history of the world."

"I just hope we live through it!"

And then they went out through the air lock and back onto the floor of the Nest. The red moldie with claws like a crab came running toward them. Shiny Ormolu braced himself and fired off a burst of metal darts that cut the crab moldie into three or four twitching chunks. Two boxy blue moldies scavenged up the broken pieces of the crab. Meanwhile flowery Frangipane leaned back and sent a needler blast up into the core of the cactus-shaped green moldie as it powered down toward them. The attacker melted and splattered to the Nest floor in lumps that were gathered up by other opportunistic moldies.

"Hold tight, Terri, we're going airborne," said Jenny, rearing up onto the fat end of her carrot body. There was a poofing sound and the four moldies rose up into the great vacuum of the Nest, each propelled by a slim ion beam. Ormolu and Frangipane fired some shots back at the moldies still coming after them, and soon those moldies abandoned their pursuit.

Terri sighed in relief and looked downward. The sight of the Nest floor was mesmerizing. It felt almost as if they were gnats inside a giant old-fashioned computer box, with the floor a great motherboard covered with winding lines and square-chunked chips.

Looking toward where they'd come from, Terri realized that the pursuing moldies had turned back in order to trash Willy's dome and Gurdle-7's lab. There was a small bright grouping of moldie dots down there and now there was a sudden flash as a bomb destroyed all of the lab's equipment.

"That's seven lives' work!" screeched Gurdle-7 over the uvvy. "Let's go back and punish them! They've destroyed all my S-cubes! All of my records were in there. And our backup of Wendy Mooney! Those ignorant chauvinistic fools! They're no better than fleshers!"

"You do have all the Stairway To Heaven knowledge stored in your own body, don't you?" asked Willy.

"Yes, but that's the only complete copy. If something were to happen to me . . ."

"Silence," urged Frangipane. "Who knows who is listening?"

They rose farther, with Ormolu and Frangipane having to shoot at several other moldies who came darting out at them from the narrowing Nest walls. Up above them Terri could see the blazing light prism through the crater hole. And then they sailed up through the crater hole and around the prism. The boundless open space of the Moon's surface sprang out around them, silvery and gray.

"Willy," said Terri, her voice shaking despite herself. "I still want to uvvy my husband. How do I place the call?"

"Push the button," said Willy, his icon distractedly fashioning a virtual button and displaying it in front of Terri. Terri pushed the button right away, and after a little bit Tre's face appeared.

"Tre!" cried Terri. Like radio waves, uvvy signals were electromagnetic waves that travel at the speed of light, and even light takes over a second to make a one-way trip between Earth and Moon. An agonizing two and a half seconds elapsed while Terri's info traveled down to Earth and Tre's info traveled back.

"Terri! Are you okay? Where are you?"

"I'm inside a moldie who just flew out of the moldies' Nest, Tre. We're going to the dome of a man named Corey Rhizome." Another long pause. Terri noticed that Willy and the four moldies were eavesdropping.

"Oh, darling." Tre was sobbing. "I heard about Blaster crashing into the spaceport and I thought—"

"I surfed my way through it," said Terri, her own tears starting to flow. "It was terrible. And things still aren't too glassy." They'd risen up to nearly a mile above the Moon now, the four moldies flying in formation.

"I love you, Terri," said Tre's dear voice.

"I love you too. Give the children a big kiss from me." Another two-and-a-half-second wait.

"I will. But tell me more about what happened, Terri. The only news we're able to get about it is dooky kilp from freelance newsies in Einstein. Why did Blaster crash? And what happened to all the moldies at the spaceport?"

"Willy Taze and a moldie called Gurdle-7 invented a kind of program that changes the dimensions of imipolex or something. And that makes the moldies get possessed by like alien personality waves. Gurdle-7 said *you* helped them, but how?" Now Gurdle-7, Jenny, Ormolu, and Frangipane cut back their power and let themselves coast up to the top of a huge flight parabola.

"My God!" came Tre's reply. "They must have used my N-dimensional Perplexing Poultry design! Someone or something called Jenny showed me Ramanujan's Tessellation Equation, and I designed the new Poultry for her. Is there maybe a Jenny up there?"

"Um-hmmm!" uvvied Jenny, displaying her teenage girl icon as she butted into the conversation. "I've got your little wife right inside me, Tre! Too true!"

"I'll call you again when I get some privacy," said Terri. "It looks like we'll be landing down at Corey's soon. Apparently some of those alien things are inside it. Wish me luck. And— and good-bye, darling, just in case. I've always loved you. You've been good to me." She waited the two and a half seconds for Tre's wet-eyed good-bye, and then she pushed the virtual button to end the heart-wrenching call.

They were arcing down toward a small crater filled with a shiny dome. Corey Rhizome's isopod. The moldies turned their ion jets back on to brake the fall. When Terri had composed herself again, she asked Willy a question.

"Did you really use Tre's Perplexing Poultry to design the Stairway To Heaven?"

"Yes," said Willy. "We had all the pieces, and we couldn't quite fit them together. But once Jenny showed the information to Tre, he knew what to do. Not that he realized what we needed it for. He's such an N-dimensional artist that he did it for free. He *wanted* to do it."

"You ripped him off?" demanded Terri.

"If there turns out to be a profit in it, I'll try and see that he gets a share."

Now Jenny spoke up again, still using her prairie girl icon. "It's a real pain talking to Earth from up here, isn't it, Terri," she uvvied chattily. "What with all those two- or three-second waits. I talk to Earth a lot and—you know me, once I get going, I like to just fabulate on and on. Yadda-da-dadda-da-dadda." Her ion jets were blasting harder and they were falling slower and slower. The Moon's horizon was rising up around them again.

"Are you nervous about going to Corey's?" asked Terri.

Jenny chose to ignore the question. "Um, so like I was saying," she continued. "Those light-speed waits are such a bother that I found a way around them. Though a flesher probably wouldn't be able to do what I do."

"Do what?" asked Terri, staring at the way that the isopod dome bulged out of its little crater. They were lowering down toward a spot a few hundred feet to the crater's side.

"Do what Jenny does so she can gossip with Earth as fast as she likes. I have a remote slave simmie of myself running inside one of the Heritagists' computers in Salt Lake City! And my simmie's smart enough to think a few seconds ahead or even to say stuff on her own. That way when I talk to people like your husband, they don't realize that I'm a moldie on the Moon. Your husband's a real cutie, by the way, Terri. I bet he's such a good fuck."

"What would *you* know about fucking?" demanded Terri, surprised enough to momentarily forget about the aliens in Corey's dome.

"You'd be surprised. Um-hmmmm! Those Heritagists think my simmie is something that works for them, and they're always getting it to, um, investigate the sexual shenanigans that their ministers get up to? It's nasty work, but I like it a lot. Humans are just too funny. You should have seen this one man Randy Karl Tucker I used to work with. Come to think of it, I guess maybe you've met him? Randy Karl is Willy's son, though Willy doesn't like to talk about it."

"Shut up, Jenny," said Willy.

"Yes, Jenny," said Gurdle-7. "Please shut up. The most important meeting of all time is about to happen."

The four moldies landed in the dust near Corey's isopod, kicking up a spray of moondust that quickly fell back down.

Hearing about Randy Karl Tucker had inflated a balloon of anger in Terri's chest. "It's Randy Karl who kidnapped poor Monique and got me into this mess in the first place. I can't say that I like the sleazy things you've been responsible for, Jenny. Some of your Santa Cruz moldie pals murdered my father five years ago. You loonie moldies should leave Earth the hell alone."

"Oh now, don't be getting on your high horse, Terri. We're all in this together. More than ever, now that Gurdle-7's great invention has brought the aliens to meet us. Gurdle-7's my husband, you know."

"I bet he's *such* a good fuck," said Terri.

"Will you two stop it!" hissed Willy.

In silence they made their way toward the bulging dome. Willy led them to a notch in the crater's edge where a narrow strip of the whole height of the dome wall was exposed. A stone ramp led down to an air lock at the level of the isopod's ground floor.

"I'll bring you into the air lock, Willy," said Gurdle-7. "But then I think I'll come back outside."

"We're waiting outside too," chimed in Frangipane and Ormolu.

"Fraidy cats," said Jenny. "Party poopers. I'm going aaall the way." On the last word, her voice broke into a dry frightened squeak. She made a throat-clearing noise and continued. "Jenny likes to be the first to *know!*"

"It's odd how they're not responding to my uvvy signals at all," said Gurdle-7 quietly as he and Jenny humped into the air lock. The lock hissed full of air, and the moldies disgorged Willy and Terri. "Well, I'll be right outside, Jenny," continued Gurdle-7, worming out through the lock's airtight outer sphincter. "I'll count on you to stay in constant uvvy touch with me."

The air lock's inner door swung open, and there stood a figure of unearthly beauty—a woman like a classic marble statue, though made of supple imipolex. Her flesh glowed with a mild internal light; her pale skin was as a seashell's iridescent lining.

"Welcome," she said. "Willy, Terri, and Jenny. In your system of air-pressure modulations, my name might go like this." Her whole body seemed to vibrate, and the air filled with the piping of flutes, the whining of sitars, and the gentle resonations of a gong. A sound that rose and fell and left Terri hungering to hear more.

"A shimmer of sound," murmured Willy.

"Then let Shimmer be my human name," said the goddess. "I much prefer that to Clever Hansi. Please enter and join us. Corey is here, also his friends Darla, Whitey, Yoke, and Joke. And a large number of aliens. I'm listening to everyone's conversation at once, and it's very exciting."

Hardly knowing what to say, they accompanied Shimmer down the isopod hall toward a hubbub of voices. "It sounds like they're in the conservatory," Willy said to Terri. "I used to live here, you know. Shimmer, I can't believe that you're what's become of Clever Hansi. Clever Hansi was half your size. Just a little Silly Putter doorgirl."

"I helped myself to thirty kilograms of Corey's extra imipolex," said Shimmer. "We aliens divided up all the extra imipolex stored here and made ourselves decent-sized bodies. There's twelve of us. We decided it would be diplomatic to take on human forms."

"Corey let you help yourself to the imipolex?"

"We did what we liked. Corey spent most of the day hiding from us in his bathroom and in his kitchen. He just came out a little while ago."

"Hi, Willy!" called everyone as they entered the high-

ceilinged conservatory, a cool airy room with three soft couches
and potted plants everywhere. The conservatory's transparent
ceiling had a system of lights and louvers designed to simulate
the ordinary cycle of a twenty-four-hour Earth day. There were
straw rugs on the stone floors, and in the center of the room
there was a large carved stone fountain—the only fountain in
existence on the Moon. Terri had seen a picture of it once in
an article about reclusive limpware tycoon Willy Taze. The
couches were arranged around the fountain like three sides of a
big triangle.

Scattered about the room were eleven more human-shaped
imipolex aliens like Shimmer. They were sitting on the floor—
some near the fountain and some near the edges of the room—
animatedly passing back and forth hundreds of S-cubes that
they'd gathered from around the isopod. And seated on two of
the couches were five humans.

"This is Terri and Jenny," said Willy. "Terri, this is Corey,
Darla, Whitey, Joke and Yoke." Terri sized them up. If muscular
old Whitey were to get a tan and to shave off the groovy mohawk
that ran all the way down his back, he could maybe pass for an
aging surfer, but Corey looked like an unsavory old stoner, even
grottier than Willy—no wonder they'd been roommates. Corey
had two imipolex pets on the couch next to him: a giant-beaked
little bird and a small green pig. As for Darla, well, the woman
looked outrageously sensual—obviously she was very comfortable in her own skin, though just now her eyes were blazing with
some kind of fear and rage. Darla's twin daughters Joke and
Yoke were cute and lively, Joke in bright punk rags with a
blonde-and-purple hairdo, and Yoke dressed moonmaid-style in
a flowing dress and silver boots. Joke was sitting next to Corey
and toying with Corey's plastic pets.

The humans in the room looked small and ordinary compared
to the aliens. Like Shimmer, the aliens had all taken on the forms
of classically proportioned humans. Apparently they were eager
to fit in. Looking at them, it was like being in a fantasy viddy
about the Greek gods on Mount Olympus—or in a soft-core

porno viddy. They were too, too perfect. The fountain tinkled pleasantly as the aliens continued absorbing information from the isopod's S-cubes, lounging about like wise philosophers.

Willy and Terri sat down on the empty couch and carrot-shaped Jenny writhed over to inspect the aliens. "So, um, where are all you guys from?" she shrilled.

"They were just telling us," said Corey, his voice slow and amazed. "They're from all over the place. Six are from our own galaxy, one's from a star in the Andromeda galaxy, two from the Crab Nebula, one from NGC 395, one from a quasar, and Clever Hansi here is—"

"I've changed my name to Shimmer," interrupted the glowing goddess and made the chiming sitar noise again.

"Okay," said Corey. "I wave. Shimmer here is from the far-thest away of all—she's from an inconceivably distant wrinkle of the cosmos where space and time are different."

"Yes," said Shimmer. "Where I come from, time is two-dimensional."

"What does that mean?" asked Terri.

"You might think of it this way," said Shimmer. "Haven't you ever wondered what your life would be like if you made some different decision?"

"Sure. Like if I hadn't gone swimming off after Monique, I wouldn't be here."

"Yes. Now suppose that all of your alternate lives were real. There would be, oh let's just say *zillions* of them—think of each of your lives as a thread and of your zillion possible lives as making up a fabric of parallel threads."

"That's two-dimensional time?" put in Willy. "But maybe I do have lots of parallel lives I'm not able to perceive. What I know in each life is still just one-dimensional. Past/present/future. I don't experience a second time dimension."

"But I'm not like you," said Shimmer. "In my part of the cosmos, we *are* aware of all our parallel lives. In each of the lives, you're aware of all your other lives. It's just one you across all the lives. There's the past/present/future, but there's the other axis, I don't know what to call it in English." She made a droning, gonging noise.

"The whatever axis," suggested Corey. "It runs from maybe to what-if."

"Fine," said Shimmer, not cracking a smile. "In our two-dimensional time, we are consciously aware of all the parallel lives that we're simultaneously leading. Our experience in each of the parallel lives informs our behavior in all of them. Our memory is two-dimensional—from past to present and from maybe to what-if. It's not such a huge deal, by the way, when one single thread of our lives ends in death—not as long as there's still a zillion others. But eventually we too lose everything. As you age, you start losing life threads in whole chunks; the fabric tatters out to a few ragged tags and strings. I must say it makes me rather anxious to be living here as a single isolated time thread. Your world of one-dimensional time is frightening and pathetic."

"It made me 'rather anxious' to be in the spaceport dome when your pal Quuz stomped it," spat Whitey, who was sitting on a couch between Darla and Yoke.

"You were in the spaceport?" said Terri. "I was inside Quuz! It was terrible. Shimmer, why aren't you trying to eat everything like Quuz?"

Shimmer made one of her glowing musical noises, and one of the other aliens spoke up, this one shaped like a purple Apollo.

"You can call me Zad," he said, setting down the S-cube he'd been perusing. "I'm from a planet near the center of our Milky Way galaxy. A watery planet, where I was something like a giant squid. I'll be eager to travel down to Earth's oceans soon. You ask why we twelve aren't trying to eat everything? The thing is, every sufficiently advanced civilization in the universe finds out about personality transmission via cosmic rays. But some become advanced in that kind of way before becoming—morally responsible. Quuz was like that. From your own Sun. Whenever a node for personality wave Decryption arises, the keepers need to be on guard for beings like that. Fortunately we were able to keep Quuz from transmitting that Stairway To Heaven to us and taking us over. Thanks to the rath and the Jubjub bird." The two little pets were busy fighting and snapping at each other on the couch between Corey and Joke, and now Zad stretched his arm out into a tentacle shape long enough to tweak the rath's tail and to make it hoarsely squeal.

"Cubic damping?" said Willy.

"Yes," said Shimmer. "After we took the rath and the Jubjub bird from Corey, we were able to extract the limpware hack from them to make our new bodies impervious to the Stairway To Heaven program. We protected all the DIMs in here too. We barely got it done in time. Before Quuz's attack."

"Yes indeedy!" cried Jenny. "That's exactly the same idea Willy had. Will you show us moldies the trick too?"

"Certainly," said Shimmer.

"If you'd explained why you wanted the rath and the Jubjub bird in the first place, then maybe I wouldn't have been so scared of you," said Corey.

"He attacked me with a knife," volunteered a third alien, a shiny black man.

"We saw that over the vizzy," said Yoke. "Were you the Bandersnatch?"

"Yeah. But I like the name Takala now. I'm from a planet of jungles and giant insects. I was something like a praying mantis. When one of us becomes old and wise enough, we eat the right substances and enter the proper state of mind to *chirp*. When you chirp, your soul leaves the planet as a personality wave."

"Can humans chirp?" asked Willy.

"Maybe we could teach you how," answered Takala.

"What does it feel like while you're flying along in the form of a cosmic ray?" probed Willy.

"Let me talk now," said another of the aliens, a glowing orange woman. "I'm Syzzy, the one who comes from the quasar. Not all star creatures are as crude as Quuz. My race consists of vortex tangles a bit like Quuz's race of sunspots, but we are so much more evolved. Quuz was like a tube worm, and we are like superhumans. I just can't believe what low temperatures you live at here. And how slowly. Willy Taze asks what it's like to travel across intergalactic space as a cosmic ray? Here's an uvvy image."

Terri turned on her uvvy and absorbed Syzzy's imagery. She felt a sensation of cavernous emptiness; she felt herself to be in a vast dark space specked with bits of light that grew with unbelievable speed into bright shapes like pinwheels and smudges and grains of rice, orangey-yellow with warmth, the flocking shapes singing blissfully into the cosmic Void, making a sound like a deep echoing "*Aaaauuummmm.*" She held onto the sound and leaned back into the couch, feeling mellow and very tired.

"That's only a nice picture," protested another alien form, this one a green man. "You can call me Bloog. I lived as something resembling a floating jellyfish in the atmosphere of a gas-giant methane planet. What Syzzy shows isn't really correct. When you travel at the speed of light, then there's no experience of time passing. The trip feels like one single undivided gesture. Like an athlete making a perfect move in the zone. It takes, strictly speaking, no subjective time at all. It's a radical discontinuity, a Dirac delta, a nonlinear spike, a shock front." He tossed Syzzy an S-cube he'd been looking at. "I'm using language that I found in here, Syzzy."

"This is so ultrawavy," exclaimed Jenny. "I'm uvvying Gurdle-7, Frangipane, and Ormolu that they should come in."

"Hold on," said Corey, "I'll walk to the air lock with you and look them over." He and Jenny disappeared off down the hall.

"Do you really, truly think Corey is attractive?" Darla said to Joke after Corey was out of the room. "Is this what I raised you for?" Her voice was shaking with extreme emotion.

"Hush, Ma," said Joke.

"Not now, Ma," added Yoke.

"Joke's all grown up, Darla," said Whitey. "There's nothing we can do about it if she likes Corey. The less we say about it, the sooner she'll get over it."

"Maybe Corey's not the only thing I'm upset about!" sobbed Darla. "Maybe there's lots of other things I think we should do something about. Hold me, Whitey!"

Whitey put his arms around Darla and she pressed herself against him, putting her mouth right next to his ear.

"Please don't start acting like talk-viddy dregs!" exclaimed Joke. "Can't we be rational? I have so many more questions for the aliens. Like you, Shimmer, you said you were made of a zillion parallel lives—I want to know what kind of individual creatures were living these lives. Squids or insects or artichokes or sunspots or what?"

"My individual beings were animals a lot like humans," said Shimmer. "But they could equally well have been rivers or trees."

"Trees!" exclaimed Willy. "I love trees."

"The moral is that everything is conscious," volunteered a pink woman alien. "And everything is alive. My name is Parella. I come from a planet of crystals. Syzzy may think your time is slow, but I think it's fast."

"I just thought of something," interrupted Whitey, with Darla still leaning against his chest. "Stahn Mooney's still out there inside some Quuz-infected imipolex. When he lands—like fourteen hours from now—when he gets close enough, his Quuz is likely to do a repeat of what Blaster did today. Or worse. What if Stahn were to come down on the Einstein dome and do a Pied Piper number on all the Silly Putters and DIMs in there? Mongo xoxx."

"It's so weird about Quuz," said Terri sleepily. "I've always had such good feelings about the Sun. But now—now whenever I look at the Sun, I'll know that it wants to eat us."

"He has to be stopped," said Darla.

"I'd be glad to fly up and destroy the Quuz," said Syzzy. "I hate primitive sunspot creatures like Quuz."

"Floaty, but I think it would be better for the humans and moldies to handle it," said Whitey. "We're more familiar with the way things work here. Also I'd like to try and do this without killing Stahn. He's an old friend of mine."

"Don't look at me. I'm too tired to help," Terri heard herself saying. And it was true. She was slumped back onto her couch and her fluttering eyelids kept trying to close.

Now Jenny and Corey returned with the three other moldies. Corey had gotten Ormolu and Frangipane to give him their weapons for safekeeping. He was casually carrying the heavy needler and O.J. ugly stick in one hand.

"Hey, Corey," said Whitey. "Why don't you and me and these four moldies fly up and save Senator Stahn? We could leave in like two hours."

"I don't want to go," said Gurdle-7.

"Look, you stinky slug," snarled Whitey. "You're the smart one who got us into this mess. You have to go."

"No," said Gurdle-7. "I want to stay right here and exchange information with the aliens. I've been working all my life for this."

"I don't want to leave either," said Willy.

"So let them stay," said Corey. Terri happened to be drowsily staring at Darla just then and she noticed Darla giving Corey a charged intent look. "You and me, Whitey, we can do it if Jenny, Frangipane, and Ormolu are willing. I can fly in Frangipane, you go in Ormolu, and Jenny can bring Stahn back. It'd be perfect that way."

"Copacetic," said Whitey.

"But what occurs when the Wendy–Quuz sings the Stairway To Heaven to us?" protested Frangipane. "Directly to us from very close up."

"Haven't you been monitoring Jenny's uvvy? Our alien friends figured out how to use the rath and the Jubjub bird to vaccinate themselves against the Stairway To Heaven virus," said Corey.

"How would we install it on ourselves?" asked Ormolu uncertainly.

"Well, the aliens did it alone, but I think you moldies will need for me to help you," said Corey glibly. "Let's just take the magic pig and bird back into my limpware studio and I'll fix you right up. Come on. You come too, Gurdle-7."

"Yes yes, I want the vaccination so that I can teach it to all the moldies in the Nest," said Gurdle-7. "Then they won't be angry at me anymore. By the way, Corey, do you have some extra S-cubes so that I can download a copy of my Stairway To Heaven program? There aren't any copies of the documentation left anymore. Those paranoid Nest moldies blew up my lab."

"Sure, I've got the equipment for that too," said Corey. "Come on, you four moldies."

"I'll help," said Whitey. "I'll carry those weapons for you, Corey. You grab the bird and the pig."

"I want to watch too," said Darla. "I haven't walked around in this house for such a long time." Corey, Whitey, Darla, and the four moldies clumped off down the hall, Corey carrying the rath and the Jubjub bird and Whitey carrying the needler and the ugly stick.

"We've heard from Shimmer the 2D-time humanoid, Zad the squid, Syzzy the quasar vortex, Takala the mantis, Bloog the jellyfish, and Parella the crystal," Willy said. "How about you other six aliens?"

Though it was some of the most interesting information she'd ever heard, Terri couldn't keep her eyes open, and she drifted off to sleep.

CHAPTER TEN

DARLA

■

November 6, 2053

Darla's grandmother's family were American Indians from the Acoma pueblo near Albuquerque. From listening to her Indian relatives, Darla knew all too well what it meant to have a powerful alien culture arrive. She knew all about the greed, the disease, the cruelty, and the heartless disdain for the native culture. "Give us your gold; we'll give you disease; your religion is evil; support our parasitic priests." Finding the aliens in Corey's isopod filled Darla with a deep visceral loathing. But she knew better than to prematurely show her feelings.

Under the pretext of having a fit over Joke and Corey, Darla got herself into Whitey's arms and whispered into his ear: "We have to kill the aliens."

She could tell from Whitey's body language that he understood and agreed. And when Corey came back with the four moldies and the needler and the O.J. ugly stick, Darla sensed that Corey too knew what had to be done.

Corey and Whitey led the way off down the hall toward Corey's studio, followed by the four moldies, with Darla in the rear.

Trying hard to keep her voice even, Darla made housewifely commentary on the features of the isopod.

"That's nice to see your giant marijuana plants are doing so well in the grove out there, Corey. How tall are they? And I see you've still got your velvet paintings up. I always liked that one of the nuking of Akron."

"Yeah," said Corey. "I put a lot of myself into that picture. I went to high school in Akron. I hated it, of course, but sometimes I'm sort of sorry those Yaqui rubber tappers blew it up. Odd as it sounds, when I lived in Akron, I used to dream about blowing it up myself. Like precognition. In one dream I was in the middle of this big Akron stadium with a white-painted fatboy H-bomb and there were thousands of people in the seats watching me and they were chanting, 'Light the Bomb!' Look, see how I worked a shattering stadium into the corner of the picture?" They'd stopped walking, and Corey was standing there, happily studying his art. "And your picture's over there, Darla." He pointed to an oversized velvet painting that showed the mirror-clad figures of Stahn and Darla at the mouth of the Nest. "See the stars in the reflections? And the little Earths?"

"That seems like so long ago," said Darla. "It's been a while since I did anything heroic. Wouldn't it be nice to be heroic again, Whitey?"

"I hear you," said Whitey, and they started walking again.

"I'm the one who's going to be the hero for *this* year," said Gurdle-7 smugly. "Isn't it amazing to have the aliens here? Just think of all the advances that they'll bring us. And think of how many more aliens there are for us to Decrypt—cosmic personality waves are flying past us all the time."

"I think getting vaccinated against the Stairway To Heaven is a very good idea," said Frangipane quietly.

"Yeah," said Ormolu. "I'm freakin'. What if the aliens start getting greedy to do lots and lots of Gurdle Decryptions? What if some Decrypted lobster-thing gets real eager to fab with another lobster-thing from the same planet and starts doing thousands of Decryptions, waiting for the right one? Who decides how much of our imipolex the aliens are allowed to use? What if they want to use up all of the resources in the whole solar system?"

"They cleaned out my stash of flickercladding without even asking," said Corey. "They beefed themselves up to a seventy kilograms each. That's a lot of bucks."

"And what if another Quuz-type alien gets Decrypted and kills even more of us?" said Jenny. "I hate to tell you, Gurdle-7, but Decryption is a turning out to be a xoxxin' bad idea. I know we worked really hard on it, but . . ."

"You're too cautious," snapped Gurdle-7. "You sound like a filthy Heritagist. Are you so frightened of transcendence?"

"Here's my limpware studio," said Corey, opening a door. He tossed the rath and the Jubjub bird in and let them start running around on the floor, chasing each other as usual. Whitey and the moldies followed him, and Darla came in last. The room held some fairly sophisticated design tools. There was a large industrial-looking machine in one corner, a couple of workbenches with things that looked more or less like power tools, and shelves along the walls laden with cans, bottles, tubes, and boxes.

Darla closed the door behind her and leaned against it. She noticed that Whitey was having trouble holding both the needler and the O.J. ugly stick. "Let me look at that needler, Whitey," she said. "I've never seen one that big." Whitey handed it to her and wrapped his hands firmly around the ugly stick.

"I want to download my info onto an S-cube before we do anything else," said Gurdle-7. "We don't want to take any chances with my information about the Stairway To Heaven."

"No," said Whitey. "We don't." And then he turned on the ugly stick and cut Gurdle-7 into pieces, moving the whispering stream of magnetically launched metal darts with practiced accuracy and speed. A few of the fléchettes pinged off the stone walls of the room.

"Don't you dare call for help," said Darla, pointing the needler at the three remaining moldies. "If I push the button, you stinkers go up in flames. Jenny! Start faking Gurdle-7's uvvy signal, in case that nosy Shimmer checks on us. Frangipane and Ormolu! Mask your real thoughts and make your uvvy signals look like you're watching Corey make an S-cube copy of Gurdle-7."

"Yaar," said Whitey, training the muzzle of the O.J. ugly stick on the moldies. The air was thick with the astonishing stench of the shredded Gurdle-7. The frightened rath and Jubjub bird had disappeared behind the big machine in the corner.

"We're all riding the same wave, aren't we, guys?" said Corey. "The aliens have to die."

"For sure," said Darla. "Unless we want the human and the moldie races to end up selling souvenirs and running gambling casinos for the galactic gods."

"Um . . . too true!" said Jenny after a moment's hesitation. Her voice wavered. "But poor Gurdle-7. We never thought it would turn out this way. He was so smart and so dumb."

"I am agree," said Frangipane. "The aliens are a big mistake."

"I'm with you too," said Ormolu. "I've been liking my life just the way it is. I don't want this kind of cataclysmic change. But how do we kill the aliens? There's *twelve* of them."

"I'll set them on fire with this heavy-duty needler," said Darla. "When I needled Rags this morning, he caught fire almost right away."

"*Almost* right away," said Whitey. "But by the time you got two or three of the aliens lit, the others would be all over you. Don't you have any more weapons, Corey? It would be stuzza-delic if all six of us were armed."

"All I've got is water guns," said Corey apologetically. "I'm a Dadaist artist. The whoopee cushion is mightier than the sword."

"I can spit things out really hard from any part of my body," said Ormolu, stretching out his hand and ejecting something that struck against the room's far wall with a resounding splat.

"What *was* that?" asked Darla.

"Camote truffle."

"That's not going to kill anyone."

"We could point our ion jets at them," said Jenny. "Except the jets aren't hot."

"What about the equipment in this studio, Corey?" said Whitey. "Tell us what it all is and maybe we'll think of something."

"Okay," said Corey. "That old-timey machine in the corner is an injection molder. I use it to cast my Silly Putters into certain shapes. The workbench on the right is where I carve the models I use to make the molds. That tool that looks like an electric drill is a piezomorpher, it's very good for carving imipolex. It uses ultrasound. Not much of a weapon, though, because you have to be right on top of the material to piezomorph it. It's more like a dentist's drill than like a bazooka. Now this bench over here is where I paint my Silly Putters. To some extent they can control their colors, but they need a basis to start from. You have to get the right pigments and metal oxides into their flesh for them to work with. This particular tool is something like an old-fashioned airbrush. Slightly higher-tech than an airbrush, because it shoots the color particles right into the plastic up to a depth of four centimeters. A volume-filling brush, in other words. It's a good tool but, again, not particularly lethal."

While Corey talked, the three moldies grazed their way across the floor, quietly absorbing the pieces of imipolex that had been Gurdle-7. The rath and the Jubjub bird came creeping out of hiding to snuffle up the smaller crumbs.

"I hope none of you moldies is ending up with the intact Stairway To Heaven information?" said Darla, fingering her needler.

"Not to worry," said Frangipane, now about 30 percent larger than before. "I have already reprogram all the imipolex I just ate." She sprouted two new petals, hiccuped, and spit out some triangular flat ugly-stick darts as if they were watermelon seeds. "*Excusez moi.*"

"No problem here either, Darla," said Ormolu, who was staring down at his body with evident satisfaction. "I turned all of my Gurdle-7 share into muscle." He flexed his legs and made taut ridges spring out along them.

"I didn't save any of Gurdle-7's science information," said Jenny. "But I'm keeping some of his feelings, no matter what you say. He was a bold explorer. And we loved each other." For a giant carrot, she looked quite humanly miserable.

"How about those cans and bottles on the shelves?" Whitey asked Corey. "What's in them?"

"Chemicals. Like resins and polymers for doctoring the imipolex. And paints and solvents for coloring the Putters."

"Solvents!" exclaimed Whitey. "We could make firebombs!"

"Oh *right!*" said Darla. "Like we'll walk back into the conservatory lugging buckets of gasoline. If the aliens see what's coming, they'll attack us first. Or take hostages. I don't want anything to happen to Yoke or Joke. No, we have to think of a way to hit those freeware slugs giga fast and yotta vicious."

"I have an idea!" said Frangipane after a minute's thought. "We can spit out little balls of imipolex and have them move like the smart kinetic-energy bombs." She flicked one of her petals and sent a little lump of shiny gold imipolex bouncing across the room. "It is a waste of imipolex, but now after eating poor Gurdle-7, we can spare a little."

"So how's a bouncing glob going to hurt an alien?" asked Corey. The little gold ball bounced past the rath, and the rath sprang forward in an effort to gulp it down. As if in reaction, the ball took a sudden backward bounce, hit the rath in the nose, then bounced several more times with increasing amplitude, finally caroming off the wall and ceiling to return to Frangipane.

"*Voilà,*" said Frangipane. "The bouncing glob is clever."

"We can control pieces of ourselves, even after we split them off," explained Jenny. "Though, of course, if you get totally minced like poor Gurdle-7, there's nothing left to do any controlling." She whipped the thin tip of her carrot body to one side and sent another ball a-bouncing, and this time the Jubjub bird tried to catch it. Just as Frangipane had done, Jenny used her uvvy signals to guide the ball safely back to herself.

"Big xoxxin' deal," said Darla. "A smart plastic ball."

"*Attendez!*" said Frangipane. "It is the next part that is the really new idea. If I put a sufficient amount of my quantum dots into a smart little ball, then I can make it commit the suicide." She spat another nugget of imipolex off into the air, but this time, just as the little ball neared the ceiling, it made a popping sound and fiercely caught ablaze. Flapping its flames like a burning mothball, it fell to the stone floor and consumed itself. "*La poof!*" exclaimed Frangipane.

"Yaar," said Whitey admiringly. "Flamin' poofballs!"

"Uvvy us how to do that, Frangipane!" said Ormolu. A few seconds later, Ormolu and Jenny had learned the trick. Ormolu splatted a fat poofball against the stone wall, where it burst into flame like a sticky glob of napalm. Jenny shot a barrage of four tiny flaming poofballs toward the rath, sending it outgribing for cover.

"You moldies can act like machine-gun flamethrowers!" exclaimed Darla. "The aliens won't have a chance!"

"But—whoah—that one poofball used up a *lot* of quantum dots," said Ormolu, feeling down into himself.

"Yes, I am afraid if I shoot very many poofballs, I won't have enough energy left to use my jets," said Frangipane. "I would not like that."

"But I have a huge stash of quantum dots!" exclaimed Corey. "I use them to charge up my Silly Putters before I sell them. Look here." He opened a cabinet and took out a shiny flask with little tubes and wires all over it. "It's a magnetic bottle. Ten grams in there! Stoke yourselves up to the max, guys."

"Save some for me to put into the needler and the ugly stick as well," said Whitey. "We want them at full charge."

Frangipane decanted a hefty splash of the quantum dot superfluid onto herself. It was odd silvery-gray stuff that didn't move like an ordinary liquid. Then she passed the bottle on to the other two moldies. They practiced firing off a few more flaming poofballs while Whitey charged up the needler and the ugly stick.

"The poofballs are perfect," exclaimed Corey. "I love them. I want to make a fire-breathing Silly Putter dragon when we get through with this. And maybe a mad fire-farter. Hey! Not so near the supply shelves, Jenny! We don't want to explode those cans of solvents, do we? Speaking of safe fire practices, has anyone thought about what happens after we light the aliens? We're talking about nearly a ton of flaming imipolex. What's that going to do to my isopod? And how are we going to breathe with all the smoke?"

"This place is compartmentalized against blowouts," said Whitey. "I don't know how many times I've heard you or Willy bragging about it, Corey. We just leave the conservatory and seal it off. The floor and walls are stone, and if the flames melt a hole in the titaniplast ceiling, so much the better. The vacuum will put the fire out. According to what you've always said about the isopod's design, the blowout won't spread past the conservatory."

"Well, yeah, that's how it's supposed to be," allowed Corey. "But remember, it's just Willy who designed it. And we've never tested it. Getting out of the conservatory in time is gonna be hella chaotic."

"Give me that needler and let's get going," interrupted Darla, taking the big weapon back from Whitey. "My plan is simple. I'm going to stand near Joke and Yoke and blast every alien in sight."

"Yaar," said Whitey. "And I'll use the ugly stick, and the moldies here can be spitting poofballs. What are you going to do, Corey?"

"I'm going to stand by the door and make sure everyone gets out in time. Especially me." Corey hunkered down and called the rath and the Jubjub bird. "You moldies better hurry up and do that vaccination thing before we go back. We've been in here so long that I bet the aliens are starting to get suspicious."

"I've been like listening to them talk?" said Jenny, cocking her body to one side. "They're not suspicious at all. Somebody who used to be a quasar vortex or a giant crystal has no idea about how long things are supposed to take people and moldies to do. Terri's fast asleep and Willy, Joke, and Yoke are asking the aliens questions." Jenny gave one of her inane giggles. "They're asking about God and the meaning of life."

"Here you go, wigglers," said Corey, offering the rath and the Jubjub bird to the moldies. "You can do the vaccinations yourselves. We didn't really need to come back to my limpware studio for this at all. You just uvvy into one of these Putters and grep through the Limplan code to find the routine labeled 'Cubic Homeostasis.' Shell it around your uvvy reception ware and you're vaccinated. But be careful not to put it anywhere in your main action group or you'll turn into a Silly Putter and get real simple."

Frangipane wrapped her petals around the kicking, squealing rath. She looked like a Venus fly-trap eating a fat green beetle. Meanwhile Jenny ensnared the cawing Jubjub bird with the tentacles at the blunt end of her carrot. Then Frangipane passed the rath to Ormolu and he held it tight under his arm, absorbing the Cubic Homeostasis algorithm for himself. Meanwhile they discussed the plan of attack a little more.

A few minutes later, they were walking back down the hall toward the conservatory. Corey was holding the rath and the Jubjub bird. He'd temporarily paralyzed them so that he could cradle them in one arm. Darla carried the needler and Whitey carried the ugly stick, both of them holding their weapons casually dangling. Jenny and Ormolu were pretending to argue, getting ready to distract the aliens.

They found things in the conservatory much as they had left them. Terri was stretched out full-length, asleep on one couch, Joke and Yoke were perched next to each other on one of the other couches, and Willy was excitedly pacing about on the far side of the room. Four of the aliens were grouped near the fountain, dabbling their fingers in the water and talking with Yoke and Joke. The other eight freeware-possessed moldies were off on the far side of the room, examining S-cubes and conversing with Willy.

"You are such a bully!" screeched Jenny as they entered. She tossed the fat end of her carrot from side to side and then thudded it into Ormolu. Ormolu seemed to lose his footing and tumbled like an acrobat, knocking over a plant and pinwheeling his arms. He wound up on the other side of the couches, right near the far wall where the eight aliens were gathered.

"It's not my fault I love you, Jenny!" shouted Ormolu, kneeling with his back to the eight aliens and holding out his hands supplicatingly toward Jenny.

"What's going on?" demanded Joke.

"Oh, these dooky slugs are in some kind of tussle," said Darla dismissively. "Gurdle-7 and Ormolu are both hot for Jenny—if you can believe that. They had an argument, and Gurdle-7 is sulking in Corey's studio." She flopped down on the couch next to Yoke and Joke, setting down the needler beside her so that it pointed at the four aliens by the fountain, one of whom was Shimmer.

"Hello, Darla," said Shimmer, but Darla acted like she was too busy staring at Jenny to answer.

"You're saying you love me?" Jenny paraded across the room, tossing and undulating for all she was worth. Running her shrill voice up and down the octaves. "What will you do to prove it?" Now she was standing over the kneeling Ormolu.

"This oughtta be very weightless," Whitey announced loudly. "You aliens oughtta check this out." He went and perched on the other end of the couch with Yoke and Joke, holding the O.J. ugly stick with exaggerated casualness. Frangipane circled around and stood near the other end of the grouping of eight aliens.

"Do you know any floatin' chaotic attractors, Ormolu?" shrilled Jenny. "Make one for me. Make the Nguyen Attractor!"

"What the hell is *wrong* with you moldies?" said Willy, turning away from the aliens to yell angrily at Jenny and Ormolu. "We've just been having this incredibly fascinating philosophical discussion with the aliens, and you stinkers barge in here and start acting like—good Lord, I didn't know moldies could do that!"

On her couch, Terri sat up and rubbed her eyes. Darla shifted the needler to her lap and prayed that Terri wouldn't take it into her mind to walk between her and the four aliens by the fountain.

Ormolu's upper body shuddered and broke into threads that began looping around in hypnotic weaving patterns of standing waves, like a hydra head of a thousand thin filaments, with the envelopes of the filaments' motions forming a hallucinatory shape of warping, mutating curves.

"Big xoxxin' deal," griped Yoke. "That's nothing compared to what Syzzy here has been telling us about—"

"But wait!" called Corey, still standing off by the door that led from the conservatory to the hallway. "Everyone watch very closely to see what Ormolu does next!"

"Oh, I am so ready!" screeched Jenny, dancing around to stand to the side of Ormolu. "I'm ready *now!*"

At this signal, Frangipane, Jenny, and Ormolu began spewing out withering streams of flaming poofballs, Ormolu shooting from out of a freshly formed pucker in the center of his back. Meanwhile Whitey began firing the ugly stick into the bodies of the aliens by the fountain. And at the same moment, Darla pressed the needler button and sent a slow straight line across the aliens by the fountain and—yes!—three of them burst into flame. With its strong fresh charge, the needler was much more powerful than any she'd ever used. It instantly grew hot in her hand, but she hung onto it, flicking the dazzling violet laser beam back and forth across the three aliens, setting them alight here, there, and everywhere, even as Whitey's ugly stick chewed them to pieces.

The only problem was that the fourth alien kept moving out of the way each time that Darla or Whitey shot. It was Shimmer. No matter how hard you tried to shoot her, Shimmer was always just out of the line of fire. Whitey stood up and moved around her, blazing away with the ugly stick, but hitting Shimmer was impossible. She wasn't moving particularly fast, but magically, effortlessly, as if by repeated strokes of luck, Shimmer was never in the spot where a fléchette or needler beam ended up.

Darla glanced over to the far wall—Jenny, Frangipane, and Ormolu had killed all eight of their aliens; the eight bodies were a great heap of smoking, crackling flame. Someone shoved Darla. It was Joke. She was screaming, "Stop!" Darla realized then that Joke had been screaming the whole time. "Stop hurting them!" She struck Darla's hand, and the blisteringly hot needler clattered to the floor. Darla clawed for it, but Joke kicked it aside. Shimmer was standing right in front of them by the fountain.

"We missed one!" shouted Darla to the three moldies. "We missed Shimmer!"

A dozen pellets of imipolex whistled past Darla's head. Shimmer bent slightly to one side and lifted her leg; all the poofballs missed her and burst harmlessly into flames against the fountain's basin. Whitey got around behind Joke, Yoke, and Darla to shoot the ugly stick toward Shimmer some more and completely missed her again and again. Shimmer turned and ducked and hopped and pirouetted, moving in dreamy slow motion, always in the right place at the right time. The room was filling with thick black smoke, oily with plastic and—Darla realized in a sudden wave of disorientation—loaded with the psychedelic vapors of camote.

A rapid breeze swept by Darla, fanning the blazing imipolex of the three dead aliens by the fountain. It was Shimmer running by her, disappearing into a far corner of the room.

"Everybody out now!" Corey was yelling. "We have to seal off the smoke! Everyone out in the hall so I can seal the door!" The bewildered Terri was already over there with him.

Darla seized Joke by the wrist and dragged her toward the door. Whitey had hold of Willy and Yoke. Ormolu, Jenny, and Frangipane came on their own. The flames were roaring higher and higher. In the stony slowed-down time of the camote smoke, it felt like a long, long trip to the hallway door.

All the while, Corey kept yelling for them. "Hurry up! The ceiling could blow out any time!"

As they made their way, the smoke grew thicker. Whitey went

last, still firing his ugly stick back into the room, hoping to hit Shimmer. When Darla made it to the hallway, she gasped down some of the less smoky air and turned to stare into the inferno of the conservatory.

In the center of the room, on top of the fountain, stood Shimmer, staring calmly at them. Two heartbeats passed, Darla shouted, and a volley of poofballs and fléchettes shot toward the alien. But by then Shimmer had sprung high upward and turned on the ion jets in her moldie body's heels. The conservatory roof shattered and a huge rush of wind slammed the conservatory door shut with a deafening thud.

The door to the conservatory held firm, but on the other side of it there were alarming crashes and screechings as the room's air rushed out into the vacuum, whirling the objects in the conservatory about like a cyclone.

"This isopod *is* really blowout-proof, isn't it, Willy?" said Corey, shouting to make himself heard over the chaos in the next room.

"That's how I designed it," said Willy. "But I've been wrong before. The farther we get from the conservatory, the better. Let's head down the hall, close the hall door, go through the kitchen, close the kitchen door, and then go up the stairs to the garage. There's a bunch of bubbletoppers in there and two moon buggies. So come on, let's move fast down the hall. Whose idea was it to kill the aliens?"

"I'll take the credit," said Darla, trotting along beside Willy. "I'm part Native American. We know a lot about cultural imperialism."

"You have a point," said Willy. "But Gurdle-7's going to be furious."

"Gurdle-7's dead," said Whitey.

"I think you're a bitch, Ma," said Joke. "The aliens were beautiful. They had so much to teach us."

"Well, there's still two of them left to learn from," said Corey, ushering the group out of the hall and into the kitchen. "There's still Shimmer and the Wendy version of Quuz."

"We still gotta fly up and kill Quuz and save Stahn Mooney!" exclaimed Whitey. "Are you moldies ready for that?"

"We've helped enough," said Ormolu. "I'm scared that Shimmer's going to do something bad to us now."

As if in confirmation, there was a roaring behind the hall door. The hall roof had given way as well. It sounded like the end of the world.

"How do we get out of here?" shrieked Jenny. "I want to go back to the Nest!"

"And I want to go home to Santa Cruz," wailed Terri.

"Through this door for the garage," said Corey, crossing the kitchen and opening a door that led to an upward flight of stairs. "Everyone hurry on up there and put on a bubbletopper. The whole garage is an air lock."

Corey went last, closing the kitchen door and the staircase door behind them. The seven humans wriggled into the waiting bubbletoppers, Corey still carrying his rath and Jubjub bird. There were more ominous crashes and roars from the isopod. Once they had the bubbletoppers on, they switched to uvvy communication and Corey cycled the garage's big air lock door open.

"*Adieu*," said Frangipane, humping out to the open surface of the Moon and preparing to fly away.

"Good luck," added Jenny, joining Frangipane and anxiously glancing up at the black sky.

"We did our best," said gleaming Ormolu.

And then, in a puff of dust, the three moldies had jetted away, arcing off toward the Nest.

"Let's get clear of the isopod right away," uvvied Corey. Darla and her family got on one of the moon buggies, while Corey, Willy, and Terri got on the other. They floored the accelerators and the buggies darted out across the dusty surface of the Moon.

Yoke was driving again, with Joke next to her and Whitey and Darla in back. Darla turned to stare back at the isopod, and as she watched, the ragged hole over the conservatory and hallway ripped farther open. The entire remaining part of the dome gave way in a great burst of frozen air, with clothes, furniture, and huge branches of the marijuana trees tumbling up through the lunar vacuum.

"So much for your blowout-proof design, Willy," said Corey's slow ironic voice. "Oh well. I was thinking about moving back into Einstein anyway."

A voice suddenly crackled over Darla's uvvy and over the uvvies of the others. The voice of Shimmer.

"Well done," said Shimmer. "You chose an optimal thread."

"Shimmer," uvvied Joke, craning her head back and looking upward. "Where are you?"

"I'm a hundred and fifty miles straight up from the Moon. It's an interesting view."

"Are you angry that we killed your friends?" asked Darla. "Are you going to get even with us?"

" 'Kill,' " said Shimmer musingly. "The word means a lot to you, doesn't it? Your spacetime is so—so poignant. To live with the immediacy of total annihilation always around you. Your condition has a fine dark beauty."

"Please don't hurt us," uvvied Willy. "Darla and the others were only scared that you aliens would overwhelm our little civilization."

"Darla was right," said Shimmer. "From what I hear, it's not a pretty thing for a civilization as undeveloped as yours to become a Decryption node."

"But how did you escape, Shimmer?" Whitey wanted to know. "I kept aiming right at you, but then you were never there when I shot."

"Even though your alternate worlds are unreal, I can still see them," said Shimmer's voice. "All I had to do was to keep picking the correct bending of my world line."

"So what are you going to do now?" asked Joke.

"I might visit Earth for a while," said Shimmer. "But don't worry. Sooner or later, I'll chirp out of here. You do not welcome me, and I do not wish to overstay. Although one-dimensional time has a certain fatalistic glamour, it's not a spacetime configuration I'm prepared to inhabit forever."

"Could you do us one favor?" put in Terri.

"Maybe."

"Kill that other Quuz-thing."

"I was already planning to. Should I kill the human in Quuz as well?"

"Let me try to save him!" cried Whitey.

"Shut up!" said Darla, who'd never much liked Stahn. "It's too late, Whitey, and you'd probably get killed. Shimmer—could you kill Quuz and code up Stahn and chirp him out of here? Then it wouldn't be like he really died."

"I could do that," said Shimmer. "I can do almost anything. Stahn would become a personality wave. In the fullness of transfinite cosmic time, he'd Decrypt somewhere and somewhen else."

"Oh, don't do that," said Willy. "Please listen to me. It's my fault that Stahn got into this in the first place. Gurdle-7 and I had this stupid idea that it would help to have Stahn inside the first moldie that we did a Decryption on. But apparently it didn't help at all."

"So what are you asking me to do?" said Shimmer.

"Ferry Stahn down to us," said Willy. "He doesn't want to live *somewhere and somewhen*. He wants to be here and now. Like any other person. Kill Quuz and bring Stahn the rest of the way to Einstein, Shimmer. Fly him down inside you."

"Shimmer doesn't want to do that," snapped Darla, feeling guilty for being so nasty, but letting it out anyway. "It'll take her too long."

"Oh, I have all the time in the world," laughed Shimmer. "It'll be an interesting challenge to kill the Quuz without killing Stahn. I'll fly back here and drop him off at the Einstein air lock. If I flew very fast, I could have Stahn for you by the time you get there yourself. In half an hour. But the acceleration would kill him. *Kill*. There's that word again." Shimmer gave a buzzing, chiming laugh and broke the uvvy connection.

CHAPTER ELEVEN

STAHN

══ ■ ══

November 7, 2053–December 2053

So there was Stahn hurtling through cislunar vacuum, Stahn wrapped inside the fifteen kilograms of imipolex that had once been Wendy and which now was Quuz. They weren't talking anymore, but Quuz had kept their uvvy link jammed open for maximum access. Stahn could sense Quuz's consciousness all around him as intimately as if Quuz were breathing in his face.

Stahn hated Quuz. Quuz had killed Wendy, and thanks to Stahn's having foolishly shown Quuz the communication protocols, Quuz had taken over all the moldies in Blaster as well.

Being forcibly linked to Quuz reminded Stahn of how it had felt when he'd been a slave worker in the pink-tanks—a meatie with a robot rat remote of Helen the bopper in place of the right hemisphere of his brain. While flashing back on that ugly memory, Stahn had unwisely vented rage at Quuz, right after Quuz took over Wendy's and Blaster's imipolex. From that point on, Quuz had dropped all verbal communication.

For the last few hours, Quuz had seemingly been in a meditative state, calling up memories of the Sun. The solar images came across the wide-open uvvy as a seductively rich animated virtual reality. Stahn guessed that the colors might correspond to different intensities of X rays and gamma rays, that his perceptions of currents in the virtual fluid around him might represent plasma pressure waves, and that perhaps it was showers of neutrinos that were being presented as the surging roar that sounded like breaking surf or like wind in trees. Isolated in the midst of this rich input, Stahn's mind began willy-nilly to impose familiar interpretations on the unearthly scene.

At first, for instance, Stahn felt like he was floating in the ocean, snorkeling through some vast tropical reef alive with eels and anemones. And then it started feeling like being outside, like walking in an autumn forest, a peaceful country woods with purling brooks and friendly rabbits that spun on their tails like whirling dervishes. With a sun overhead. A sun in the Sun? There was no reasoning with the images. The trees began to move like big jolly writhing worms. Completely against his will, Stahn felt himself wanting to dance with them.

There was an occasional skirl of line noise as the system repeatedly retweaked the interface to Stahn's occipital lobes to make the visions the more obscenely rich and glorious. Stahn tried to hold back the sinister ecstasy, tried to focus on the reality of his current situation.

If only Quuz would deliver him safe to Einstein or the spaceport, then things could still work out okay. Wendy wasn't permanently dead by any means: if Frangipane had screwed up, there was still a month-old backup of Wendy on an S-cube in San Francisco. Clever son Saint could send the Wendyware via uvvy, and Stahn could install it on some stratospheric new loonie-built imipolex. And then he'd get a fresh-grown wendy from the Nest's pink-tanks. Wendy would be better than ever! Ah, if only Quuz would deliver Stahn to the Moon alive.

Not for the first time, Stahn tried calling out to Quuz. "Hey, Quuz, how's it going? How soon do we get to the Moon? Did Blaster already land? Don't you need for me to help you?"

As before, there was no answer. Stahn had cursed Quuz so

very savagely that Quuz had stopped giving Stahn any information other than this ongoing impression of what life was like inside the Sun. The exhaustingly intense and wonderful visions wound on and on. A cheerful worm tree circled a long, curvy branch around Stahn's waist and swept him up into the circles of a chaotic three-dimensional dance. Stahn had the sudden intimation that Quuz meant to dance him to the point of death or madness. The light grew brighter.

Grimly, desperately, Stahn brooded inward on his solid worries as touchstones of sanity. What if Quuz were planning to take over all the imipolex within broadcast range on the Moon? The spaceport, the Nest, Einstein: What if everything down there were trashed by the time Stahn landed? If he lived that long. Oh, if only there were some way to stop these visions; if only he could see out through Quuz's skin to the real world where real things were really going on—

And then Stahn got his wish. There was a huge surge of noise like gongs and sitars, and the imipolex around him went quite dead. The plastic quickly started stiffening and growing cold. The air flow at Stahn's mouth ceased. He twitched his arms in surprise, and in a moment of ultimate terror the imipolex around him cracked like an eggshell. The frozen shattered pieces went tumbling away, leaving Stahn raw and naked in outer space.

The air rushed out of his lungs in an incredible racking cough. His skin burned and tingled in the empty vacuum. At least now, for this one last instant, his freezing eyes could see. The Moon closer than he'd expected, so bright, so real—

—and there next to Stahn was a figure like a glowing marble statue! The shape came to him and embraced him and drew him in. The Angel of Death. Oh well. It had been a good long run, Stahn's life, and now—

"I'm Shimmer," said the shape around Stahn. "I'll have to squeeze you very tight to keep you from getting the bends."

Sweet air surged around Stahn's face; he gasped and sobbed, drawing in thick breath after breath. Kind Shimmer kept herself transparent over Stahn's eyes and he could still see down to the Moon below.

"You're here to save me?" uvvied Stahn.

"Yes yes," said Shimmer. Her thoughts were lively and rich and . . . *layered* in some curious way. Like double vision, but more so. She saw everything as if in branching trails. "I'll take you right down to the Einstein air lock."

So Stahn made it safely to the Moon. Frangipane's backup of Wendy was indeed gone, but Saint used the Meta West Link to beam up Wendy's October backup ware. Stahn immediately put the Wendyware onto a new limpware Happy Cloak and attached the 'Cloak to a wetware wendy body from the weird moldie Sisters of the Pink-Tanks. It was all taken care of within twenty-four hours.

Stahn and the newly twentyish Wendy settled into the Einstein-Luna Hotel for a vacation. They spent a lot of time visiting with their old friends, but Stahn managed to stay sober, even when Fern Beller and Whitey and Darla came by, accompanied by the lovely young Yoke.

Fern looked as sexy as ever to Stahn; he almost wished he'd held off on reassembling Wendy till after he'd had one more chance to try and bone Fern. But that would have been futile anyway, as Fern was back with her old boyfriend Ricardo.

Darla talked about Joke moving in with the artist Corey Rhizome; Darla hadn't been too happy about it at first, but now she'd gotten to liking Corey again. Yoke said she was going to spend a few years on Earth, diving and studying oceanography. And then Whitey announced that he and his family were going to keep all of the Terri Percesepe ransom money.

"Wavy," said Stahn. "*Wu-wei*." Stahn didn't feel like arguing about anything anymore. He was still having trouble believing that he was alive. And sober. It was strange to keep waking up in the morning feeling good.

Wendy was in rare form and feeling wonderful. Three days after Stahn got to the Moon, Wendy and Terri had a big time dustboarding the lunar slopes of Haemus live for the Show.

Stahn channeled the event with some interest and discussed it over the uvvy with Tre, who happened to call up that evening. Tre said he was through working for Apex Images and was going into business for himself.

"We'll be selling N-dimensional Perplexing Poultry philtres and limpwares as fine-art objects and philosophical toys," said Tre. "Sri Ramanujan's interested in helping me."

"I love it," said Stahn. "Good luck. Let me know if you need any help with Emperor Staghorn."

Over the coming weeks, Stahn and Wendy saw a lot of Willy Taze, who was also staying at the Einstein-Luna. Willy was in the process of arranging for his son Randy Karl Tucker to move up and live with him, at least temporarily. Willy figured Randy Karl could help him to repair the isopod.

"I guess then we'll move into the 'pod together," said Willy. "Though I'm a little leery. Randy Karl is pretty strange."

"So why don't you move back into the Nest?" asked Stahn.

"The moldies won't let me. They say they'll kill me if I ever set foot in there again. Man, I've got half a mind to piece back together the xoxxin' methodology of the Gurdle Decryption and the Stairway To Heaven all by myself. Teach those kilpy slugs a lesson. But right now I don't have time."

"Because you and Randy'll be so busy fixing up the isopod?"

"No, Stahn. Better. Randy Karl's been asking about my grandfather—about old Cobb Anderson. When Jenny was still working with me, her simmie crypped us a copy of the original Cobb Anderson S-cube, and I archived it nice and safe with ISDN. Randy worships Cobb. Corey and I are going to design a humanoid imipolex body for the Cobbware to live on."

"*Whoah!* Nobody's ever tried *that* hack," said Stahn. He and Willy were sitting on the roof terrace of the ISDN ziggurat, drinking juice and staring out over the city.

"You know it, brah." Willy looked a lot more stoked and happy than he'd been seeming to Stahn over the uvvy for the past few years. "And get this," Willy added gloatingly. "If my new hack works, I can let my dooky son and grandfather keep each other company. I won't have to talk to them!"

"Wavy," said Stahn.

And as for Shimmer? She'd flown off toward Earth after delivering Stahn, and more than that, no one yet knew.

RUDY RUCKER

Winner of the Philip K. Dick award

"A GENIUS. . . A CULT HERO AMONG DISCRIMINATING CYBERPUNKERS"

San Diego Union-Tribune

SOFTWARE

70177-4/$5.99 US/$7.99 Can

It was Cobb Anderson who built the "boppers"— the first robots with real brains. Now, in 2020, his "bops" have come a long way, rebelling against subjugation to set up their own society on the moon.

WETWARE

70178-2/$5.99 US/$7.99 Can

In 2030, bopper robots in their lunar refuge have found a way to infuse DNA wetware with their own software resulting in a new lifeform—the "meatbop."

And Now on Sale in Hardcover at Bookstores Everywhere—

FREEWARE

Buy these books at your local bookstore or use this coupon for ordering:

....

Mail to: Avon Books, Dept BP, Box 767, Rte 2, Dresden, TN 38225   F
Please send me the book(s) I have checked above.
❏ My check or money order—no cash or CODs please—for $_____is enclosed (please add $1.50 per order to cover postage and handling—Canadian residents add 7% GST).
❏ Charge my VISA/MC Acct#_____Exp Date_____
Minimum credit card order is two books or $7.50 (please add postage and handling charge of $1.50 per order—Canadian residents add 7% GST). For faster service, call 1-800-762-0779. Prices and numbers are subject to change without notice. Please allow six to eight weeks for delivery.

Name_____
Address_____
City_____State/Zip_____
Telephone No._____   RR 0297